I0681989

Allon

Book 3

Heir Apparent

Shawn Lamb

Allon Books

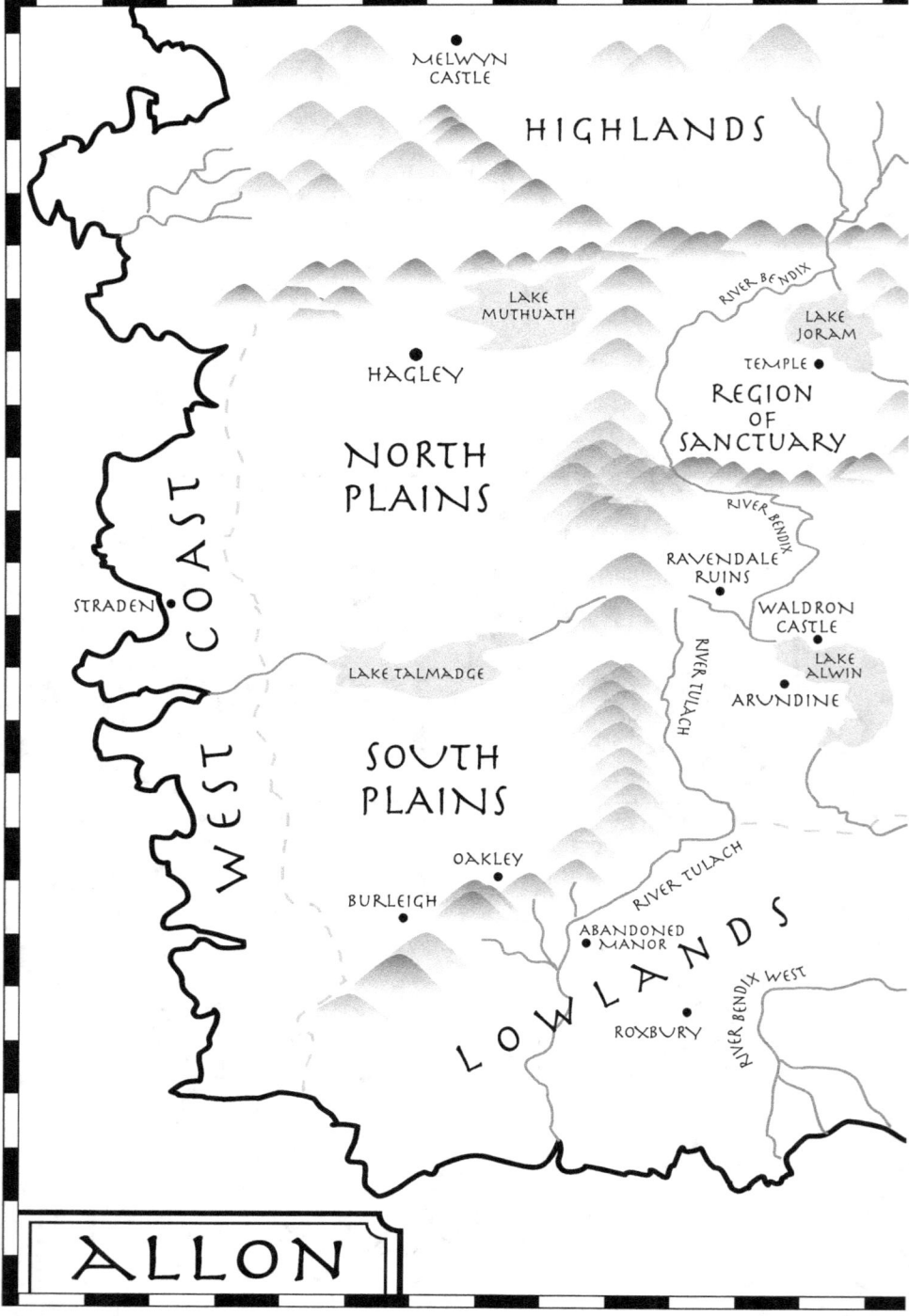

MELWYN CASTLE

HIGHLANDS

RIVER BENDIX

LAKE MUTHUATH

LAKE JORAM

TEMPLE

HAGLEY

REGION OF SANCTUARY

NORTH PLAINS

RIVER BENDIX

RAVENDALE RUINS

WALDRON CASTLE

WEST COAST

STRADEN

LAKE TALMADGE

RIVER TULACH

LAKE ALWIN

ARUNDINE

SOUTH PLAINS

OAKLEY

BURLEIGH

RIVER TULACH

ABANDONED MANOR

LOWLANDS

RIVER BENDIX WEST

ROXBURY

ALLON

UPPER GLACIER LAKE

CLIFTON CASTLE

GLACIER LAKE

RIVER BENDIX

NORTHERN FOREST

LAKE DENLEY

DENLEY CASTLE

RIVER OLC'BURN

DORIGRITH

RIVER DEIGH

GARWOOD

LACHLAN

SOUTHERN FOREST

RIVER CONN

DRYFESS

PRESLEY MANOR

RIVER CONN

LEITH

TRI'AIBHNE LAKE

PICKFORD

MIDESSEX

EAST COAST

CONN'CHEUG RIVER

RIVER BENDIX

MEADOWLANDS

LAKE MILTON

MILTON CASTLE

DELTORIA CASTLE

RIVER BENDIX EAST

DELTA

PANOS POINT

WAUFORD ISLAND

ALLON ~ BOOK 3 ~ HEIR APPARENT by Shawn Lamb
Published by Allon Books
209 Hickory Way Court
Antioch, Tennessee 37013
www.allonbooks.com

Cover design by Robert Lamb

Library of Congress Control Number: 2011920438

International Standard Book Number: 978-0-9829204-1-1

Other Books by Shawn Lamb

ALLON ~ BOOK 1
Published by Creation House
A Strang Company

Published by Allon Books
ALLON ~ BOOK 2 ~ INSURRECTION

*Coming in 2011
from Allon Books*

ALLON ~ BOOK 4 ~ A QUESTION OF SOVEREIGNTY

MORTALS

King Ellis – age 38
Queen Shannan – age 37
Prince Nigel – age 16
Princess Ellan – age 15
Princess Tristine – age 12
Princess Necie – age 10
Lady Arista – wife of Darius, age 39
Angus – son of Darius & Arista, age 11
General Wess – age 32

COUNCIL OF TWELVE

Vicar Archimedes	Region of Sanctuary
Darius, Duke of Allon – age 41	Southern Forest
Baron Erasmus	Delta
Baron Mathias	West Coast
Baron Hollis	East Coast
Lord Zebulon	Lowlands
Sir Gareth	South Plains
Lord Malcolm	North Plains
Baron Ned	Northern Forest
Lord Fagan	Highlands
Lord Allard	Meadowlands
Lord Bosley – age 30	Midessex

FOREIGN VISITORS

Lord Bijan – Ambassador for Emperor Kamu of Morven
Princess Kaleana – royal daughter of the emperor, age 16
Ambassador Lanzo of Tunland, age 33

IMMORTALS

GUARDIANS

Captain Kell – Commander of the Guardians of Jor'el and
King's Champion
1st Lieutenant Armus – Overseer of Princess Tristine
2nd Lieutenant Avatar – Overseer of Prince Nigel
Mahon – Overseer of Princess Necie
Morrell – Overseer of Princess Ellan
Vidar – Overseer of Queen Shannan
Eldric, Guardian Prime Physician
Phoebe, Eldric's assistant

TRIO LEADERS

Gresham	Midessex
Priscilla	East Coast
Chase	West Coast
Egan	Northern Forest
Wren	Southern Forest
Jedrek	Delta
Zadok	Region of Sanctuary
Zinna	Meadowlands
Barnum	Highlands
Derwin	Lowlands
Mona	North Plains
Auriel	South Plains

Chapter 1

THE TWENTIETH YEAR of the reign of King Ellis of Allon experienced a number of challenges. It began with a petition for military aid from an ally in fear of being overrun by a warring neighbor. The resulting complications from the aid brought a wave of diplomatic envoys coming and going from Waldron Castle. Due to the great political tension, Ellis decided to take his family on a holiday to the East Coast before the situations impacted their relationships.

For two young girls, ages twelve and ten, fun replaced the business of diplomacy and war. They scampered over the rocky dunes along the beach near Leith in a game of hide-and-seek. Tristine and Necie were trying to elude their brother, sixteen-year-old Nigel, who at any moment would come looking for them.

Necie was the youngest of Ellis' four children and a slip of a girl with brown hair and large doe eyes easily capable of melting her father's heart when she chose to use her girlish wiles. She didn't hike up the skirt of her dress to climb the dune and squeezed under a rock to hide.

At twelve, Tristine was third born and the most unlady-like of Ellis' three daughters. She would wear breeches, shirt, and doublet all the time if it were permissible, but being a princess required decorum. For today, she placed aside convention and wore breeches to frolic on the beach, her long

8

golden hair partially pulled back. She climbed the highest dune to lie in wait, hazel eyes alert to any movement.

Not far from where the girls hid, two Guardian warriors sat on a large flat rock at the base of the dunes. When standing they reached seven-and-a-half feet tall. One was burly and ruggedly handsome with brown hair and unusually bright chestnut eyes, the other blond-headed with vivid light blue eyes set in a boyish face. Instead of the royal uniforms of blue and silver, they wore the Guardian suit of their station, embossed tan close-fitting, knee-length jackets trimmed in gold with slits in the side from the hem to the hip. The tan breeches were tucked into leather boots and armed with swords and daggers. They appeared amused in their watchfulness of the girls.

From the inland pass Nigel came jogging toward the dunes. He was tall and athletic with golden brown hair and blue eyes set in a pleasant face. His doublet was partially opened and he wore shoes instead of boots. He did carry a small-sheathed dagger on his belt. All gentlemen used a dagger for various reasons during the day, be it for cutting an apple or opening a letter.

He frowned at seeing the Guardians and said, "You're not supposed sit where I can see you. Now I know the girls are not far off."

"How do you know we're sitting anywhere near them, Highness?" teased Armus, the burly one.

"Ay, this may be just be a ruse," said Mahon with an impish smile.

"If you believe that, then I'm not here either," said Avatar, the bronze-haired, goateed Guardian warrior who followed Nigel. His silver eyes twinkled in merriment. He took a seat beside Armus.

Nigel continued his trek up the dunes, shouting, "I'm going to find you both! You can't be far." Hearing a familiar yet stifled giggle, he stopped.

Necie. She never could hide well, too anxious to be found. He followed her giggles until he noticed her left foot sticking out from under a rock formation and feinted a disappointed sigh.

"Well, Mahon, I guess Necie found a good place to hide this time because I don't see her."

"Keep looking, Highness," said Mahon playing along.

Nigel sat on the rock where Necie hid and pretended to grow concerned. "I don't know. She may really be lost this time. What will I tell Father and Mother if I can't find her?"

Underneath, Necie covered her mouth to stop a squeal and moved in reaction to what Nigel said, inadvertently kicking his leg.

"What's this? An animal?" Nigel got down on his knees to look under the rock.

"I'm not an animal," she insisted while giggling.

"You must be, that hole is only big enough for a mouse." He laughed and helped her to crawl out.

"You always find me first."

"You give yourself away by laughing."

"I can't help it. Hiding makes me giggly."

Nigel chuckled. "Wait with Mahon while I find Tristine."

"You won't find her," she said before going to join the Guardians.

Nigel rolled his eyes. Whereas Necie was not good at hiding, Tristine was a master. With her, he must be more diligent and alert. He climbed further up the dune, his eyes shifting about for movement or strange shadows. When he reached the top, there were no signs of her. She may have gone down the other side and out of Armus' view. Typical. She constantly vexed him with her ability to slip off unnoticed. Armus often bore the brunt of jokes by mortals and Guardians about a girl eluding an elite Guardian warrior, and not just any warrior, but the second-in-command. No, with Tristine, Nigel had to be careful. He took his time searching the top before beginning to go down the other side.

Someone jumped him from behind and both went tumbling to the sand. Tristine ended up on top of him, pinning his arms to the ground.

"You have to be more careful," she teased.

"You have to stop being so aggressive."

"What's that supposed to mean?"

"It means you can't tackle every man who comes along and expect him to like it."

"Who's a man?" She roughly released him and stood.

He frowned and wiped off the sand from his hair. "Some day soon we won't be able to play games like this and you'll to have to start acting more mature. You're going to be thirteen in a couple of months and you know what that means."

Hurt, she scowled. "Why do things have to change?" She ran back down the dune.

"Tristine!" He scrambled to rise and follow her.

She didn't reply and kept running, past the Guardians and up the inland path.

Nigel wasn't far behind her and Armus asked, "What happened, Highness?"

"I don't know! She's acting touchy and temperamental; just like Ellan when she proclaimed she was a woman." Before Nigel finished speaking, he realized what he was saying and groaned.

Avatar patted Nigel's shoulder, yet attempted to curb a wry smile. "Happens to every mortal female."

"What does?" asked Necie.

"You'll learn soon enough," said Mahon.

She didn't like the answer and tugged on her brother's sleeve. "Nigel?"

A fond smile appeared as he gazed at her. "Please don't grow up too soon. I don't think Father and I could take it."

"Why?"

Instead of answering Nigel lifted her on the rock and turned around to offer her a piggyback ride. "Time to return." She climbed on his back and repeated her question. "Ask Mother to explain." They all headed back up the inland pass.

Inside a large manor house at the end of the inland pass a quarter mile from the beach, Queen Shannan relaxed before an open window in the drawing room doing some needlepoint. At age thirty-seven she was a pretty woman with fawn colored hair, green eyes and a rosy complexion. The front door flew open and Tristine rushed in.

11

"Tristine?" she called, but was ignored when Tristine ran upstairs, followed shortly by the sound of a slamming door.

Ellis entered from an adjacent room shuffling through papers he carried. He was a year older than Shannan—six feet, two inches tall, handsome and in peak physical condition. Tristine favored her father with golden hair and medium complexion; only he had blue eyes compared to her hazel. "Who was that?"

"Tristine."

The front door opened again and this time Nigel and Necie entered, followed by the Guardians. Armus continued upstairs while Nigel and Necie entered the drawing room. Avatar and Mahon waited in the hallway.

"Did something happen on the beach?" Shannan asked Nigel. The resemblance between mother and son was strong.

"Tristine had a girlish reaction to a comment I made about how she needs to grow up," he sarcastically replied.

Ellis snickered, shaking his head.

Shannan gave her husband and son each an admonishing glance. "Becoming a woman isn't easy."

"Nigel won't tell me why," said Necie.

"Because you're still young. And we'd prefer you stay that way," said Ellis, indicating himself and Nigel.

"Nigel said the same, but why?"

Shannan placed aside the needlepoint to take Necie's hand. "I'll explain when I talk to your sister."

At the bottom of the stairs Shannan and Necie met Ellan, the eldest girl at age fifteen. She was a brown-haired, blue-eyed beauty with all the feminine charms and grace Tristine lacked. "Mother, you have to speak to Tristine she's being unruly."

"I'm just on my way upstairs."

Ellan entered the drawing room and glared at Nigel. "What trouble did you let her get into this time?"

"I didn't let her get into any trouble. She's very capable of doing that on her own."

12

Ellis sat on the window seat and tried to hide his amusement behind the papers, but Ellan noticed.

"Father, why do find her antics amusing?"

"Because most are harmless. Tristine maybe independent and headstrong, but she is intelligent and has a good heart—not unlike someone else I know," he said with a fond smile.

Nigel sat in the chair. "You mean Mother."

"Ay. She used to romp about Dorgirith with the same reckless stubbornness, confronting anything and everything that moved."

Ellan sat beside Ellis. "It's hard to imagine Mother acting like Tristine."

"She did, which is why I hold out hope that Tristine will someday mature into a sensible and confident woman like your mother. Besides, it took you time to adjust to being an adult and look how well you are doing."

Ellan slightly blushed. "You think I'm doing well?"

"Ay," he said, smiling and squeezing her hand. "By extending some patience to Tristine and helping her, she might do as well as you."

Upstairs, Tristine sat on the bed and wiped tears from her face.

Armus stood beside her. "What upset you?"

She snorted in annoyance, but didn't answer.

"It can't be the fact Nigel found you."

She shook her head. The door opened and she sneered at seeing Necie enter with Shannan. "Why did you tell?" she accused Necie, who looked hurt and pouted.

"Necie didn't tell me anything. Your blustery entrance and slamming the door did," began Shannan. "Why did Nigel's comment about growing up upset you so?"

Tristine set her lips, reluctant to answer.

"So that's it," Armus said. He explained to Shannan, "They were playing hide-and-seek on the dunes. He wasn't certain what upset her, only mentioned her behavior was *touchy* like Ellan once acted," he said with emphasis on the word touchy.

13

Shannan flashed a smile of understanding and sat on the bed. She took Tristine's hand. "Answer me. What did he say to upset you?"

"He said someday we'd have to stop playing games and I needed to act more mature since I'm going to be thirteen."

"Was he mean?"

Tristine shook her head.

"He's right. He is heir to the throne." She gently brushed the hair off Tristine's shoulder. "Despite these clothes and childhood games, you are a princess."

"I know! I just hate that things have to change. We have so much fun together."

Shannan chuckled. "You can still have fun, nothing's stopping that."

Necie crawled onto the bed to sit beside Tristine. "Nigel and Father say I'll change too."

Tristine rolled her eyes in frustration. "Of course, you're a child."

"You're not an adult yet. And you're crying because you can't play any more children's games," Necie lashed back.

"That's not true! You don't understand!"

"Peace," warned Shannan.

The girls clamped their mouths shut. Tristine cast an angry side-glance at Necie, who folded her arms and turned away in a huff.

"Both of you will mature," Shannan firmly began to get their attention. Once she did, her voice grew kind. "Many things change as we get older, but some things will never change. Nigel will always be your brother, you will always be sisters, and we will always be your parents."

"How long does it take to change from a girl to a woman?" groused Tristine.

Shannan smiled. "Depends upon the person. Ellan blossomed quickly but I took longer."

Armus chuckled.

"I don't think it's funny about Ellan. She's annoying," Tristine chided him.

14

"He's amused because of me," said Shannan. "He met me when I was young and exploring the forest, honing the skills I would one day need to fulfill my destiny."

"You are much like your mother, skilled with a bow and keen to nature," said Armus.

Tristine smiled, large and pleased. "I'd like to think so."

"You haven't become that way on your own," said Shannan. "I'm teaching you just like my grandfather taught me. But, I also had to learn how to adapt those skills and apply them to being queen. Same as you will do in becoming an adult."

"I suppose," she groused. "Father says I remind him of you as a girl. But was he cocky like Nigel when growing up?"

Armus heartily laughed and said; "Your father was much more stubborn and thickheaded than Nigel."

"Indeed," agreed Shannan. "It took nearly being gouged by a boar for him to admit I was a better archer than he."

The girls laughed and Tristine said, "I can't imagine Father not being good at anything."

"I didn't say he wasn't good, just I was better." Shannan again stroked Tristine's hair. "Since Nigel wasn't mean, you need to come down and apologize for your rude behavior."

"Only don't tell him about the boar," teased Armus.

In the drawing room Ellis sighed and tugged at his chin, his focus on what he read. Nigel and Ellan remained only Ellan now sat in a chair near the window reading a book.

Nigel approached at hearing Ellis' sobriety. "Is the news bad?"

Ellis cocked his head and indicated the papers. "Not good. These are reports from Iain and Roarke dated a month ago. I just got them earlier this morning while I've not heard from Darius in two months."

"It's doesn't mean anything has happened to Uncle," Nigel tried to sound encouraging.

"It doesn't mean it hasn't," muttered Ellan.

"Ellan," scolded Nigel in a hushed voice.

She was surprised at being heard and Nigel's warning glance to Ellis, her father looking stern. "Father, don't imagine the worse about uncle."

For a moment Ellis's gaze shifted between Nigel and Ellan. Nigel tried to be supportive, and her apology sheepish. All the same, he was concerned about Darius; but for his son's sake he flashed a cheerless, forced smile. "You're right. Darius is too ornery."

"You don't sound convinced."

Ellis pursed his lips, once more regarding the papers wondering how much he should tell of the situation. Before he could say anything further, Ellan groused.

"Why did you go to war anyway? It's Tunlund's problem, not ours."

This time Nigel forcefully rebuked her. "The king responded to a petition for help from an ally."

"Indeed. A king must honor his word, whether verbal or by written treaty," said Ellis, looking from Ellan to Nigel.

"I understand, sir," said Nigel.

Ellan capitulated. "Ay, sir."

A Guardian warrior appeared in the threshold. His hair was black, and linked with strong amber features, made an impressive setting for golden eyes. Although he wore the Guardian uniform, he also wore the amulet of the King's Champion, the royal eagle clenching the symbols of the Temple, a crown surrounding a sword.

"What is it, Kell?"

The Guardian smiled. "His Grace has returned.

Ellis looked greatly relieved, as did Nigel and Ellan. "Where is he?"

"I'm here."

Darius, the Duke of Allon entered the drawing room covered in road dust and appeared weary, but in one piece. Being foster brothers there was little resemblance between Darius and Ellis. Darius was three years older with dark brown hair, brown eyes and more rugged features while Ellis stood four inches taller and more athletically built compared to Darius' broad frame.

16

Ellis embraced Darius. "Thank Jor'el. That took too long."

"Ay," agreed Darius, although his expression exceedingly burdened.

"It's good to see you whole, Uncle," said Nigel.

Darius embraced Nigel and also greeted Ellan.

"Uncle!" exclaimed Tristine. She rushed to embrace Darius. Shannan and Necie arrived with her.

For a moment Darius held onto Tristine and kissed her cheek before embracing a chattering Necie. "No, I'm afraid all I brought back from this trip is myself," he replied to Necie's question.

"That is enough." Shannan eyes grew misty. "It is good to have you home." She embraced Darius and kissed his cheek. "You look tired. I'm sure you'd like to rest."

He shook his head. "Not yet. We need to speak." His prompting glance passed to Ellis.

Ellis steered Tristine and Necie toward the door. "Run along. You'll see Uncle at supper." He also motioned for Ellan to join her sisters.

Darius crossed to a side table upon which sat a pitcher of ale and tankards. He helped himself to a drink.

"I can tell the news is bad," said Ellis. He, Shannan, and Nigel waited in anticipation of the answer while Darius greedily drank.

Darius drained the tankard and sat, a poignant glance to Ellis. His voice was thick with emotion. "Jasper is dead. So are, Iain, Ferrell and Roarke."

Ellis winced at hearing about Jasper, the loyal master-of-arms of Garwood, who helped his foster father Angus rescue him as a baby. Jasper taught him and Darius how to fight using all manner of weapons, and helped to guard his identity until he came of age to claim his royal birthright. Jasper even lost his left eye in defense of Ellis. Iain commanded the royal army while Ferrell and Roarke were prominent Jor'ellian commanders. He regretted their loss, but Jasper's death was painful.

The sorrowful news forced Shannan to sit and Nigel bit his lower lip to contain his emotions. As soon as Nigel could hold a sword, Jasper helped train him in combat just like he had Ellis and Darius.

"How?" Nigel forced the word from his mouth.

17

Darius shrugged and drank before answering. "The campaign was hard fought and our losses higher than anticipated."

"How many?" asked Ellis.

"Almost three thousand killed, over fifteen hundred wounded, and six ships lost with all hands."

Shannan's breath caught in her throat and she grew teary-eyed. Nigel placed a hand on her shoulder in an effort to comfort her yet he too was distressed.

Ellis swore under his breath. "What about Hollis and Mathias?"

"Mathias suffered serious wounds, but will survive. The six ships lost came from Hollis' command and he's taking it hard." Darius grew passionate, pushing himself up from the chair. "I wish to heaven you had ordered Jasper to stay home! Why didn't you? You knew his remaining sight was failing."

Visibly pricked, Ellis turned to the window, battling to maintain his composure.

Shannan took Darius' arm, her face and voice sympathetic. "Do not be cross with Ellis. Jasper came to him a few days before departure asking him not to agree with you and forbid him to go. He knew it would be his last chance to serve Ellis and protect you before completely losing his sight."

"We didn't protect him when he needed it."

Ellis turned from the window to face Darius. "If you were in his position, would you have done any different for those you love?"

"No," droned Darius.

"Which is why I didn't have the heart to refuse him."

Darius went back to the chair, plopped down and took another drink.

"Where are Hollis and Mathias now?"

"In Leith. The surgeon forbade Mathias from traveling until he is recovered."

"Tomorrow you, Nigel, and I will ride into Leith."

Darius nodded, trying to stifle a yawn, despite his grief and agitation.

"Maybe now you'll rest," insisted Shannan.

"Only if Kell tells Eldric to put some Guardian concoction in this drink to make me unconscious."

Ellis drew Darius to his feet. "Please, do as she says. You'll need all your faculties to help me in honoring Jasper and the others."

"Some question why we aided Tunlund since they didn't seem very appreciative."

"We'll address the matter after speaking to Hollis and Mathias. For now, rest." Ellis escorted Darius to the threshold where he motioned for Kell, who took charge of the duke.

Shannan moved to comfort Ellis. "I'm so sorry about Jasper."

He blinked back tears. "I had a hunch something terrible would happen to him."

"Before or after you agreed?" asked Nigel.

For a moment Ellis regarded his son, then replied, "During our conversation. But you heard the reasons I couldn't refuse. In fact, Jasper said, if he died, he did so without regret and for me not be remorseful in granting permission." He moved from Shannan to Nigel, taking his son by the shoulders. "Sometimes a king must make personally painful decisions for the good of others. Jasper didn't want to spend his remaining years as a useless blind man."

"He wasn't useless."

"In his mind he was since he couldn't do what he had all his life: be a soldier and pass on those skills." Ellis took a steadying breath to quiet his passion. "Despite my hunch, knowing he died in service is far easier to accept than watching him lose all hope and desire for life."

Nigel's face was somber. "I understand why this is so painful for you, especially considering Uncle's reaction."

"Let's not speak of the matter at supper, rather enjoy the meal and celebrate Darius' return. Tomorrow will be soon enough to deal with such matters."

"Ay, sir."

Supper came and went with no military talk since all were eager to welcome Darius home. Normally the family dined together three times a week with the rest being state or private dinners meant for adult members of the family: those thirteen and older. On those nights Tristine and Necie either dined in the family salon or in their chamber. When a royal child reached the proper age, a banquet was held to announce their coming of age. In two months, they would celebrate Tristine's birthday with a Coming of Age Banquet.

It was very late when Darius retired to his chamber. He found Tristine in her dressing gown curled up in a chair asleep. The oil lamp on the table next to her was turned low. Despite the lack of blood relation, the strong bond between Darius and Ellis reflected in their families. He smiled, sat on the footstool, and touched her cheek.

"Tristine."

She stirred and woke. "Uncle."

"What are you doing here? You should be asleep."

"When we were going to bed, I heard Father say something about you leaving in the morning. I was afraid I wouldn't get to talk to you before you left for who-knows-where."

Darius chuckled. "Silly child, we're going to Leith to visit Baron Hollis and Baron Mathias."

"Oh," she muttered with embarrassment.

"What do you want to talk to me about that you couldn't say at supper?"

She grew sheepish. "It's about my banquet. I don't know that I want to grow up. It means everything is going to change. It did with Nigel and Ellan."

"Ay. They joined the adult world—but still indulge a clever little sister."

"Not Ellan," she said with a deep, sour frown.

"Nigel does."

"He says that will change."

"Has Nigel changed since his banquet?"

Her brows grew level in through and she frowned. "Some. The older he gets, the more responsibility father gives him."

"I mean in the way he treats you. Does he ignore you? Bully you? Or does he treat you the same as before?"

She sighed in resignation. "The same."

"So what makes you think he'll change after your banquet?"

"Nothing, I guess."

"Not in your relationship, but there will be changes regarding your responsibilities as a princess."

"Mother said the same thing."

Darius gave her a mild, scolding glance. "Did you expect me to tell you something different than she? I think you know better."

She flashed an impish smile. "Ay."

He shook his head with a snorting laugh. "One of these days, you'll try my patience."

"No, I won't." She giggled and hugged him.

After a quick knock at the door, Armus enter. The Guardian grinned. "I'll take her back to her room now, Your Grace."

"Ay, but can you keep her there?"

Chapter 2

GRAYDON CASTLE, the home of Baron Hollis, Lord of the East Coast, dominated Leith from the heights about a mile from the harbor. Gun emplacements on the battlement pointed out to sea, although nearly ninety years past since Allon was attacked. Ten years ago the small aging cannons were replaced with newer more effective artillery. Ellis encouraged military advancements along with growth in commerce, medicine, and education for all Allonians regardless of class or rank. The amount of education was tailored to the different areas of commerce, science, medicine, etc.

Leith prospered more in the twenty years of Ellis' reign than it did in the previous century. Trade expanded and brought a variety of goods from the far off corners of the world. Allonian wool, timber, cloth, iron and woodworking were in high demand. Fortunately, the sending of military aid to Tunlund did not have a detrimental impact on trade since the campaign only lasted a year. Quite the contrary, it produced a positive affect by contracting ship merchants to haul cargo and troops to Tunlund and back.

Although the war proved successful in the commercial arena, the loss of five ships and crew proved a harsh blow to the inhabitants of the East Coast. Ellis would make his appreciation known by having the local priest arrange a memorial service so he could address the families and personally thank them.

22

He also issued an order for each Fortress Master of the Twelve Provinces to hold a memorial service for the fallen sailors and included a hand written statement expressing his gratitude.

Darius, Ellis, and Nigel joined Hollis in the drawing room. Kell and Avatar stood by the door. Hollis was a forty-year-old man of moderate disposition and average looks.

"That is very generous of you, Sire," he said.

"It is a small thing to do after such suffering."

After a short knock, a servant entered. "Sire, Baron Mathias is awake."

Ellis left the drawing room to follow the servant upstairs to Mathias' chamber. Darius, Nigel and Hollis accompanied him. Outside the chamber a heavy-set middle-aged mortal man in physician's robes met them.

"Please be brief, Sire. He needs to rest."

Ellis said to the others, "Nigel only."

In a well-furnished chamber, Mathias lay upon a large bed. He appeared older than his early forties. In peak health he was a dashing man with dark hair and neatly trimmed goatee. Although dulled by pain and fatigue, the green eyes watched Ellis approach. He began to sit up.

"Sire."

Ellis stopped him. "No, Mathias. You need to save your strength for recovery."

Mathias slowly and painfully settled back into bed.

Nigel observed Mathias' pain. "Where do you hurt?"

"Everywhere, Highness."

Nigel flushed with embarrassment. "Sorry. Silly question."

"We came to thank you. Your service is greatly appreciated and we're glad you survived," said Ellis.

"Maybe I shouldn't have," groused Mathias. "If not for my blunder, Hollis would not have been forced to cover my mistake and lose so many ships."

"You made a decision in the heat of battle that saved more lives than were lost."

The statement puzzled Mathias. "Did Hollis say so?"

"Ay. So did Darius, other commanders, and a personal note from Ambassador Lanzo commending your actions. According to them, if you had not made the defensive maneuver most of the fleet would have been lost and changed the outcome of the war."

Mathias' brows furrowed, trying to let the news sink in. "I don't remember much past giving the order. Captain Banning told me of our losses when I briefly woke in my cabin."

"Do you know where you are now?" asked Nigel. Mathias simply looked at him, making the prince frown. "Sorry. Another silly question."

Mathias smiled, weak and thin.

The door opened and the physician entered, giving Ellis a prompting glance.

"You did well, Mathias. Rest and recover," said Ellis.

"Take care, Baron." Nigel and Ellis left.

"How is he?" asked Darius.

"He only remembers giving the order and is unaware of anything else," replied Ellis.

"The surgeon wondered if he'd it make back alive," said Hollis, growing melancholy. "It was hard enough losing the others, I couldn't image losing Mathias also."

Ellis clapped Hollis' shoulder. "Jor'el dealt mercifully with him."

"Ay, and Mathias would scold me for brooding. Will you be staying to dine, Sire?"

"Not this time. We leave for Waldron tomorrow. But the holiday was much appreciated and needed."

Hollis smiled and a bowed to the compliment. "I shall order your horses."

Ellan sat lounging on the manor terrace overlooking the beach. The aroma of fresh bread and roasting meat floated on the breeze. She took a deep whiff. "Smells like a good dinner, Morrell," she said to her Guardian warrior overseer.

24

He sat on the terrace stonewall gazing out to sea. Although good-looking like all Guardians, he had a slight weather-beaten aura to his face, golden haired, a thin beard and bright amber eyes. He cocked a grin. "I wouldn't know, Princess. Armus is a better judge of mortal food than I am."

"You have a sense of smell," she teased.

"Ay," he chuckled and turned back to the vista.

"What are looking at with such interest?"

"Nothing really, just taking in the view."

"You have no appreciation for food but enjoy a good view? You're a hard Guardian to figure out."

He heaved a casual shrug. "I could say the same about mortals. Especially one as unpredictable as Princess Tristine." He pointed over the wall.

Ellan moved to join him. Tristine trudged up the inland path, soaked from head to toe, face smudged and looking fretful. As usual, Armus followed her. "What have you done now?" she asked when Tristine reached the terrace. Instead of a reply, she received a withering glare. Ellan's displeasure turned to Armus, but the Guardian said nothing.

Nigel hurried from the house "Tristine? Are you hurt?"

"Hurt? She's completely ruined her clothes," chided Ellan.

Tristine made an angry, upset snarl at Ellan and began to bolt toward the house when Nigel caught her. "No. Father and Uncle are in the study talking to Mother about the visit. Go through the kitchen and up the back stairs."

Tristine sniffled a sob and nodded before changing course, Armus following.

Ellan prevented Nigel from leaving by stepping in front of him. "Why do you indulge her?"

"I'm not indulging her."

"Of course you are. You don't even know what happened yet you're shielding her. Just like you always do!"

Nigel's temper flared. "Didn't you see how upset she is? I think she's lucky only her clothes are ruined."

"Because she did something she wasn't supposed to."

"Or could have been hurt by something *not* her fault."

"It's always her fault."

He snarled in annoyance. "You may not care about her welfare, but I'm going to find out what happened before Father sees her." He pushed past Ellan to return to the house.

"I do care—only differently!" she called after him but was ignored. Her scowl of disapproval turned from the departing Nigel to Morrell. "I don't know who is more incorrigible, Nigel for protecting her or Tristine for being reckless."

A hive of activity took place in the kitchen during preparations for supper. Being wet and looking miserable, the servants didn't seem to recognize Tristine, and said nothing as she made her way around them to the back stairs. Even the sight of Armus didn't stir much attention.

He snatched a towel and pitcher of water before heading upstairs. In the room, Tristine removed her doublet. He poured water into a basin, but stopped when the door opened. Nigel quickly entered and shut the door.

Tristine grew anxious at his entrance. "Did anyone see you?"

"No, and you haven't much time to clean-up and change before supper."

"Finish undressing. I'll fetch your clothes," said Armus. She moved behind a changing screen and he went to the wardrobe.

"What happened?" asked Nigel. She made an angry snort, but didn't reply. He turned to Armus for an answer.

The Guardian took a dress and other garments from the wardrobe and placed them on top of the screen for Tristine to reach. "She wanted to take a last walk on the beach before leaving. The queen only agreed to give permission if she promised not go too far and be back in time for supper."

"How far did you go?" asked Nigel, but again she didn't answer.

"The wading pool," said Armus.

Nigel huffed in exasperation. "The only way in and out of there is to climb."

"Ay. When Tristine realized she would be late, she tried to hurry, but slipped—"

"And fell into the water," Nigel concluded.

Tristine loudly growled at his sarcasm, still behind the changing screen.

"She narrowly missed hitting her head on the rocks," said Armus with emphasis, his chestnut eyes direct on Nigel. "She was out of my reach to prevent the fall. I jumped in after her and pulled her up before rocks dislodged by her climb could strike her."

Nigel's brows drew level in fearful concern. "So it could have been worse."

"Ay. Thank Jor'el it was not."

"Indeed," murmured Nigel, momentary discomposed by the statement. "How did you get back in time?"

She came out from behind the screen wearing a loose fitting dress and turned so Armus could finish lacing up the back. She spoke for the first time. "Dimension travel from the pool to the end of the house path."

"I'm glad you weren't hurt," said Nigel in all sincerity.

She nodded and moved from Armus to the vanity to brush her hair.

"How did you expect to get inside without being seen?"

"The same way I've gotten in before—my Guardian shield."

"You are fortunate Armus was there, but one of these days you'll get him into serious trouble for helping with your little covert acts."

"Like Avatar helps you?" she shot back, looking at him in the mirror.

"Don't change the subject. This is about you; not Avatar and me."

"Did I hear my name?" asked Avatar.

She gasped in fear at seeing Avatar's reflection in the mirror as he stood in the threshold. She whirled about. "Did anyone see you come in here?"

"The king asked where Nigel went; so I said I'd find out."

Her worried look passed to Nigel, who said, "I'll tell Father I went to freshen up for dinner." He turned to leave.

"Wait, Highness," began Armus. He tossed Tristine a prompting glance. "Are you going to let him lie for you?"

"No. I'll say Nigel was visiting me."

Armus didn't relent in his stern regard. "You may have changed clothes, but your hair is wet and it won't be dry in time."

She grew fretful. "I'll get in trouble if I tell the truth."

"Falling into the pool was an accident."

"I went too far!"

Armus gripped her shoulders, making her look up at him. "Part of growing up is accepting the consequences of your actions, whether right or wrong. You didn't mean to go so far, but you did, which caused you to hurry and fall into the pool. Now you must admit to making a bad choice."

"I've learned it's better to tell Father the truth. He may get angry at first, but he prefers to deal with issues directly than learn the truth later," said Nigel.

Hesitant and indecisive, she bit her lip before asking, "Will I still be punished?"

Nigel shrugged in uncertainty. "Maybe. Only the punishments I've received were less severe when telling the truth than being caught in a lie."

"Really?"

"Ay," he replied with a soft grin.

She sighed in resignation. "Let me finish brushing my hair then we'll go downstairs." Being wet and tangled her hair was hard to brush and difficult to style, so she simply pulled the sides back from her face using ivory combs.

They were the last to arrive in the drawing room. Proper attire and decorum for dinner was part of training, so she knew her wet hair would be noticed. Nervous, she gripped Nigel's hand.

Sure enough, Shannan looked puzzled and asked, "Tristine, did you wash your hair before supper?"

Tristine felt Nigel squeeze her hand for support. "No, Mother," she began, her voice a bit stressed. "I had an accident on my outing."

"Accident? Were you hurt?"

"She wasn't hurt. She came back wet from head to foot. Her clothes are ruined," said Ellan in contempt.

Angered by the callous comment, Nigel refuted. "She fell out of Armus' reach and he jumped in to pull her out before rocks fell into the water on top of her."

"What?" Ellis' concerned glance changed from Nigel to Tristine. "Tell us everything."

Nigel encouraged Tristine with a smile, and she replied; "I asked Mother for permission to go on one last walk along the beach. She said I could if I didn't go too far and was back by suppertime. Well, I went further than I intended and when I realized I wouldn't be back I time, I tried to quickly climb out from the pool. The rocks gave way and I fell."

"It could have been worse if Armus wasn't there," said Nigel, tossing a scolding glance to Ellan, although his primary focus was on Ellis.

Ellis cocked a brow and turned to Armus, who stood by the door. "I take it after pulling her from the water you brought her back."

"Just to the end of the path, Sire."

Nigel spoke, "She arrived on the terrace looking very upset and I went to see if she was hurt. Thankfully not. I urged her to calm down and change before telling you what happened."

Tristine bit her lip, on the verge of tears but spoke when Ellis' gaze shifted to her. "I'm truly sorry, sir. It was unintentional. Are you going to punish me?"

Ellis pursed his lips to the question and Shannan said, "Ruined clothes are a small price to pay for an innocent mistake in judgment that could have been more serious."

"Besides, he did something similar as a boy," said Darius, pretending to speak into his cup while taking a drink, yet loud enough to be heard.

"You did?" asked Tristine in guarded curiosity.

Ellis frowned at Darius. "As I recall, you lent a helping hand in the stunt resulting in ruining my clothes and leaving me bruised and sore for a week."

Darius laughed. "You have a selective memory."

Tristine's curious, yet guarded gaze shifted between Ellis and Darius. "Then you won't punish me?"

Ellis smiled. "For clothes ruined in an accident? No. Thank Jor'el Armus was present. And it took courage to admit your mistake."

Tristine was relieved. She received a cup of mulled cider from Darius, along with a wink.

29

Nigel noticed Ellan frown and approached her to speak privately. "Did you expect her to be punished?"

"She usually does things worthy of punishment."

"This was an accident."

Her eyes narrowed in suspicion. "Did you know this earlier?"

"No. By her expression I didn't think what happened was on purpose."

She sarcastically snickered under her breath. "I think everything she does is on purpose."

"There's the difference. Father and I give her the benefit of the doubt, you don't. Tristine isn't mean, just reckless at times. You may try being a little kinder and a more supportive. I helped you during your transition and you've done well. Even Father complimented you."

Ellan's shoulders sagged and she nodded. "I'll try."

When dinner was over, they went back to the drawing room, signaling time for Necie and Tristine to withdraw for the night. Before leaving, Tristine approached Ellis.

"Thank you for understanding, Father. I truly didn't mean to be late or ruin my clothes."

"I know. However, the time is growing short for such antics."

"I only hope I don't disappoint you too much when I try to act like an adult."

Ellis chuckled. "Just make the effort to minimize those mistakes."

"Ay, Father. Goodnight." Tristine and Necie left.

"It's going to take more than *effort* to change her ways," murmured Ellan to herself.

Ellis cocked a scolding brow. "That's the second derogatory remark you've made about your sister this evening. Why?"

Although surprised he heard, Ellan had to answer. "She's headstrong and stubborn. I can't imagine her changing just because she turns thirteen."

"You didn't change overnight," said Nigel.

"I'm not reckless."

30

"Recklessness doesn't make her incapable. Believe me, I understand what a reckless, younger sibling is like," said Darius.

Ellis frowned in rebuke at the reference.

"I thought you said Tristine is like Mother?" Ellan asked Ellis.

"There is a bit of both of us in her. Each of you do to one degree or another."

"Yet you are also individuals," began Shannan. "You will each mature in your own way and time. You are doing well, even though you needed help at the beginning. Tristine may require a little more patience." She spoke the last sentence to Ellis.

"The patience of Jor'el," he snickered.

"Which is what Father said about you," quipped Darius.

In spite of his earlier annoyance, Ellis laughed.

"Mother and Uncle are right. We need to be patient with Tristine," said Nigel to Ellan.

"With help, she too will do as well as you," added Ellis.

"Ay, sir."

Kell entered. "Sire. Baron Hollis is here."

"Send him in."

Hollis was booted and spurred, and looking serious. "Sire."

"Hollis. Do you bring news of Mathias?"

"Mathias is well. An envoy from Morven arrived in Leith about an hour ago. My men brought him to me when he requested directions to Waldron with a message for you from Emperor Kamu."

Ellis' questioning glance passed to Darius who said; "I have no knowledge of the emperor wishing to have a dialogue."

"According to Lord Bijan, he means no harm, only to offer tribute to the victor," said Hollis.

"Is he alone?"

"Ay, Sire. He yielded his sword and submitted to being searched for any hidden weapons."

"Is he still in Leith?"

31

"No. I took the liberty of bringing him here under guard in case you wanted to speak to him." Seeing Ellis' disapproval, he added; "I thought it would be better to deal with him here where he could be put on a ship and sent back if there were trouble, rather than inland at Waldron."

"Stated that way, I appreciate your consideration."

"Ellis, the Morvenians are not inclined to deal openly around women. In fact, they view it as an insult," said Darius, tossing a wary eye to Shannan and Ellan.

Shannan took mild offense. "Why?"

"Morven is a patriarchal society. Women are treated with respect but not permitted to be included in the affairs of men."

She set her chin. "This is Allon. Here men and women are treated equally in all aspects of life."

"I know, but—" began Darius but was stopped by Ellis, who addressed Shannan.

"I will be certain to let Lord Bijan know about the difference. However, for the first encounter, let me feel him out and learn what the Morvenians want."

Shannan wasn't pleased by the suggestion, yet yielded. "If you insist. Come, Ellan. We'll leave the men to the affairs of state."

Ellis snorted an ironic chuckle yet waited until his wife and daughter left. "You may bring him in, Baron." Ellis spoke to Kell. "This should be interesting."

Lord Bijan was a short man with thin, wiry black hair, beard and dark brown eyes. He wore an ornate red, gold, and green robe over a long dark green tunic with a large red sash. The gold pants were bloused at the top and draped over the top of the black leather boots. On his head was a red, green, and gold feathered skullcap.

"Sire, Lord Bijan of Morven," said Hollis.

"Most noble king," said Bijan in heavily accented Allonian. He offered Ellis a low, deep bow. He gave a respectful nod to Nigel and Darius.

"His Royal Highness, Prince Nigel and the Duke of Allon," said Ellis.

"Most Exalted Highness," said Bijan, bowing to Nigel. "My Lord Duke, it is pleasure to meet you again."

"Lord Bijan, this is an unexpected visit, especially so soon," said Ellis.

"It is emperor wish time not pass too much before making tribute for great victory."

"Indeed, the powder is not yet dry," mused Ellis yet saw by Bijan's puzzled look he didn't understand the expression.

"How soon after we left did the emperor dispatch you?" asked Darius.

"Next day. After tribute was decided. I was sent before tribute to make certain to be received by king. Often enemy not received well by victor who is suspicious of trouble."

"According to Baron Hollis you willingly placed yourself in his charge," said Ellis.

"It is of little trouble when duty to respect emperor and king."

"What are the emperor's intentions?"

"His Imperial Majesty Emperor Kamu wishes to make gift to king by offering an alliance by marriage to royal princess."

Ellis took note of Nigel's surprise at the offer and the young's man attempt to curb his surprise when they made brief eye contact before Ellis replied. "The emperor is generous. However, I'm already married."

"King have one wife?" asked Bijan in confusion.

"Ay."

"Young prince also have one wife?"

Nigel flushed with embarrassment at the question. "I'm not married yet."

"Prince is age of man, no?"

Ellis pursed his lips to stop a laugh before speaking. "My Lord Bijan, His Highness is not yet of age for marriage according to Allonian custom, and when he marries, he too will only have one wife."

Bijan appeared to be trying to comprehend. "Emperor have many wives and many children. King have one wife, one child?"

"I have four children. All from one wife."

Bijan was surprised. "This is different. In Morven, it is one wife for one child."

33

"How many children does the emperor have?" asked Darius.

"One hundred and three," replied Bijan.

"What?" exclaimed Nigel in astonishment.

Ellis placed a hand on Nigel's shoulder to calm him, but spoke to Bijan. "That is very different from Allon, my lord."

"Then king will not take royal princess as wife?"

"I cannot accept such a generous offer. To do so would go against Jor'el's law."

"For prince perhaps?"

Ellis pursued his lips in a brief moment of consideration, moving from Nigel. "That is a suggestion requiring thought and prayer."

Nigel stared in surprise at Ellis. Darius discreetly took him by the elbow, giving him a careful warning with a shake of his head. Nigel forced his face to relax. Neither Ellis nor Bijan noticed the exchange as Bijan continued to speak.

"Emperor instruct I tell king: emperor greatly desire treaty with king. We have seen power of king's army and Jor'el and have respect. The royal princess is one part of tribute. Perhaps by seeing king will consider again."

Ellis paced as if thinking when in fact he tossed a glance to Kell after turning his back to Bijan. The Guardian Captain paid close attention to Bijan. Guardians were keen judges of mortal character, and if there were duplicity in Bijan's manner or voice, Kell would know. A shake of the captain's head indicated trouble, while a nod meant all was well. Kell did neither. Rather he made a small shrug. To keep up his façade of consideration, Ellis paced for a few more steps and took note of the others. Darius appeared undecided, Hollis passive and Nigel anxious. Ellis stopped pacing to face Bijan.

"When does the emperor expect an answer?"

"At king's pleasure. The tribute can wait long as necessary."

"Wait?"

"Only word from king will bring it to Allon."

34

The word *it* did not go unnoticed by Ellis, Nigel, Hollis and Darius, only Nigel spoke first. "You said the tribute is marriage to a princess. How can you refer to her as *it*?"

"Princess is property of emperor."

"Property?" said Ellis with ire.

"I believe he meant to say daughter," said Darius in a corrective tone of Bijan.

Bijan bowed, his face apologetic. "My speech in Allonian not perfect. Please, king, forgive mistake. Princess Kaleana is obedient daughter of emperor who wishes to please emperor and king."

Ellis tugged on his lower lip and regarded Bijan. "How long will it take for you to return with Princess Kaleana?"

"Shortly of month."

"You mean within the month?"

"Ay. Does this mean king accept tribute?"

"Let's just say, I will consider an alliance with Morven, and am undecided about the exact terms."

Bijan smiled. "I understand. Will king be here for my return?"

"No, come to Waldron. Baron Hollis will escort you."

Bijan bowed. "By king's leave I return."

Ellis motioned to Hollis, who left with Bijan.

The moment they were gone Nigel asked; "Father, you're not seriously considering I marry this princess? You heard the way they treat their women."

Ellis put up a hand to stop Nigel. "I said I will consider an alliance, I didn't say marriage."

"Oh," said Nigel, suddenly deflated.

Darius chuckled and clapped Nigel on the shoulder. "You need to learn the art of diplomacy. When a defeated enemy comes bearing gifts and offering to make an alliance, you proceed with cautious respect. You never know if that former enemy will one day prove to be your best ally."

Ellis grinned at the explanation and looked to Kell. "Well?"

"I don't believe I sensed any duplicity, Sire. However, their beliefs are so foreign and deeply rooted he is difficult to completely read."

"I sensed the same." Ellis returned to Nigel. "Despite the fact the emperor has over one hundred children, offering a royal marriage is very serious. As a fellow monarch, I should listen and consider."

"Is that all you will do?"

"That is all I can do at present. Until I know the Morvenians better, their motives, customs, and character, I will not make a final decision." He snickered at seeing Nigel look relieved. "I have no intention of forcing you into a marriage but I must consider all options. In time Jor'el will show me the best choice. Be at ease until then, but learn from this meeting what will some day be required of you."

"Ay, sir."

Darius snorted a laugh. "You convinced Nigel, but what about Shannan?"

"Ay," added Nigel, widely smiling. "Mother didn't look pleased."

Ellis slyly grinned. "Leave her to me, I have a way of convincing her."

"May I watch so I can learn?" quipped Nigel, making both Darius and Ellis laugh.

"That is a lesson only learned by the experience of marriage," said Ellis, to which Nigel flushed.

36

Chapter 3

WALDRON CASTLE stood as a wonderful reminder of the victory twenty years ago that restored the House of Tristan to Allon's throne. In tribute to his ancestor Tristan, Ellis rebuilt Waldron on the original spot. With help from the Guardians, the sprawling splendor was completed in a mere five years, a feat mortals could not have accomplished since the compound enclosed fifty acres. However, a brief interruption during the construction could have altered the future of Allon.

According to Prophecy the next heir would be born at Waldron and Ellis insisted the forthcoming birth of their first child happen there, although construction was not yet complete. Two months after Nigel's birth, Sir Owain, a member of the Council of Twelve, mounted a coup. Aided by the Dark Way, he and his forces easily breeched the incomplete walls and gates during a night attack when Ellis was away dealing with a crisis in the North Plains. The quick action of a few Guardians and bravery of handful of Jor'ellian Knights and Royal soldiers allowed the queen to flee with Nigel before the castle fell.

Learning of the attack, Ellis mustered his army intent on taking back Waldron. One false move and civil war could erupt. Fortunately, the remaining members of the Council stood against Owain. Although outnumbered at fifty thousand to two thousand, Owain fought. The assault

37

to liberate Waldron lasted less than an hour, with Owain and most of his men killed. The stench of the Dark Way lingered over the royal castle so Ellis ordered construction completed before the royal family returned to take up permanent residence.

The enormous splendor and strength of Waldron dominated the plain. It sat slighted elevated and surrounded by forest and rolling countryside. A manicured driveway led to an elaborate oak and wrought iron gate flanked by two impressive gatehouses. From the gatehouses stretched fifteen-foot high walls, ending in massive square corner turrets at each intersection. Past the main gate lay the Grand Courtyard of white marble cobblestone with a cascading fountain in the center. Directly beyond the main gate, across the Grand Courtyard, stood the Great Hall, a stone structure of grand proportion to impress the visitor with the strength of Allon's King. To the right of the fountain was the Castle Chapel honoring Jor'el. This structure was more elaborate in carving, stained glass, and awe-inspiring architecture than the Hall.

A less ornate, but finely crafted gate stretched diagonally from the Great Hall to the Chapel. The gate separated the armory, stables, carriage house, soldiers' barracks, and servants' quarters from the Grand Courtyard. Another smaller wrought iron fence and gate ran between the Chapel and the right gatehouse. This area housed the Jor'ellian priests' quarters and the Chapel gardens. Accessible to the Chapel, yet outside the main walls, were the family cemetery and royal crypt. The only occupant of the crypt was Sir Niles of Pollux, Shannan's grandfather, killed just prior to Ellis' victory.

A two-story enclosure ran from the left front side of the Great Hall leading to buildings on the west wall. This corridor served to divide the Guest Quarters from the Family's Private Quarters on the west and south walls. The lower level served as a galley way, while the second story housed Waldron's steward, the King's study, Captain of the Guard's office, and the private quarter's of the King's Champion. The galley way also formed the final section enclosing the Family's Courtyard and Garden.

It was a beautiful, late summer's day when the royal family returned from Leith. Almost immediately, Ellis informed his steward of visiting royalty from Morven expected to arrive by the end of the month. Ellis also dispatched messengers to the Council of Twelve, inviting them to Waldron in anticipation of the royal reception. He knew Mathias would be absent. Hollis informed him Lady Rhea arrived in Leith to care for Mathias. Darius would not appreciate time at home with his family being cut short, but such was the lot of being brother to the king.

The same night of their return, Avatar accompanied Nigel to his chamber to retire. Nigel acted moody since leaving Leith five days ago. He spoke little, even when addressed by others. Nigel normally grew quiet when troubled or agitated; but rudely dismissing the servant helping him change for bed was unusual. Despite personal feelings, he usually treated his servants kindly.

Avatar closed the door upon the servant's departure and asked; "What's troubling you?"

Nigel glanced at him, awkward and uncertain. "Do you know anything about the Morvenians?"

"A little. What do you want to know?"

"Are they like us?"

"You mean mortal? Ay." Avatar's attempted humor was met with a sour frown.

"No, I mean their beliefs, customs, lifestyle."

"From what I recall hearing over the centuries, they believe in multiple gods, more numerous than the Gormanites or Tunlundians. There is a god for almost every day and everything imaginable."

Thoughtful, Nigel sat on the bed. "Sounds complex and confusing."

Avatar sat beside him. "Ay. In what does one place their faith? The sun, the moon, or some beast?"

Nigel stared side-ways at Avatar and chided, "Father's going to hear their proposal for an alliance."

"As king, he must listen and consider all options."

"He said the same, but I'm not ready to get married!" When Avatar chuckled, Nigel bolted off the bed. "I don't see what's so funny."

"Once again, you're jumping to conclusions without knowing all the facts. You must curb your tendency and this is a good opportunity to start. Besides, I know what will guide the Son of Tristan's decision, same as it should yours."

"Verse and prayer." Nigel waved his hands in frustration and paced. "I know!"

"Then you also know what Verse says about not joining oneself with those who profane the truth."

"Father's made alliances with other nations who don't worship Jor'el. Are you saying he violated Verse?"

"That part speaks of marriage."

"Oh," said Nigel, sheepish.

Avatar made a sarcastic scowl. "To think, Master Hampton boasts you are his best royal pupil when it comes to Verse and Prophecy."

"I listen and memorize—"

"But don't retain." Avatar stood and gripped Nigel's shoulder. "What's in your head must penetrate your heart in order to guide you. I thought you knew better."

"I do! You are a great reason I do. Still, the older I get, the more I understand how complex life really is. How heavy a burden Father bears as king. A burden I don't know I can bear, or I'm supposed to." He spoke the last sentence with a fading voice.

"What?" asked Avatar, not certain he heard correctly, rather, hoping he had not heard correctly.

Nigel shook his head, moving from under Avatar's grasp to pace again. "My feelings and head are confused and conflicted."

"How so?" Agitated, Nigel he didn't immediately reply, so again Avatar made Nigel stop and look at him. "Tell me."

Nigel grew fretful and apprehensive. "I don't think I can."

The expression told Avatar he heard correctly so he pressed the matter. "You said something about the burden of a king. What do you mean?"

Nigel's head lowered and replied in a shaky voice. "I have a deep sense I'm not to be king."

For a brief moment, the statement stymied Avatar, but more important was dealing with Nigel's agitation. When Nigel cautiously looked at him, he asked; "When did you start to sense this?"

"Recently, only it's vague, almost counter to the knowledge I'm to continue in my duties and be the son and brother I've always been." His agitation heightened. "As heir I am responsible to continue the lineage! In light of this sense I don't see how that's possible and what I wrestle with. How can I not be king but still be son and brother? I even wondered whether to tell you."

"You know you can tell me anything in complete confidence."

Nigel flashed a small but mirthless smile. "What does this mean? And what should I do?"

Avatar's brows leveled in disturbed thought. More often than not, he anticipated what Nigel was thinking or at least what troubled him. This was something he did not expect. "I'm not certain. But I will find out. If not from Kell then directly from Jor'el."

"Should I tell Father?"

"No. At least not for the time being."

"But this alliance—"

"I don't believe will result in your marriage," insisted Avatar. "Continue as normal and leave the rest to me. You do trust me, don't you?" he asked in his usual dry humor, prompting a low chuckle from Nigel.

"Of course."

"Then get some rest." Avatar guided him to the bed. Nigel climbed under the covers and stopped him from turning off the oil lamp beside the bed.

"I don't know what I'd do without you, Avatar."

The Guardian cocked a grin. "I don't think you want to find out."

Nigel smiled and settled into bed, closing his eyes.

Avatar turned out the lamp and took his place beside the door. What Nigel said unsettled him. Being a warrior, he understood battle and his role in defending Jor'el, Allon and the mortal population; but Nigel was his first assignment as a Guardian Overseer. Charged with the life of a single mortal

41

from infancy was a new and different experience; and not just any mortal, the heir to the throne. Since the first day, he diligently oversaw Nigel's care.

In fact, his appointment came a few days prior to Owain's coup. During the escape, he was not only responsible for Nigel's care, but also the queen, Lady Arista, and the boys, Wess and Bosley. Hardly a good beginning, yet as a result he felt closer to Nigel than any mortal in his more than eighteen hundred years of existence. The bond grew since, and anything that upset, caused harm, or disturbed Nigel, he took personally. Thus when he was confident Nigel slept, he left to find Kell.

Kell wouldn't be hard to find, especially considering the time of night. After the royal family retired, the captain went to his quarters located on the upper galley way. Normally one waited for a reply to a knock, but Avatar wasn't in a patient mood and entered. Kell sat on the floor at the end of his bed in the Guardian meditation position.

"I need to speak to you."

Kell cocked a brow at Avatar's demanding tone and fixed features. "Is there a problem with Nigel?"

"Ay, and I want answers!"

Kell stood, his features stern and shoulders square. "Pardon me?"

Avatar scowled in frustration. "I'm sorry, Kell. I didn't mean it the way it sounded."

"What's wrong?"

"I don't want to betray his confidence. However, Nigel said something about his future I had not anticipated and is deeply troubling. Have you any idea what he's talking about?" His look was direct, almost insolent, making Kell's brows furrow in guarded concern. "Well?" he pressed, seeing Kell's expression change.

"In a manner of speaking, only I don't think I can give you a satisfactory answer because it's not definite, nor final. Still, there is a vagueness concerning his future. What it means has been part of my nightly mediation for the past week but with no clarification."

"Could there be a connection to this Morvenian marriage alliance?"

"Agreeing would violate Verse and I don't believe the Son of Tristan will do so."

"I told Nigel the same. I just wanted to speak with you to be sure."

Kell clapped Avatar's shoulder. "To be honest, I'm not sure. However, I am sure Jor'el is in control and if we are to know, we will be told in time."

Avatar became sober, almost melancholy. "I never cared so much for a mortal before. It hurts to think his future is unclear."

"I understand. I felt the same when Latham captured Shannan and I couldn't help her. In the end, it worked out. It may do the same for Nigel, for I don't sense finality. You've done well with him. Even Jor'el is pleased."

"Thank you. Again, I'm sorry for my earlier rudeness."

Kell laughed. "That was mild. A few times I thought Armus would become violent with me concerning Tristine."

Avatar smiled, his goatee winkled with irony. "Can you blame him? She's left him looking like a fool often enough. A Guardian warrior incapable of corralling a mortal girl."

Kell chuckled and shook his head. "She is precocious and independent, but with a good heart."

"Of his sisters, Tristine is Nigel's favorite."

"Unfortunately, he's made it obvious. Morrell says Ellan grows resentful."

"I'll tell him. Necie seems the same.

"She's too young to understand the difference yet."

"She's spoiled by everyone's attention."

"Ay. There's a gentleness and innocence about her." Kell guided Avatar to the door. "For now, just continue as you have and wait."

While the rest of Waldron went about preparing for a royal visit, Tristine and Necie continued their lives as usual. Not being of adult age yet, was mildly frustrating at times and Nigel's inability to either play with Necie or go riding and exploring with Tristine proved irksome. However, duty required his attention.

43

Tristine enjoyed the family holiday on the coast, but missed hunting the familiar grounds surrounding Waldron and took advantage of her free time to do just that. Covered in road dust, her hair windblown, and cheeks rosy from a day of riding, she returned to Waldron leading a limping black mare. She wore breeches, boots and spurs, a bow and quiver across her back. Armus walked behind, keeping watch over his charge. Two geese hung over the saddlebow.

A groom hastened to take the horse once she removed the geese from the saddlebow.

"Rub her well and look at her right foreleg. She pulled up lame," she said.

"You did well, Princess," said Wren, the beautiful green-eyed Guardian huntress. Her long auburn hair was pulled back at the sides, falling loose behind her shoulders. She stood a few inches shorter than Armus and unlike the warrior, wore forester brown and green, armed with a crossbow and quiver.

"Ay, but I could have done better. I nearly got a stag this time."

"Really?" Not completely convinced, Wren glanced at Armus.

"Ay," he affirmed.

Wren smiled warm and generous at Tristine. "Let me take them to Cook."

Tristine yielded the geese to Wren. "Do you know where my parents are?"

"The queen and your sisters are in the family salon while the king and prince are in the study."

Tristine beamed. "I'll tell Mother first."

The family salon was a warm intimate room of cherry wood with special mementos and miniatures of various family members at different ages. The most endearing aspect of a room was a painting of Ellis and Shannon together. The late Vicar Archimedes commissioned the portrait after the coronation to save for history the likeness of the Son of Tristan and the Daughter of Allon at the moment of their victory. Ellis was nineteen and Shannon, eighteen. Both wore the forester clothes from their days hiding in

Dorigirth until the appointed time in Prophecy. Ellis' golden hair was longer and a bit unkempt. He held a common sword, not the weapon of a King or Jor'ellian knight. He hands rested on the pommel, swordpoint resting on the ground. Shannon stood at Ellis' left shoulder, brown hair loose and the sides pulled back. In her right hand she held her bow, and upon her left arm sat Kato, the majestic eagle. Torin, a large magnificent wolf, stood in front of them. Together, they would topple the worst evil Allon had seen since Dagar's Great Rebellion. Archimedes meant well, but the painting invoked too many personal feelings and emotions to share. Thus they chose to keep it private. Once they passed to the heavenlies, and if their children agreed, the painting could be viewed publicly.

When Tristine and Armus arrived, Shannan and Ellan were doing needlepoint while Necie tried to manage her hoop, needle and thread.

"Mother, I'm back."

Shannan accepted Tristine's hug and kiss. "I gather from your greeting the outing was successful."

"Ay! I downed two large geese." She used her hands to show their size.

"That big?" snickered Ellan in disbelief.

"Ay," she said with triumphant confidence. "Wren is bringing them to Cook. You'll see them once they are prepared."

"See what?" asked Ellis. He and Nigel entered unnoticed.

"Father." Tristine gave him an enthusiastic greeting.

"Something good must have happened for that greeting."

"Tristine said she downed two large geese." Necie used her hands to give a visual measure. In doing so she not only exaggerated the measurement, but also dropped her hoop.

"They weren't that big," said Tristine. She used her own hands to show Ellis. "But, Father, that's not the best part. It was the stag."

"Stag?"

"Ay. Ten points at least," she said, excited. "I pursued it near the old widow's place and cornered it ready to shoot—"

"Ay, ay!" said Necie in giddy anticipation.

"She didn't down a stag," Ellan rebuffed Necie.

"Let her finish," chided Nigel.

Tristine frowned in disappointment. "Ellan's right. I had perfect aim but just when I released, Caleigh stumbled and pulled up lame. I wounded the stag, Father. With your permission I'll get a better horse to pursue and finish it."

Ellis gave a moment's consideration. "If it was earlier in the day—"

"I can't leave the poor animal wounded."

"You've not camped out alone at night."

"You said if I did so you would take me hunting with you and Nigel. Now's my chance."

Ellis pursed his lips. "I know what I said and I stand by it. However, plans have changed since you left this morning."

"How?" she asked with guarded curiosity.

"Uncle, Aunt and Angus have arrived, which means the Council is all present. We decided to change our family dinner to this evening and have a Council banquet tomorrow night."

Her displeasure faded at the news of Darius and Arista's arrival. Ellis placed an arm around her shoulders. "That wasn't too big of a disappointment, was it?"

"No, but if my horse wasn't so old and I had a better bow, I would have downed the stag."

"I believe you." Ellis tossed a sly glance to Shannan, who smiled.

"Can I try tomorrow and camp out?"

Again, Ellis hesitated. "Now is not the best time with visitors expected any day."

"Then when?"

"After our guests leave."

"I'll go with you. I'll need a night out after this," said Nigel.

"It's settled. Now go clean up for dinner."

"Ay, Father." Tristine gave Ellan a triumphant smirk and departed.

The family dining hall was at the rear of the west wing on the first floor and a relatively small room for Waldron, decorated in warm rosewood

46

paneling with a beautiful tapestry carpet. Tristine retold her tale to 'uncle' and 'aunt'. Arista, the Duchess of Allon and great granddaughter of Vicar Archimedes, was a comely woman of thirty-nine, well certain of her mind yet discreet. She served as lady-in-waiting for three years before marrying Darius. Upon marriage she received the affectionate title 'aunt' and appointed 'godmother' to the royal children. Their son, Angus, was a gangly boy of eleven and favored his father in feature with thick brown hair and brown eyes.

Ellis and Shannan sat at each end of the table with the family arranged accordingly. As heir, Nigel sat on Ellis left, Darius to Ellis' right. Tristine sat beside Nigel with Ellan beside Darius. Arista sat to the left of Shannan with Necie and Angus.

Darius spoke once Tristine finished her story. "Perhaps Wren should find the beast and put it out of its misery."

"I already instructed her," said Ellis.

"When?" asked Tristine.

"After you left the salon. She found it dead with your shot still in it. Venison will serve for the main dish at the Council banquet tomorrow."

Tristine's proud smile stretched from ear to ear.

"Only six points, not the ten you claimed," said Ellan.

"Six? I thought I saw more."

"The number doesn't matter. You're credited with your first stag. I will make certain everyone knows who provided the meat," said Nigel.

"That is the king's prerogative," bantered Ellis.

Tristine tossed a triumphant glare and smile at Ellan and returned to eating.

The door opened and a servant entered carrying a letter. Kell, Avatar and Armus stood just inside the door where Kell intercepted the servant, who gave the letter to the captain before withdrawing.

"A letter from Baron Hollis, Sire."

Ellis paused in eating and held out his hand for the letter. His brows raised in surprise upon reading. "Well, that was a quick month."

"They're here already?" asked Shannan.

"Arrived five days ago with much cargo. Hollis sent a messenger ahead with warning. They should be here in two days."

Nigel's fork slipped from his hand and he sat back in his chair, brows level. Avatar noticed his reaction and made a slight motion for calm.

Tristine also noticed. "Nigel?" she asked in concern, taking his hand.

He sat upright in an attempt to act natural. In doing so he caught Ellis' glance.

"Nothing to worry about," said Ellis.

"Ay, sir." Nigel forced a grin at Tristine and squeezed her hand. "I'm fine," he said to her.

"Appears the Council arrived just in time," said Darius, his glance shifting between Nigel and Ellis.

"Indeed." Ellis folded the letter and handed it back to Kell. "Inform the Council of the baron's message."

"Ay, Sire." Before departing, Kell gave Armus and Avatar a look of concern and short nod to remain alert.

Vidar, Mahon, and Morrell waited in the hall. Vidar was the premier Guardian archer and the Queen's protector. Like Wren, he carried a crossbow. He won the position for his bravery in saving Shannan just prior to Ellis' battle with Marcellus, Latham and Dagar. Trim and athletically built with auburn hair and brilliant copper eyes he stood a head shorter than the warriors.

Guardians divided the duty of standing watch inside or outside of a room where the royal family gathered, although mortal soldiers also stood watch in the corridors. The only exception was Kell, who always accompanied the king. Kell emerged form the dining room, and they noticed his serious expression.

"Trouble, Captain?" asked Morrell.

"Hollis sends advance word of the Morvenians' arrival."

"That bothers you?" asked Vidar.

"Anything that isn't clearly known and can impact Allon bothers me."

Morrell and Mahon exchanged snickering glances. Kell scowled and glared at Vidar.

The archer shrugged. "You do tend toward the dreary side of consideration."

"As captain it's my duty," insisted Kell, which didn't change their amused mood. "Perhaps my calling a meeting of Trio Leaders will convince you both."

To this Mahon and Morrell did look more concerned. The Trio Leaders were the Guardian counterparts of the mortal Council of Twelve. "Why?" asked Morrell.

"Because foreigners who do not worship Jor'el are in Allon. Is that reason enough?"

Morrell and Mahon were subdued. "Captain, we didn't mean any disrespect. Our swords are at your command," said Mahon.

"I have a task." Kell indicated the letter and left.

"What was that about? We were only joking," Morrell said to Vidar.

"He'll tell us in time. Still, if some sense is troubling the captain, I suggest you curb your humor, stay alert and close to your charges."

Later that night, Tristine peeked out her bedchamber. Royal guards stood at either end of the hall, but they rarely made a sound. Her parents and Nigel paused before the royal chamber with Kell, Vidar, and Avatar not far behind. Nigel gave Shannan a goodnight kiss before going to his bedchamber. Kell and Vidar remained in the hall; Avatar accompanied Nigel. Tristine shut the door, brows thoughtful and chewing on her lower lip. She crossed to her bed put on slippers and grabbed her dressing gown.

"What are you planning now, my little mouse?" asked Armus, suspicious.

"I'm worried about Nigel. He was quiet through dinner. In fact, he's been moping since we got back." She didn't wait for Armus to answer and left her chamber.

Kell and Vidar became alert at seeing her, but she ignored them and went to Nigel's chamber. Armus waved a friendly hand at his fellow Guardians.

At the chamber door, she carefully called. "Nigel." Receiving no immediate answer, she spoke a little louder. "Nigel?" Upon hearing voices inside, she tried the door, only to find it locked. "Nigel, let me in," she insisted. From behind the door came muffled voices that sounded like arguing. The door opened and Avatar motioned her inside, but with a hand, stopped Armus from entering.

Only a few lamps were lit and Nigel sat in a chair beside an empty hearth, his doublet off. By his expression he wasn't pleased to see her.

"Why aren't you in bed like you're supposed to be?"

"Because I know something is troubling you."

He turned away to stare into the hearth. "You wouldn't understand."

She moved so she could see him. "Does it have to do with the Morvenians?"

His look was sharp. "What made you ask about them?"

"I'm not stupid. You became upset when Father said they were on their way here. Why?"

"I said, you wouldn't understand."

"Why? Because I'm not yet an adult? *T'iseanpoup!*"

Although shocked by her speech, Nigel couldn't help a chuckle. "What did you say?"

"*T'iseanpoup,*" she repeated. "Wren said it about Cook earlier. Now I say it about you."

Nigel tossed an amused glance to Avatar, who tried to keep a straight face as the he discreetly said, "Princess, the word means *chicken poop* in Ancient."

"Oh," she muttered, then became annoyed at hearing Nigel laughing. "Well, your stubbornness is still *t'iseanpoup.*"

"Don't let Mother or Father hear you."

"I'll say it louder," her voice rising.

Nigel bolted to his feet and covered her mouth before the word came out. "You're incorrigible." He tightened his grip when she tried to speak again. "If I tell you, will you promise you won't say that word again?" She nodded and he released her. He motioned to the chairs and she sat. Before

50

resuming his seat, he noticed Avatar's guarded concern and made a quick, curt shake of his head to the Guardian before sitting.

"What was that about?" she asked at the exchange.

Nigel ignored her question to ask, "Do you know why the Morvenians are coming?"

"To make a treaty with Father because they lost the war."

"Do you know the terms they are offering?"

"No. I thought the victor made the terms. That's what Armus said."

"Father may end up doing so but Lord Bijan came with a offer from Emperor Kamu for Father to marry a Morvenian princess."

She gaped, shocked. "What? Father agreed to marry another woman?"

"No!" he insisted. He motioned at Tristine yet spoke to Avatar. "You say I jump to conclusions?" He turned back to her not allowing Avatar to answer. "Father refused. In Allon, one man and one woman make a marriage, but it is different in Morven."

"Does Mother know?"

"Will you let me finish?" he chided. "When Father refused, Lord Bijan asked about me." When her breath caught in her throat and she stared at him, he balked in speech. "Father told him I'm not of age yet, and when I do marry it while be according to our laws. Still, he agreed to listen to the Morvenian proposal. That is what troubles me."

Her surprise turned to concern. "You can't marry. Not now! Not ever!"

He snorted a humorless laugh. "I will marry some day, same as you."

"I don't want to get married. It doesn't sound like any fun. Unless he can hunt, fish, and ride all day, of what good is he?"

This time his grin was genuine. "Maybe you will be lucky, but my marriage is important since I'm the royal heir."

She became fretful. "You said you'd go camping with me. And what about my banquet? You promised to dance with me like you did Ellan."

He took her hand for reassurance. "I will keep my promises. Even if, and I stress *if*, Father agrees, I wouldn't marry until I am of age, two years from now."

"Neither of you need to worry. The Son of Tristan will not violate Jor'el's law by agreeing to such a marriage," said Avatar.

"I suppose not," she murmured.

Nigel pulled Tristine to her feet. "Time for you to get back to bed." He led her to the door where she stopped and hugged him, hard and long. "It's all right. Nothing's going to happen overnight."

Still sheepish and upset, she nodded and left.

"You handled her well," said Avatar.

Nigel was cross with the Guardian. "You thought I was going to tell her about my nightmares, didn't you?"

"I was uncertain of the extent of your explanation."

Nigel rolled his eyes. "Of course I won't burden her! The reason for the Morvenian visit will be made clear soon enough. Although I rather not involve her, it's best she learns the facts from me rather than by rumor."

"Indeed. She already bemoans her upcoming change into adulthood, and fears it will affect your relationship. She views marriage as losing you completely."

"She's not the only one who fears being lost." He waved off Avatar when the Guardian began to speak. "I'm going to bed."

Armus joined Tristine in returning to her chamber and noticed her disturbance. "Did you find the answer?"

She shrugged, fighting her emotions. "It can't be what he said."

"What?"

"The Morvenians are coming to offer a marriage of him to one of their princesses!"

Armus briefly considered the news. "Did Avatar say anything?"

"Only that Father wouldn't make a decision that violates Jor'el's law."

"And he won't."

"Oh, Armus!" She sobbed, hugging him. "Everything is changing so fast. I don't know if I want to be an adult and I don't want Nigel to get married."

"Unfortunately, you can't stop the mortal aging process." He knelt to look at her in the eyes. "As for the Morvenians, you must trust your father.

He will consider Jor'el's law, and he loves his children. He won't make a decision that would compromise or hurt any of you."

She nodded, sniffling and wiping her eyes.

"Now try to get some sleep." He accompanied her to the bed, and when she slipped under the covers, lowly spoke in the Ancient to put her to sleep. He waited a moment before leaving to approach Vidar and Kell.

"What was the visit about?" asked Kell.

"She was concerned for Nigel. He told her the reason for the Morvenian visit, which upset her. I put her to sleep rather than wait so we can speak. What do you make of this proposal?"

"Difficult to say. They are a closed people and I couldn't sense much from Bijan at the first meeting."

"Avatar assured her Ellis will not violate Jor'el's law and I concurred. Still, this visit is upsetting the family."

"Exactly," said Kell, his gaze shifting to Vidar, "why I am calling the meeting."

Vidar snickered. "I didn't question you. I know better."

The tall grandfather clock at one end of the hall chimed the half-hour at eleven-thirty.

"Stay alert. I have a visit to make before seeing you both at the meeting." Kell left the family quarters heading down the outer galley way stairs, into the Grand Courtyard and across the compound to the office and residential quarters of the royal officers, specifically General Wess.

Although granted an estate about five miles from the castle where his family lived, Wess worked at Waldron everyday. During times of peace he split his nights between Waldron and home. In times of unrest, he spent most of his time at Waldron. Since Darius and the fleet returned, peace returned. He would have left for home except for the news concerning the Morvenian visit required planning for extra security. Thus Kell knew Wess would be hard at work in his office.

Kell knocked and briefly waited before entering. Only a few oil lamps were lit; those needed for work. At thirty-two, Wess was Allon's youngest general. Although Iain's nephew, he worked his way up the ranks after receiving an appointment as a king's squire for his service to the queen and prince. With youthful clean-shaven features, Wess didn't look his age, which often caused an enemy to under estimate his skill and cunning. Being a general didn't stop his daily sparing with Ellis in mock bouts of hand-to-hand combat. Staying in top physical condition was a priority.

Wess sat back, wryly observing Kell. "I thought you left for the Trio meeting."

Kell flashed a knowing grin. "You've heard."

"No, you always call a meeting when something happens, so why should this be different?"

"The meeting is set for midnight and shouldn't be more than an hour."

"Gaynor, a half-dozen more guards to the royal quarters," Wess said. He waited a moment for Gaynor to depart. "Do your Guardian senses expect trouble?"

"I always err on the side of caution."

Wess motioned to the paperwork. "I canceled all leaves and in the morning will post the roster for a double portion of guards around the clock."

"Once the Trio Leaders are alerted, that is all we can do."

Wess leaned forward on the desk, his expression serious. "Tell me truly, Kell, what do you make of this overture? After all, their guns sank our ships, killing our sailors and marines."

"And your uncle."

Wess steadily regarded Kell before sitting back. With a lamenting sigh he said, "Ay. Learning of Iain's death has been difficult; more for Bosley and our sisters."

"He's always had a softer side."

"Oh, and I'm heartless?"

"You know what I mean."

Wess nodded. "Death is part of a soldier's life whereas politicians would rather negotiate than fight."

"Bosley has done well in his position. Iain was proud of both of you."

Wess remained silent for a moment, the impact of Kell's statement rippled across his brow. At Kell's studious regard, he cleared his throat to regain his composure. "Back to my question, what do you make of this?"

Kell replied in a considerate tone and expression. "I'm not certain. I didn't sense direct evil or malicious intentions on the part of Lord Bijan. They may truly desire peace, which Uriah will view as a missionary opportunity."

Wess chuckled. "I'm surprised at your skepticism, Kell. Being Jor'el's Captain I thought you would welcome the chance to bring the knowledge of the Almighty to another country."

"I do. I simply want to assess their heart and intentions before making such a commitment."

"Agreed. The Vicar might wish to jump at the opportunity, but we must take it slow and cautious, as I'm certain the king will."

"Time to leave. I'll speak to you afterwards." Kell vanished in a flash of light, temporarily blinding Wess.

"I hate when he does that in the dark," he grumbled, rubbing his eyes.

❧

In the forest of Midessex, in the heart of Allon, stood Arundine, Council Hall of the Guardians, a small, domed shrine of white marble, similar to the Temple of Providence. Before Ellis became King, Arundine vanished into the mist of legend. Since Ellis' coronation, the Guardians returned to their former station among the mortals and Arundine reappeared.

The interior was larger than anticipated by the exterior. Twelve pillars held up the dome and between each pillar stood a marble chair. Different colored marble were used in the floor to construct a map of Allon, naming each province in front of its respective chair.

From the high chair, Kell watched the Trio Leaders assemble. Priscilla, Guardian of Fair Winds from the East Coast whose beauty and flowing sea foam and dark green gown made a lasting impression on mortal sailors. Mona, Guardian of Legends of the North Plains was a shape-shifter, one who could change personas to suit any given situation. Zinna was a highly skilled archer with a longbow from the Meadowlands. Auriel of the South Plains was a female warrior. Finally, Wren of the Southern Forest made up the female contingent of the Guardian leadership.

Barnum of the Highlands was brawny like Armus with a grizzled beard and good-natured sneer. Gresham and Jedrek appeared together. Gresham was a shrewd vassal Guardian of Midessex. He displayed his intelligence by supplementing his russet and tan vassal uniform with modest ornamentations, including a jeweled, hilted dagger. Jedrek was a fair-haired youthful Guardian of the Delta, whose appearance belied the mind and heart of a cunning warrior. A Sea Guardian, Chase commanded the West Coast. Derwin of the Lowlands possessed a temperament directly opposite Chase, fiery and outspoken. He and Zadok got along well. Zadok was hardly what one would consider the most likely Guardian to be entrusted with Allon's most treasured province, the Region of Sanctuary. Many considered Zadok a surly warrior, fully of retorts and complaints, but with the stubbornness of a mule and sword of iron. Egan of the Northern Forest, a quiet unassuming warrior rounded out the Guardian leadership. Actions and not words, spoke for Egan.

Kell wondered why Armus, Vidar and Avatar had yet to arrive? His second-in-command and aide were rarely late, while Vidar's duties to Shannan sometimes kept him from the meetings. A flash of light at the door, and Armus and Avatar arrived together. He acknowledged their arrival and waited a moment for them to make their way to their customary places flanking the high chair.

"The king received word this evening of the Morvenians arrival in Leith. They should be at Waldron in two days." He asked Priscilla, "Have you been able to get a sense of them since their arrival?"

She shook her head. "I didn't want to appear intimidating or unfriendly, so I've tried not to be too obvious in my observation. I maintain contact with Baron Hollis and he's not certain what to make of them. They look and act very different from other foreigners he knows, and they brought a lot of baggage."

"If they pose no immediate danger, then all we can do is watch and wait," said Barnum.

"Ay, which makes this meeting pointless," groused Zadok.

Kell rebuked Zadok. "No meeting is ever pointless, even if only to alert you to possible danger."

"Ay, Captain."

Curious, Wren leaned forward in her seat. "Captain, is it true the Morven emperor offered the king a princess to wed?"

Her question stirred reactions of shock, surprise, and outrage among the Trio Leaders. So much so that Kell had to call for quiet.

"Ay, but the Son of Tristan diplomatically refused by citing Jor'ellian law. Lord Bijan proceeded to inquired about the prince, but again the king wisely answered along with granting permission to hear the complete Morvenian proposal."

"How so, if what they offer compromises Jor'ellian law?" asked Derwin.

"Because a defeated enemy willing to offer a royal marriage should be taken seriously. Neither the king nor I sensed evil intention at the first meeting. This could open the door to a fruitful relationship."

"So this meeting isn't pointless after all," said Jedrek to Zadok.

Kell covered a smile by pretending to tug at his upper lip in a thoughtful gesture. Wren didn't bother to hide her amusement, neither did Chase, Barnum, or Zinna, all laughing out loud. Others either chuckled or grinned.

Zadok scowled. "So what are we supposed to do, Captain?"

Kell sat upright, his smile gone. "Gresham, alert your Trio members and lower team leaders to keep a keen eye for anything out of the ordinary around Waldron. Priscilla, return to your watch. The rest of you stay alert for as long as they are in Allon."

Zadok pushed himself out of his seat and headed for the door. He vanished just outside the threshold.

"What caused the delay?" Kell asked Armus and Avatar.

"I waited for Nigel to fall asleep," replied Avatar.

"Why didn't you make him sleep, like Armus did Tristine?"

57

Avatar arched a private glare at Kell. "He is more disturbed by the Morvenian visit than Tristine and I didn't want to force him. Vidar volunteered to remain."

"Does he fear the thought of marriage?" teased Armus, which drew an immediate and irate response from Avatar.

"Mortal political alliances are no laughing matter! How would you feel if your charge was being used as political pawn?"

Kell intervened. "It is a delicate time for the family and we must stay extra vigilant."

"Then I'll be getting back." Avatar took a few steps away and vanished.

"He is unusually defensive. Why?" asked Armus.

"He already answered you."

"I thought it was something else. In the past, he's teased Nigel about marriage."

"Teasing about a possibility and seeing it play out in reality are different. You and I know from experience, Avatar doesn't. Nigel is his first mortal charge and he's taking things very personally."

"I'll make sure not to tease him again."

"Come, we should return." Kell held Armus' shoulder and they vanished together.

Chapter 4

OLLIS DISPATCHED A RIDER ahead to inform the king they were an hour from arriving. This sent everyone at Waldron scrambling to get to their places for receiving the guests. On this occasion, Tristine and Necie joined the family in the Great Hall, but stood to one side with Armus, Mahon, Avatar, and Morrell. They wore formal gowns and adornment befitting princesses. Most children of the Council and Court were not permitted to attend state functions until reaching the adult age of thirteen. The only exception was Angus, due to his relationship to the king and queen. He stood beside Tristine and Necie.

Ellis and Shannan wore all the trappings of royalty and sat on their thrones. Nigel stood beside Ellis, and Ellan beside Shannan. Nigel wore the coronet of his position as royal heir.

Vidar took up position in his usual place next to the wall behind Shannan's throne. Vicar Uriah, a virile-looking man of forty-three who became Allon's religious leader upon the death of Archimedes, stood on the floor directly in front of the royal couple. The Council and members of the royal court assembled in the hall with Guardians and soldiers at their respective posts.

The loud pounding of a large gold staff on the floor echoed in the hall and followed by a call from the back the room for attention.

59

Darius appeared, bowed and said, "Sire, the Morvenian delegation."

At the announcement, Nigel tossed a guarded glance to Avatar. He dreaded this moment. Avatar flashed a small smile of encouragement. Nigel turned back to observe the arrival of the Morvenians.

They were elaborately and colorfully dressed in flowing gowns, long robes and sparkling jewelry. A procession began with servants bearing ornate chests, cloth, trinkets, and other items unfamiliar to the Allonians. Servants placed the gifts on the floor in front of the platform, and offered deep bows to the royal couple before backing away on their knees. Behind the first wave of gift bearers, Kell and Darius escorted Lord Bijan and a veiled female who delicately held onto Bijan's arm. She was a few inches shorter than Bijan and wore a striking gown of a brilliant light blue shimmering fabric embossed with silver thread and diamonds. Long black hair cascaded down her back from under a matching headdress. Morvenian servants and standard bearers followed Bijan.

Kell, Darius, Bijan and the princess stopped ten feet before the platform. The servants and standard bearers stopped and knelt. Kell assumed his position to the right of the king and Nigel.

Darius introduced the Morvenians. "Sire, Your Majesty, I have the honor to present Lord Bijan of Morven." After speaking, he bowed and stepped aside.

"Welcome to Allon, Lord Bijan," said Ellis.

"Most Noble King Ellis." Bijan bowed very low. "Emperor Kamu sends greetings and gratitude to king for agreeing to accept tribute."

"The emperor overwhelms us with such generosity."

"It is small token. This is emperor's true gift. Princess Kaleana." Bijan removed the veil to reveal Kaleana, a stunningly beautiful young woman in her late teens with black hair, clear, crisp hazel eyes, flawless tanned complexion and delicate features.

"Most Excellent King," said Kaleana in forced Allonian. She lowly bowed.

Ellis and Shannan exchanged careful glances, both noticing Kaleana's extreme, exotic beauty. "Welcome, Princess." Ellis motioned to his right. "This is Prince Nigel, our royal heir."

"Royal Highness," said Kaleana.

Nigel stared at Kaleana and almost forgot to reply. "Princess," he said with a nod of acknowledgement and impulsive smile.

Ellis took note of Nigel's thunderstruck reaction, but kept going with the introductions. "Standing beside the queen is Princess Ellan, the eldest of the royal daughters."

Ellis introduced Tristine and Necie, who followed protocol in acknowledging the Movenians. Tristine's gaze shifted to Nigel. He stared at Kaleana.

"The royal family welcomes you, as do the lords and ladies of Allon." Ellis gestured to the crowded hall.

"Here, here!" said Darius on cue.

"Such welcome is appreciated," said Bijan to Darius before addressing Ellis. "If king permit me to read message from emperor to king and people of Allon."

"You may."

Bijan pulled out an ornate scroll tucked in his sash and opened it. "To Most Noble King Ellis and most excellent people of Allon, greetings from imperial majesty Emperor Kamu, the bright and shining light of all Morven. King's recent victory in defeating emperor's most distinguished army has brought to the mind of all Morvenians that most noble King Ellis is equal to emperor in power of divine light. As such, Emperor Kamu offers tribute to appease king's wrath—"

Ellis raised a hand up to halt Bijan's reading. "Wait! Did I hear you correctly, this is an offering to me for divine appeasement?"

Bijan was surprised, and a bit confused by the question. "King showed divine power as great as emperor so we bring gifts in token of worship."

Ellis's face flushed with indignation and Shannan piqued. She was the first to speak. "You worship your emperor as a god?"

Bijan stiffened at Shannan's address and replied in a thinly disguised tone of pride and arrogance. "Emperor is supreme god of Morven."

The answer brought shock and offended murmurs from those assembled in Hall. So much so, that Ellis stirred in his seat and declared, "Jor'el is the only god who is worthy to be worshipped and receive offerings."

"Does king not reign in Jor'el's name?"

"I reign by Jor'el's grace. If you wish to present these gifts in a show of respect from one kingdom to another I accept, but I will not receive them for myself as a divine offering!"

Bijan clenched the scroll and bowed. "Forgive for offending king."

Ellis paused for a moment to regain his temper. "There are great differences between our countries. So before we proceed with any negotiations I suggest we take time to become acquainted."

"As king commands." Bijan rolled up the scroll.

Shannan cordially spoke, "You have traveled far. Please accept our hospitality until the banquet this evening and we can begin to become acquainted."

Again, Bijan stiffened in irritation at her address. Kaleana's brows furrowed, her cautious gaze shifting between Shannan and Bijan.

Darius stepped forward and drew Bijan's attention from Shannan to depart. "My lord."

Bijan bowed and turned to accompany Darius from the Hall. Kaleana tossed a curious glance to Shannan. In doing so, she caught Nigel's eye and his smile before hastening after Bijan.

Everyone present remained silent until the Morvenians left.

"My lords and ladies, I bid you good day until the banquet," said Ellis. He stood and extended his hand to Shannan. All bowed when the king and queen left, followed by Nigel, Ellan, Tristine and Necie.

Ellis briskly walked from the Great Hall and through the main hallway, Shannan by his side. Nigel lagged behind, walking with his sisters, his brows level and thoughtful.

Tristine noticed his preoccupation. "Are you angry because they insulted Father by their offering?"

Nigel made a distracted negative grunt.

"The offering is annoying but such nerve of Lord Bijan to be offended when Mother spoke to him. Is that what bothers you?" said Ellan.

He gave a scowling, "No."

"Since the offering and insult doesn't matter, it's *her*," declared Tristine.

Nigel sent Tristine a withering glare, but before he could speak, Ellan asked, "You mean the princess?"

"She is so beautiful," said Necie in awe.

Nigel rolled his eyes, fighting to maintain his temper.

"Tristine's right. You were taken by her," said Ellan.

Nigel stopped near the rear-intersecting corridor. Their parents turned left into the adjacent hall, unaware of the dispute. Still, he kept his voice low. "I was not!"

"You were too," argued Tristine.

"Mind your tongue! Too often you forget yourself."

Stunned and hurt by his harsh rebuke, she set her chin. He turned on his heels and marched off in the other direction. Avatar gave Tristine a passing pat and smile of reassurance before pursuing Nigel.

"Why was Nigel so mean?" asked Necie.

Angry, Tristine turned and hurried to the back stairs, Armus close behind.

Nigel's pace didn't slow until he reached the lower gallery way. Across the private garden, Darius, Bijan and Kaleana headed toward the Guest Quarters and paused to observe.

Avatar joined him. "She did capture your attention," he said, making Nigel growl in anger. "Why take it out on Tristine because she noticed?" Nigel did not answer, rather picked up the pace; Avatar in pursuit. "So you would rather wound your sister than admit being attracted to the princess?"

Nigel stopped, whirled about and glared at Avatar. The Guardian didn't flinch, rather stared back, his silver eyes probing. Guardians not only had unusual colored eyes, but also invoked their heavenly sense of insight and prompting when needed. Nigel sighed, his shoulders sagging. "I don't know why I snapped."

"You were apprehensive about meeting the Morvenians. Only it wasn't as bad as you feared."

"They came to make a peace offering to Father like he is a god. You heard how they worship the emperor."

"That wasn't what I meant and you know it."

Nigel shook his head with uncertainty. "I don't know what to think."

"Lack of thought caused you to act cruelly to Tristine."

"To apologize I have to admit she is right." Avatar cocked a rebuking brow and Nigel scowled. There was no escaping the compelling look of a Guardian's eyes. "Why do you do that to me?" he snapped in frustration.

"I can only do what I was created to do and would be derelict in my duty to you and Jor'el if I did otherwise. However, it is not what is in my eyes that troubles you, rather what's in your heart. Pride made you lash out and wound someone you love, and who loves you. Will you let it prevent you from healing the hurt you caused?"

Nigel sighed and shook his head. "No."

He changed his course and crossed the garden to the back the hall and the family salon. He wasn't certain if his parents went to the salon, but it was the logical choice considering the direction they headed. Seeing Vidar and Morrell standing outside the door, told him he made the correct assumption.

"Is Tristine here?"

"No, Highness. She ran to the backstairs after you left," replied Morrell.

Nigel made his way to the family quarters. More than likely she went to her room. He knocked on the door and waited for an answer. Armus' expression was stern. He could be more intimidating than Avatar and Nigel flashed an apologetic smile.

"I came to see if Tristine's all right."

Armus' features softened and he waved them inside.

She paced in front of the hearth, hurt and anger rippling her brow. She stopped. "What do you want?"

"I came to apologize. I shouldn't have scolded you."

Her emotions were slow to subside and she started pacing again.

Nigel took her arm to stop her, but she jerked away. He seized both her arms to make her face him. "I was wrong and … you were right. I found her beauty stunning."

"Why? I thought you said you didn't want to marry her?"

"I don't! Sight of her caught me by surprise."

"So seeing her gave you second thoughts?"

"No," he began then balked at her steady suspicious regard. "Well, maybe, but only for a moment. When he read the greeting and we learned the meaning behind the gifts I became greatly offended."

"By Kell's expression, I thought he would strike him down."

"Kell wasn't the only one," said Avatar, tapping his sword.

"What would that do for international relations?" quipped Nigel.

"Aside from immense personal satisfaction, nothing."

Nigel chuckled, only short-lived as he continued speaking to Tristine. "Father did right to adjourn the Hall. We don't know much about the Morvenians."

"I don't want to."

"Kell told the Trio Leaders this may be an opportunity to bring the knowledge of Jor'el to another country. Only time and prayer will tell," said Armus.

"For everyone else, but not me. I'm not old enough to attend the banquet and see for myself," she complained.

"Oh, so now you want to be an adult?" teased Nigel, for which he received a hard jab in the ribs. "If you like, I'll speak to Father and ask him if you can attend."

She shrugged and sat in a chair. "I'd like to see what happens, but they make me uncomfortable." She rubbed her arms like warding off a chill, her face a bit disconcerted.

"How so?"

"Some of those small statues and carvings are strange. We have nothing like them." She noticed Avatar and Armus exchange careful, wary glances. "Have either of you seen such things before?"

Armus shook his head. "We've heard about them and seen trinkets with similar images. However, I didn't sense any danger about them. Did you?

"No," said Avatar. "Still, it is good to be cautious with unknown beliefs."

"Even they agree," she insisted to Nigel.

Nigel gave the Guardians a brief annoyed scowl before speaking to Tristine. "Kell wouldn't make such a statement if he sensed trouble."

"Of course not," affirmed Armus. "He will act with prudent caution. So will the Son of Tristan."

Nigel smiled at Tristine. "There's nothing to worry about. I'll tell you everything that happens." His smile grew teasing. "So, am I forgiven?"

"Ay," she said with smirk. "I can never stay mad at you, even when I should."

He laughed and embraced her. "The feeling is mutual. Now, we need to make an appearance in the salon since they're probably wondering about us."

"You can depend upon Ellan to tell them," said Avatar dryly.

"That's what I'm afraid of."

"You go. Ellan makes me too mad. At least she talks nice to you."

Nigel chuckled. "All right. I'll tell them something." He kissed her cheek and left.

Meanwhile, Darius was gracious yet formal at seeing the Morvenians to the guests quarters. Two Guardian warriors, Ewert and Bailey, accompanied them.

"These rooms are adjacent," Darius said, and moved to a door. He opened it to reveal a short hall of about five feet. "Both doors can be locked." He demonstrated, but left it unlocked when closing the door.

Bijan's scrutinizing gaze went around the room viewing the grand design and rich decoration of the finest Allonian furniture and craftsmanship. "It is adequate."

Darius raised an offended brow but managed to keep a level voice. "If you or Her Highness require anything please inform Ewert or Bailey and it will be promptly complied with."

Bijan frowned to the contrary. "Guardians must stay?"

"They are at your disposal for protection and assistance. Do you object to them?"

"Please to understand, Morvenians are unfamiliar with Guardians."

"I do understand. However, in Allon they are a very important and intricate part of our society. They are Jor'el's loyal servants and help to protect Allon."

Skeptical, Bijan eyed Ewert and Bailey. "Does king command Guardians?"

Darius grinned. "In a manner of speaking. By his orders they are assigned to you and the princess while you are in Allon."

Kaleana touched Bijan's arm and lowly spoke in Morvenian. He replied to her then addressed Darius. "Princess concerned Guardians see her when not appropriate."

"They will be respectful of the princess' privacy."

Bijan's scrutinizing and disapproving gaze of the Guardians was obvious.

"Your Grace. We can stand just outside the door and still perform our duty," said Bailey.

"Very well," said Darius, a bit begrudging. "Will that suffice, my lord?"

Bijan spoke to Kaleana, who replied and Bijan addressed her concern to Darius. "That will suffice. Yet, if princess need Guardian, how to speak? Princess not very good in Allonian speech."

"We speak many languages," said Bailey in Morvenian, surprising Bijan and Kaleana.

Darius flashed a satisfied smile. "Any more questions?"

Bijan looked to Kaleana, who shook her head.

"Then I bid you rest well until the banquet." Darius bowed then he and the Guardians departed.

Kaleana moved about the room, looking at the furnishings. "This is a strange place," she said in Morvenian.

"Remember you are here at the emperor's command," replied Bijan.

"I remember and I will honor my father the emperor with complete obedience. As such when shall I give the prince his present?"

"Let me see what I can arrange." Bijan left.

67

Nigel and Avatar just left Tristine's chamber heading for the back stairs, intent on heading to family salon, when Bailey intercepted them.

"Highness. Lord Bijan requests a moment of your time."

"Me?"

"He says 'He take king at word to become acquainted'," said Bailey, mimicking Morvenian speech.

Nigel chuckled. "Very well." He and Avatar went with Bailey to Bijan's quarters on the guest floor. At the door, Bailey detained Avatar.

"You might want to wait out here. They are rather shy of Guardians."

"Shy?" began Ewert in his droll wit. "Dislike, aversion, abhorrence even."

Bailey sent a jab into Ewert's arm to stop further words. "Ignore Ewert, Highness, he's in one of his jolly moods."

"If this is jolly, I hate to see sour," snickered Avatar.

Ewert smirked at his fellow warrior, baring teeth.

Nigel waved for Bailey to knock. They heard Bijan's inquiry. "My lord, Prince Nigel," said Bailey in response.

"Come."

Bailey entered first, holding the door for Nigel. Bijan and Kaleana bowed to Nigel, who acknowledged them.

"Lord Bijan. Princess. You wish to speak to me, my lord?"

"By princess request. But meeting man alone is prohibited."

Nigel smiled at Kaleana. "We have a similar rule with our women. For discretion and prudence."

She blushed and smiled and indicated a settee. Nigel understood and sat. Kaleana sat the other end of the sofa. She glanced with uncertain timidity to Bijan, who stood across the room to allow for decorum and privacy. Bijan nodded, so she forced herself to speak in broken words.

"I speak little Allonian."

"I'm afraid I don't speak any Morvenian," said Nigel.

"Oh," she sighed, looking a bit frustrated.

"Bailey does. He can translate."

Kaleana glanced with hesitancy at Bailey, who remained just inside the door. "Guardian strange creature."

"Some stranger than others," snickered Nigel. He waved the humor aside at seeing by her expression she didn't comprehend. "Sorry. Bad joke."

"Prince know Guardian long?"

"All my life. Each member of the royal family is assigned their own Guardian Overseer."

"Which one prince?"

"You mean which Guardian is my Overseer? Avatar."

"Avatar?" she tried to repeat the name.

"Ay. Tall, goatee, silver eyes," he said, making hand gestures on his face. She imitated his gestures in an attempt to comprehend.

Nigel looked hapless at Bailey, but the Guardian averted his eyes in pretended ignorance. "Why did you want to speak to me?"

"For present," she said motioning at Nigel.

"You mean as in gift? I'm not a gift."

She grew nervous and frustrated by her inability to clearly communicate. "No. Kaleana give prince present." She snapped her fingers and a male Morvenian servant brought a large box and knelt, holding it out to her. She took the box and the servant scurried away. "For future shared by Morven and Allon."

Nigel took the box and was surprised by the heavy weight. Opening the lid revealed a large jade stone statue. He put the box down on the floor and took the statue out. The stone was a highly polished figure of an animal he had never seen before, large with big ears and a long appendage he guessed to be a nose. What appeared to be horns came from its face along side the elongated nose. A platform was on top of the animal's back.

"Interesting. What is it?"

"*Olifa*," she said in Morvenian, with an ignorant shrug of what else to say.

Bailey translated. "Elephant. A large beast that doesn't live in Allon." His eyes narrowed in caution at the statue.

Nigel examined the statue again. "Must be very large."

"Olifa strong," she said.

69

"What does an elephant do?"

She made a walking sign using her fingers.

"A beast of burden?" he asked in confusion. He again regarded the statue. "How do you tame such a large animal?"

She shrugged. "Prince like?"

He flashed an awkward smile. "Thank you." He began to place it back in the box when she stopped him.

"Keep by bed. For luck," she said with a charming smile.

"Very well. Is there anything else?"

She glanced to Bijan, who shook his head.

"Then I bid you good day until the banquet." Nigel rose and bowed to Kaleana.

She went to reach for the box when he reached for it also. Their hands came together. She was shy yet direct in her glance and he gallantly smiled. "I wasn't going to leave without the box." He straightened, box in hand, and nodded to Bijan before leaving. Bailey followed him.

"What is that?" asked Avatar.

"A present," Nigel replied. He walked away not seeing Bailey sneer and shake his head in disapproval to Avatar.

Avatar didn't have time to inquire of Bailey when Nigel called for him. Once in his chamber, Nigel placed the box on the bed and pulled out the statue.

Avatar's brows leveled in cautious regard. "An idol?"

"An elephant statue." Nigel placed it on the table beside his bed.

Concerned, Avatar hastened across to the bed. "An animal idol."

"I don't know if I'd call it an idol. Kaleana didn't mention anything about worship. She asked me to place it beside my bed for luck and as a symbol of the future between our countries."

Avatar stiffened, silver eyes narrowing in anger. "It is an omen and should not be in here!" When he reached for the statue, Nigel stopped him.

"This is a gift from a Morvenian princess to me, the royal heir of Allon as a gesture of good will."

Avatar jerked away, scowling to contain his temper.

70

"To refuse would be an insult. Besides, I don't believe she meant any harm."

Avatar still didn't appear convinced. In fact, the Guardian moved to the other side of the room so he couldn't see the statue.

"Why does this trouble you?"

"It should trouble you to have a foreign idol in your room."

"It's not a idol. Simply an ugly stone carving of some animal." He crossed to Avatar and gripped the Guardian's arm. "I don't believe in statues or objects. My faith is secure in Jor'el."

Avatar's features softened. "Your faith does not worry me. I sense the Morvenians are a closed people."

"They came here seeking an alliance that could open their world."

Avatar shook his head. "Open in trade perhaps. I'm not sure about their hearts and minds."

"So you don't agree with Kell this could be an opportunity?"

"Let's just say I'm not as convinced as the captain."

Nigel snorted a chuckle. "To be honest, I'm not sure what to make of them either. Father and Cook agreed on the menu last week, then Lord Bijan informed Father of the strict Morvenian diet. Meat is limited to pork or lamb, although fowl is common. Bread is almost non-existent, mostly fruits, vegetables and rice. Cook flew into a tizzy when Father told him. Lord Bijan offered the assistance of several of his cooks, but they don't speak Allonian."

Avatar laughed. "So Armus is stuck with them."

"Ay," said Nigel with a teasing grin. "Perhaps there is a downside to Guardians being able to speak any language.

"Joined with his mastery of mortal cooking. Oh, I look forward to hearing what he has to say after this."

Avatar's desire to hear Armus' tales of the Morvenians would have to wait since he wasn't at the banquet, being too busy in the kitchen.

The Hall was transformed into a large dining room filled with tantalizing aromas, chattering voices, and pleasant background music. Lord Bijan and Princess Kaleana sat at high table alongside the royal couple, Nigel and Ellan.

The rest of Morvenian delegation sat with other Council Members. Morvenian servants fetched the special meal prepared for them.

"My compliments to Guardian for preparing Morvenian food. What spice used?" said Bijan to Ellis.

"You will have to ask Armus."

"Please, if king permit, to learn."

Ellis told Kell, "Send for Armus."

A few moments later Armus arrived. "You sent for me, Sire?"

"Lord Bijan wishes to speak to you."

Armus turned to Bijan. "Is the food unsatisfactory, my lord?"

"No, food very good. Please, what spice used? Is unfamiliar taste."

"I used the spices provided by your cooks, my lord. Nothing else."

"How Guardian cook?"

"I followed instructions and said a blessing while cooking," replied Armus matter-of-factly.

"Blessing?" echoed Bijan, disturbed

Upset, Kaleana spoke Morvenian to Bijan, who responded in quick phrases.

"Is there a problem?" asked Ellis.

"Morvenians only speak blessing on food offered to gods in hope of good fortune, not normal meal."

"Why didn't you say something earlier when I asked Jor'el's blessing upon the meal?"

"King speak for Allonian people food. Morvenian people food different."

Ellis regarded Bijan with sudden understanding. "You knew I would ask a blessing which is why you insisted your meals be specially prepared and served after we began eating."

"Like king does not wish to compromise beliefs, we wish same. Guardian speak blessing make food bad for Morvenians to eat."

Armus stiffened, but Shannan spoke. "Armus meant no offense, my lord. He did what he normally does."

Bijan's jowls tightened in noticeable anger at her address.

72

Irate, Nigel leaned toward Bijan. "My lord, why do become angry when my mother, the queen, speaks?"

"Again, difference between countries, Highness. Women do not rule in Morven like in Allon."

"You don't appear angry when Princess Kaleana speaks to you," said Ellan.

"By emperor's command," his voice filled with restraint. His eyes showed he didn't like dealing with Ellan either.

Ellis sat up straight, his face firm. "What if I command you to show more respect to Allon's queen and royal princesses?"

Bijan inclined his head in submission. "It will be as king commands."

Ellis nodded and relaxed his posture.

"If king please. We cannot eat food blessed to unknown god." Bijan motioned to his and Kaleana's plates.

This time Armus wasn't the only Guardian offended. Kell's golden eyes narrowed on Bijan. Vidar shifted in his stance as if ready to arm his crossbow and Avatar rested his hand on the pommel of his sword.

At their reactions, Ellis said, "Since no one purposely tried to offend your conscience, have your servants return to the kitchen and prepare a new meal."

Bijan spoke in Morvenian and servants scurried to heed his command.

Ellis gave Armus a smile of encouragement and said, "Thank you. Return to Tristine."

Armus bowed, tossing a wary glance from Bijan to Kell before leaving the Hall.

"Guardians unique creatures. Guardians advise king?" asked Bijan.

"Sometimes. Kell is not only the King's Champion but also the Captain of Jor'el's Guardians and in direct contact with the Almighty."

Bijan looked with wonder at Kell. "Captain talk to god directly?"

"Ay, but so do the mortals, in prayer."

"I thought you said, you pray to your gods?" asked Nigel.

"We pray to—how you say—shape or like?"

"Idol?"

73

"Ay. Idol serve as link to god. Never direct speech."

Nigel's brows furrowed in thoughtful concern. He glanced from Bijan to Avatar, who stood at the end of high table nearest to him. The Guardian stared at Bijan so Nigel turned back to the conversation and asked, "Do all idols and carvings represent your gods?"

"Many do, but not all. Some mean other things."

"Such as?"

Bijan shrugged. "Courage, strength, things of life."

Ellis and Shannan noticed their son's interest in the subject so Ellis added, "You place a value on the image?"

"It can be said that way. Does not king place value on items for memory?"

"You mean sentimental value? That's different."

"How different?" asked Kaleana.

Ellis paused for a brief moment of thought before answering. "The item becomes a symbol of remembrance for a person, not something to be worshipped."

"Still it have value," said Bijan.

"Ay, to the individual, but not necessarily the whole population."

"Not so different in Morven."

Shannan grew disturbed. "Are you saying, each home can ascribe value to an image or item and it becomes the god of that family?"

"Ay."

Stunned, Nigel asked; "What about the gifts you brought? Were all offerings?"

"No. Some represent friendship."

"Sounds like a complex system. How do you keep everything straight?" asked Darius.

"Not easy. Learn from childhood."

"But it can change, depending upon how one views the object," insisted Shannan.

Bijan's reply stopped when the Morvenian servants returned with fresh plates of food for Bijan and Kaleana.

74

"Please, enjoy your meal," said Ellis.

Nigel picked at his food considering the conversation. *Perhaps Avatar is right to be concerned. But it doesn't have to mean anything. It's what the person makes it and it doesn't mean anything to me. To Kaleana ...*

He glanced to Kaleana. She was beautiful. Even when eating there was a charm and grace to her movement and countenance. She caught his eye and discreetly smiled, her face brightening. At that moment he couldn't imagine her harming anyone or even intending to do harm. The gift was purely for friendship. He returned her smile.

After feasting, dancing, and entertainment, the banquet ended around midnight. Before retiring, Ellis announced the Council would assemble in the morning to interview Lord Bijan and consider the Morvenian's offer.

Once in his chamber and changed for the night, Nigel paused before climbing into bed to regard the statue. He grinned at recalling Kaleana's charming smile at dinner. He heard a low grunt from Avatar, who assumed his usual place beside the door. The Guardian said nothing about his conversation with Bijan regarding idols. Still, he saw heightened disapproval in Avatar's steady, silver gaze.

"I told you, its means nothing to me."

"Then let me put it some place else, preferably out of the room."

"It's not that bad. Ugly though."

Avatar became puzzled. "I thought the conversation with Bijan changed your mind."

"Why? When I'm telling you for the third time, the statue means nothing to me."

"Your private smile tells me you are attaching some feeling to it. The princess, perhaps?"

"Tread lightly, Avatar."

"Why? Will you scold me like Tristine for confronting you about a foreign princess?"

Nigel rolled his eyes, more in an attempt to avert them from the Guardian's stare. "Keleana is charming and sweet, but I'm not swayed to the point of being smitten. While this," he moved to the statue and rapped his knuckles on the platform portion, "is merely a carved stone. It can't do any harm."

"The stone doesn't concern me."

"Well," began Nigel, sarcastic, "Since it means nothing to me and neither my faith nor the stone concerns you, then there is nothing to be concerned about." He climbed into bed.

"Why are you being stubborn?"

"It is a gift, given in sincerity and kindness. For that, it will stay beside my bed!" He huffed and lay down, turning his back to Avatar and facing the statue. "Turn out the lamp." He heard Avatar approach the bedside table. Before the Guardian turned out the oil lamp he spoke an evening prayer.

"Jor'el, grant peaceful sleep as I trust my soul to your watchful eyes."

Now dark, Nigel closed his eyes and slept; only sleep was not peaceful. Then again, Nigel wasn't certain if he was awake or asleep. All he knew was he had to get away before being captured by the dark, formless image chasing him. The closer the image came, the more frightened he became. He cried out and sat up. In the darkness it took him a moment to realize he was in his room and in bed. Avatar wasn't in his usual place and Nigel's gaze swept around the room looking for the Guardian. He noticed the statue missing. Did Avatar taken it against his wishes? What still frightened him? He was awake and in his own room.

He tried to push aside the covers to rise, but couldn't. No matter how hard he tried, the blanket wouldn't budge. In fact, the blanket began to grow up his torso, pulling him back onto the bed. He fought against the constraint and when his head hit the pillow, he felt his breath being smothered out of him by the constricting blanket. He tried to call for Avatar, but his voice was muffled and everything went dark.

Suddenly he sat up, gasping for air. Once again he found he was in his room and in bed. Only this time Avatar sat beside the door in the Guardian meditative position with his legs crossed, eyes closed and his sword across his lap. Nigel tried to speak only his mouth was dry and the words wouldn't come easily. This time he could push aside the covers. However when he

76

stood, his legs gave way and he grabbed onto the bedpost to keep his balance.

"Avatar," he managed to say.

The Guardian's eyes snapped open. He rushed to help Nigel sit on the end of the bed. "What's wrong?"

Nigel shook his head, face disconcerted and his voice shaky. "I thought you were gone. I didn't see you when I woke and the blankets ..." He motioned back toward the head of the bed and noticed the statue.

"The blankets what?"

Befuddled, Nigel regarded Avatar. "I thought you took it away and the blackness got you."

"What are talking about?"

Nigel shook his head trying to comprehend. "It must have been the dream."

Avatar sat beside him. "You had a nightmare?"

Nigel looked along his shoulder at Avatar. "Didn't you hear me before?"

"There was no sound until you said my name."

Nigel's befuddled gaze shifted between the statue and Avatar. "Have you and the statue been here the whole time?"

"Ay. Is that what you thought I took away?"

Nigel grew upset. "I woke up when it reached to grab me. You and the statue were gone. When I tried to get up to find you, the blanket pulled me back and began smothering me. I tried calling for you, but I couldn't speak."

"Relax," soothed Avatar, stroking Nigel's hair. "It was just a bad dream. I haven't gone anywhere and I'm not going to leave. *That* going somewhere else is up for debate," he said in reference to the statue, only to be met with annoyance from Nigel. "What were you running from?"

Nigel shrugged, awkward and tentative in answering. "The same thing I've been running from lately. Only the image is getting closer and more frightening."

"Any clearer?"

"No."

"If you can describe it perhaps I can discern what it means."

"A dark, scary indescribable shape! How should I know? It's more a sense than anything!"

"Easy. Perhaps after a good night's sleep, we can consider it better." He guided Nigel back to bed.

"I hope so."

Nigel lied down. Avatar placed a hand on Nigel's forehead and spoke in the Ancient. "Sleep in Jor'el's peace. I'll be right beside you." Within a moment, Nigel fell asleep.

Chapter 5

THE COUNCIL CHAMBER was located behind the Great Hall. Beautiful stained glass windows depicted each province in its unique manner. Under each window stood a handsomely carved wooden, cushioned chair. The chair to the right of the king's high chair belonged to the Region of Sanctuary in whose window shone the Temple of Jor'el. Next came the Highlands with mighty mountains dominating its window. Beside the Highlands was the North Plains, flowing fields of grain marked its window. Its sister province of the South Plains was known for it abundance of vegetables, including grapes for wine. The West Coast displayed its naval contributions in bold colored glass. A large figure of cattle from the Meadowlands completed the west wall.

In a place of prominence to the left of the king's chair, was the Northern Forest, whose quarried marble and stone help construct Allon's Temple and Waldron. The Southern Forest window displayed massive timbers and woodcraft. Midessex was renowned worldwide for exceptional horses and the best wool. The Lowlands took the wool and boasted of extraordinary tapestries. The East Coast imported and exported fine goods. Finally, came the Delta, where many Allonians and foreigners flocked to for its spas and minerals deposits. Down the middle of the tiled floor, a multicolor patterned carpet led the way to the king's high chair.

Vicar Uriah wore his official priestly robes, looking sober and stoic as he conversed with Darius. Their speech paused when Lord Gareth of the South Plains accompanied his brother, the gruff Lord Zebulon of the Lowlands to his seat. An age difference of ten years separated Gareth and Zebulon, so the family resemblance was slight. Baron Ned of the Northern Forest kept company with Baron Erasmus of the Delta, Lord Fagan of the Highlands, and Baron Malcolm of the North Plains. Fagan was Ned's younger brother by two years, and between them the family looks were evident.

Hollis occupied the East Coast chair and spoke to Lord Bosley of Midessex. Earlier Hollis reported to Ellis that Mathias' wife Rhea sent word her husband was recovering nicely and asked the king to excuse his appearance from the Council. The request was naturally granted. Thus the West Coast chair would be empty during the meeting.

Kell entered. "Lords of Allon, give heed." At his announcement, the Council Members stood in front of their chairs. "His Majesty, King Ellis and His Royal Highness, Prince Nigel."

The lords bowed when Ellis and Nigel entered and made their way to the platform. Ellis sat while Nigel remained standing beside the throne.

"Sire, the Lords of Allon are assembled," said Kell. He bowed and took his place.

"What is the will of the king? Speak, and we, the Lords of Allon, will obey," said Uriah in formal greeting.

"Be seated, my lords, and hear my will, that we may take council together and seek Jor'el's guidance in the matter before us," replied Ellis. He waited a moment so they could take their seats. "This day a petition from Emperor Kamu on behalf of Morven is to be presented." He raised his right arm and waved his hand, looking toward the back of the chamber.

Bijan and five members of the Morvenian delegation entered. Ewert, Bailey and four royal soldiers escorted them. Pausing at the base of the platform, the Morvenians made their traditional low bow to Ellis.

"Welcome, Lord Bijan, my lords of Morven. The Council of Twelve is assembled to hear the petition. The notable absence is Baron Mathias, who is still recovering, yet hopes to be with us shortly." Ellis spoke on purpose

80

about Mathias to gauge the Morvenians' reactions. None came. All remained formal in feature and form. That could bode well or ill depending upon the petition and the mood it invokes from the rest of the Council. "Proceed."

Bijan nodded his acknowledgement and began speaking the flowery phrases of Morven. "Most Noble King Ellis, Royal Highness, and gracious Lords of Allon, by will of Imperial Emperor Kamu, greetings and thank you for kindness in hearing emperor's humble servant."

"It is an honorable and worthy opponent who seeks peace in defeat," said Darius.

"And a gracious and noble victor who listens," returned Bijan.

"Please, proceed. You have our attention," said Ellis.

Bijan pulled a scroll out from his sash. The scroll was different than the one that caused the earlier controversy. In a loud voice he read the same grandiose, formal speech they came to expect from the Morvenians praising Kamu and Ellis for their positions and wisdom.

Ellis' brows grew level at divine references to Kamu and a few to himself. Clearly the wording bothered him, but he allowed Bajin to continue. He made his point the day before, but the Morvenian's way of thought and phrases would not change overnight and these documents were written weeks before.

After a lengthy introduction and compliments, Bijan came to the heart of the matter. Kamu desired an alliance with Allon by offering trade routes, commerce license to any Allonian merchant willing to set up shop in Morven, and any military assistance should Allon require. The alliance would be sealed by a marriage between the Princess Kaleana and Prince Nigel.

During the reading, Nigel stood with a casual hand on the back of the throne. His grip tightened at hearing the final point of the petition and moved in reaction, slightly bumping the throne.

At the jostling, Ellis took brief notice of Nigel, his attention focused primarily on the varied reactions among the Council. Some listened, looking passive. Zebulon scowled or frowned at some of the phrasing. Hollis and Erasmus appeared agreeable to certain points.

Bijan could not view the response unless he stopped reading and turned around. "This is the will of Emperor Kamu to his most noble majesty King Ellis," he said in conclusion.

"Those are generous terms. Would you be willing to answer some questions from the Council?" asked Ellis.

"Of course."

Questioning lasted an hour and concerned trade law restrictions, types of goods and all manner of details, except the marriage proposal. That was until Uriah asked, "By what means would this marriage take place?"

"According to Morven custom."

"Which is?"

"A detailed ceremony with many parts over a week to complete in grand celebration."

"What parts?" asked Nigel, speaking for the first time.

"Parts representing life in Morven."

"So this ceremony would take place in Morven?" asked Ellis.

"It is required."

"Required?" repeated Ellis in displeasure.

"King disapprove?"

Ellis took a deep breath to calm his reply. "The differences in our marriage customs will have to be explored more closely before I can answer your question."

"As king commands," said Bijan with a submissive nod.

"Are they any more questions?" Ellis asked of the Council. Upon receiving negative answers, he spoke to Bijan. "My lord, if you will go with Ewert and Bailey, the Council will begin deliberating the emperor's petition."

Bijan and the delegates made their customary stiff bows before leaving. The door no sooner closed upon departure than a debate began concerning the finer points of trade, shipping, gains and losses.

"This is all well and good, but didn't he say the alliance is contingent upon the marriage being agreed to?" said Fagan.

"I should hope not," said Nigel in an impulsive reaction.

"Highness?"

82

Nigel was momentarily surprised at being heard, but recovered and replied. "It is the victor who dictates the terms of an alliance not the defeated. Despite personal and national loss, we are in the position of strength. The Morvenians came here hoping to appease us. Why should we accept their terms when they are offensive to our ways?"

Ellis grinned in approval at the argument.

"His Highness is correct. Agreeing to a marriage of convenience and according to Morvenian custom violates our laws and Verse," said Darius.

"No one is suggesting the prince marry her without thought or consideration," said Erasmus.

"However, the generous terms are difficult to ignore. Not to mention Kamu is powerful. Our victory was hard won and only by the slimmest margin," said Hollis.

"Jor'el does not deal in odds or margins, my lord. Faith and obedience win battles," said Uriah.

"Tell that to the thousands of widows! And Mathias nearly lost his life," rebuffed Hollis before turning to Ellis. "We would be hard-pressed to stand against the Morvenians in another battle."

Nigel stepped forward to confront Hollis. "The king was not there! Put the Sword of Allon in his hands, and the Morvenians would think twice before attacking us."

Ellis curbed the impulse to smile at his son's rebuke. He spoke to Hollis. "Baron, Allon values your opinion and deeply appreciates your sacrifice. I told Lord Bijan I will hear more about their marriage customs …"

"Father—" began Nigel in protest, but stopped when Ellis sent him a hot, rebuking glance. He knew it wasn't for speaking, rather his informal address at an official function. He bent his head in a submissive apology. "Sire."

Ellis continued speaking to Hollis and the others. "Only after I have gained full knowledge of their mindset, hear the opinion of the Council, and make prayerful consideration of all aspects, will I be able to render a proper decision."

"Sire, it is the Council's opinion that a alliance with Morven would be economically and militarily beneficial. However, we will not risk national stability to accept the alliance," said Darius.

Erasmus, Fagan, Ned, Uriah, Allard, Malcolm, and Bosley agreed with Darius.

"I see no risk," said Hollis.

"Nor do I," said Gareth.

"Nor I," added Zebulon.

Ellis glanced at the individual members. "That makes three to eight. My lords, I thank you for your service to Allon this day. The Council is adjourned until I have reached a decision." When he stood, the Council rose and bowed. He and Nigel left the chamber. Kell followed.

Ellis and Nigel headed toward the galleyway. Avatar fell in step beside Kell. He waited in the hall during the meeting.

"Sir, I'm sorry for my outburst," said Nigel.

"You must learn how to conduct yourself in a Council meeting. Diplomacy and logic rule, not emotion. You did well in your reply to Fagan." Ellis stopped walking and placed both hands on Nigel's shoulders. "I understand your feelings in this matter. Please try to understand my position. Often the head and heart of a father does not agree with what must be done as king. The dilemma is trying to reach a compromise where both can be satisfied and content with the decision. That is what I face regarding this marriage proposal."

Nigel swallowed back his disturbance.

At the reaction, Ellis' hands dropped off his son's shoulders. "Go. Find something to occupy yourself while I speak to Bijan privately."

"Father—"

"Go!" Ellis abruptly waved, turning to resume his course.

Agitated, Nigel hurried toward the main entrance.

In the courtyard near the barrack, just off the Grand Courtyard, Tristine and Angus practiced archery under the instruction of Wren. Armus watched.

Nigel rushed from the main building. Tristine was about to call a greeting when he grabbed a soldier about to mount a horse, pulled him aside and vaulted into the saddle. He sent the horse galloping toward the main gate. Avatar ran after him.

"Nigel!" Tristine hurried toward the gate.

"I wonder what made him ride off?" asked Angus. He, Armus and Wren joined Tristine.

"Something must be wrong."

"Or Uncle sent him on an errand."

Tristine shook her head. "No, Father uses vassals or soldiers."

"Whatever it is, Avatar will see to him," said Armus.

Tristine gave the bow to Wren and ran inside the main building. She raced up the stairs, down the upper galleyway and burst into the king's study.

"Father!" She pulled to a halt at seeing Ellis wasn't alone. Lord Bijan and Darius were with him. "Oh, sir!" she stammered, her face flush with embarrassment yet worried in expression.

Ellis didn't reprimand her, her agitation obvious. "A moment, my lord," he said to Bijan and approached Tristine. "What's wrong?"

She flashed a guarded glance at Bijan and replied in a low, hurried voice. "It's Nigel. He's gone."

He drew her further away from Bijan. "What?"

"He tossed aside a soldier about to mount and rode off on his horse. Avatar ran after him. Father, what's wrong?"

Ellis scowled in disapproval at the news. "Nothing for you to be concerned about."

"He ran off!"

"So have you on occasion when upset."

She frowned in frustration. "You know why he's upset but won't tell me."

"Not now." He tossed a warning glance back to Bijan.

"I'm truly sorry I interrupted. I didn't know what else to do, I'm concerned for Nigel."

85

Ellis nodded, a small, kind smile appearing. "Run along. Nigel will be well. Avatar will see to him."

Nigel pressed the horse for miles, his mind a whirlwind of emotions. Perhaps the harder he rode the quicker he could clear his mind. The sense of uncertainty gnawing at him grew more dreadful during the Council meeting, turning to utter fear at hearing Ellis' intention to listen to the marriage proposal! If that wasn't enough, the Morvenians were so different and unnerving in ways he couldn't discern. True, Kaleana was beautiful and harmless, but Bijan and his description of the Morvenian's beliefs and customs were disturbing. How could his father even consider listening to them?

He said a king must listen and consider all sides before making a decision. I don't know that I can ... or that I want to.

He didn't realize how far or how long he rode until the horse became unsteady and faltered in step. He slowed the animal and dismounted before the beast collapsed. The horse was lathered in sweat, pink foam dripping from its mouth where the bit cut, its nostrils slightly bleeding from exertion. He almost pressed the horse beyond its limits. He walked the horse to keep it on its feet and recover its breath.

Avatar drew alongside Nigel. Guardians easily kept pace with a horse, capable of running all day if necessary without exhausting their energy, so he wasn't sweating or breathing heavy. "Feel better?"

Nigel didn't reply, more concerned for the horse's condition.

Avatar shrugged in pretended indifference. "You'll tell me eventually."

"Why are you so sure of everything?"

"Not everything, just you."

"You may not know me much longer if Father agrees to this marriage. According to Morvenian custom," he said in mocking tone.

Avatar's brows rose in surprise. "The Council agreed to the proposal?"

86

Nigel shook his head, still concentrating on the horse and not looking at Avatar. "Not all, some did. The usual: Gareth, Zebulon and Hollis. Darius tried to talk reason while Father just sat and listened."

"It's the Council's duty to advise the king in matters of national concern."

"Why should my marriage be of national concern?"

"You know the answer."

Disgruntled, Nigel sat beneath a large oak tree and let the horse drink from a stream. "He said the heart of a father doesn't always agree with the duties of a king. He practically told me he's going to consent. Why else make such a statement except to prepare me for it?"

Avatar sat next to him. "Because it's true. The Son of Tristan has great responsibilities, both personal and national."

"I know." Nigel sighed, leaned his head against the tree and closed his eyes.

"You're still troubled by the sense of doubt about your future. That's probably why you had the nightmare."

Nigel nodded, his eyes still closed.

"I spoke to Kell. He felt a similar sense." While Avatar spoke, Nigel's eyes opened, expectant for an answer. "Only he doesn't sense anything definite or final, just unclear."

"That doesn't help much."

"He says he'll keep praying, so will I. The answer will come in time."

"Time enough to stop this marriage?"

Avatar looked askew to Nigel. "Did he say he agreed? Or are you jumping to conclusions again? And what about Tristine?"

The abrupt shift in question surprised Nigel. "What about her?"

"Didn't you hear her call to you when you left? You probably scared the wits out of her, tossing the soldier aside to jump on the horse and gallop off."

Nigel rolled his eyes. "As if she never left in a huff before."

"You're supposed to be a man. She's still a girl, although not for long. And someone promised to help her," said Avatar. His silver eyes direct on Nigel.

"Must you remember everything I say?"

Avatar impertinently grinned.

Nigel scowled again, leaning his head against the tree. In doing so, he saw the sky through the branches. The sun was past its apex. "Well past noon."

"Ay. You pushed the poor beast for several hours. It's a wonder it didn't die under you."

Wren appeared from behind a nearby tree. "I'll take the credit for that. And Avatar's right, you did scare Tristine."

"No need to ask how much of the conversation you heard," chided Nigel.

She squatted in front of him, her bright green eyes direct. "You should be getting back, Highness. The king will start asking questions if you don't return before tonight's banquet."

"Oh, the banquet!" he said in frustration, lightly hitting the back of his head against the tree. "What about the horse?"

"You don't need the horse, I can take you back," said Avatar.

"No, I'll ride."

"You won't return in time."

Nigel became annoyed. "During combat training you and Father speak of how a Jor'ellian must prepare himself to face trouble. Well, I'm not ready to face what I feel is a conflicting future wrapped up in a marriage contract! I'll prepare myself as I ride."

Avatar made no further argument so Wren approached the horse as it chomped on the grass. She lifted its head and spoke in the Ancient. The horse responded, snorted and pawed the ground.

"He's fit to ride now, Highness. Only he asks you let him set the pace this time."

"Gladly." Nigel took the reins from her and mounted. He knew they would follow, but let the horse set the pace.

The animal mostly cantered rather than a full gallop with several intervals of walking. It took more time to return, and although that was fine with him, he imagined his father's furious reaction at being late to the banquet. This was not only a slight against the king and the Council, but an insult to royal guests. He may not care about the Morvenians, but he was concerned about how to approach his father. He also thought about his mother and her feelings in the matter. Oh, he would have a lot of explaining to do.

By the time they returned to Waldron, the formal dinner in the Great Hall was well underway. Being road dusty and sweaty Nigel left the horse in Wren's care and went to his chamber for a bath and change of clothes. With all servants occupied at the banquet, Avatar prepared the bath. It was better this way, since Nigel didn't want to draw too much attention to his return before he could speak to his parents.

While bathing, he heard a brief knock at the door. He sat up in the tub wondering who could be calling upon him. He hoped his father had not learned of his return before being ready to present himself. Hearing Tristine's voice, he relaxed back in the tub; that was until she entered the privy. Angus tried to detain her. Avatar stood in the threshold beside a bashful Necie.

"We heard you were back. Are you all right?" asked Tristine.

Red-faced with embarrassment, Nigel submerged himself until the water reached his chin. "Why did you let her in?" he demanded of Avatar.

The Guardian just smiled. Startled, Necie ran from the privy. Tristine folded her arms in defiance.

"I told her not to bother you," said Angus to Nigel then scolded Tristine. "I told you. Now you've scared Necie."

"Get her out of here!" snapped Nigel to Angus.

Tristine shook off Angus' attempt to steer her out. "He's fine all right." She huffed on the way out. Angus tossed an apologetic look to Nigel before following her.

Nigel glared at Avatar. "Hand me the dressing gown." Shortly, he appeared in the bedchamber. Tristine, Necie and Angus waited. "You should *not* have let them in," he scolded Avatar. Again the Guardian grinned.

"I tried to stop her," said Angus.

"Where did you go and why?" asked Tristine.

"I went for ride," snapped Nigel. He crossed to his wardrobe.

She followed him, beginning to speak when she caught sight of the jade statue. She screwed up her face in repulsion. "What is that *ugly* thing?"

Nigel selected clothes and handed them to Avatar. "A gift from Princess Kaleana."

Necie moved to see what they were talking about. She had a similar adverse reaction to Tristine, only not as demonstrative. "A gift of what?"

"A statue of an elephant."

"What's an elephant?" Necie approached the statue for a closer look, curiously tilted her head to view it at different angles.

"A beast of burden not found in Allon." Nigel moved behind a changing screen.

Tristine frowned in disapproval, surveying the statue. "Never heard of it."

"Apparently it's common enough in Morven," Nigel spoke from behind the screen. In order, Avatar laid the clothes over the screen for him.

Angus joined the girls in viewing the statue. "Why place such an ugly thing beside your bed?"

"Because the princess asked me to."

Annoyed, Tristine rolled her eyes. "Are you going to do everything she asks you?"

"There are affairs of state and diplomacy you don't understand."

"Oh, and you do?"

"Ay." Nigel stepped out from behind the screen dressed in breech, shirt, stockings and fastening his doublet. "I attended the Council meeting this morning."

There was another knock at the door and this time Ellan entered. Her angry glare found Nigel. "Here you are! Where have you been? Do you realize you left me to endure the endless ramblings and insulting questions of the Morvenians? Where is the prince? And all the while Kaleana acting forlorn and abandoned."

Nigel's shoulders' sagged at the chastening. "Father must be furious."

"Furious doesn't begin to describe it! The royal prince not present at a formal state banquet for a foreign dignitary is outrageous."

"Is the banquet over?" He took his boots from Avatar and sat to put them on.

"No. I pretended to feel ill to get away from them because of you."

Nigel set his chin and left the chamber. Tristine caught him in the hall. She appeared worried, almost to the point of tears.

"What will happen with Father?"

"I don't know, but I must face the consequences like a man. A boy ran from here. Now I have to do what I convinced you to do at Leith, own up to my mistake and accept the punishment."

"That could mean marriage!"

He couldn't reply, and squeezed her hand before continuing on his way.

Ellan, Necie and Angus joined Tristine. She lashed out at Ellan. "I hate you!" She ran to her chamber.

"What did I do?"

"You told on Nigel," rebuffed Angus.

"I didn't tell on him. He failed in his responsibility." Ellan marched down the hall toward her chamber.

Necie sniffled. "Why is Ellan always so mean?"

"Some people are just that way. Don't let her upset you," soothed Angus.

Nigel made his way to the Great Hall but stopped short of entering. He sent Avatar to inquire on the progress of the banquet. Learning Ellis and Shannan were still engaged with the Morvenians, Nigel decided to wait in the king's study. He did not fear facing Bijan or Kaleana, but dreaded seeing the look of disappointment on his mother's face and his father's anger for his foolishness. This subject was better dealt with in private.

91

He mentally went through the Jor'ellian Knight drill to prepare himself. Yet if not for the horse on the point of collapse, he would have followed his impulsive to run away and spare his family from whatever deeply disturbed him. Now, it was impossible and he didn't know which was worse, leaving them without warning, or seeing their disappointment in his cowardly behavior. Tristine was frightened and Ellan angry. Who can blame her?

I placed her in a bad position by not being there and doing what I'm supposed to. And I'm sure she bore the brunt of Father's displeasure. Serves me right if she doesn't forgive me.

He paced the chamber, occasionally looking at door in anticipation at hearing footsteps or voices. Avatar didn't say anything. Then again what more could he say? In fact, what will he say to his father to explain his actions? The Jor'ellian meditation gave him the determination to face his father, but it didn't give him the words to speak and no matter how many times he tried to form the words in mind, nothing seemed right. He didn't understand what frightened him or what his dreams meant, so how could he explain it to his father?

During his pacing and internal debate he caught Avatar's studious regard. He appreciated Avatar more than he could say, but some times his presence and silver eyes were unbearable. Not to mention the fact that the Guardian always knew the right thing to say whether he wanted to hear him or not. Finally, he stopped and faced Avatar.

"Go ahead! Say I look like a fool mumbling to myself."

"You look at war with yourself and the words you know you must speak."

"Ay," Nigel admitted. He sat on the window seat and gazed out into the Courtyard.

Barely, a moment passed when the door opened and Nigel bolted to his feet. Ellis and Darius arrived. For a long moment father and son regarded each other. The anger, hurt, and disappointment in Ellis' eyes made Nigel look down at his feet in shame. The words he formed left him and all he could say was, "Forgive me, sir."

Ellis waved Avatar out before closing the door, hard. "You easily ask forgiveness, but I don't think you fully understand your actions."

"I offended you and insulted our guests by my absence."

"That's putting it mildly. What were you thinking when your rode off?"

"I wasn't."

"Ay! Imagine my surprise when Tristine bursts in here when I am speaking to Lord Bijan, very upset and tells me you're gone. Galloping off to who knows where!"

Nigel was initially surprised to hear Tristine reported his departure. Then he recalled Avatar asking him if he heard her call and Wren telling him she was scared. Of course she'd run to Ellis.

"You compounded your foolishness by not being at a formal state banquet!"

"I have no excuse, sir."

"That's not true. You had a reason to leave. Was it because of the Council meeting?"

Nigel again found himself at a lost for words so he nodded.

Ellis swore, "Foolish, boy! If you listened to me the decision would have been easy. Now I can't do what I wanted and decline the marriage."

Nigel was thunderstruck. "What?"

"You have so insulted the Morvenians nothing short of your marriage to the princess will undo what you have done!"

Overcome, Nigel sat on the windowsill.

Ellis took several deep breaths to calm his temper, his gaze shifting to Darius, who watched in concern. "I don't want this marriage."

"Then don't agree. You are king," argued Nigel.

Ellis' look was sharp. "A king dishonored and disgraced by his son."

Nigel fought back tears of shame and fear. "I'm sorry! I never meant to dishonor you."

Ellis' jaw slackened at the distress. "I'm sorry too, for I must give them my answer in the morning before they leave."

Nigel bolted to his feet. "No!"

"Don't you understand? Your action may result in war!" declared Darius.

Nigel grimaced, yet kept his course. He had to. "I do understand, but I won't sit by and see him forced into a decision because of my foolishness, especially with Allon's future at stake."

"You should have thought of that before you left."

"I realize that now." He approached Ellis. The effort on his face to maintain his composure evident yet he managed to keep his voice level. "Sire. I ask you to let me set things right by speaking to Lord Bijan. If I fail to convince him, then I will do as you command."

Ellis regarded Nigel, long and steady.

"He owes them an apology," said Darius.

Ellis turned on his heels and opened the door. "Kell!" The captain waited in the hallway with Avatar. "Has Lord Bijan retired for the night?"

"I just saw him heading the Guest Quarters, Sire."

Ellis motioned for Nigel and left the study. Nigel hurried to follow; Darius accompanied them. Kell and Avatar fell into step behind the mortals.

In hall of the Guest Quarters, Ellis halted a few steps from Bijan's chambers and took hold of Nigel's arm. "Choose your words carefully," he warned.

"I will, sir."

Kell knocked on the door and when a servant answered, he spoke in Morvenian. The servant bowed and backed away to allow Ellis, Darius, Nigel, Kell and Avatar to enter.

Bijan was speaking to several other members of the delegation. Conversation stopped at seeing the king, duke, and prince. The Morvenians formally bowed, however severity filled their faces and glances at Nigel.

"My Lord Bijan, forgive this late call. The prince wishes to speak to you and your noble lords," said Ellis.

Despite seeing Bijan's stern features and glance pass from Ellis to him, Nigel spoke. "My lord, I owe you, Princess Kaleana, and your noble lords a most sincere and humble apology for my absence this evening. There is no excuse to undo what I have done."

After a moment's pause, Bijan replied. "You speak well, but insult grave."

Nigel squared his shoulders. "Upon my word of honor, I never meant to insult you or to dishonor the king. My action was sheer foolishness of youth."

"How old prince?"

"Sixteen."

"By time emperor sixteen, emperor rule Morven for two years."

"And I'm sure because of that he has more wisdom and maturity than I do at present."

Bijan nodded with a small sly smile. "It is good prince recognize faults. Although that not always make things right."

"No, so I ask for you not to leave Allon under these circumstances and allow me to correct my fault and make right the injury I caused."

Bijan turned to Ellis. "King agree to this?"

"I agreed the prince should come and apologize. The decision to leave or stay is yours. However, if there is to be a future relationship between our countries, I will consider it an act of kindness to allow my son, and heir, this opportunity."

"If no opportunity, no marriage?"

"I didn't say that."

Nigel intervened. "My lord, this is between you and I, not the king. I have dishonored him. To make amends he graciously granted me permission to speak to you. Now I ask you to let me redress the wrong I have done you and your delegation."

Bijan again turned from Nigel to Ellis. His look and voice sharp. "What punishment for prince who dishonors king?"

Ellis' brows leveled and he replied. "That is for me to decide. All that concerns you is to allow him to redress the insult or not."

"If Morven give opportunity, king give punishment."

Ellis' whole body stiffened in outrage, bringing Kell to stand beside him, a hand on his sword. Avatar placed himself at beside Nigel, also at the ready.

"You presume to order the king?" demanded Kell, golden eyes flaring in intensity.

95

Bijan's boldness faded at seeing the Guardian captain's wrath. "Only fair after such insult," he managed to say.

"I shall decide what is fair in Allon!" rebuked Ellis. "I convened the Council, heard your petition, given you every royal courtesy, and endured your rude speech. I will not be told how to deal with my son, the next king of Allon."

Nigel flinched at Ellis' pronouncement of his being king. Only Avatar noticed his disturbance, and touched his elbow in support. The others continued the confrontation.

"Would the emperor tolerate such insolence from a visiting dignitary as the king has from you?" demanded Darius.

Bijan balked. "Emperor ... no," he admitted.

"Then consider it a wise move to give the prince his opportunity." Ellis turned on his heels and the Morvenians bowed very low in a more subdued attitude.

Once in the hall, Darius glanced back to toward the room. "That turned out better than I expected."

Ellis snorted with irony, looking side-ways at Nigel. "Your punishment is to endure Bijan's arrogance every moment of every day for as long as they remain."

"Ay, sir," he replied with a relieved chuckle. "Then will I have redeemed myself in your eyes?"

Ellis threw an arm about Nigel's shoulder, a smile appearing. "You started by the way you handled yourself just now. Continue and all will be forgiven and forgotten."

"Thank you, sir. I promise, I won't fail."

"What about Shannan, Ellan and the Council?" asked Darius.

"I'll speak to all of them. You being first, Uncle."

Darius laughed. "Tend to your mother and sister, I am well."

They parted company, Darius and Ellis to return to the king's study and Nigel to speak to Shannan and Ellan.

Since the hour was late, Nigel knew his mother's habit of nightly prayers before retiring. Thus he headed to the royal apartment antechamber. He waited for his knock to be answered, and as suspected, it was by Vidar. The archer said nothing. Like all Guardians his eyes conveyed his meaning, making words unnecessary. Under such scrutiny, Nigel couldn't tell which pair of eyes were more convicting and unnerving, Avatar's silver gaze or Vidar's copper stare. Still, they didn't come close to Kell's intimidating golden glare.

He forced the words from his throat. "I'm here to apologize."

Vidar glanced over Nigel's head and no doubt to Avatar, but Nigel dared not watch the exchange and kept his focus on the archer. Again, Vidar said nothing in shifting his gaze back to Nigel, rather stepped aside to allow him entrance. Nigel didn't even look to see if Avatar followed him, although he didn't think so at hearing the door immediately close.

Shannan rose from a chair upon sight of him. The moment their eyes met, Nigel fought back tears at seeing the tremendous disappointment he expected. Oh, there was anger also; so much so, Shannan didn't speak only stared at him. The bond between his parents ran strong and deep. Whatever injured, hurt or in anyway touched one, the other felt it. He now wished Avatar accompanied him, wanting an ally since Vidar would not intervene for being staunchly loyal and protective of Shannan. After all, as the Daughter of Allon, her bond was as great with the Guardians as with Ellis. Fortunately, he had not often incurred her wrath. Still, like with his father, he chose to address her in all humility and formality.

"Your Majesty, I just came from speaking to the king, duke and the Morvenians."

Her brow wrinkled in curiosity at mention of the Morvenians, but she remained silent.

He went on to explain the cause of his foolish action, the conversation with Ellis and Darius upon his return, the encounter with the Morvenians and finally the outcome.

"Upon my word of honor, I will do everything I can to redress the wrong I have done." His voice grew passionate, almost desperate as he continued. "Madam, believe me, I never meant to hurt or bring dishonor to you or the king."

Shannan's rigidity softened during his speech though did not completely vanish when she spoke for the first time. "What did your father say to the Morvenians' agreeing to stay?"

Nigel suppressed a smile of relief at hearing her say *father* rather than *the king*, a hopeful sign of swaying her anger. "To quote him, 'Your punishment will be to endure Lord Bijan's arrogance for every moment of every day for as long as they remain.'"

She smiled, yet she tried to hide it under a fake cough and covering her mouth.

He was winning and continued. "When I asked if that was sufficient, he said it would. Will my punishment suffice for you ... Mother?" he asked, a knowing, prompting grin appearing.

She broke into a touched smile, choking back emotion, "Ay."

He embraced her and kissed her cheek. "I'm really sorry."

She held his face in both hands. "Stay the course, fulfill your punishment and don't ever do anything like this again. Oh, the look of hurt in his eyes when he realized you would not return in time."

"I know. I wanted to crawl under a rock. Just like seeing your disappointment was nearly unbearable. I never want to experience those looks again." He hugged her, holding tight. "I love you, Mother. I love Father. With Jor'el's help, I promise never to act so foolish in the future."

"I love you. And so does he, deeply, which is why your absence was so painful."

Nigel nodded, his attempt to contain his emotions muting him.

She flashed a teasing smile, turning him toward the door. "Now, you need to get some rest if you're going endure your punishment beginning tomorrow."

Nigel chuckled, more for relief than humor. "After I speak to Ellan."

"She may be asleep by now."

"I'll wake her. My mind won't be at ease until I at make amends to my family." He kissed her cheek and left. "All is well with Mother," he told Avatar.

"I'm sure the Daughter of Allon did not let you get off easy."

98

Nigel shook his head. "Not by the way she looked. I was more frightened by her silence than Father's anger."

"I'm not surprised. She can command Guardians by a mere glance. I never met such a formidable female mortal."

Nigel sarcastically grinned. "Tell that to Ellan." He knocked on the chamber door and softly called her name. Morrell opened the door. "Is Ellan awake?"

"She's just getting into bed."

Nigel entered. For some reason Morrell didn't intimidate him like the others. Not to mention, Morrell didn't bar his entrance or even appear put out.

Ellan sat up and scowled. "I told Morrell I didn't want to see to you!"

"If he kept calling he would have woken your sisters," said Morrell.

Her rolling eyes passed from Morrell to Nigel. "What do you want?"

"I came to apologize. What I did was wrong and it placed you in a bad position."

She folded her arms, expression fixed and unflinching.

He sat on the bed. "I don't blame you for being angry."

"Blame? Of course you can't blame me. You were wrong."

"I know, which is why I'm apologizing" He watched her fold her arms further and avoid direct eye contact. "Why are so angry?"

She scowled, unable to look at him. "You wouldn't understand."

"Try me." He reached for her hand in an effort to coax her, but she jerked away. "Please, Ellan. You are my sister. There isn't anything you can't tell me that I wouldn't at least try to understand."

"You say that, but isn't how you treat me. You more tolerate Tristine's antics than listen to anything I say."

His brows furrowed in confusion. "I didn't think so. Although you tend to be mean to her."

"I'm not trying to mean, I'm trying to correct her bad behavior. You and Father indulge her, but she must grow up."

He snickered. "I think Necie is more indulged than Tristine."

"Necie is beside the point. You told me at Leith to try and be more understanding and supportive, but whenever I do, you interfere. Father finds her amusing, Mother instructs her, and Necie follows her everywhere. It's as if the world revolves around you as heir and Tristine's antics. I'm completely ignored."

For a brief moment he was stymied by her outburst. "I'm at a loss of what to say. I didn't realize you felt this way. I'm sorry."

She drew her knees up to her chest and pouted. "A lot of good being sorry does."

"It's a start, isn't it?"

She shrugged.

He moved closer to take her hands and when she wouldn't yield, he persisted. "Now that I know, I can change my behavior."

"Maybe, only it doesn't change Tristine."

"She'll have to change with her banquet coming up."

"I can't wait to see that."

He cocked a guarded brow at her crossness. "Do you hope she fails?"

She shrugged. "I'm just weary of her reckless, childish behavior."

"Perhaps, if we join forces instead of being at odds—" he began, which made her grin. "I like seeing you smile. At least you and Mother were easier to deal with than the Morvenians."

"What about them?"

He told her about the events of the evening, all of which she reacted to in various degrees of surprise, annoyance, and finally pleasure with the outcome. "Do you think that sufficient punishment for the errors of my ways? Father and Mother agree. What about you? Am I forgiven?" he asked with a rakish smile.

She playfully smirked. "Perhaps."

He kissed her cheek. "Now, I need sleep to face them tomorrow. Good night."

When the door closed, she lay down, staring at the ceiling as images of the day and the conversation with Nigel ran through her mind. True, he apologized, and perhaps some good can come of him finally understanding how he treats her and favors Tristine.

Still, both are blind where Tristine is concerned, she thought of Nigel and Ellis. *But he says he's proud of me,* she continued about Ellis. *Why should I let her antics take that away?*

Her mind argued back and forth about Tristine, Nigel and Ellis. Although her parents expressed how well she was doing, how could she make them see Tristine the way she does, childish and obnoxious? True, she might not be mean-spirited, but her reckless nature is unfit for a princess, especially with royal guests present. Add to that Nigel running off and being put on and alone in her stance to make a good impression on the Morvenians.

Perhaps that's the answer. By playing a dutiful hostess and respectful daughter of the king, I can show everyone the difference between Tristine and me. With her mind settled, she closed her eyes and fell asleep.

Chapter 6

NIGEL WAS RIDING. He was running. He was in the forest. He was in a building. All was confusion. All was muddled. Whatever was happening, he had to get away. No matter where he turned, or what he did, it kept following him, drawing closer and more terrifying. Someone touched him and he cried out, trying to jerk away even though the urgent voice sounded familiar and the hold on him persistent. Finally his eyes snapped open, his breathing labored with fright. It took a moment for his eyes to focus in the dim yellow light and for his faculties to realize who called him and held him.

"Avatar?"

"You were having a nightmare."

Nigel's confusion grew at seeing he lay in his own bed. The images were so real. His mind struggled to comprehend while his heart pounded in his chest. "It was horrible!"

"What about?"

Nigel closed his eyes and swallowed back his fear. "I'm not sure. All I knew is I had to get away, but no matter where I turned, I couldn't escape."

"From what?"

Nigel sat up, his face pale and a bit sweaty; his voice unsteady. "I never saw it, only felt it close and horrifying. I've never being so scared of anything."

Avatar sat on the bed, a comforting hand on Nigel's shoulder. "Easy, you know I will let nothing harm you."

"In reality, ay, but my mind?"

Avatar cocked a grin. "Reality is all that matters. Imagination is harmless."

Nigel grunted in annoyance. "Easy for you to say. Guardians don't dream."

"The mind can be controlled and mastered by your will while the actions of others is out of your control." Avatar stood and pulled back the covers. "Come." He took Nigel's hand, drew him to his feet and led him to the nearest chair. "Sit and begin the meditation."

Nigel arranged himself with his hands in his lap and eyes closed. "I hope this works."

"Don't hope, do," said Avatar. His voice grew softer. "Recite the Jor'ellian Creed after me:

'There is one Lord.
He is the Infinite, the Almighty.
By his Will I live.
By his Power I serve.
And his Honor I defend.
My mind, heart and strength belong to him.'

"Now think about what blessings you have in your family and in Allon." He heard and watched Nigel repeat each phrase. Soon Nigel's body began to relax, his face softening into a peaceful expression. "Well done."

Nigel opened his eyes and smiled. "Thanks."

Avatar gregariously grinned and shrugged. "You allowed your mind and spirit to be changed, I simply pointed the way."

"I may need more direction before this day is done."

The Great Hall was set up for a breakfast buffet along the far wall with servants manning the table to serve the royal family, nobles and guests. Nigel purposed to fulfill his word and responsibility in good order. He even managed to beat his father to the Great Hall and Ellis was known for early rising and prompt attention to the day's duties.

Erasmus, Fagan, Ned and Wess were similar in habit, so they were the first group to hear Nigel's apology and intention. They were also among those more favorable toward the royal family since Fagan and Ned were Darius' cousins by blood, making them foster cousins to Ellis. Erasmus married Erin, aunt to Ned and Fagan. The brothers eagerly accepted Nigel's apology with Erasmus a bit sterner, but willing. Wess' expression showed disappointment; and the general had yet to say a word.

Next to his father and Darius, Wess was the man Nigel most admired. At age sixteen, Wess, along with his younger brother, Bosley, risked their lives protecting Shannan and the infant Nigel during the coup. Since then, Wess rose through the ranks from Ellis' squire to general. Not once did he take advantage of his relationship to the king nor his own royal heritage and lineage. If anything Nigel should be bowing to Wess, third in line to the throne under the House of Unwin. Fate intervened when Ellis deposed Marcellus and took mercy on Wess' father Hugh. Whereas Jasper instructed Nigel every time he visited Garwood, Wess took direct charge of his formal training in arms, and befriended the younger prince.

"General?" asked Nigel, hopeful.

Wess gave his companions a nod before placing a hand around Nigel's shoulders to draw him aside. "You're young. Though I understand the reckless impulses of youth and can personally forgive you, on behalf of your father and seeing him dishonored and deflecting comments regarding your absence, I should box your ears!" His voice never rose in volume, but his intention clear in expression.

"I welcome a thrashing from you compared to enduring Lord Bijan for the remainder of their stay," said Nigel, a chuckle began but stopped at feeling Wess' grip tighten about his neck.

"Dishonor the king again, and you will get that thrashing."

This was no idle threat. Wess always meant what he said. "I won't fail, General."

"Good," said Wess, now grinning. "Because I'm letting Lord Allard use my corral for some scheme you and he are plotting."

This time Nigel didn't suppress his pleasure and smiled. "Thank you, General."

Wess motioned to the far end of the room. "Your parents have arrived." With a nudge, he sent Nigel on his way.

"Good morning, Sire. Majesty." Nigel bowed.

"It appears you've begun speaking to people." Ellis motioned toward the group Nigel just left.

"Ay, sir. I will not let a morsel of food pass my lips until I have spoken to all concerned." The arrival of Hollis, Malcolm and Bosley caught his attention.

Ellis and Shannan also noticed. "Don't let us stop you," said Shannan.

Nigel left his parents, and with all congeniality, offered his apologies and proclaimed his desire to make amends. Bosley willingly accepted what he said, but Malcolm received it in silence. Then again, due to illness, he frequently appeared silent and thoughtful, so Nigel tried not to make too much of the solemn reception. Hollis was a different matter. Although, he possessed a jovial and kind nature, the consummate naval officer suffered devastating losses. In an unusual, reserved manner he accepted Nigel's stated purpose. Where Nigel was accustomed to Malcolm's disposition, he wanted to press Hollis. But the baron used his wife as an excuse to continue to breakfast.

"Don't let Hollis discourage you," said Darius. He and Arista arrived unseen. "You are taking responsibility and that is what matters, not how others receive it."

"I'll need to remember that when I speak to Zebulon and Gareth."

"Speaking of the contentious duo." Darius pointed to the brothers. "They see you."

Nigel took a deep breath, squared his shoulders and approached them. "My lords, good morning."

Zebulon's combative expression matched his sarcasm. "Your Highness. You're looking well. I thought maybe you were ill last evening."

"No, my lord, not ill. Unless you consider being possessed by a inexcusable youthful impulse an illness?"

"Depends on the outcome of the illness. And last night's outcome could prove debilitating, if not fatal."

At that moment, Bijan, Princess Kaleana, and the Morvenian delegation arrived.

"Or could result in complete recovery." Nigel motioned to the Morvenians. "They don't appear to be dressed for departure."

"Indeed not. Did you speak to them?" asked Gareth.

"And convinced them to stay?" added Zebulon.

"You see the result with your eyes, my lord," said Nigel.

"Did the king help you?" Zebulon continued his aggressive interrogation.

Nigel stiffened and stared at Zebulon. "Despite my youthful mistake, I can hold my own."

Zebulon returned Nigel's stare. "I should hope so. It is upon that mettle the responsibility of Allon will one day rest."

Nigel's jowls flexed and he withdrew from the brothers. The reference to his future as king pricked him. His apprehension grew as the nightmares increased in frequency and intensity, making his feelings more and more difficult to mask.

"Your Highness. How are you this morning?" said Uriah.

At the Vicar's address, Nigel's attitude softened. "Vicar. I owe you an apology—" Uriah's hand on his shoulder and friendly smile stopped further speech.

"The king spoke to me last night in private."

Nigel glanced to high table before discreetly asking, "How troubled is he about this proposal?"

"To answer you would betray his confidence in me as spiritual advisor."

Nigel's own trouble rose to his lips. However, this was not the time and place to speak. Perhaps later if the Vicar could spare moment, he would ask for advice and prayer.

106

Allard arrived. "Highness. Good morning, Vicar."

Uriah replied to Allard with a nod. "Highness." He bowed and took his leave.

Allard of the Meadowlands was the shrewdest member of the Council and good friend of his father, thus Nigel said, "My Lord Allard, you would be the first one I look for, but I last I find."

Allard heartily laughed, giving Nigel a friendly poke in the ribs. "I know better, Darius is the first. I might rank a close second, but you're being gracious."

"It is you who are being gracious to forgive me with a jest after my foolishness last night."

"Darius told me everything before breakfast. Keep your word and the Council may be persuaded to dictate different terms." His tone changed to one of warning as he spoke.

Nigel flinched at the change. "I will."

Allard drew closer to speak privately. "You placed us all in a difficult position, so my words should come as no surprise."

"No. I only hoped you would understand."

"I do. But that understanding doesn't negate my responsibility to the Council and to Allon. Do you *understand?*"

"Ay."

"Good," said Allard, his countenance brightening. "I have complied with your request. The best of my herd is awaiting your inspection at General Wess' estate."

"He told me when I spoke to him earlier. I'll inform Father and we'll inspect the herd at the first opportunity."

"Speaking of, the king is trying to get your attention."

Ellis discreetly motioned for Nigel. Bijan and Kaleana now sat at high table with his parents. He left Allard to approach them.

"Good morning, Lord Bijan, Princess."

"Good morning, Highness," replied Bijan. Kaleana remained silent.

"Have you not spoken to the princess?"

"I have."

Nigel turned to Kaleana. A hint of melancholy crossed her features, her glance at him timid. "Most noble princess," he began using Morvenian phrases, "my absence last night was inexcusable but in no way meant as a personal offense against you or your countrymen. I offered my humble apologies to Lord Bijan last night, and I do so to you. All I can do now is give you my word I will be a most attentive host."

In uncertainty, Kaleana glanced to Bijan, who nodded, so she returned to Nigel. "I accept prince apology," she said in broken Allonian.

Nigel smiled and came around the table to take his place.

Tristine, Necie and Angus entered the Great Hall. Breakfast was less formal than dinner, so they were permitted to mingle with the guests. Nigel sat at high table speaking to Kaleana, and seemingly in good spirits. Tristine scowled in annoyance.

"They make a striking couple," said Ellan.

Tristine gaped in disbelief at Ellan, who kept moving toward the buffet. She followed. "You don't really think that, do you?"

Ellan selected her breakfast before replying. "Why not? She is beautiful."

"She's not Allonian."

"What does that have to do with it?"

"Princess?" a servant asked Tristine.

"The usual," she said, distracted, her focus on the conversation with Ellan. "I thought being Allonian and believing what we do has everything to do with it."

Ellan laughed in ridicule. "You are naïve in your belief. Nigel is heir and his marriage will be more political than religious."

"What about believing in Jor'el?"

Ellan sent Tristine a rebuking glare. "You barely pay attention to the lessons so why should it matter now?"

"I do too pay attention," she insisted, but it was obvious Ellan didn't agree. In fact, with a disdainful smirk Ellan headed towards high table. Tristine wanted to pursue the matter but saw the interested way her father watched them. Further conversation could cause a stir and he wouldn't approve of that in public.

"What did Ellan mean?" asked Necie.

"I don't know, but Father sees us." Tristine smiled and approached high table. "Good morning, Sire. Majesty," she addressed her parents.

"Fa—Sire," Necie corrected herself at a nudge from Tristine and offered a quick curtsey to Ellis.

"Sire." Angus bowed.

Ellis flashed a private smile and used his fork to wave them to take their seats. With the guests occupying high table, they would sit at the table closest.

Tristine tried to catch Nigel's eye before leaving to take her seat, but he focused on Kaleana. Even after sitting, she kept watch of Nigel, who still didn't notice them. Finally he looked their way; only a short glance with no acknowledgement.

"Nigel is ignoring us," she groused.

"Maybe that's what Ellan meant," said Necie.

"I don't think so. I can't image him favoring her over family," said Angus.

"I hope you're right," said Tristine.

Breakfast passed, giving way to the activities of the day. Some of the Morvenian delegation was shown military weapons and uniforms by Wess and Darius. Ellis engaged Lord Bijan concerning matters of interest to the ambassador. Princess Kaleana and her female servants kept company with Shannan, Ellan, Arista and other ladies of the court.

Tristine, Necie and Angus were too young to be officially included, leaving them free to pursue their own entertainment. This usually included hanging around the fringes to observe the guests. Necie was curious but easily distracted. Angus played mediator when Tristine complained about the Morvenians or attempted get Nigel's attention.

Staying true to his word, Nigel successfully divided his time between Lord Bijan and Princess Kaleana during the course of the day. By late afternoon, he accompanied Kaleana for a stroll in the family garden, rich in full summer bloom. Shannan left to tend to duties requiring Ellan and

Arista's presence, leaving Nigel with Kaleana. Two Morvenian guards and three of the princess' female servants remained and pretended to be otherwise occupied so they could speak semi-privately. From an archway between the lower galleyway and garden, Avatar kept watch of everything.

"Her Majesty gracious woman. Very believe," said Kaleana.

"What do you mean?"

"Believe your god."

He smiled. "Ay, she is a devoted follower of Jor'el. We all are."

"Hard to believe one god."

"Actually, I think it's harder to believe in many gods. How do you keep them straight in your head?" When she stared at him in befuddlement, he tried to rephrase his question. "Do you know all your gods?"

"No. Not know gods," she said a bit disturbed. "Cannot know."

"Then how do you believe if you can't know?"

She frowned in frustration. "Believe. Then know."

"Ay, wisdom often follows belief. Still, there must be something known beforehand to make you believe."

She lightly bit her lip in vexation over the difficulty of communication.

"Princess." Necie hastened over. She carried something and looked at Nigel with big doe eyes and said; "I have something to give her, if you'll let me." He grinned and nodded in approval. She held out a handkerchief with rather uneven embroidery on it. "I made this for you."

Kaleana took the handkerchief and examined it.

"Those are the symbols of Allon: a wolf, an eagle and a crown. It's not very good, but it is a gift."

"It's fine. Thank you," said Nigel, giving her a wink of encouragement.

"Thank you," said Kaleana sweetly.

Necie smiled, and after a quick curtsey, scurried away.

In watching Necie leave, they caught sight of Tristine in the shadow of the lower galleyway. Her stoic expression turned to Necie, who ran up to her and said something, pointing back at them.

"Old one like me not," said Kaleana.

"I don't think that's true. Tristine is cautious," said Nigel. He steered Kaleana away from Tristine yet sent Tristine a private rebuking glare. She sneered at him and left.

"What Tristine mean in name?"

"Bold, fearless. She was named after our ancestor."

"Then not cautious."

Nigel frowned at his failed diplomacy. "No, but she's not spiteful. What does Kaleana mean in Morvenian?"

"Pure and true," she said, looking at him with large open eyes.

How captivating and alluring were her eyes and Nigel found himself speechless, feeling warm and awkward. "Do you like picnics?" he blurted out.

"What pic-nic?"

He scrambled for words, still flustered by her look. "Picnic. Eating in the open." He tried to explain, but she still looked uncertain. "Eating outside not in a hall. Tent." He used his hand to make an exaggerated illustration of a tent.

"Oh, pic-nic," she said with understanding.

"I'll make the arrangements." He gave her a hasty bow and left the garden, his sudden embarrassment puzzling. He just rounded a corner when he ran into Tristine, who spoke to Armus and had her back turned. "Sorry," he grumbled, but tossed a glance back to the garden.

"What's wrong? Did the princess not like her gift?"

"No, no, she liked it fine."

"Then why do you look like you got caught at something?"

He became annoyed. "You're too young to understand."

"More affairs of state?"

He scowled at her. "I was thinking of allowing you to come on the picnic, but if you can't act mature I may reconsider."

"What picnic?"

"The picnic I'm going to arrange for Princess Kaleana." He moved off.

"Did Father approve?" she called.

"He will," he answered over his shoulder without looking back.

111

"Avatar." She stopped his departure. "What's gotten into him? He's behaving strangely."

"I'm not entirely sure."

"It's her, isn't it? She's somehow bewitched him."

Avatar's interest became piqued by her statement and visible concern. "What made you say that?"

"She's so different. And that ugly statue she gave him to place by his bed."

"You sound jealous," said Armus.

Disconcerted, Tristine folded her arms, staring in the direction Nigel went. "No. I just can't imagine him married. At least not to her."

Armus grinned at Avatar, but Avatar appeared serious when speaking to Tristine, "I'll find out and place both our minds at ease."

Avatar left, but unfortunately, didn't get the opportunity to ease either his or Tristine's concerns as Nigel and Ellis began planning the picnic. Ellis not only approved of Nigel's suggestion, but also added more events until it became a full-blown summer fair where local merchants could show off their wares and all participants could take a chance in a game of skill. He considered it a great way to show the Morvenians Allonian society and give them a sampling of trade goods. By the end of a week, all would be ready on the Plain of Hereford three miles west of Waldron.

Chapter 7

THE ROYAL FAMILY GREETED GUESTS and participants; with Ellis giving a short speech of introduction. The best way to deal with the Morvenians was to segregate them. So, while he, Nigel, Darius and Wess entertained Lord Bijan and the males of the delegation, Shannan, Arista and Ellan tended to Princess Kaleana and the Morvenian females. Again, Tristine, Necie and Angus were left to themselves for the day. Sometimes they were with the women, other times they followed the men, often distracting Nigel.

"Princesses free to do as please. Does king approve behavior?" asked Bijan, watching Nigel speak to Necie. She showed him some doll at a booth.

Ellis smiled. "Today is a fair. There are enough serious matters in life to confront. Time for rest and recreation is good. And I confess, I enjoy seeing my children having fun. Does the emperor not take pleasure in his children?"

"Court of Morven much different. Although we have celebrations."

Nigel returned. "Necie found something to amuse her."

"Necie has a knack for finding amusement in everything," quipped Ellis, making Nigel, Darius and Wess laugh.

Lord Allard approached. "Sire. All is ready."

113

Ellis turned to Bijan. "You spoke of how the Morvenians take pride in being expert horsemen and your herds are dwindling. What would you say to seeing the best horses Allon has to offer?"

Bijan grinned with enthusiasm. "King make most interesting offer. Where are horses?"

"Two miles from here. We can be there and back before tonight's feast."

Bijan spoke Morvenian to the other noblemen, who were also pleased at the prospect.

"This way, Sire, Lord Bijan," said Allard.

At a nearby makeshift corral behind the royal pavilion, ten horses were saddled. Once mounted Bijan noticed Kell and Avatar remained on foot. "Guardians not go with us?"

"They don't need a horse."

Soon Bijan understood what Ellis meant since Kell and Avatar easily kept pace, and by the time they reached General Wess' estate, weren't even breathing hard.

"Guardians are remarkable creatures. Do they ever tire?"

Ellis laughed. "I don't think so."

One of Bijan's companions remarked on the brick and timber construction. "Please, king. What is this place?"

"This estate belongs to General Wess."

"Welcome to my home. The horses are in a corral just behind the stables."

The large corral easily held the twenty horses Allard brought from the Meadowlands. The Allonians listened to the Morvenians converse, pointing at the horses.

"They are larger than Morvenain mounts. What about endurance? Speed?" asked Bijan.

"The shorter, broader ones are bred for endurance. The taller, leaner horses are bred for speed. Racing, if you like," explained Allard.

"We have one breed. Still, we see others, not like these. Big, pull wagons," said another Morvenian.

"Those are bred for strength and war. Please, feel free to examine them."

The Morvenians entered the corral, eager to get at the horses. Wess accompanied them.

Allard turned to Nigel. "There are four I thought would interest you." He moved to a pale horse with a white mane and tail. "She is three years old with a quiet and agreeable disposition."

Nigel laughed. "She won't do for Tristine."

Ellis chuckled and Darius verbally agreed.

"There is another mare, a yearling and not yet broke but with more spirit." Allard moved to a black filly, which shied when he reached for her.

"Doesn't seem like spirit. More skittish," said Ellis.

A loud angry whinny caught their attention. One of the Morvenians tried to examine the teeth of three-year-old sorrel gelding that kept pulling his head away. The Morvenian irately spoke to his companions.

"What about that one?" asked Nigel.

"Dunstan? I don't think so. He's too contrary." The moment Allard said the word 'contrary' he rolled his eyes at Ellis.

Dunstan broke free of the Morvenian and began to trot off when Nigel caught the halter. "Whoa, boy." Dunstan snorted and pawed the ground, glaring at Nigel almost daring him to do something. "What do you think, Father?"

Ellis came alongside Nigel and looked the horse in the eye. "He has spirit, but for Tristine?"

"Why not? He can match her temperament. Besides, Caleigh is too old and Malin too slow and stubborn."

"She's not ridden any other horses," said Ellis. Nigel grew sheepish and Allard coughed to one side. "What other horses has she ridden I don't know about?"

"Actually, Sire. She rode Balin," said Allard.

"What?" exclaimed Ellis in surprised concern.

"Father, nothing happened. She did well."

"Ay. In fact, she stayed on longer than you and Darius," said Allard.

"She was thrown?"

"No, Sire," insisted Allard, trying to calm Ellis. "I remained beside her and when Balin grew intolerant I made her get off. Still, she managed to ride him for fifteen minutes."

Ellis' incredulous look turned to Darius, who appeared amused. "Balin. The beast that threw you and me." Hearing a low chuckle from his son, he suspiciously asked, "Is there more I should know about her riding habits?"

"Twice I caught her on Cutler."

Ellis' brow cocked at hearing about his warhorse. "Anything else?"

"No, sir. Maybe now you'll see why I think Dunstan would be perfect. He offers her a challenge."

Darius tried to keep from laughing.

"I suppose you agree?" Ellis asked Darius.

"If she did what you and I failed to do, why not? She has Shannan's way with animals."

Again Ellis studied Dunstan. The horse pricked its ear forward and snorted at him. "Very well. Bring him to Waldron for her banquet."

Nigel widely smiled, patting Dunstan. "You're going to meet your match."

◈

Meanwhile at the fair, Shannan, Vidar and Armus stood off to one side watching Tristine take part in an archery game of skill.

"You taught her well, Daughter of Allon," said Armus.

Shannan smiled with great pleasure. "Soon she'll be better than me." She sighed and smirked in annoyance. "Well, enough selfish pleasure, I must get back to our guests."

"They disturb you?"

She looked up at Armus. "I'm not sure what to make of them. Superficially they are polite, generous and very formal, but their hearts and souls are unlike any people I've ever met."

"Centuries ago I heard about them, during Heith's reign. They were simple nomadic people who banded together. Only I don't recall their religious system being as complex." Armus turned to Vidar for confirmation.

116

"I heard the same," said the archer.

"It's not a system I am comfortable being associated with," she chided.

"Have you told Ellis?" asked Armus.

"Naturally, and he agrees. For a moment it appeared Nigel's mistake would cost us, but he is doing very well in making up for it. Oh! Good shot!" she cheered at Tristine nearly make a bulls-eye. "I wonder why Angus isn't competing since he and Tristine practiced with Wren."

"He wanted to try his skill in the manly art of wrestling, or so he said," said Armus with a chuckle.

She laughed. "If he fills out in the shoulders and chest like Darius, he will someday be a formidable wrestler. Well, back to duty."

Morrell's brow levelled and he winced at a sharp pain in his head. His eyes darted to where Ellan sat engaged in conversation with Kaleana. Everything appeared well with his charge so what sensation poked at his brain? Guardians didn't experience what mortals called 'headaches' yet something caused him pain. The pain stopped as suddenly as it started, but his countenance grew placid, almost blank. He turned and walked into the woods.

Necie won the game of tossing the balls through a hoop. Three noble children her age competed against her and voiced disappointment in losing, yet showed forbearance toward the bubbly princess.

"For the little princess." The gamekeeper gave her a small trophy.

She giggled and left while the other children continued to play. She ran up to Mahon, who stood a few yards away. "Look what I won. I'm going to show Ellan and Kaleana."

Mahon smiled and watched her scurry off. He shivered and turned to where he knew Morrell stood, only he wasn't there. Ellan and Kaleana remained engaged in conversation unaware of Morrell's absence. Giddy, Necie approached the older girls. It was unlike Morrell to be absent from duty. With the princesses safe, he honed in on Morrell's essence and moved to find him. He became concerned when the essence led him from the fair to the edge of the woods. He glanced back, unable to see the girls, but did not sense danger to them so he continued into the trees.

After about a hundred yards, he found Morrell sitting on the ground cradling his head. "Morrell?" When Morrell didn't respond, he knelt and touched him on the shoulder.

Morrell bolted up, startled. In confusion, his gaze swept around the vicinity, seeing trees and nothing else. Dazed, he swayed and Mahon caught him to steady his balance. "Mahon? How did I get here?"

"I don't know. When I saw you weren't at your station, I came looking for you."

"Ellan?"

"Fine. When I left Necie—" Mahon stopped, suddenly alert, his head snapping around. Grabbing the hilt of his sword, he raced off

Unaware of Mahon's departure, Necie continued on her way, carefully holding the trophy. Ellan and Kaleana didn't notice her approach and kept talking. But Necie could hear them.

"Do sisters always trouble brother?" asked Kaleana.

"Oh, ay," said Ellan in disapproval. "Tristine especially. I don't know how he tolerates her. Necie is a spoiled brat."

Necie slowed at hearing Ellan complain about Tristine, which was not uncommon. They often complained about each other. She stopped when Ellan called her a 'spoiled brat', looking wounded.

"Such trouble not known in Morven. Brothers and sisters have little contact."

"How is that possible?"

"If brother heir, rudeness punished and sent away."

"Father should punish them and make them learn proper behavior. I'll speak to him about it."

Hurt, Necie gasped, dropped her trophy and ran off into the woods.

Tristine finished shooting and made her way back to the main area, the bow over her shoulder. A short distance ahead, Necie dropped something and dashed into the woods. She hurried after Necie only to pull up at not seeing the direction she went after entering the trees.

"Necie?" She received no answer so she called again. "Necie!" Hearing a whimper, she headed in the direction from which it came. In a grove of trees, Necie sat at the base of an oak, weeping. Tristine knelt beside her. "What's wrong?" Necie didn't reply. "Tell me why you're crying."

Necie shook her head and stubbornly set her mouth.

Snap! A branch broke. Tristine turned from Necie but saw nothing. A low, strange, snarling screech came from nearby. "Come. We must get back." She drew Necie to her feet.

"I won't go back!"

Tristine's glance darted about the grove at hearing more snarling. "We have to." She took Necie's arm, but Necie bolted away.

She only took a few steps from Tristine when she stopped. In front of her appeared a strange creature. The body and tail resembled a lion with the head and wings of an eagle. Feathers covered the body and a feather fan at the end of the tail. Petrified, Necie stared at the creature.

Tristine loaded her bow. "Necie, move back!"

Necie was too scared to move. Another angry screech came from behind Tristine. A second creature appeared. Necie screamed and ran to hide behind Tristine. The creatures began to circle them.

"What are they?" Necie's voice quaked with fright.

"I don't know." Tristine held her bow ready, anxiously watching the creatures.

One suddenly lunged at them and Tristine fired, wounding the creature in the shoulder. The second one came at Necie from the other direction. She tried to run when the creature swiped at her with a massive, clawed paw, sending her flying through the air and crashing into a tree.

Tristine was reloading her bow when the wounded creature came at her. She dodged the swipe at her head, but took the brunt of the blow to the left shoulder, ripping her clothes and tearing flesh beneath, the force sent her tumbling sideways. Before the creature launched at her, a flash of white light appeared between she and the creature. Armus arrived, his sword drawn. Angry, it screeched and leapt at him. He only moved one foot and swung at the creature, decapitating it. It fell to the ground with a hard thud before vanishing in yellow light.

Although grateful for Armus' intervention, Tristine saw Necie lying in a huddled mass at the base of a tree and the second creature about to strike her. "Necie!"

A sudden blast sent the creature flying some twenty feet away from Necie. It scrambled to get up before Mahon attacked, but instead, Mahon stood between the creature and Necie, drawing his sword. The beast charged Mahon, then, in mid-stride, rose on its hind legs to lunge at him. Mahon sidestepped, and with a mighty swing, cleaved the creature in half. In a surge of yellow light, it vanished. Mahon knelt beside Necie, who was unconscious, a large bloody gash on the left side of her head. He first felt her cheek for body temperature then her neck for a pulse.

Tristine hurried over and fell to her knees beside Mahon. "Necie?"

"Alive. I'm taking her back to Waldron."

"They both need to go back," said Armus.

Vidar rushed over, loaded crossbow in hand. "What happened?"

"They were attacked by unknown creatures. We're taking them to Waldron for medical treatment," replied Armus. He took hold of Tristine. Mahon lifted Necie in his arms. In a bright flash of white light all four vanished.

At Waldron, Eldric, the Guardian physician arrived in Necie's quarters. His assistant Phoebe accompanied him. Necie lay on the bed and Tristine sat in a chair. Phoebe moved to tend Tristine and Eldric to examine Necie's injuries. Her pupils were uneven and her breathing irregular.

Upset, Tristine shooed off Phoebe's attempt to treat her wound to speak to Eldric. "Will she die?"

He kindly smiled. "Not if I can help it, princess. Now let Phoebe medicine your shoulder."

The door burst opened and Shannan rushed in. Vidar, Ellan, and Morrell at her heels. "How badly are they hurt?"

"Necie is unconscious with a serious head wound," replied Eldric.

"I thought you said she wouldn't die!" clamored Tristine, on the verge of tears.

"She won't."

"I tried to shoot it," Tristine told Shannan.

Shannan knelt beside her. "I'm sure you did. Now calm yourself. If Eldric says Necie won't die, then she won't."

"Where's Father?"

"I sent word to him and Nigel. They'll be here soon." Shannan motioned for Phoebe to continue her work and moved to stand beside the Guardians. Compassion showed on Armus' features but Mahon appeared troubled. She lowered her voice to ask, "What attacked them?"

"I've never seen the creatures before. They were half lion, half bird," replied Armus.

"That's why you left," Morrell said to Mahon.

Mahon's initial glance was sharp, and for a long moment he stared at Morrell. The latter backed away to where Ellan watched her sisters being treated. Worry filled her face in respect to Necie, whose head was being bandaged.

Bright white light filled the room, more than normal for the arrival of a single Guardian, placing Vidar, Mahon and Armus on alert. Morrell stepped in front of Ellan in anticipation of arrival. The light faded to reveal Kell and Avatar holding Nigel and Ellis. Father and son were dazed by the dimension travel, a typical mortal state when defying time and space.

The others relaxed but Tristine shouted, "Father!" and ran into his arms, weeping.

Ellis held her close, looking to the bed and Necie, then to Shannan for an explanation. "Necie?"

"She'll recover."

Ellis sighed in relief. "What attacked them?"

"Armus said he'd never seen the creatures before. Some cross between a lion and bird. Tristine shot at it."

"I only wounded it, Armus killed it," she sobbed.

Ellis tightened his embrace. "Still, that was very brave."

Nigel sat on the bed, anxiety filling his face in watching the sleeping Necie. "How did this happen? How did she get like this if you were with her?" he asked Mahon.

Mahon grimaced and didn't reply.

"You were with her, Mahon," said Ellis firmly.

"He was with me, Sire," said Morrell.

"You? Why?"

Necie stirred, agitated, but still unconscious.

"Sire, this is best done elsewhere. She needs to rest undisturbed," said Eldric.

Ellis released Tristine to approach the bed. He bent down and whispered to Necie, "Rest and recover, my little one. All will be well, I promise." He kissed her cheek. Upon standing, he made a curt wave for Mahon and Morrell to follow.

Tristine held Nigel's hand when the family and most of the Guardians departing, leaving Eldric and Pheobe to care for Necie.

In the hall, Ellis confronted Mahon. "You better have a good explanation for your dereliction of duty."

Shannan eyed the soldiers standing watch and others lingering in the hall awaiting news of the princesses. "Ellis not here."

Darius, Arista and Angus hurried over. "Tristine! How bad is your wound?" asked Darius.

She accepted his hug and complained, "It's hurts, but Necie is much worse."

"How bad is she?" asked Angus, great fear evident in his face and voice.

"She is unconscious with a nasty head wound, but will recover," replied Shannan.

"Thank Jor'el," said Arista.

"May I sit with her, Uncle? Someone should be present when she wakes."

"Of course." Ellis guided Angus to the door, nodding to the guards to admit the boy. "The rest of us have matters to discuss." He turned on his heels and led them to his study.

Nigel helped Tristine to a chair and she sat yet kept hold of his hand.

Ellis' harsh gaze found Mahon. "I want to know everything."

"Princess Necie told me she was going to show Princesses Ellan and Kaleana the trophy she won at one of the gaming booths."

"We never saw her," said Ellan.

"You didn't?" he asked, confused.

"Then where did she go?" asked Ellis.

Ellan shrugged but Tristine spoke up, "She went running into the woods."

"Why?"

"I don't know. I was returning from the shoot when I saw her approaching Ellan and Kaleana. She dropped her trophy and ran off. I went after her and found her crying. I asked her if something had happened with Ellan—"

"I didn't speak to Necie!"

"Did she say what happened?" asked Darius.

"No, she wouldn't tell me. Then the creatures appeared."

"Is this when you were with Morrell?" Ellis asked Mahon.

"Ay, Sire. I sensed something wrong when I didn't see him where he should have been. Necie was happy in her victory and approaching the princesses, so I went to find Morrell and learn why he abandoned his post. I found him deep in the woods sitting on the ground holding his head in hands in pain."

"Where you injured?" Kell asked Morrell.

Morrell wore a timid and confused expression. "No, Captain. I was surprised when Mahon found me. I don't even remember leaving the area."

Armus' quizzical gaze passed between the speakers. "That's strange."

"Ay," mused Ellis. "You remember nothing?"

123

"No, Sire. I'm truly sorry. If Mahon hadn't come to find me the princesses wouldn't not have been injured. So if any one is derelict in duty, it is I, not Mahon. And I don't know why."

For a moment Ellis regarded Morrell, the Guardian's distress visible. He then turned to Armus. "You said you never seen these creatures before."

"No."

"Kell?"

"No, Sire."

"I take it you and Mahon destroyed them," Darius asked Armus.

"Ay."

"Sire," began Vidar. "Eldric is sure the princesses will recover. In the meanwhile, permit us Overseers to confer with Kell and determine who is responsible and why they intend harm to the royal family."

There was a brief pause as Ellis regarded Vidar before giving permission. "Ay, go."

"Father, Tristine needs to rest," said Nigel.

Tristine adamantly shook her head. "No! I don't want to be by myself. I'll go to my room when Armus returns."

"I'll stay with you."

Ellis approached Tristine and softly smiled. "Go with Nigel. I'll look in on you later."

Tristine yielded and left with Nigel.

"I hope the Guardians can learn the answers. It could have been so horrible," said Arista, a quiver in her voice.

"Do you know why Necie ran off when she told Mahon she was going to see you and Kaleana?" Shannan asked Ellan.

"No."

"What were you and Kaleana doing?"

Ellan grew offended. "Nothing. Talking, that's all. I can't help it if my little sister goes running off for some unknown reason."

"There's no need to get defensive. I simply wanted to know what upset her because she ran into danger and could have been killed."

Ellan deeply frowned. "I said I don't know, and I'm sorry Necie got hurt. Maybe she ran off for the same reason Morrell was drawn away."

"That's possible," said Ellis. "The only one who can tell us is Necie. We'll have to wait until she wakes and is strong enough to talk. In the meantime, I need to speak to Bijan and Kaleana about what has happened."

"No, let me. You stay with the girls," said Darius.

In the captain's quarters, Kell, Armus, Mahon, Morrell, Vidar and Avatar gathered.

Kell's thoughtful glance fell on Vidar. "I agree this was an attack upon the royal family, and I don't recall seeing such creatures before. But why did you ask to speak in private?"

Vidar reached into the pouch on his belt. "I found these on the ground in the clearing. I'm not sure where they came from, but they don't look Allonian." He handed Kell two unusual looking crimson jewels.

Kell examined them. He drew Mahon's attention to the gems. "Some foreign trinket Necie won at the gaming booths?"

"She only won the trophy."

"You said you found these at the attack site?" Armus asked Vidar.

"Ay. One was near a tree where Necie lay and the other about ten, fifteen feet away."

"You believe the jewels are connected to the creatures?"

"Jewels don't sprout from the ground or fall off trees, so how else, unless someone or something brought them? Mahon said Necie only won the trophy. Besides, Dagar forged a talisman for mortals to use as a conduit of power, so why not some strange looking jewels?"

"Ay," agreed Mahon. "Like he did with the tardundeen that tried to kill the queen and Nigel years ago. The creatures were contained for future use by either a Shadow Warrior or a mortal trained in the Dark Way."

Avatar's voice was tight when he spoke. "It may not be the Dark Way. The Morvenians have unknown gods. Not to mention the hideous statue Princess Kaleana gave Nigel. I get an uneasy feeling every time I look at it."

"You think the statue is connected to the jewels?" asked Morrell.

"Why not? It's as plausible an explanation as the Dark Way."

Suddenly a bright flash of white light filled the room, placing them alert. From the light, appeared Priscilla and Gresham. The warriors relaxed and Vidar lowered his bow; but neither Priscilla nor Gresham seemed aware of the reaction their arrival caused.

"Captain, uneasiness stirs the forest around the ruins of Ravendale," said Gresham.

"The Dark Way," said Mahon to Avatar's chagrin.

"Not exactly. The sensation is different. Not like Dagar or Latham," said Gresham.

"There's also something stirring among the Morvenians I can't quite place. Then again, I'm more tuned to the wind than mortals," she added flippantly then became defensive at Kell's immediate disapproval. "It doesn't mean I can't find out."

"Do so, because someone tried to kill Necie and Tristine."

Priscilla looked stricken. "I didn't know."

Kell took a deep calming breath. "I'm sorry. We're trying figure out who commanded the two magical creatures that attacked them. Armus and Mahon didn't recognize them. Neither do I by the description."

"What were they like?" asked Gresham.

"Half lion, half bird," replied Armus.

"So it can fly?" asked Priscilla.

"I suppose. Although I didn't see it fly rather it leapt at me."

"Me too, but the wings appeared big enough to fly," added Mahon.

"We'll learn the source of evil we sense," said Gresham, taking Priscilla's arm. They vanished.

Kell regarded the jewels, golden eyes narrowed in deep consideration. "Something dark and dangerous is stirring. Return to your charges and stay within arms reach."

In Tristine's room, Nigel summoned a female maid to aid Tristine in changing for the evening. Armus and Avatar entered and stood in the archway between the sitting area and bed area. The door again opened, this time Ellis and Darius arrived.

"Where's Tristine?" Ellis asked Nigel.

"Changing."

Ellis approached the Guardians. "Any results from your meeting?"

"Not complete answers, Sire, but Kell sent Gresham and Priscilla to investigate. Hopefully we'll know something soon," replied Armus.

Now in a dressing gown, Tristine joined Nigel, Ellis and Darius in the sitting area.

Ellis softly smiled. "I told you I'd come by." She didn't return his smile so he took her hand and led her to the sofa to sit. "You were very brave."

"I don't feel brave. I was scared. I thought it would kill us!" she sobbed.

He held her. "I'm so glad it didn't."

"We're all glad," said Darius.

"I don't know about Ellan," she groused.

Ellis wiped the tears from her cheeks. "Why do you say that?"

"Necie ran from her. She must have said something mean."

"You heard Ellan speak to Necie?"

"Not exactly. Ellan and Kaleana were talking but Necie was near enough to hear."

"So you're assuming she overheard something said between Ellan and Kaleana."

"What else would make her run off crying and refuse to tell me?"

"Only Necie can say. Remember what Mahon said about Morrell. There may be a connection to what happened to him and not anything Ellan said or didn't say."

"I suppose," she begrudgingly admitted.

"Now, I'm going to see if Necie is awake yet. I'll come by again later." Ellis kissed her forehead and left.

Darius remained and waited until the door closed to sit beside Tristine. "You really believe Ellan said something to upset Necie?"

"Ay. She's been acting meaner lately and Nigel—" she clamped her mouth at seeing Nigel's curiosity.

"What about me?"

"Preoccupied."

"I haven't much of a choice. They're our guests."

"Then you don't favor her over us?"

Nigel laughed. "Don't be ridiculous. You're my sisters."

She frowned, rueful. "Armus says I sound jealous."

"Well, aren't you?" asked Armus.

She shied away, shrugging.

Nigel smiled and sat on the footstool in front of the sofa. "No one will ever take your place, my incorrigible rascal." He grew serious and hugged her. "I could have lost both of you today and I don't mind saying it terrified me."

"Reminds me of what happened when you were a baby," said Darius to Nigel. "We nearly lost you to—what was that enormous creature called?" he asked Avatar, but answering his own question before the Guardian replied, "Ah, a tardundeen."

"What's a tardundeen?"

"An enormous bull-man like creature taller than the ceiling, perhaps fifteen feet, standing erect and holding an enormous axe." Darius moved his hands for illustration.

"You said this happened when Nigel was a baby?" asked Tristine.

"Ay."

She recoiled in fear, which made Avatar warn, "Your Grace," only to be ignored as Tristine further questioned Darius.

"You think what happened to Necie and me is like that? Someone tried to kill us on purpose?"

Her panicked voice brought Armus to stand behind the sofa and place both hands on her shoulders. The Guardian lieutenant's chestnut eyes were direct on Darius and his voice authoritative. "That's enough."

Darius flashed an apologetic smile at Armus before speaking to Tristine. "I spoke hastily. I didn't mean to upset you. Get some rest. The Guardians will discover the truth." He gave Nigel a prompting look.

"Ay." Nigel hugged her, holding her tight for a moment before kissing her cheek and leaving with Darius and Avatar.

In the hall, Nigel couldn't let the subject go and stopped Darius from departing. "Tell me everything about the night Mother fled with me."

Darius regarded Nigel, curious. "Don't you know?"

"All Mother told me is how Wess and Bosley helped Avatar with our escape and Avatar took me to Melwynn for a time. From the sounds of your version, she left out some details."

Darius took Nigel's arm. "In your room." Once there, he asked, "Has Ellis told you anything?"

"No."

Darius drew a deep contemplating breath. "I'm not surprised. He felt responsible since his desire was to fulfill prophecy by having the heir born here. If we remained in the Highlands the coup would not have happened." He asked Avatar, "Have you told him?"

The Guardian shook his head. "There's been no need."

"No need?" echoed Nigel with incredulity. "According to Uncle I was almost killed by a beast and now my sisters nearly suffered the same fate."

"Guardian modesty," said Darius.

"Wess and Bosley haven't spoken of it either," said Nigel, his patience waning.

"Bosley won lordship of Midessex for his courage. Although, Ellis held the province in trust until he came of age. I tutored him in politics. Wess became Ellis' squire and the rest is well known of his rise in the ranks."

"I like Bosley, but with his moderate temperament, I hardly see him as courageous. Wess, naturally."

"Bosley can be roused when he feels threatened."

"Indeed. He charged the Shadow Warrior holding you," said Avatar.

"Bosley?!?"

"He and Wess helped to protect you, your mother and Lady Arista. Even at sixteen, Wess possessed a stouteartedness and determination beyond his years. Bosley grew into his role as protector."

"What of the tardundeen?"

129

"I hadn't seen one since the Great Battle. I thought all were destroyed when Dagar was imprisoned in his nether dimension."

Thoughtful, Nigel pursed his lips, his gaze shifting to Darius. "What little I heard about the coup is how Owain wasn't skilled in the Dark Way, but the person helping him. Who?"

"To this day we don't know."

"Did Father have any clue what Owain was planning?"

Furious, Darius scowled. "No, although he aided Marcellus and Latham's attempt to thwart Ellis' in becoming king."

"Why did he remain on the Council? Why didn't Father deal with him like the others?"

"He did. At the coronation, Owain renounced his actions and pledged fealty. Ellis granted mercy with a four-year probation and suspension of his Council seat. The first two-years he served under the watchfulness of Archimedes. Since he proved repentant to the Vicar, Ellis restored him to the Council, with the final two-years of probation directly answerable to Ellis. When trouble began, some thought Owain had something to do with it, but there was no proof."

"Not until he took Waldron," said Avatar.

"How? Surely Father fought him."

"Waldron was under construction and none of us had any clue to what extent the Dark Way still existed," began Darius. "Shadow Warriors caused an uprising in the North Plains drawing Ellis from Waldron. We learned en route of the attack."

Avatar added, "Shadow Warriors were also used to take Waldron. While helping in our escape, Mahon and Vidar were seriously wounded, which left me five mortals to protect alone. The tardundeen was only one obstacle to our survival."

"Stop being modest, Avatar," said Darius.

Nigel added his prodding of the Guardian. "What *did* you do?"

Avatar answered, nonchalant. "Since you were born in winter, we contended with the cold and snow along with kelpies, Shadow Warriors and pursuing enemy soldiers."

Since Avatar avoided going into detail, Darius took up the explanation. "According to Arista, despite being paralyzed from the hips down by a kelpie bite, he used his special power to destroy the Shadow Warriors and kelpies and freed you from one of the Warriors. The one Bosley charged."

"Not paralyzed, numb," said Avatar in a tone of correction.

Awed, yet curious, Nigel regarded Avatar. "What power?"

"My name means *He of the Lightning Sword*, and is only used under extreme circumstances. Each Guardian has a power is equal to their station and responsibility. Being a warrior I tend to be stronger. However, calling upon our power can be dangerous, since it is a drain on our life force, thus is used sparingly. The wound seriously depleted my strength."

"Your wound and depleted strength didn't stop you from making a stand again the tardundeen. When you dove on top of Shannan to protect her I thought for certain its axe would cleave you in two," said Darius.

"Wren and Vidar arrived before anything worse happened."

"Modesty again," complained Darius then spoke to Nigel. "Just like then, your sisters are safe thank to divine intervention. Not to mention the unknown whereabouts of the talisman."

Brows furrowed in wary consideration, Nigel asked, "So that's why you think there may be a connection to Necie and Tristine, because of the talisman?"

"Ay. The similarities are too hard to ignore. I'm certain Ellis thinks the same since we never learned who helped Owain."

"We will learn who or what is behind this," said Avatar with certainty.

Darius flashed a small, yet confident smile. "I'm sure. Now, I'm going to look in on Necie. Do you want to come?"

Nigel didn't answer, the worry on his face preventing speech.

"He needs time to digest what he has learned," said Avatar.

"I thought as much." Darius gave Nigel a clap on the shoulder before leaving.

The door closing brought Nigel from his stupor and he regarded Avatar in admiration. "I don't what to say, but thank you."

Avatar flashed a droll smile. "Just doing my job."

131

Nigel visibly warred with what to say next.

"Don't let the past trouble you. We don't know if there is a connection."

"What about my nightmares? Could they be the connection?"

Avatar thought for a moment before replying. "I can't think of how since your sisters were attacked, not you."

Again, Nigel's expression showed conflict. "I feel there is something more sinister."

"Do not allow your feelings to run wild. If there is a connection, either myself or Kell should sense it, and we don't."

"I feel powerless just doing my duty."

"You're not powerless. Faith in Jor'el and prayer can prevail over any Guardian sense or lack thereof."

"You believe that?"

"I have witnessed seemingly hopeless and devastating events turn on a mortal's simple prayer when Guardian strength failed. Your parents are examples. When Niles was killed, Ellis seriously wounded and Shannan captured by Latham, we believed all was lost since we could do nothing to change the situation. Only when Ellis cried out to Jor'el in despair and accepted the Almighty's challenge of faith and trust was he healed, and we could go forth united into battle."

Nigel chewed on his lower lip. Avatar took him by the shoulders to make him look up. "Kell and I will do what is necessary to discover who and why. However, you must not forget to seek Jor'el and look to your faith for help."

"I suppose that's all I can do, for now."

"It'll be more than enough, you'll see."

"I wonder if I should check on Tristine. Uncle's words upset her."

"No. More than likely Armus helped her to sleep. Before seeing either her or Necie again, you need to gather your wits. You'll be no comfort or help to them if you are unsettled in mind and spirit. They need you to be strong."

Nigel wryly grinned. "And will you put me to sleep like you did the night of the Trio meeting?"

"I didn't put you sleep. I waited until you fell asleep naturally."

Nigel's expression immediately changed to disturbed. "Then whose hand was on my forehead speaking the Ancient before I fell into a dreamless sleep?"

"Vidar volunteered to remain. You must have woken after I left."

The answer didn't convince Nigel. "The voice didn't sound like Vidar's tenor, more a baritone like your voice."

"Vidar didn't report any trouble when I returned, so don't imagine worry where there isn't any."

"Could you ask him if he did?"

"I can, but I see no need. He would not allow anyone or anything to harm or influence you so he must have put you to sleep when you woke." Avatar took Nigel by the shoulder and turned him toward the privy. "Take a bath and relax. But, if you persist in this mood, I *will* put you sleep."

Morrell returned to Ellan's room after the meeting. She climbed into bed, annoyed. He couldn't blame her after blanking out and wandering off, leaving them vulnerable to attack. In contrition he spoke, "Princess. I'm deeply sorry for abandoning my post ... for everything. I don't know what came over me."

Ellan shrugged and frowned. "Kaleana and I were so engaged in conversation, I didn't even notice you were gone. Then to hear how badly Necie is hurt. The worse part is Mother thinks I'm somehow to blame."

"Why?"

Ellan shook her head in great frustration. "After you left she questioned me about not seeing Necie and what Kaleana and I were we talking about, as if our conversation was somehow involved." She grew bitter. "Tristine accused me of making Necie run off."

Morrell snorted a half-mocking snicker and sat on the bed. "Tristine has little room to talk when it comes to misbehavior."

"Ay. But I didn't say anything to Necie."

He cocked a rebuking brow. "I do know that before I blanked out, you and Kaleana were talking about your sisters in a most unflattering way."

Her look was sharp at first then she sighed in resignation. "I wondered if she overheard what was said."

"That's possible, but we won't know until she wakes up."

She became upset and insisted, "I would never want to hurt Necie. She maybe a spoiled brat at times but has her bright moments and is less trouble than Tristine. I hope that wasn't the reason."

He looked directly at her. "Do you wish Tristine was the one more seriously injured?"

She balked at the question. "No. I just wish she'd learn not to be so reckless and impulsive, getting all the attention and belief, while I rate only questions and doubt."

"That's not true. I've heard your parents praise you."

She frowned and slowly agreed. "Ay. It doesn't change Tristine's behavior."

"No, but neither should it affect how you feel about your parents. Her banquet is only a month away and she'll have to mature. I watched you change after you came of age."

She rolled her eyes. "I don't hold out much hope for her changing no matter what age she is."

Morrell chuckled. "I've seen stranger things happen over the centuries, so don't give up hope."

"I can't give up something I never had with Tristine," she quipped.

Mahon sat beside Necie's bed. He would not be any further than arm's reach. Shannan retired but Angus insisted on staying and slept on the sofa. With the exception of Angus' presence it could have been a normal night, only it was anything but normal as Mahon regarded his charge. Over the centuries he experienced and performed many pleasant and unpleasant tasks, the worse was suffering imprisonment in the nether dimension for four hundred years. His training as Avatar's apprentice helped prepare him for surviving his captivity. However, like Avatar, this was his first assignment as Guardian Overseer to a mortal. Until today, all went smoothly. Necie's sweet nature, charming wiles and winning smile were endearing qualities. Perhaps the one aspect he endured, for lack of a better term, was her chatter. She talked endlessly without saying much of anything, yet always jovial and optimistic.

Of Ellis and Shannan's daughters, Necie was the most bubbly and engaging. Ellan tended toward brooding and Tristine was a rogue in petticoats. The thought brought a smile to Mahon's face. For all her challenging ways, Tristine was the one Necie gravitated to and in turn Tristine indulged and accommodated Necie. Not surprising they were together when the attack occurred. Ellan's fastidious nature barely tolerated either Tristine or Necie; while the older Nigel grew, the more occupied he became with royal duties, less time to spend with his sisters like in their younger days.

At a stirring, Mahon looked across to Angus. He couldn't quite place his finger on the attraction between Angus and Necie. True, they grew up cousins, though of no blood relation; but Angus acted protective toward Necie in a different way than Nigel. For all his centuries among the mortals, he still couldn't clearly discern the key to their relationships. Whatever formed the bond between Angus and Necie, it was strong and capable of lasting a very long time.

Mahon became alert at hearing a low moaning from Necie and leaned forward. She remained asleep, moving restlessly. He gently placed his hand on her forehead. "Peace, my dear little charge. I'm here." Necie grew still.

He stroked her cheek, his brow furrowed in compassion. Who would want to hurt such a lovely child? He knew the answer lay in the dark machinations of the mortal heart and mind. His absence when the attack happened gnawed at him. True, he sensed something wrong with Morrell and wanted to learn what made him leave his post. Now something dark and sinister threatened the royal family and he would not leave Necie again.

The door opened. Mahon stood, wary of who entered. Morrell. He met him between the bed and door. "What are you doing here? Has something else happened?"

"I came to inquire how the little princess is feeling."

Mahon's gaze turned sympathetic. "Although Eldric assures me she will recover, I can't help but wonder what her state of mind will be when she wakes. I wasn't there to protect her."

Morrell clapped Mahon's shoulder. "I take full responsibility and will tell her so."

Mahon nodded, watching Necie sleep. Morrell approached the bed, bent down and place a hand on Necie's cheek. He heard Morrell say something, which sounded like the Ancient, only he couldn't hear distinctly. After Morrell's strange behavior earlier, Mahon moved to the bed. "Why were you speaking the Ancient?"

Morrell grinned and guided Mahon away from the bed to reply. "I wished her a speedy recovery, that's all. Nothing to get upset about."

"Sorry. I'm just edgy."

"I understand. I feel responsible for everything."

"You're not at fault if the Dark Way or something or evil is involved."

"Perhaps—still," He glanced back at the bed, "Eldric is right. Upon touch, I sense she will recover. So be at ease. I'll see you in the morning." With that Morrell left.

136

Chapter 8

THE BRILLIANT, FULL MOON rose to its apex by the time Priscilla and Gresham arrived at the ruins of Ravendale, the one-time castle of deposed King Marcellus. The bright moonlight created long, eerie shadows among the ruins. Ellis ordered Ravendale razed to the ground after his victory. For a hundred years, Marcellus' family ruthlessly ruled from Ravendale; the castle alive with the Dark Way. The accursed ground became a scorned place by mortals and Guardians.

Day or night did not inhibit a Guardian's eyesight; still Gresham's hand hovered above the hilt of his dagger. Being a vassal, he wore no sword, while Priscilla was completely unarmed. However, as Trio Leaders, they possessed power equal to their station.

"The sense of evil is growing stronger," he said.

"Ay," she agreed, rubbing her arms as if chilly. "Some of the Dark Way still emanates from this place, but there is something different."

"Ay. If the sense can take physical form, then it is powerful."

A loud screech came from over head and they caught a glimpse of the creature Armus described diving at them directly from out of the moon's gleaming sphere. Gresham shoved Priscilla aside but was unable to draw his dagger before being taken down by the creature and pinned to the ground.

137

Against the powerful beast he needed all his strength to hold its chin at bay and keep from getting bit.

"Gresham?" she called after recovering from his shove.

He didn't answer, his focus on the creature. He managed to move his legs so his feet were under the belly. He kicked it off of him, scrambled to his knees and drew his dagger. Angry, the beast screamed at Gresham and swiped a massive, clawed paw at the Guardian. Gresham rolled under the attack, got quickly to his feet and jumped on the back of the beast, striking it in the neck with his dagger. In painful rage, the beast reared in an attempt to throw him off, but he held on. When it fell back onto all fours, he again drove his dagger into the beast's neck. The beast took off, vigorously flapping its wings, Gresham clinging to it. His eyes grew wide at seeing the ground about fifty feet below.

"Hang on!" Priscilla called. *"Gaoth beuc, thoi a' torit!"* she shouted. The wind swirled, tossing the creature off course.

"Don't do that!" Gresham shouted in surprise.

"Trust me!"

He closed his eyes and clamped his mouth to stifle an outcry when the beast turned upside down in midair. Then the direction dramatically changed. His eyes snapped open to see the ground coming up fast. "Priscilla!"

"Suas!" she commanded.

The wind violently lifted the beast straight up, away from the ground. The move was so violent that Gresham lost his hold and fell backwards thirty feet to the ground. He lay stunned, his breath and dagger knocked away on impact. Priscilla knelt beside him. He was pale and wildly looking at her unable to breathe. She struck his chest and he took in a loud gulp of air and began breathing heavily. Helping him took her focus off the beast. It dove at her, back claws catching her right shoulder, sending her tumbling.

Gresham pushed himself to his knees and seized his dagger. The beast turned for another attack on Priscilla. Taking aim and waiting until the last possible moment, he threw his dagger, striking the beast squarely between the eyes. A dying scream, and the creature vanished in a bright yellow light, his dagger and a shiny object falling to the ground.

He shielded his eyes against the light, squinting to see the object. His first concern was Priscilla. He made his way to her and helped her sit up. The talons gouged her right shoulder, which appeared to be the extent of her injury. "You all right?"

"I think so."

"Your shoulder doesn't look too bad."

"What about you? That was a nasty fall."

He smirked. "Aside from the pain in my chest where you struck me, I'll be fine." He retrieved his dagger and discovered what else dropped from the sky. An unusual-looking crimson jewel lay beside his dagger. He sheathed his dagger before picking up the jewel and returning to Priscilla. "This fell when the beast disappeared."

"It doesn't look Allonian."

"No. We better take it to Kell and tell him what happened."

"You're going tell him I hurt you?"

"Are you kidding? I'd never hear the end of it if I said your slap hurt."

At Arundine, Kell stood behind the high chair watching the Trio Leaders assemble. Gresham and Priscilla would be absent, tending to their special assignment. He also dispatched Wren to scout the forest surrounding Waldron. Armus, Vidar and Avatar remained at Waldron. He preferred them being near their charges. In fact, he wanted to return to Waldron quickly. Thus he spoke to get attention. His voice stern and expression grim.

"It appears my caution of informing you to the Morvenians' arrival didn't help to avoid trouble. Two unknown creatures attacked and injured Princesses Tristine and Necie this afternoon. Mahon and Armus destroyed the creatures and prevented the attack from becoming deadly."

"How badly were they hurt?" asked Jedrek.

"Tristine's wound is minor," he motioned to his arm. "Although sore from the encounter. Necie is more serious, suffering a head injury, but Eldric is confident of her recovery. Priscilla and Gresham are following leads of a disturbance at Ravendale and among the Morvenians."

"The Dark Way?" asked Barnum.

"We don't know yet, and until we do, Allon is on full alert." His intense golden gaze swept over the Leaders, his voice thick with deadly authority. "Any mortal or hint of evil so much as twitches, quell it, dispatch it if needed. Not one more incident will touch the royal family. Now, go."

Kell didn't even wait for the Leaders to disperse before vanishing.

Ellis couldn't sleep and went to the chapel. He was grateful his daughters would recover, but he wanted to meditate. Kell returned from Arundine in time to accompany Ellis and waited in dutiful attendance as Ellis sat on the front pew, staring at the altar.

Who and why? Morrell's behavior is puzzling. What power affected him could affect the others. Unfortunately, the answers would have to await the result of the investigation.

Priscilla and Gresham arrived, entering through the front door rather than in dimension travel. They and Kell were respectful in their approach of Ellis.

"Sire. Priscilla and Gresham are back."

Ellis stood, his regard hopeful. "Have you accomplished the task already?"

"We're not certain, Sire. We encountered another beast at Ravendale. We defeated it, and when it vanished this fell from the sky." Gresham handed the jewel to Ellis.

Ellis examined jewel, then held it up for Kell to see. "Looks foreign. Have you seen anything like this before?"

"Earlier this evening. Vidar found two identical stones at the site of the attack."

"Why didn't you tell me?"

"I was not sure of a connection and asked Mahon if Princess Necie won some foreign trinkets at one of the gaming booths. He said no. Avatar believes the stones could be connected to the Morvenians."

"Why?"

"Something to do with a statue Princess Kaleana gave the prince."

"Nigel made no mention of a statue."

"According to Avatar it's ugly and makes him uncomfortable."

Ellis's brows furrowed, looking at the jewel then back to Kell. "Send for Avatar."

While waiting for Avatar, Ellis' focus divided between the jewel and the altar. Images of the past few weeks crossed his mind, beginning with Bijan's arrival in Leith. He and Darius were surprised by the quick visit of the Morvenians offering an alliance after suffering defeat. Perhaps this visit was a ruse to plant some evil in Allon and threaten his family.

"You sent for me, Sire?" asked Avatar.

Deep in thought, Ellis was briefly startled by the speech. "Gresham found this after he and Priscilla defeated a beast like the one that attacked Necie and Tristine." He handed the jewel to Avatar.

Recognizing the stone, Avatar immediately turned to Kell.

"I told the king about the other stones and what you said about them."

"Tell me about the statue Princess Kaleana give Nigel," said Ellis.

"Well," began Avatar in deliberation of what to say. "It is a rather ugly jade carving of an elephant, an animal native to Morven."

"I've heard about them. What about the statue troubles you?"

"I get an uncomfortable sensation every time I look at it. I know the Morvenians make deities out of practically everything and I told him so. However, he doesn't believe anything is wrong because the princess gave it to him as a symbol of Morvenian and Allonian friendship."

"You think Nigel is wrong to believe her?"

Avatar pursued his lips in consideration. "He is naïve in his worldly views, and as such wants to believe the best of people."

"Diplomatically phrased, Avatar. Now, I want to hear your true feelings in the matter—to a father concerned for his son, not as king for his heir."

Avatar cocked an easy smile. "Nigel is being foolish because she made an impression on him."

"How much of an impression?"

"Difficult to say. I'm still learning how to gauge the depth of mortal emotions, especially a teenager."

Ellis waved a finger at the Guardian. "You're being diplomatic again. I said I want direct answers. How infatuated is he?"

"Enough to cause some confusion, but not enough to go against Jor'el's law."

"Do you believe this statue may be influencing him?"

"That's a possibility."

Ellis sent a glare to Kell. "You agree with his assessment?"

"Avatar is Nigel's Overseer, he would know better than I."

Ellis' temper exploded. "Blast Guardian double-talk! I nearly lost two daughters today! I want straight answers!"

"Sire, we don't know yet," began Kell. "Nor are we trying to avoid answering your questions and concerns. You wanted Avatar's assessment of the statue and he gave it. We need time to investigate and discover if there is a connection between the stones and the statue. And if there is, who and why?"

"Sire, I would not withhold any information, nor place Nigel's life in jeopardy, nor any royal family member," insisted Avatar. "What I am sure of, is the statue makes me very uncomfortable, and these stones make me suspicious. The rest is speculation."

Ellis' eyes narrowed, his face fixed but voice more controlled. "Well-founded speculation, and I completely trust your instincts. Kell is right, we need a direct connection before pursuing the matter."

"Until then, Sire, you and the Council should proceed with caution," said Kell.

"Indeed." Ellis turned to Gresham and Priscilla. "Continue to keep a sharp vigil. Avatar, tell me the moment anything unusual happens whether you believe it deals with the statue or not."

"Ay, Sire."

Priscilla, Gresham and Avatar bowed when Ellis left the Chapel, Kell at his heels. Avatar kept a respectful distance from Ellis and Kell in heading back to the family quarters. Before Kell followed Ellis into the royal apartment, Avatar intercepted him.

"I need to speak to Vidar."

"Why?"

"Just get Vidar and bring him to your room!" Avatar turned on his heels and marched off, preventing the captain from making further inquiry.

Kell complied with the abrupt request and when they arrived at his chamber, Avatar accosted Vidar.

"Why did you put Nigel to sleep?"

"What?"

"The night of the Trio meeting. You failed to mention it."

"Because I didn't."

Already irate, Avatar drew a step too close to the archer for Kell's liking and he jerked Avatar back and rebuked him.

"You said Nigel fell asleep naturally."

"He did."

"Why would he say I put him to sleep when he never woke up?" asked Vidar.

Avatar glared incredulously at the archer. "Are you saying Nigel's lying?"

"No. I'm saying I didn't put him to sleep since he remained asleep the entire time you were at the meeting."

"He said a hand touched his forehead and spoke the Ancient. So if it wasn't you then who did you allow into the room to have access to him?"

Vidar rose to his full height and squared his shoulders. "No one!"

"Enough!" snapped Kell, his ire directed at Avatar. "I've been tolerant of your concern in dealing with Nigel and his problem, but ordering me and accusing Vidar, I will not allow. Now, in rational words and tone explain what Nigel said and why?"

Avatar lowered his head, closed his eyes and took a long deep breath and slowly exhaled. Upon regaining his temper, he spoke. "First of all, I apologize, Captain. Vidar, I was out of line."

Kell gave a curt nod, Vidar vocal and willing. "Accepted."

"After visiting Tristine, we returned to Nigel's chamber and Darius told him the entire story of our escape from Waldron when Owain attacked."

"Why?"

"Darius thinks there is a connection to the present since we never learned the identity of the individual who possessed the talisman."

"Interesting," mused Kell. "What does that have to do with Vidar?"

"I managed to allay Nigel's concern about Darius' theory and told him to take a bath and get some rest. He teased me about putting him to sleep like the night of the Trio meeting. I told him I didn't but he insisted someone did."

"You told him I did?" asked Vidar in confusion.

"No. I said you volunteered to remain after he fell asleep so I could attend the meeting." Avatar grew thoughtful. "He said the voice didn't sound like you, rather similar in quality to me."

"You say he never woke up?" Kell asked Vidar.

"No."

Kell took hold of Vidar's shoulder and steered him to the door. "Return to duty."

Vidar started to object, but at the staunch resolve on Kell's face, thought better of doing so and left.

"Why did you dismiss him?" asked Avatar, his voice short of demanding.

"Out of respect for what I'm about to say to you. This may be connected to Nigel's continuing dreams about his future and not the stones or statue."

"How can someone speaking the Ancient to put him to sleep be connected?"

"You said he fell asleep naturally but Vidar says he never woke up, nor did anyone else enter the room. Vidar would not allow any harm to Nigel, and you know that. However, Nigel is experiencing frequent, disturbing dreams about his future; so dreaming is an explanation when reality doesn't support his claim of being put to sleep."

"It's not the only explanation," said Avatar, his earlier rigidity returning. "Darius maybe right and Vidar unaware of another presence."

"Don't jump to conclusions."

"Kell, those creatures, jewels and that statue are not jumping to conclusions!"

"I think you're becoming too emotionally involved."

"Oh, like you and Vidar aren't emotionally involved where Shannan is concerned?"

"Enough, Lieutenant!"

Avatar seized the hilt of his sword in an effort to contain his temper. Every fiber of his being grew tight, silver eyes blazing.

"You know the dangers and eternal consequences a Guardian faces due to unbridled emotions. Dagar is a prime example." Kell watched for the impact of his reference. Some of Avatar's passion subsided, but not enough. "If you do not get a hold of your emotions, I will reassign you." He put up a hand to stall Avatar's objections. "I don't want to, but for your own good, I will."

"And Nigel's good?"

Kell held a steady eye on Avatar. "Consider this: how is losing control and facing punishment for doing so going to help him? Goodnight, Lieutenant."

Chapter 9

THE FOLLOWING MORNING Angus left Necie's chamber to freshen up. Necie woke and complained of a headache so Mahon sent for Eldric, who made her a tonic.

She handed the cup back to Eldric. "Will it make me sleep again?"

The Guardian physician smiled. "No, just help your headache. However, you should remain in bed for the rest of the day. Tomorrow you can get up for a while."

Mahon waited until Eldric left before sitting on the bed to speak to Necie. All night he rehearsed his lines of apology. "Necie, I'm sorry for what happened."

"It wasn't your fault—I think," she said with uncertainty. "Although I don't remember much."

"Really? What do you recall?"

"Winning the trophy. Then I woke up in bed feeling awful. Can you tell me what happened?"

Mahon briefly considered what to say. If she didn't remember would it be wise to tell her about the creatures? Eldric told him lack of memory is common among mortals suffering head injuries. Sometimes they recalled events at a later date, sometimes not. Thus he answered, "You had an accident in which you hit your head and Tristine was injured."

"Tristine? Is she all right? Was it a bad accident?"

"Bad enough to affect your memory. Eldric is certain you'll make a complete recovery. Tristine received a bad cut on the arm."

A knock at the door stopped further discussion.

"Mahon?" said Ellan.

Mahon didn't reply to Ellan, instead he asked Necie, "Are you up for a visitor?"

"I think so. Especially if what happened makes Ellan concerned enough to visit me."

Mahon chuckled and went to open the door. Princess Kaleana accompanied Ellan, and carried a brightly painted ceramic jar.

"Is Necie awake?" asked Ellan.

"Ay. She says she is up for a visit, although Eldric gave her a remedy for a headache, so please, keep the visit short."

"Of course." Ellan moved inside, followed by Kaleana and approached the bed. "How are you feeling?"

Necie's gaze shifted from Ellan to Kaleana and the jar then back to Ellan. "I have a headache so Eldric says I must sat in bed today. What's that?" She pointed to the jar.

"Morven remedy for you," replied Kaleana, having difficulty with the word remedy. She moved close to give the jar to Necie when Mahon stepped in front of her and took the jar.

"Thank you. The princess appreciates the gesture."

Ellan sent the Guardian a disapproving frown but he remained in place between Kaleana and the bed. Mahon sent his own prompting look to Ellan to convey his concern. Despite that, or maybe because of it, she took Kaleana's hand to step around him to stand beside the bed. He didn't object. Ellan wouldn't harm her sister, but considering the strange nature of the stones and beasts, he wasn't going to take any chances with a Morvenian remedy. Add to that what Avatar said regarding the jade statue making him uncomfortable. Ellan's usual stubbornness would not stop him from being right beside his charge. He moved beside the bed, opposite Ellan and Kaleana.

Ellan spoke to Necie. "Do you know what happened?"

"No. Mahon said I had an accident and I hit my head and Tristine cut her arm. I only recall winning the trophy. Did you see what happened to us?"

Mahon cleared his throat to catch Ellan's attention. He carefully shook his head.

"No," she said in a moderate huff, "And neither did Mahon."

"You didn't?" Necie asked him.

"No," he said, sending a direct admonishing glance to Ellan. The intense look of his sky blue eyes made her shy away. He returned to Necie with a kinder, gentler expression. "Excited about winning the trophy you ran ahead of me to tell Ellan and Princess Kaleana. For a moment you were out of my sight, which is why I apologized. If I were closer I could have prevented the accident. Armus and I brought you and Tristine back for immediate medical attention."

"Oh." Necie's brows furrowed trying to recollect then groaned in pain.

"Enough for now. She needs to rest," he said firmly. He moved to usher Ellan and Kaleana away from the bed.

Ellan stiffened under his action and jerked away from his touch on her arm. "Very well. Come, Kaleana."

"Please, better get," said Kaleana to Necie before leaving with Ellan.

Mahon was about to shut the door on their departure when Angus returned. His face brightened at seeing Necie sitting up in bed.

"Necie! You're awake. How are you feeling?"

"A little tired with a headache. Eldric said I can get out of bed tomrrow. At least for a little while. Oh," she said, seeing Mahon return to his position by her bed and still holding the jar. "Princess Kaleana brought me a Morvenian remedy. Come to think of it, I don't know what it's for."

"I'll give it to Eldric and he'll determine how to use it for your recovery," said Mahon. "For now, do as he says and rest."

"I'll read to you," said Angus.

"Ay." She smiled. "You know my favorite stories."

As Ellan and Kaleana made their way from Necie's chamber, Kaleana said, "Sad sister not remember."

"Perhaps. At least she's awake and will recover," said Ellan.

Morrell waited by the door and began to follow when Bijan arrived and drew Kaleana aside to speak privately in Morvenian.

"Are you distressed about Necie?" Morrell asked Ellan while Kaleana and Bijan spoke.

"No, I'm relieved. I thought I'd be in trouble if she remembered I did say something to upset her and make her run off."

Morrell grinned. "I took care of that possibility."

"What? How?"

Morrell placed a finger to his lips for discretion when Ellan's voice rose. He cast a cautious side-glance to Kaleana and Bijan. "Last night I visited and told her subconscious not to remember the events. No harm done."

Ellan smiled with gratitude, but didn't say anything since Kaleana and Bijan finished their brief conversation and they all proceed to the Hall for breakfast.

"Lord Bijan say poultice will help," said Kaleana, touching her head to indicate the location of Necie's head wound.

"I'm sure it will. I'll be certain Father knows of your generosity."

Kaleana bowed her head to the compliment. "What about fair? Much enjoy. Like see Allon more."

"I'll speak to my father about what arrangements can be made." Kaleana smiled but Bijan appeared indifferent so Ellan asked him, "Did you not enjoy the fair, my lord?"

Bijan attempted to contain his rigidity to Ellan's question. "Seeing horses enjoyable. However short."

"Perhaps you can finish the inspection today."

Bijan again exhibited his reluctance at dealing with females in a curt answer. "Perhaps."

Ellan frowned at Bijan's obvious dislike of speaking to her. She caught Morrell's encouraging eye so she didn't press the matter, at least for the moment.

149

When they arrived at the Hall, Ellis, Nigel and Darius sat at high table in their usual places, eating. Some of the Morvenian delegates gathered at another table, chatting and eating

"Father's almost finished with breakfast," said Ellan.

"King fast eater," said Kaleana, making Ellan laugh.

"No, he's an early riser. He claims he gets more done in the morning without interruptions."

Bijan and Kaleana paid their respects to Ellis, Nigel and Darius. "Most noble king, royal prince, duke," began Bijan. "It is good to hear little princess better. Princess fortunate lion not injure her more seriously."

Since Ellis ate, he acknowledged Bijan with a nod and motioned for them to be seated. Ellan sat beside Nigel. Bijan and Kaleana took their seats beside Shannan's empty chair. Once seated, Bijan gave orders for his and Kaleana's food to a Morvenian servant then spoke to Ellis.

"King. Are lion attacks common in Allon?"

Ellis took a drink to wash down his food before answering. "No. It is a rare occurrence this far south since most live in the upper Highlands."

"Sad to say, very common in Morven."

"Princess Kaleana gave Necie a Morvenian poultice," said Ellan.

Ellis cocked a curious brow. "What is in the poultice?"

"Morvenian herbs used for a lion's bite. Mahon took it before Necie could receive it," she said, annoyed.

Ellis smiled and turned to Kaleana. "I'm sure Mahon will give it to Eldric, who will make good use of it. Please, enjoy your breakfast."

Kaleana's returning smile was sweet and willing.

Ellan continued, "Kaleana told me how much she enjoyed the fair—until Necie was hurt, that is."

"And Tristine," said Nigel.

Ellan's look at Nigel was momentarily sharp, but she kept a neutral tone in reply. "Of course, but Necie is hurt worse."

"Older sister look goodly," said Kaleana to Nigel.

"Ay, Tristine is doing better."

"You said you enjoyed the fair?" asked Ellis.

Kaleana smiled in genuine pleasure. "Different than Morven, fun."

Ellis chuckled, glancing to Bijan. "Ay, Allonians know how to conduct a fair where all can have fun."

Bijan formally nodded his acknowledgement of Ellis' meaning.

"King, fair today again?" asked Kaleana.

"No. Under the circumstances I cancelled it."

"What a shame," began Ellan, "Princess Kaleana expressed her desire to see more of Allon." She then added, "Perhaps I could take her to Hereford and visit the shops?" She watched for his reaction.

He was thoughtful; a good sign since he did not immediately dismiss the idea. She knew Ellis was concerned for his family. Still, the Morvenians were guests and due proper treatment. Thus she continued in a low but respectful voice.

"Sire, the danger is over. We can't confine our guests to Waldron. How would that set with the emperor?" When he pursed his lips in serious consideration she spoke a bit louder. "You and Lord Bijan can finish inspecting the horses."

To this Bijan made a favorable grunt of consideration. "Lion attack not follow another too close. Since lion killed by Guardians, unlikely another nearby."

There was only a moment's pause during which Ellis changed his focus from Bijan to Ellan. By his look, she was winning the argument so she added, "Send as many Guardians and soldiers with us as you like."

Ellis called to Wess, who sat at near by table. He promptly presented himself to the king. "Lord Bijan and the others would like to finish inspecting the horses. I believe it may be helpful for morale."

A hint of surprise crossed Wess' face, but he submitted. "As you wish, Sire. We can leave after breakfast."

"King most generous, thank you," said Bijan.

Ellis grinned. "Thank the princess." He leaned close to Ellan and said, "Well done."

Ellan beamed. Darius nodded and raised his goblet in salute.

Nigel leaned close to Ellan to speak privately. "Well done, indeed. You gave good, sound reasoning without demanding or demeaning the king."

Her smile held a hint of sarcasm as she concentrated on her food. "Thanks. Nice to finally be noticed."

He sighed in mild frustration. "I suppose I don't say it often enough, but I am proud of you and how you've matured."

She regarded him in cautious scrutiny. "What brought this on?"

"Our conversation. I honestly didn't realize how I was treating you, or rather how you thought I was treating you. I want to change."

For Ellan, his admission was a pleasant surprise. "Thank you," she said in genuine gratitude.

"You two conspiring about something?" quipped Ellis.

Nigel grinned. "No, Sire. Just discussing the day."

A mischievous gleam grew on Ellan's brow, her voice low so only her brother and father heard. "Good luck with Lord Bijan."

Nigel wore a tight sarcastic smile and Ellis chuckled.

Again, Kell and Avatar accompanied Ellis, Darius, Nigel, Lord Bijan and the Morvenians. This time a dozen mounted royal soldiers rode in the front and the rear of the group for added security.

"Are you sure this is a good idea?" Wess asked Ellis.

Ellis glanced over his shoulders to Bijan and the others. He, Darius, Wess and Nigel rode ahead of the Morvenians. Allard accompanied the guests, Bijan picking his brain about the horses. "They believe a lion attacked, not magical beasts. Perhaps by playing along we can discover if they know more than they're letting on."

"You could be taking an awful risk. More with Ellan than us, especially after Morrell blanked out the way he did," said Darius.

Ellis slyly glanced at Darius. "Which is why I sent Ewert and Bailey along."

Upon reaching the estate, the Morvenians were eager to inspect the horses. Kell and Avatar casually leaned on the corral fence watching Ellis,

Darius and Nigel examine Dunstan again. On the far side of the corral, the Morvenians grew aggressive and active in their inspection. Allard and Wess tried to contain the enthusiastic guests.

"They are suddenly a lively bunch," said Darius.

Nigel's face screwed up in distaste. "Such a guttural language, sounds like gibberish." Dunstan snorted and tossed his head. "Oh, you agree?"

"Or maybe he can understand them," joked Ellis.

Dunstan made low grunted noises.

"He says they have rough hands," said a female voice.

They turned to see the new arrival.

Ellis wryly grinned. "Hello, Wren."

"Sire. Highness. Your Grace." She passed her fellow Guardians without even looking at them to enter the corral.

"How do you like that? We don't even get a hello," remarked Avatar to Kell.

Wren grinned. She ran a hand along Dunstan's neck when the horse whinnied. "You're right about them," she said to Dunstan, a glance back to Avatar and Kell.

"Right about what?" asked Kell.

"I don't think we want to know," quipped Avatar.

Loud, excited Morvenian exclamations and chatter caught their attention.

"Now what?" asked Darius.

Two Morvenians sat bareback on the horses they tested and sent the animals into a gallop, jumping the far corral fence. Allard and Wess shouted after them.

Nigel pointed across the field. "A stag!"

Pandemonium broke loose when the Morvenians raced back to the horses they rode to the estate to begin pursuing the stag.

"They don't have bows, how do they expect to down it?" said Nigel.

Ellis ran to his horse. "I don't know! But we can't let them gallop all over the countryside." He vaulted into the saddle. "Stop them!" he commanded the soldiers before snapping the reins to gallop in pursuit. The soldiers instantly responded.

Nigel and Darius quickly mounted their horses to help pursue the Morvenians chasing the stag. Allard and Wess were close behind with the Guardians following on foot. It became a mad chase through the field and into the woods about a mile away. The Morvenians were going in every direction imaginable while Ellis, Darius, Nigel, Wess, Allard, the soldiers and the Guardians tried to keep track of their wild guests.

Ellis lost sight of everyone just after entering a thick patch of woods. "All right! This has gotten out of hand," he complained to no one.

He turned his horse to go back the way he came. A large creature leapt onto the path in front of him. A huge, hulking, gray, hairy, man-like beast stood on two legs, perhaps ten feet tall. The beast let out a roar and the horse backed away, whinnying in fear.

Ellis steadied his horse and drew his sword. The beast swiped at the horse, making the animal rear. Another swipe and a massive hand clipped the horse's head with enough force to stun the animal and send it falling sideways, pinning Ellis. He grimaced in pain from the fall and tried to push away from the horse, which didn't move and remained on top of him. Seeing the beast approach, he readied his sword. Although at a great disadvantage, he would make what defense he could. The beast started to swing down at him when—*Twang! Whiz!* An arrow struck it in the right shoulder making it stagger back, screaming in pain.

Wren moved beside the horse, touched it and said, *"Saus!"* The horse stood, blocking the beast's path so she could pull Ellis to his feet. The horse bolted when startled by the beast's roar.

The beast struck out at Ellis and Wren, but Kell caught the arm in both his hands. Since the beast was bulkier and larger than the Guardian captain, it took all Kell's strength to keep it from attacking. The beast went to strike him with the other hand, but Avatar caught it. Both warriors strained against the powerful beast as it began bringing its arms together. They dug in their heels, but kept sliding closer to the beast. With a mighty roar it flung its arms wide, tossing them aside. This left the torso exposed. Ellis landed a savage slash that cut deep into its body. The beast grabbed the blade. Ellis held onto the hilt. Using the sword, it lifted him off his feet and tossed him sideways.

Twang! Twang! Wren's first shot struck the beast in the throat while the second hit it between the eyes. A loud gargling gag of death, and the beast vanished in a flash of bright, yellow light, a jewel falling to the ground where it stood.

"Ellis!" called Darius. He and Nigel pressed their mounts through the trees.

Wren helped Ellis to his feet.

"Father?" Nigel leapt from his horse before the animal stopped. Darius also dismounted.

"I'm all right."

Nigel examined Ellis for himself. "What attacked you?"

"I don't know. Have any of you seen such a beast before?" Ellis asked the Guardians.

Kell and Avatar stood, brushing dust and leaves from their clothes and hair. "No," said Kell. Avatar shook his head and spat dirt off his lips.

"Something fell when it vanished." Wren picked up an identical crimson jewel to the others that were found.

Ellis fiercely scowled, taking the jewel from her and showing it to Kell and Avatar. "There must be a connection. This is too coincidental."

"What is?" asked Darius.

Ellis didn't answer for a moment at hearing horses and voices approaching. "I'll explain after we return to Waldron." He gave the jewel to Kell and fetched his horse, which wandered off, but remained nearby.

"Sire. We managed to round up the Morvenians," Wess said of himself and Allard. The soldiers arrayed behind the Morvenians. All the Allonians were stoic in feature with Bijan and the Morvenians looking sheepish, even ashamed.

His ire aroused, Ellis demanded of Bijan, "What was that all about?"

"Please, king, forgive enthusiasm. Morvenians cannot control self when hunting."

"We didn't come here to hunt!"

155

"Again, accept apologies." Bijan offered a bow over the saddlebow. The other Movenians also bowed to Ellis and spoke apologies in either broken Allonian or Morvenian.

"We're returning to Waldron," declared Ellis, and mounted.

"As king commands," said Bijan.

Nothing was said on the return ride. Once at Waldron, Bijan again offered apologies to Ellis, who dismissed the Morvenians until dinner. Ellis, Nigel, Darius, Allard, Avatar and Wess made their way toward the study. Ellis dispatched Kell to fetch Shannan.

She was prompt in arriving and noticed everyone's fixed and stern expressions. Her gaze found Ellis. "Should I ask why so short a trip?"

He proceeded to explain about the three jewels and his discussion with Avatar about the statue. Nigel momentarily went wide-eyed in surprise then glared at the Guardian.

"Avatar did nothing wrong by telling me. You should have told me."

Chastened, Nigel said, "Ay, sir. But I don't see the connection."

"We still haven't made a direct connection, but finding a fourth stone today with a different creature makes it more probable than before."

"What fourth stone? You only mentioned three," said Shannan.

Ellis' expression softened towards her when telling about the beast that attacked him. She turned ashen with concern, her hands tightly clenched.

"First the girls, now you."

"Please, Mother, sit," said Nigel.

She waved him off, her focus on Ellis. "What now?"

"Find that connection." He held the stone for her view.

"How?"

His look grew sly. "Perhaps an accidental viewing of the stone at dinner may cause a reaction from our guests."

"How can it be by accident?" asked Wess.

156

The color returned to Shannan's face, along with determination. "Give me the stone," she said, holding out her hand and Ellis complied, a private look passing between them. "This requires a woman's touch."

"If she succeeds and the connection is made the Council should be informed," said Darius.

"It wouldn't be hard to convince most of us," said Allard.

"One step at a time," began Ellis. "Now find something to occupy yourselves until tonight."

At dinner, Shannan noticed that since the fair and spending the day in Hereford together, Ellan and Kaleana chatted like old friends. The language barrier didn't seem to affect them. This gave her an opening to implement their plan.

"Oh," she began in sudden thought. "Speaking of shops and booths. A merchant said you dropped this after visiting his booth at the fair and ask I return it to you." She waved Vidar forward and he handed her a bundled handkerchief. "Because of what happened yesterday and being gone today, I have not had the opportunity to do so." She unwrapped it and gave Kaleana the jewel.

At first Kaleana appeared confused, but upon receiving the jewel she gasped in fear and immediately passed it to Bijan.

His face grew harsh. "This not belong to princess."

"You mean it is not Morvenian?" asked Shannan.

"Morvenian, but not me," said Kaleana in distress.

Bijan gave Kaleana a scolding eye before speaking. "This could not have come from royal princess. It is *dibla*," he sneered, tossing the stone down the table at Shannan.

The answer made Vidar stiffen and Kell moved beside Ellis to translate. "That means evil stone, Sire."

Bijan's mouth clamped shut and his eyes narrowed at Kell.

"Why bring such a stone to Allon if you seek peace?" demanded Ellis.

157

"We not bring," refuted Bijan. Seeing Ellis' anger, he curbed his temper. "Merchant is mistaken. This come from someone else. Many things at fair not from Allon."

Ellis' gaze shifted from Kell to Shannan. She wore a satisfied expression. If not a direction connection to the beasts at least the stone was confirmed to be of Morvenian origin. He assumed a more casual attitude. "Possible." He reached for the jewel, and after a brief look at it, gave it to Kell and said; "Keep it until we learn the owner's identity."

Kell backed away from the table drawing Vidar with him.

Ellis flashed a friendly smile to Bijan and Kaleana. "Please, finish your dinner."

After dinner, Ellis and Nigel entered the Council Chamber. Although the Council was privately summoned by Darius to gather after dining, the majority was surprised by the king's unannounced arrival.

"Be at ease, gentlemen. This isn't a formal meeting since I've not reached a decision concerning the Morvenian proposal. Rather to inform you of a disturbing discovery confirmed this evening."

He proceeded to inform them of Gresham and Priscilla's encounter with the beast, finding the jewels, the attack on him at Wess' estate, finding the fourth jewel and their plan to confront the Morvenians with a jewel at dinner.

"We had to determine if the jewels were connected to the Morvenians without direct confrontation or informing them about the incidents. Kaleana became upset at the sight of it and Bijan angry. He confirmed the stone is of Morvenian origin but they didn't bring it because they consider the jewel an evil stone."

"Evil? How?" asked Erasmus.

"He didn't say. However, he pointed out that the jewel could have been brought here by a merchant who attended the fair."

"You don't believe that, Sire," said Ned.

Ellis' face grew stern. "Two of my daughters and I could have been killed in less than twenty-four hours. Until I learn who is responsible and why, I view everything with suspicion. The coincidence is not to be ignored."

"Nor should it be ignored, Sire," began Uriah. "We must proceed with caution concerning their proposal."

"Exactly my reason for informing the Council." Ellis cast a harsh look at those who favored the proposal, Hollis, Zebulon, and Gareth.

"We would not agree to anything placing the royal family in jeopardy, Sire, and we are appalled these attacks took place," insisted Hollis.

Ellis' glare passed to Zebulon and Gareth to which Gareth said; "Hollis is correct, Sire. The safety of the royal family and Allon comes first."

"But should we totally refuse the offer?" asked Zebulon in his usual surly manner.

"My lord, did you not hear what they king said? He and my sisters might have been killed. If that is not reason enough to refuse their offer, what is?" rebuffed Nigel.

Zebulon didn't reply rather Allard said to Ellis; "You want a counterproposal."

Ellis slyly grinned. "That shouldn't be too difficult."

Allard also grinned. "We already started formulating such a proposal." He pointed to those nearest him, Darius, Ned, Erasmus and Fagan.

"Why haven't you told the rest of us?" chided Zebulon.

Ellis cast a rebuking glance to Zebulon but spoke to Allard. "Where is the document?"

"In my quarters, Sire."

"Fetch it. We shall complete the terms."

Allard was quick in fetching the document, and by the time he returned, the others assumed their proper seats. What began as a discussion, turned into a formal Council meeting. He read aloud the contents thus far.

To trade proposals the Council agreed, with minor alterations more favorable to Allonian merchants. In addressing the matter of marriage, it stated such a marriage would only be considered after a royal ambassador visited Morven to become acquainted with their lifestyle and customs much like Bijan and Princess Kaleana on their visit to Allon.

159

The terms pleased Ellis but Nigel's reception was less than enthusiastic. For a long moment Ellis regarded his son before his attention was drawn aside by Allard's concluding statement and inquiring of his opinion.

"My compliments, gentlemen, you found an excellent compromise. This gives us time to consider the alliance more carefully, investigate these attacks, and gain knowledge of their society, while not completely rejecting them."

"We're glad you are pleased, Sire."

"Any suggestion on the ambassador?"

"Lord Emery," said Darius. "He's as shrewd as Allard, though less opinionated."

Allard snorted a good-natured snicker and bowed his head to Darius.

Ellis glanced at the others, focusing specifically on Hollis, Gareth and Zebulon. "Any objections?"

"No objection, Sire, but a question. How long should this take?" asked Gareth.

Allard answered, "A few weeks, perhaps. We can make this a formal statement from the king and Council, inform the Morvenians, and dispatch Emery with them when they return bearing the counterproposal." He turned to Ellis for approval or correction.

Ellis tugged at his lower lip, his expression thoughtful.

"Sire," began Nigel. "Princess Tristine's coming of age banquet is in three weeks. I don't believe this should interfere with her special day."

"My thoughts exactly. There has been enough upheaval. She will not share her special time also." Ellis then spoke to the Council. "Lord Emery will be instructed to probe and delay according to our timetable. Gentlemen, we leave you to formalize the document. Once the Council has signed and stamped full approval, I will present our counterproposal to the Morvenians and begin the process on our terms."

Ellis rose, so did the Council, and bowed as he and Nigel left the chamber. Nigel's face and brooding silence told of his disturbance as they made their way to the study. Once in the study, Ellis spoke.

"You're not pleased about the compromise."

"No, I'm not, especially after nearly losing you, Necie and Tristine. I believe it is wrong to even offer a counterproposal considering their devil stone is involved."

Ellis curbed the impulse to smile. "I appreciate your passion and protective nature toward your family. And you know I will not place our family's welfare in jeopardy to favor foreigners. Still, there is much to consider. Despite Kaleana and Bijan recognizing the stone, there is no proof they knew the beasts to be magical or were directly involved. To accuse them without poof is dangerous to national security. This way I can protect our family and Allon from more attacks, while saving face and avoiding unwanted consequences."

Nigel's brows deeply furrowed with disturbance. "But why is the marriage still included?"

Ellis cocked a brow and snickered. "My boy, you better get used to the idea of marriage, it will happen one day."

Nigel gaped at his father. "I thought you said you don't want this marriage? If they intend us harm, why should I marry her?"

Ellis took Nigel by the shoulders and looked him squarely in the eyes. "Whether Kaleana or another princess, you will someday marry. The future of Allon depends upon it."

Nigel winced, turning away and biting his lower lip.

The sudden change made Ellis curious. "Does that trouble you?"

He was awkward in reply. "I don't know if I can be as good a king as you."

Ellis smiled, tossing an arm about Nigel's shoulder. "I didn't know if I would be a good king either. It's natural to doubt one's ability, but the true mettle of man pushes through those doubts to do what is necessary." His face grew thoughtful in remembrance. "Learning my destiny to take back Allon according to Prophecy overwhelmed me at first. At times I thought I couldn't go on, that I couldn't fulfill everyone's expectations. Yet a deep sense in my soul told me I would be more miserable if I didn't embrace my destiny than if I failed in battle." He smiled, warm and tender. "Your mother is a great part of why I succeeded. Her faith in Jor'el and belief in me kept

161

me going. The disappointment of others I can accept, but not Shannan's. Our destinies are linked. I had to succeed if only for her."

"I felt her disappointment and never want to again," said Nigel before casting a sheepish glance to Ellis. "So you don't consider me weak for doubting my future?"

"No." A kind smile crossed Ellis' lips. "It is natural at your age to struggle with doubts and fears. But you can't let those rule you. You must push forward."

"I'll try."

"Good. Now let's look in on Necie and Tristine."

Necie sat up in bed. Arista sat beside her. Tristine and Angus sat in nearby chairs. Shannan stood on the opposite side of the bed. All were laughing.

"Well, I like the sound in here. Feeling better?" Ellis asked Necie.

"Ay, just tired."

He smiled and touched her cheek. "I'm sure you'll be fine in a few days. And most definitely recovered in time for Tristine's birthday."

"You haven't forgotten?" asked Tristine.

"What makes you think I would?"

She heaved an awkward shrug, turning to Nigel, then back to Ellis.

"Because of the Morvenians."

She shrugged again, looking away.

Ellis moved to her chair, knelt and lifted her chin to make her look at him. "Nothing will make me forget or neglect my family. We will celebrate your banquet and with no foreigners present."

"They're leaving?"

"Ay, and very soon."

"You and the Council have reached an agreement?" asked Shannan, a hint of trepidation in her voice.

"Ay," replied Ellis then added at seeing Tristine's frightened glance to Nigel, "Don't worry, it's not what you think. A counterproposal is drafted stating our terms for an alliance."

"With no marriage?"

"In a manner of speaking. It's rather complex, but trust me, Nigel isn't getting married any time soon."

Tristine's faced brightened in relief and she hugged Ellis then Nigel.

Nigel said nothing; he couldn't speak since he wasn't convinced the counterproposal provided the answer. Thus his hold of Tristine was more for his own comfort than her relief. When she looked at him with a big smile, he said, "When I do get married, it won't change anything between us, I promise."

"I hope I at least like her," she said, which amused him.

"Necie appears ready for sleep. We should all leave," said Shannan. "Including you, Angus. You need to sleep someplace other than a chair."

He frowned in reluctance. "Ay, Aunt. I'll be back first thing in the morning," he said to Necie.

"I'll take Tristine to her room," said Nigel.

After escorting Tristine and bidding her goodnight, Nigel was not ready to retire and went to the training center near the barracks for some physical activity. His mind and emotions ran the gamut. The incident at Wess' estate disturbed him. In less then twenty-four hours, unknown magical beasts attacked three members of his family and somehow those attacks were believed to be connected to the Morvenian's visit. This made the marriage contract highly suspect and bothered him that it remained in the counterproposal. He knew his father tried to ease his mind by speaking about his own doubts, but this went beyond normal uncertainty to the very core of his being. The continuing nightmare confirmed his misgivings while the attacks heightened his fear.

As usual, Avatar accompanied him. When performing the Jor'ellian positions to loosen up then mock combat, Nigel's disturbance came though in angry blows. He launched a vicious attack, and Avatar disarmed him, catching him around the waist and holding him against his side.

"You fight with mindless anger. Why?"

Nigel was sweating and breathing hard from exertion but instead of answering, he tried to free himself only Avatar held fast.

"I won't release you until you answer me."

"You can't force me to speak."

"No, but I will not continue this bout." Avatar released Nigel and sheathed his sword.

Sneering, Nigel placed himself *en garde*. "I'm not ready to stop."

Avatar turned to leave.

"Where are you going? Come back!" Nigel's shout drew the attention of the few soldiers, knights and squires present. Avatar continued to walk away. Piqued, Nigel ran after him and seized the Guardian's arm. "I said come back!"

Avatar looked down at Nigel, his silver eyes intense. *"Samhchair, Nigel mac Ellis agus Tristan,"* he commanded. Nigel's face became placid, anger gone and he blinked in bewilderment. "Come." Avatar steered the now subdued Nigel from the training center.

"I don't know what came over me."

"I do. You let your emotions rule. Your deepest fears and anxieties came out with the intention to do harm."

"I didn't want to hurt you, I wanted to—" Nigel stopped, clamping his mouth shut.

"To what? Fight until you collapsed in exhaustion? Or until you destroyed what troubles you?"

Nigel was slow to answer, the weight of disturbance on his brow. "I don't know." He didn't realize until they stopped that Avatar brought him to a quiet corner of the Chapel garden.

"It can't be the jewel, you agreed to the plan, so something happened with the Council. What?"

Nigel sighed and sat on a bench. "Allard, Uncle and some others drafted a counterproposal that Father agreed to. He even said it provided the answer he was looking for."

Avatar sat beside him. "But not you."

"No. It only delays the decision of marriage."

"Isn't that what you wanted?"

"I want a permanent answer, not a delay!"

"From what I've observed of mortals, diplomacy is a delicate matter. A ruler risks war by speaking plainly but can avoid serious consequences by the words he chooses."

Nigel nodded and grumbled, "I've been told that before, only he can't even speak plainly to me!"

"Have you spoken plainly to him about your fears?"

Stymied, Nigel stared at Avatar. "No. It would hurt him too much."

"Perhaps he feels the same about hurting you and is trying to bring you into an understanding of what will one day be required of you as king."

Irate, Nigel bolted up. "Don't *you* even understand?"

"Of course I do," said Avatar. He rose to calm Nigel by taking him by the shoulders. "I'm only explaining his actions. You haven't told him, so he is continuing to instruct you as if nothing is wrong. You can't expect him to act differently if you keep him ignorant."

"But how can I tell him?" asked Nigel, almost desperate.

"That's for you to decide."

"Could you tell him for me?"

"No. I cannot interfere in this," replied Avatar, uneasiness creeping into his voice.

Nigel studied Avatar's face. Something now disturbed him. "Why?"

Avatar lowered his eyes. "I may not always be with you."

Nigel's breath caught in this throat. "What? Why?"

"I never acted as a Overseer before you." He cocked a grin. "Watching you grow up has been a unique experience and given me new insights into how a mortal thinks, acts, and feels. But watching over you wasn't the reason for my creation."

Nigel frowned. "I never considered what you did before, although I know you are a mighty warrior. Selfish, I suppose."

"No, not selfish. You've not known another way of life, whereas I've seen and experienced much in more than eighteen hundred years."

Nigel shook his head; the unction on his face filled his voice. "I couldn't imagine my life without you."

Avatar chuckled, a look of tenderness in his eyes. "I appreciate the sentiment. I too am very fond of you, more than any mortal I've ever known. But a mortal's life changes over time. You have passed from childhood into manhood and as such my role is diminishing with the more responsibilities and skills you accumulate."

"Kell and Vidar remain with my parents. Why not you with me?"

"Their duties changed once your parents became king and queen. Besides, Kell is only on temporary assignment. First and foremost, he is the Captain of the Guardians and has been from the beginning." Avatar placed a hand on Nigel's shoulder, looking him squarely in the eyes. "Some day you will marry and your life change. Will that affect the love you have for your family?"

"No, of course not.

Avatar gently smiled. "So it will be with us. My role in your life will change, but our bond remain."

Nigel lightly bit his lower lip. He knew Avatar was right, only it didn't calm his uneasiness.

"Still, that is some time away," said Avatar in a lighter tone. "For now enjoy what is to come after they leave: Tristine's banquet."

Nigel laughed, more in relief than humor. "I think I'm ready to retire now."

166

Chapter 10

THE FOLLOWING MORNING, Ellis received the Council's approved counterproposal. After reading it, he signed it and affixed the seal of the King of Allon directly above the eleven seals and signatures of the Council. Once done, he sent for Emery, a thin, wiry man of forty with boundless energy. He was not surprised to learn Darius already spoke to Emery. Sometimes Darius' pre-emptive actions were annoying, but Ellis knew he acted out of brotherly love and loyalty. Rarely did he rebuke or correct Darius for acting before he, as king, issued orders.

Whereas Darius spoke to Emery, Ellis was confident he had not spoken to Bijan. Thus, when he finished giving his instructions to Emery, he sent Kell to inform Bijan he would receive him and a representation of the delegation in the Great Hall in half an hour.

This meeting would be formal, so Ellis sat on his throne and wore his crown. Emery, Darius and Uriah were present. Darius represented the Council of Twelve and Uriah in his capacity as the Vicar of Allon.

Kell escorted Bijan and two of the Morvenian lords into the Great Hall. Bijan and the lords made the formal bow. "Most Noble King. What is your pleasure?" asked Bijan.

"A decision has been reached concerning the proposed alliance." The document lay in Ellis' lap and he picked it up. "This is our counterproposal.

167

You will take it and Ambassador Emery to the emperor with our compliments and good wishes that we can reach a mutual agreement."

"Counterproposal? King reject emperor's generosity?"

"No. However, there were points in your proposal we have addressed."

"Please, king, what points?"

Ellis casually replied. "Matters of trade laws, military consideration, marriage customs, nothing extraordinary."

Bijan flinched when Ellis mentioned marriage in the list of items. "King not agree to marriage? That will seal alliance."

"As you have witnessed, our customs are different. We simply want to know how Morvenians view marriage and your customs before making a final decision."

"That is why prince not present for decision," said Bijan, his gaze momentarily going to Darius, Emery and Uriah.

Ellis continued in his matter-of-fact attitude, not commenting on Nigel's absence. "This is Ambassador Emery. He will present our counterproposal to the emperor and explore your country, much like you have done these past few weeks."

"I look forward to enjoying Morvenian hospitality," said Emery.

Bijan didn't look happy when he turned from Emery to Ellis. "Please to understand I have instructions only to return with king's answer."

"Ambassador Emery is conveying my answer."

"What of Princess Kaleana?"

"What about her?"

"She is to remain in Allon not return to Morven."

The statement perplexed Ellis. "I don't recall you saying she was part of the agreement."

"She is emperor's divine gift to king. Gift cannot be returned."

Ellis glanced to Uriah upon hearing the Vicar mutter a prayer in the Ancient. He turned his attention back to Bijan, the casual, matter-of-fact attitude gone, replaced by displeasure. "When you first arrived I told you I would not accept any gift given as 'divine' offering. I also made it clear Allonians are not in the habit of treating people like property to be given away and you insisted the gift was the marriage proposal and not the princess. Well, which is it now?"

Bijan stirred with insult. "Emperor consider great honor to bestow royal princess to king and will be insulted if princess returned by king."

Piqued, Ellis rebuffed, "Then you will explain to the emperor Allonian customs are different and no insult is meant. Otherwise Ambassador Emery will tell the emperor of your failure to deal honestly in this matter and misrepresented the emperor's intentions."

Bijan paled and hastily bowed. "It will be as king commands."

Ellis sat back and assumed a calm posture. "How long do you need to prepare for the return journey?"

"What gift does king wish to send emperor?"

"Some trade goods from the fair. Perhaps a few of Lord Allard's horses."

Bijan grinned in pleasure. "Emperor very interested in horses. They make good gift."

"Very well. All could be ready in two days," said Ellis, looking at Darius and Emery, who both nodded.

"Then in two days we leave for Morven."

"Excellent. The night before departure we shall hold a feast in your honor and a toast to the emperor."

Bijan and the lords understood they were being dismissed and bowed before departing with Kell.

During the last two days of the Morvenian visit, Nigel spent a lot of time with Kaleana. They communicated as best they could with her limited Allonian vocabulary and his complete lack of Morvenian. Language was a part of his learning, but only included the Ancient used in knightly practice and Tunlundian, a major trading partner and ally. Guardians spoke all languages only Nigel didn't want to impose upon Avatar to act as a constant interpreter.

The afternoon of the banquet, Nigel and Kaleana strolled in the terrace gardens. She was more quiet than usual and barely looked at him.

169

"You seem melancholy," he said.

She glanced at him, confusion on her features."Mel-an-choly?"

"Sad."

She glanced down at her feet. "Sad to return to emperor."

"You don't like your father the emperor?"

She shrugged, still averting her gaze. "Do not know emperor goodly."

"You mean you don't know him well."

She nodded with an uncertain smile and gestured at him. "You know king well. Know queen well. Know sisters well."

He smiled, wide and loving. "Ay. They are my family. I guess it is hard to be well acquainted with all one hundred of your siblings."

She just stared at him.

"Do you know any of your family well?"

"No. Forbidden."

"Forbidden?" he repeated in surprise.

She grew upset at struggling to be understood. "Morven different. Family different. Too many. Learn duty not family. Not fun like fair."

Nigel's brow furrowed, distressed to hear her speak about not knowing her family. Her words drove home Avatar's point about how his life could change yet the bond he shared with those he loved would never change. Kaleana didn't share that bond.

"Kaleana make prince melancholy?" she asked, stumbling over the word.

Nigel forced a smile. "I was just thinking how sad it is you don't know your family like I do mine."

"I not know before Allon," she droned.

He took her hand and gave her a supportive squeeze. "I think I understand why you are sad to return to the emperor. There is no warmth, only duty. You're very sweet and beautiful. I can't see how he doesn't notice you or why he sent you away."

"King sent me away."

"It's not the same. You are not his child."

"Prince not sent me away." Kaleana kissed his hand, her eyes misty.

Her tender action and the pleading look in her bright hazel eyes stunned him. The word 'no' rose to his lips, but the deep sense haunting him of late, suddenly gripped him and he withdrew from her.

She clapped a hand over her mouth to stifle a surprise gasp at his action.

He whirled about at hearing her distress. "Kaleana—" he struggled to find the words. "I don't think I can begin to explain how or I why feel what I do. I don't even understand it. Until I can, it is best you return to Morven."

"Prince forget Kaleana!" She began to cry.

"No! But until I am certain of my own mind, I would not be a good husband to you, or any woman. Please, try to understand."

"Prince promise not forget. Keep gift?"

"I promise."

Her smile was soft and tender. With a delicate gesture, she wiped her eyes. "Will return to Morven and wait for prince summons."

A female Morvenian servant hurried into the garden and approached Kaleana, bowing and chattering excitedly. Kaleana turned to Nigel, and with urgency in her voice said, "Must go." She and the servant left.

"I wonder what that was about?" Nigel asked Avatar, who moved from his vigil at the garden gate.

"The matron responsible for the princess is angry at her long absence and neglectful in preparing for the banquet."

"She hurried off because a servant became annoyed?"

"The matron is given authority over the princess' life even to the point of punishment. Much like a Guardian in overseeing a royal heir's life."

"You don't punish me."

"Maybe I should have," quipped Avatar.

Ellan arrived in the garden. "Nigel? What did you say to upset Kaleana?"

"Nothing. She's upset because they are leaving in the morning to return to Morven."

"I'm not sure I understand or agree to what Father is doing."

"You're understanding or agreement isn't the issue. This is about my future," he chided.

Ellan glared at him. "Don't take your anger out on me. I've kept Kaleana from being hurt and insulted by your rude and thoughtless behavior. She's sweet and demure and has taken a liking to you despite your insufferable, selfish —"

"Enough! I have apologized and made amends. I've even tried to soothe our relationship because of what you said; but where my future is concerned, you have no say. Father and I have reached an agreement and that is the way it will be."

She momentarily gaped at him before her jowls tightened in anger and she grew rigid.

"Maybe I shouldn't have snapped, but don't let your new found position go to your head."

"What does that mean?"

"You've become friendly with Kaleana, fine. However, it doesn't allow you to interfere in this matter. You did well in reasoning with Father about Hereford. You may want to try that approach with Tristine and me rather than accusations and bullying." He marched from the garden.

Ellan glared in tearful anger at Avatar, who gave her a short bow before following Nigel.

Avatar caught up to Nigel in the armory yard. "You were rough."

"No more than she deserved. It is not her place to scold me."

"No, but you're doing exactly what you accused her of doing. She let her friendship with Kaleana lead her into overstepping her bounds, while you're allowing your dreams and feelings of uncertainty to make you oversensitive and irate."

Nigel stopped in a shadowy doorway away from on-lookers to confront Avatar. "That's rather rough of you."

"Does it make any less true than what you said to Ellan about her behavior?"

"Ellan doesn't have the responsibility I do."

"When will you stop making excuses and deal with the issue?"

172

Nigel looked Avatar squarely in the eyes and seeing the Guardian's stubbornness, recanted. "After the Morvenians are gone, I need to clear my head."

"I'll see you have the time." Avatar steered Nigel back inside Waldron to continue the day's duties.

The Morvenians were subdued at the banquet while the Allonians enjoyed themselves. Despite his own distraction of dealing with personal feelings about the situation, Nigel kept up appearances when addressed by Darius or other members of Court. Several times he caught Ellis' eye but said nothing. What more could be said? The truth perhaps? What good would it do now? The Morvenians and Emery were leaving in the morning to deliver the counterproposal. The marriage went from a necessity in the Morvenian proposal to a consideration in their counterproposal, so why complicate matters by expressing his uncertain feelings? No. It was best to wait for Emery's report. For now he played the dutiful host.

Before the planned entertainment began, Bijan asked Ellis for the Morvenians to be excused to retire early for a proper night's rest. The entire Morvenian delegation left the Hall to well wishes from the Allonian nobles.

Ellis leaned over to Nigel. "What's troubling you?"

The question momentarily caught Nigel off guard and hastily said, "Nothing, sir."

"You expect me to believe that?"

"No," he admitted, a small smile appearing. "Since you noticed, my effort not to let my concern get the better of me, failed."

"What more is there be concerned about? We gave our answer and they are leaving. Besides," an impish voice matched Ellis' expression, "we have Tristine's banquet to plan."

This time Nigel's smiled in genuine pleasure. "Ay."

Ellis laughed, a hearty pat on Nigel's shoulder.

Later in the royal chamber, Shannan questioned Ellis. "You handled Nigel well, but are you as confident as you tried to sound?"

"Why do you ask?"

She gave him a long steady regard. "Because I know you. We've discussed Nigel's future many times, so can you tell me you are convinced according to Jor'el and Prophecy, Kaleana is the one he should marry?" He didn't reply. There was no need; his contrary look provided the answer. "You are not convinced."

"No, but I'm not ready to close the door. At least not until Emery returns and I learn more about them. Kamu is powerful and his influence stretches far beyond Morven."

"Are you afraid we cannot withstand an attack?"

"That is a serious consideration."

"Allon is powerful in its own right."

"Ay, Jor'el has blessed us, but I shouldn't ignore or shun this opportunity."

She glared at him. "You are using our son as a bargaining tool."

"No, I'm not," he refuted. "Kamu began this by using his daughter in a way I find appalling. Remember, she was originally sent as a gift of marriage to me for divine appeasement." He flashed a roguish smile. "Of course, I immediately dismissed the suggestion. I am very happy and satisfied with the wife I have."

"I should hope so."

He chuckled and continued his defense. "Bijan suggested Nigel, not me. However, to reject the suggestion outright would have shut down negotiations before they began. Now, we keep an open dialogue by using their terms as a bargaining tool, not Nigel."

"Sounds like a fine line. Have you told Nigel this?"

"Of course, only I don't know if he completely understands. Diplomacy is often about fine lines and choosing one's words carefully to get the other side to listen while keeping your own integrity, honor and best interest intact." Ellis frowned and shook his head. "He's still young and such subtleties aren't easily acquired."

Pondering, she briefly chewed on her lower lip. "It may be hard for him to focus on diplomacy after nearly losing most his family to horrid, evil attacks. I am having difficulty dealing with the situation and maintaining decorum. You two must discuss the situation at length, and in private, without interference."

"I agree—" A knock at door and hurried entrance stopped Ellis' reply. "Tristine? What are you doing up this late?"

Although in a dressing gown, Tristine was giddy with excitement. "I couldn't sleep. They're leaving in the morning which means Nigel and I can go camping."

Ellis smiled at her enthusiasm. "Rather quick, don't you think?"

Her face fell. "You said we could go after they left."

"I did. And you will, only not tomorrow."

"When?"

"After the Morvenians are safely away and life is returned to normal. I want to make certain there are no more magical beasts. A week perhaps—"

"Before my banquet?"

"Ay," he said and steered her toward the door. "Now, good night." He kissed her forehead and sent her on her way.

On the way back to her room, Tristine saw Nigel heading for his chamber and ran to catch him by the arm, startling him. She didn't notice his reaction due to her own excitement. "Father gave permission for us to camping in a week."

"Oh, right," said Nigel, distracted.

"Did you forget your promise to go with me?"

"No. I just didn't think it would be so soon."

"I'll be thirteen in less than three weeks and Father said if I proved myself sleeping out at night I can go hunting with the two of you after my banquet."

Nigel grinned, but it was humorless. "I know what he said. I was there."

She held his arm as they walked. "I'm glad they're leaving and things can get back to normal."

"Let's hope that's the case." He stopped at the door to his chamber.

This time she noticed the gloominess in his voice and stood away from him to view his face. "What's wrong? I thought you'd be happy about them leaving."

"I am. Only there are matters of diplomacy you know nothing about."

"Does it still involve you?"

He shook his head in an effort to end the conversation. "It's too complex to explain."

She huffed, her hands going to her hips. "I'm not stupid."

"This doesn't have anything to do with intelligence. I'm still trying to comprehend everything."

Avatar was waiting at the door. He cleared his throat and made a brief indication behind them, so Nigel snatched a glance over her shoulder to see Armus, who looked very displeased.

"You slipped out of your room, didn't you?" Nigel said to her.

"I told you I spoke to Father."

"Without Armus' knowledge." He pointed past her.

She saw Armus and reluctantly admitted, "Ay."

"You know this can't keep happening," Nigel began to Tristine, but ending up speaking to Armus, "a mortal girl outwitting a two-thousand-year-old Guardian."

Avatar bit his lip to keep from laughing out loud when Armus' disapproving scowl passed to him. Armus took firm hold of Tristine's shoulder. She offered no resistance as he steered her back to her chamber.

Nigel playfully spoke to Avatar, but loud enough to be heard. "Maybe he should put a cow bell on her so he can hear when she moves."

"Maybe you should paint that ugly statue a bright pink so more people will notice," Armus loudly spoke over his shoulder.

This time, Avatar laughed out loud.

176

Chapter 11

NIGEL RAN DOWN HALLWAYS. He rode in the open. The nameless terror drew closer than ever before and he was scared. He bolted up, his heart racing and his breathing labored.

Avatar moved beside the bed. "The same nightmare?"

Nigel nodded, trying to steady his breathing. "Every night this week. I wish I understood what it meant."

Avatar placed a hand on Nigel's forehead. "Be at ease. Close your eyes and take a deep breath. You won't be able to discern until your mind is clear. Now try to relax and concentrate on the Creed."

Nigel closed his eyes and took in a long, deep breath before exhaling. Avatar whispered in the Ancient, the Guardian's hand remaining on his forehead. Soon he reclined against the pillows, breathing normally.

Avatar removed his hand. "Better?"

"Ay, but I still don't understand what it means."

"Any sense of what or who you're running from?"

Nigel hesitated before shaking his head. "I'm just trying to get away."

Avatar didn't say anything. His glance at the elephant statue was enough to convey what he was thinking.

"The statue has nothing to do with it. Besides, they left a week ago."

177

"So? Time doesn't matter where evil is involved. You nearly lost your father and sisters in less than twenty-four hours."

"I know that!"

"There is only one way to be sure. Let me take it out of the room for one night—"

"No! I promised to keep it."

"You're not getting rid of it, just moving it."

"You've obviously forgotten the nightmare started before she gave it to me."

Avatar didn't reply rather stared at Nigel.

"Don't try your Guardian eyes on me. You just don't want to admit being wrong."

Avatar went back to his usual position near the door.

Nigel punched the pillow to fluff it. He turned his back to Avatar, facing the statue. Despite his insistence to keep it, the carving was ugly. However, each time he saw it, he thought of Kaleana. So beautiful, gentle and sincere, it was impossible to believe she could mean any evil. Still, he couldn't deny what happened during the Morvenians' visit; and he shivered at the thought of possibly losing three members of his family so quickly. He loved and respected his father, and that love kept him from telling Ellis and hurting him concerning the sensation he would not be king. How else could Ellis take such news but that his son was rejecting the throne? No. He accepted the responsibilities given him; but how can he explain his fear of the future when he didn't understand the meaning? If the beast had killed Ellis, he would have become king immediately.

However, Necie and Tristine first suffered injury. Nigel thought about them individually. Necie's sweet nature and ability to find amusement in even the simple things was adorable. Then he thought about Tristine, the endearing tomboy who mimicked him in everything. He smiled, which faded at recalling what Ellan said about him favoring Tristine. He loved all of his sisters, equally he believed. Their conversation forced him to look at the way he treated them, and in the end, admit Ellan was right; he favored Tristine.

Now, he would take her camping to help her gain the right to go hunting with him and their father.

What if this whole scheme is a plot to kill my family and make the deaths appear accidental?

A deep, cold shiver ran through him, adding a fearful wrinkle to an innocent adventure. Tristine was so excited when they spoke before bed. Nothing troubled her, though she probably wasn't sleeping due to excitement. He wasn't sleeping because of a nameless fear.

Get a hold of yourself. You can't let her see your fear and scare her when you don't know what scares you. She'll be nervous enough once it gets dark.

He glanced to where Avatar stood. He and Armus would accompany them on the camping trip, but not too closely. Tristine had to endure the night on her own just like he did. Except for that night, Avatar remained within earshot or arms length to help him deal with trouble or fear. If not for the Guardian's soothing influence, he would still be troubled by the repeating nightmare. There had to be a reason. Until he discovered something to help his understanding, he would not be able to get back to sleep. He sat up, tossed aside the covers and reached for his robe on the chair beside the bed, then put on his slippers.

"Going somewhere?" asked Avatar.

"The Chapel library. I want to look up something."

"Master Hampton will be asleep."

"With your help, I won't disturb him."

When necessary, Guardians moved about undetected by mortals, thus they reached the Chapel's library without notice. Avatar lit the oil lamp. Nigel took the lamp from him, turned it low and searched the bookshelf.

"What are you looking for?" asked Avatar.

Nigel didn't answer, rather removed the Book of Prophecy from the shelf. Avatar moved to look over Nigel's shoulder, but Nigel drew the book closer for privacy and sent the Guardian a warning glare.

"I can't help if I don't know what it is you're looking for."

Nigel wasn't in the mood to be friendly or accommodating and after another glare, Avatar stepped back. Nigel flipped through the pages. He scanned a few in reference to his father and mother, the Son of Tristan and the Daughter of Allon.

For the king shall return unto Allon,
And the house which was once laid desolate shall be rebuilt.
And all the people shall gather to rejoice
That the time of peace has come.

Then a few pages later he read:

Those whom after his own heart shall he seek and find.
From the fowls of the air, to the beasts of prey and
The faithful shall he gather to himself the hope of Allon.
Among them shall be one whose birth
Shall be linked to his own by a season
And whose soul shall mirror his own.
The two shall become as one in desire and purpose.

He couldn't help but smile. His parents were indeed special and their love visible in how much they complimented the other in word, thought, and action. Several dozen pages later, he found what he was looking for and the words were sobering.

The house restored shall be shaken
To its foundation by calamity.
For only after sacrifice and cleansing
Of trouble brought upon itself
Can the Great King arise.
And he shall be Allon's greatest king.
Of such a heritage as to rule Guardian and mortal alike.
To unite them in purpose and heart toward Jor'el.
For he shall prepare the way for the Almighty's return.

He gasped and shivered as the words and his nightmares suddenly came together. In his heart and spirit he knew he was not the Great King, but for the Great King to be revealed, he must step aside. What about his father? He heard Avatar's question of concern but didn't respond. Feeling an urgent grip on his shoulder, he stared at the Guardian, gathering his wits to speak.

"What do you know of the Great King?"

Avatar's brows furrowed in perplexity at the question. "Not much other than what is written. Is that what you came to find out? About the Great King?"

"I didn't know what I was looking for until I read the passage," he murmured, his focus returning to the book.

Avatar sat beside Nigel. "You think the prophecy has something to do with your nightmares and sense of doubt?"

Nigel nodded. "Although I'm not sure of how or why." He stared at the passage. "I already fear Father's reaction, but what does he know or think about the Great King?"

"The only way to know is to speak to him."

Nigel shook his head, uncertainty on his face. "What if he asks me if I know who it is? Which I don't. Or how it will affect our family?"

"If your nightmares do coincide with Prophecy, the Son of Tristan and Daughter of Allon will come to accept it."

"And my sisters? They look to me for help and protection. How can I disappoint them?"

"Will having complete answers help you face what faith and trust require you to do?"

"It wouldn't hurt. But this raises more questions than gives answers."

"It gives you a direction where before you had none."

Frustrated, Nigel closed the book and pushed it to Avatar. "I've read enough for now. I must consider what I've learned.

Avatar put the book back on the shelf. "Can you get some rest before leaving?"

"Maybe."

Avatar again sat beside Nigel to get his full attention. "You said your sense included the knowledge you are to remain the brother and son you've always been. For Tristine's sake, don't let this interfere. She needs you to be undistracted for this camping trip and for her banquet."

"I know. Jor'el willing, I won't let her down."

"You can help that sentiment by getting some rest." Avatar turned out the lamp and escorted Nigel from the chapel.

181

Tristine woke at first light, her excitement palpable even though she and Nigel would not be leaving until mid-afternoon. After all, the point was to spend the night in the forest and they didn't have to travel far.

Three hours before sunset, Tristine and Nigel went to the stables. She wore a doublet and breeches, carrying a bow and quiver and a dagger on her belt. Nigel was armed with his sword and dagger. He tended to his horse, Alden, a beautiful, gray gelding while she examined a large, black gelding.

"I'll take Kerrick tonight."

"No, you'll take Malin," said Ellis, who arrived unseen.

"Why? Malin's slow and small. He's a child's horse."

Ellis laughed. He patted Malin's muzzle and spoke to the horse. "Don't mind her, she thinks she's grown-up before her time."

"Father!"

"You'll take Malin. Unless you'd prefer Caleigh?"

Tristine snatched Malin's halter and led him out of the stables.

"Hardly subtle," Nigel said to Ellis.

Ellis grinned. "She'll be more appreciative when the time comes."

"Somehow, I don't think that'll be a problem," snickered Nigel before leading Alden from the stables.

Ellis followed and watched them inspect, groom and saddle their horses. Nigel instructed Tristine on attaching the necessary equipment to the rear of the saddle. Ellis grinned. Normally such tasks fell to the grooms, but part of learning to hunt was how to take care of one's horse and equipment for those times when self-reliance became a necessity. Being of royal blood did not mean they were ignorant of elementary and needed life skills.

Shannan joined him. "You look as if you're in another world."

"Just indulging in a moment of remembrance. It suddenly seems long ago watching her chase after Nigel mimicking him in everything, picking your brain for training, and pestering Wren and Armus to teach her their skills for hunting and tracking. All shall be tested tonight; and very soon, she will be the third our children to pass into adulthood. Hard to think of them getting older."

"Or you getting old?"

"Oh, no, only the children age, you and I don't."

Shannan laughed. "She's so excited."

He leaned closely to her and privately said, "Just wait until she gets her presents. She complained when I told her she'd have to ride Malin and not Kerrick."

"Ellis, you didn't," she said in amused outrage. "You can be devious."

The conversation stopped when Tristine and Nigel approached, leading their horses. "Well, tonight is the big night," said Ellis to Tristine, who beamed. He placed one hand on her shoulder and one hand on Nigel's shoulder. "Almighty Jor'el, I ask your blessing upon this venture and that you will watch over my children. Grant success and bring them home safely tomorrow. *Tangiel.*"

"*Tangiel,*" said Tristine and Nigel. She looked to Shannan with a wide confident smile before mounting. Nigel kissed his mother's cheek then mounted.

Avatar and Armus waited by the gate, and when Nigel and Tristine rode past, followed their charges.

"Where are we heading?" asked Tristine.

"To the same spot I spent my first night," replied Nigel.

"Is it far?"

"Far enough so you won't feel so close to Waldron, but close enough should you feel the need to return," he teased, making her scowl.

"I won't return."

He laughed. "I believe you. However, the forest is very different at night. It can be a cold, lonely and frightening place."

"Are you trying to scare me?"

He balked at the question. "No, just preparing you. Are you scared?"

"I'm not scared," she said, the confidence in her voice waning. "Just nervous."

"That's natural."

"Father told me not to let fear rule me, but I've never slept anywhere but on a bed inside a house. Not even in a tent."

He snorted a chuckle. "We're not sleeping in a tent."

"We're not? Then what did you pack?" She pointed to the roll behind his saddle.

"Bedding. Unless you want to sleep directly on the ground."

She frowned and glanced at the bedroll again.

"Did you think Father and I sleep in tents?"

"Well, I didn't think the king slept on the ground."

He laughed. "You're going camping and you don't even know what it is."

Hurt, she lashed out. "You don't have to make fun of me. At least I'm going and not afraid to face my fears like you are."

His expression turned sharp. "What do you know of my feelings?"

"I've got eyes and ears. I know what's going on and why Lord Emery left with the Morvenians. You're afraid to get married."

He made a low throaty growl.

"Is something wrong, Highness?" asked Avatar.

"Nothing," snapped Nigel before looking back at the Guardians. He caught Avatar's warning glance. Taking a deep breath, he turned forward in the saddle and spoke in a more controlled voice to Tristine. "Let's not talk about it any more and enjoy this night."

She nodded in agreement. "I'm sorry for what I said. I really don't think you're afraid. It just doesn't feel right you marrying someone who doesn't at least believe in Jor'el."

He cocked a rueful grin. "That's one way of putting it. But I said enough, I don't want to spoil your fun."

For an hour they rode east, the sun growing lower in the western sky behind them.

"Feels like we're heading to Garwood," said Tristine.

"We're not going that far."

"I know. It takes four days. I said it just feels like it."

Nigel smiled. "This is where we leave the road." He turned his horse north and headed into the woods.

184

For another hour they rode deeper into the forest. Twilight gave way to night, and the sounds of nocturnal animals started to surround them. Nigel glanced over his shoulder to check the distance between he and Tristine. She kept a good pace, despite her objection to Malin's slowness. Behind her, he saw Armus and Avatar disappear into the woods.

"How much further?" she asked.

"Not much. Nervous?"

"No." She smirked in bravado, making him chuckle.

After another half-mile, he stopped in the middle a clearing and dismounted. "We're here."

She dismounted and noticed they were alone. "Where are Armus and Avatar?"

"You don't expect them to stay with us do you? What kind of test is that if your Guardian is with you?" He tied his horse's rein to a sapling in a manner so the horse could graze.

She didn't reply, mimicking what he did with her horse.

"Time to gather firewood. You start over there," he said, pointing east.

After leaving the campsite, Tristine's gaze shifted about in search for wood. Even though her pupils were adjusted to the darkness, it was difficult seeing everything. Several times she tripped over a stump, root, or half-buried log while gathering wood. Along with the unfamiliar surroundings and sounds, the nights grew chilly as autumn drew near. She didn't know how far she traveled in collecting wood when she turned to go back to the campsite. Suddenly she realized she did not pay attention to any landmarks and couldn't remember which way to go to return the campsite. A small seed of fear started in the gut, but she swallowed it back.

"I'm not alone in the dark. Nigel's nearby and so are Armus and Avatar. I only need to find my way back," she told herself.

She headed in the direction she believed she came from, but soon found it was the wrong way so she retraced her steps to where she began. She heard a loud croaking sound close to her right ear, startling her. Upon another croaking, she recognized the sound of a tree frog. Still, it forced her to listen and in doing so she heard what she thought were footsteps.

Must be to be Nigel, Avatar or Armus.

"No, Guardian warriors would not make a sound. Unless they want me to know where they are," she said to herself yet raised her voice while speaking. She paused to listen for a reply and heard more footsteps. "Nigel?"

She moved in the direction of the footsteps. When she stopped again to listen the footsteps also stopped. She saw no sign of the campsite. Turning around, her breath caught in her throat at seeing a wolf staring at her. Once the shock wore off, she recalled her mother telling her when one wolf was seen, more could be lurking about since they tended to hunt in packs.

"Torin?" she blurted out the name of the wolf that aided her parents years ago before they became king and queen. "No, you can't be Torin, he'd be old or dead by now." The wolf kept staring at her. The small seed of fear grew. "Armus," she whispered in fear, standing rock still and clenching the wood.

In the nearby trees, Armus and Avatar watched her encounter with the wolf. Armus stepped forward in answer to her call, but Avatar stopped him.

"No. Wren won't hurt her."

When Armus didn't respond, Tristine spoke to the wolf. "Are you part of the test? I hope so, because this isn't fun." Snarling, the wolf lowered its head, appearing ready to attack. She threw the wood at the wolf and blindly ran off.

"Nigel!" she screamed and burst through a set of low shrubs and found herself back at the campsite.

Nigel now wore his cloak and tended a fire over which hung a rabbit, skinned and cooking on a spit. "Took you long enough."

Flushed and confused, she tried to catch her breath. "Didn't you hear me? A wolf— " She stopped at seeing his scolding glare.

"You went in that direction, so what are you doing coming back a different way?" he asked, motioning with the stick he used to stoke the fire. She grew sheepish, so he said, "You didn't pay attention to where you were going and got lost. Worse could have happened to you than running into a wolf."

"I could have been killed," she insisted. When he simply looked at her to the contrary, she became suspicious. "Why didn't it attack?"

"Why do you think?"

"Armus and Avatar—No, Wren." Angry, she sat by the fire. "Why?"

"To teach you a lesson about paying attention to where you are in the forest, especially at night."

She frowned and tried to contain her annoyance. "Did Wren help you with the fire and rabbit?"

"I started the fire but she provided the rabbit since we arrived too late to set a trap." He reached over and took her hand. "Tristine, camping and hunting are not only about sleeping out at night. You must take all the skills you've learned and use them."

"I suppose next you'll say I'm acting like a foolish child."

"No," he said with a soft smile. "Naïve, but not foolish." He squeezed her hand before tending to the rabbit. "Don't feel bad, I didn't do so great my first time out."

She rubbed her hands and sat closer to the fire.

"It'll grow colder. Fetch the bedrolls."

She went to do as instructed, putting on her cloak before fetching the bedrolls. When she returned to the fire, he had his cowl up against the growing chill.

"Arrange them near the log."

"Why?" she asked, yet followed his instructions.

"The log will provide protection by hiding us from sight on one side. I'll sleep in front of you for added protection."

"I thought snakes and other vermin hide under logs."

187

"Some do, only you're not going to sleep with your back against the log." He grinned and pretended not to watch her move her bedroll away from where she placed it against the log.

She caught his effort to hide his amusement and gave him a mocking smirk. Returning to the fire, she sat opposite him, removed her bow and laid it on the ground beside her. The small quiver remained strapped to the side of her belt in a way that didn't encumber her sitting on the ground. "Now what?"

"We wait until the rabbit is done and eat." He partially raised his covered head while speaking.

She balked in fright at seeing the firelight and cowl casting eerie dark shadows across his face.

"What?"

"N—nothing," she stammered, looking down to warm her hands.

"No, something frightened you. What was it?"

Nervous, she glanced across to him. He moved and now most of his face was in shadow. "Your cowl. In the firelight it made strange shadows across your face. It didn't look like you. It was dark and mysterious."

"Oh, is that all," he chuckled.

"You don't have to laugh at everything I say and do!"

"I'm not laughing at you. Actually this whole experience is reminding me of my first night. I greatly amused Father by my reactions and concerns."

She scowled and huffed a disheartened grunt. "This isn't turning out like I hoped. I'm doing everything wrong."

He moved to sit beside her and embraced her about the shoulders. "No, you're not. And I was wrong to laugh. I'm sorry. I won't tease you again, I promise."

"And I'll try to do better."

"You're doing fine. The best way to learn is by doing and when you make a mistake, correct it and do it over again. Ahhh!" he exclaimed at seeing the rabbit flare in a flame. The spit was hot, and he juggled it while taking it off, trying not to burn his hands.

She gabbed a corner of her cloak and took hold of the spit before he dropped the rabbit in the dirt.

"Good catch." He blew on his hands.

She placed the rabbit and spit on top of several pieces of wood so it hung in way to easily be carved. "Are you burned?"

"No. It doesn't look too bad. Check if it's cooked through."

She used her knife and deftly cut the carcass. "Ay." She cut off a leg and gave it to him.

In silence they ate, sharing a flagon of cider. She jumped at hearing an owl's screech and its shadowy figure swoop down out of the trees. He clamped his mouth shut in an attempt to stifle a chuckle. His mirth was cut short at hearing an angry, squealing grunt and a wild boar appearing on the edge of camp about twenty feet across from them.

"Another one of Wren's tests," she snickered and continued eating.

"I don't think so," he whispered in warning. He warily eyed the beast and carefully moving his left hand to restrain her. "Stay still. Don't make any sudden moves and it won't charge." He slowly moved his right hand toward his dagger, his focus on the boar.

She sat frozen, staring at the boar, which kept grunting at them. She shifted her glance to Nigel in time to see his hand take the hilt of his dagger. "You're not going challenge it, are you?" Her whispered words filled with fear and anxiety.

"No, but if it charges, I'll distract it. You shoot it."

She inched her hand along the ground toward her bow. The moment she grabbed the bow a wolf emerged from the trees next to her. She bit her lip to keep silent, but the wolf focused on the boar. The boar pawed the ground and grunted a warning at the wolf. The wolf snarled, showing its fangs. At the same time, the animals charged each other.

Nigel seized Tristine, pulling her to her feet and away from the animals now locked in deadly combat. The battle was ferocious with the snarling wolf trying to take down the squealing, angry boar. One ear-piercing squeal made them turn from their retreat. The boar wounded the wolf, which was yelping and retreating. The boar chased the wolf and both headed straight for them. Nigel drew his sword. Tristine quickly loaded her bow, aimed and fired at the boar. The arrow struck it in the chest, making it stumble forward in mid-stride, head over heels.

Nigel stood braced and ready for the wolf but the animal altered its course and disappeared into the forest. For a moment they waited in anxious anticipation, watching the dying boar and for signs of the wolf.

"Are you all right?" he asked.

She was breathing hard, clenching her bow, staring at the boar. "I think so. You?"

"I'm fine." He approached the boar and heard guttural sounds at first then silence. He prodded the boar using the tip of his sword. There was no reaction or movement. "Looks like we'll have a boar to take back. Nice shot."

"I'm beginning to think I don't like being out in the woods. That's the second beast I had to shoot in self-defense."

"Wild animals are one of the dangers." He fetched a rope from his saddle and returned to the boar.

"What are you doing?"

"I'm going to hang the carcass from that tree. Doing so will keep it from wolves, foxes, wild dogs and other night predators. In the morning we'll cut it down." Once he securely tied the boar, he tossed the other end of the rope over a nearby branch approximately twelve feet off the ground. "Fetch Malin and bring him here."

She did so and held the bridle. He wrapped the rope around the pommel in such a way that the rope was taut, with a good bit of excess hanging off the saddle. He led Malin away from the tree, raising the boar's carcass off the ground. He made the horse walk twice around a nearby tree.

"Hold him still while I tie off the rope."

Once again she followed his instructions and saw him use the excess to secure the rope to the tree before unwinding the rope from the pommel. The carcass slipped slightly but remained suspended in the air.

"Done," he said with satisfaction. He tethered Malin beside Alden. "We can tell father you killed your first boar to go along with that first stag."

She looked at the hanging boar and smiled.

"I don't know about you, but I'm tired." He yawned and returned to the fire.

She joined him. "I'm not sure if I can sleep. Everything is so unpredictable out here."

"You should try." He stoked the fire then tossed on another log. "Lie down. I said I'd sleep in front of you for protection. There's nothing to fear."

"Tell that to the boar," she groused. She followed his instruction and lay down.

Nigel sat by the fire, poking at the embers. He thought to wait until Tristine fell asleep before lying down, but she squirmed in trying to get comfortable. Finally she grunted and turned toward him.

"Why are you having a hard time getting to sleep? I told you I'd watch over you."

"I told you I don't think I can sleep. The ground is cold and hard, and despite the sounds there is an uneasy feeling to the dark I've never felt before." She drew her cloak and blanket close about her.

He moved from the fire to lie on his back on his bedroll. "Ay. There is a different sensation sleeping outdoors than in a bed. Look up."

She rolled over onto her back. Being in a clearing, the sky was visible through the trees. Against the blackness shone numerous stars of varied brightness, some clustered together to form what appeared to be a trail, others creating shapes, while others stood alone.

"You can't see those in your bedroom," he said.

"Gulliver told me he uses the stars to navigate the sea."

"Ay." He glanced from the sky to Tristine. She focused on the stars. "Sometimes I count them to see how many there are."

"Well, there's a big one over there. And one there, two there."

He grinned. "You see how many you can count silently and I'll see how many I count."

The challenge of counting stars didn't last too long because within a few moments, her eyelids fluttered. He tried not to let her see him smile when she yawned and finally closed her eyes.

Armus and Avatar drew their swords ready to intervene when Tristine shot the boar and the wolf ran off. They stood guard watching Nigel and Tristine bed down for the night. They relaxed upon seeing Wren. At least Avatar did, Armus wasn't happy.

"Cut that a little close, don't you think?" he scolded her.

"What are you talking about?"

"What do you mean, 'What are you taking about?' The boar nearly attacked them!" he said, his voice rising.

"Shhhh!" warned Avatar.

"I didn't do anything with a boar," she spoke in a lower voice.

"What about the wolf that attacked the boar?" asked Armus, lowering his voice.

"I don't know what you're talking about. I challenged Tristine as planned, nothing else."

Armus and Avatar exchanged glances of concern before Avatar explained to Wren; "A boar entered camp and was about to charge them when a wolf appeared and attacked the boar. The boar wounded the wolf and it retreated in the direction they fled. We were about to intervene when Tristine shot the boar and the wolf ran off. We thought it was you. At least the wolf."

Her brows leveled at hearing the disturbing story. She shook her head. "No."

"Did you sense any evil from the creatures this night?" Armus asked her.

"No. You?"

Armus didn't respond, chewing on his lower lip and regarding the campsite, guarded and thoughtful.

"We didn't," Avatar said to Wren, then he spoke to Armus, "This was a coincidence, which means she can claim the boar as a trophy."

"One I wish she had gotten another way. I think they've had enough excitement for one night. We'll create a defensive perimeter."

Avatar stopped Armus when he turned to leave. "Do you really want to interfere now? She's done well. Let her finish the night without help." Armus grew rigid in resistance, so Avatar continued his argument. "I understand. I felt the same when Nigel spent his first night out and Kell prevented me from helping when I realized he was about to fall into the deep sinkhole he couldn't see. Ellis and Darius rescued him without our help and fortunately, he only caught a bad cold. Kell argued any interference could nullify Nigel's accomplishment and I didn't want that since I knew how important succeeding meant to him. It's the same with Tristine. If you interfere and she finds out she may become resentful since she wouldn't have earned the right to hunt with her father on her own."

"He's right. I don't think you want that for her," said Wren.

Armus reluctantly agreed. "All right. But if one more danger presents itself or I sense the slightest hint of evil, I will act to protect my charge."

Avatar raised his hands in a mock surrender. "I won't stop you."

At a rustling sound near his ear, Nigel's eyes snapped open. He knew he fell asleep, but didn't know for how long. By the amount of gray light, he realized it was early dawn. He heard the rustling again and close to his head. A squirrel dashed from beside the log to a tree. He felt movement beside him. Tristine awoke.

"Morning, sleepy-head."

"Morning?" she echoed in surprise. "I slept through the night?"

"That you did. I told you there was nothing fear." He stood to stretch out the kinks. "Come. Let's fetch the boar, clean up the campsite and head home."

Tristine scrambled to her feet when she didn't see the boar hanging from the tree. "Where's my boar?"

"I don't know—" he began.

"Here," a voice said. Armus and Avatar held the bridles of their saddled horses with the boar placed behind Malin's saddle.

193

"We didn't think you'd want to waste any time returning with such a prize," said Armus. He smiled and winked at Tristine.

She hugged him. "Oh, Armus! I did it!"

"Indeed you did, little one. I never doubted you."

Avatar cocked a contrary brow. Fortunately her back was turned so she didn't see his expression, but Nigel saw and privately said to Avatar, "We have to talk about last night."

Two and a half hours later they returned to Waldron. The day's activities were well under way. At the stables Tristine instructed a groom to take the boar to Cook before she and Nigel went inside the main building. Breakfast was over, but Nigel ordered food prepared and brought to the king's study, the most likely place to find Ellis. Sure enough, he was at work with Darius and Kell in attendance.

"Father! Uncle," she cheered upon entrance.

Both accepted her embrace. "I take it all went well," said Ellis.

"Better than that. I killed a boar!"

Ellis' initial pleasure turned to surprise. "What?"

"It came into camp and when the wolf—"

"Wolf?" he echoed, an impulsive glance to Avatar and Armus, who stood beside Kell.

"I think you should start from the beginning," Armus said to her.

Ellis, Darius and Kell listened to the tale with great interest, especially the part about the boar and the wolf. Armus and Avatar did not add or correct anything Tristine or Nigel said. They no sooner finished telling their tale when servants arrived bringing food.

Mixed emotions played across his face as Ellis watched them sit at a table to eat.

"You expected the night to pass without incident?" asked Darius.

"I had hoped so. It did for Nigel."

"Falling into a sink hole filled into waist deep muddy water and catching a cold is hardly uneventful," snickered Darius.

194

"Better than nearly being attacked by a boar and wolf."

"We wouldn't have let it happen, Sire," said Armus.

"So Wren sent the wolf," said Ellis, a relieved smile appearing.

"Er, no," said Avatar, which drew an annoyed look from Ellis. "Wren tested Tristine as planned, but the boar coming was not by her design and the wolf—was just a lone wolf. When the beasts fought, Nigel and Tristine retreated into the trees. We were about to intervene when she shot the boar and the wolf ran off."

"I thought you said Wren wasn't controlling the wolf?" asked Darius.

"She didn't, and was as surprised as we were."

Concerned, Ellis turned to where Tristine and Nigel ate and conversed, unaware of any disturbance. "Did you sense any evil?"

"No, Sire. There was nothing unusual about either animal. In fact, they brought the boar home and sent it to Cook for dressing."

With probing eyes, Ellis regarded the warriors. "You sensed nothing unusual all night?"

"No, Sire. We would have acted if we felt the slightest hint of evil," replied Armus.

"Then she did everything on her own?"

Armus smiled, wide and proud. "Ay. Given time, her skills will be as keen as the Daughter of Allon with courage equal to the Son of Tristan to down a charging boar by a single shot to the chest."

Impressed, Darius whistled under his breath.

Ellis gripped Armus' arm and said, "Thank you." He crossed to the table and sat with his children, Darius also joining them.

Kell motioned his fellow Guardians from the room, leaving the mortals some privacy.

"Now aren't you glad you didn't interfere?" Avatar asked Armus.

"I knew she could do it," replied Armus with a cocky grin. "Still," he continued, his smile turning into a thoughtful expression, "while we watched them I got a sense of a deeper purpose than simply passing the night outdoors. A sense of preparation."

195

Avatar sent an irked frown to Kell, the captain returning a look of warning. The exchange made Armus curious.

"Is there something I should know? If it's about Tristine, I have a right to know."

"No, not Tristine," chided Avatar.

"Then what?

"Nothing for you to be concerned about," was the rough response.

Kell's swift grab of Armus stopped him from replying. At the captain's prompting nudge, Armus withdrew a short distance, yet remained near the study door. "What's wrong?" Kell asked Avatar.

Before replying, Avatar tossed a side-glance at Armus, who pretended not to be paying attention, despite still appearing put out. Avatar's voice was tight, yet low for privacy. "For the past week, he's experienced the same nightmare. The night before we left, we went to the chapel and he searched through prophecy. Something struck him. I don't know exactly what or how, only he asked me about the Great King and believes there is a connection to his nightmares."

"Interesting. I've sensed no connection."

"It wouldn't be the first time," groused Avatar, to Kell's chagrin. "Well, you've said the Daughter of Allon can have keener senses than you in regards to some matters. Why should Nigel be different? He bears both her blood and the Son of Tristan."

"Ay. There is something happening within the family that defies my sense to understand and Jor'el isn't answering my inquiries. All we can do is wait and be ready for when it does become clear."

"That's not very helpful."

"Agreed, but it doesn't change our duty." He nodded to Armus and spoke in a marked tone of authority. "A duty we *all* take seriously, especially involving personal charges."

Avatar flashed a rueful grin. "I owe him an apology."

"Good. For a moment I thought about letting him knock some sense into you." Kell returned to the study.

Avatar approached Armus. "Sorry for being so gruff."

Armus nodded in acknowledgment. "Is there anything I can do to help?"

Avatar sighed and shook his head. "Kell can't even offer advice."

To this, Armus' brows leveled in concern. "That's unusual."

"Ay. And it's getting worse."

Armus tried to be supportive and encouraging. "The answer will come in time."

"I pray the answer is sooner than later."

In sober silence they waited in the hall for their charges.

Chapter 12

OVER THE NEXT TWO WEEKS the hive of activity around Waldron increased in preparation for Tristine's Coming of Age Banquet. Since a total of three weeks separated the Morvenian departure and her banquet, most of the Council Members remained within the vicinity of Waldron rather than returning home only to journey back shortly thereafter.

Fortunately, harvest would not begin until a week after the banquet. A time when the lords were busy in their provinces bringing in the crops and preparing for winter. It was also the start of the fall hunting season. Tristine eagerly looked forward to this time since she earned the right to finally participate with her father, uncle and brother. Being credited with her first stag and boar were added bonuses in her favor. She enjoyed the gallop and pursuit, which is why it was so frustrating riding Caleigh and Malin; older, smaller and slower horses. Perhaps now her father would permit her to ride Kerrick, Chava or any of the other horses more fit for the hunt.

The day of the banquet arrived, and Tristine rose extra early. Necie accompanied her as they made their way down the hall of the family quarters towards the back stairs. Neice yawned, listening to Tristine chatting about the day.

198

"I should ask Father to go hunting this morning and down a buck for the banquet."

Necie shrugged, yawning again.

"You can't go anywhere," began Ellan. She came up from behind them. "You must remain here to receive homage from Court."

"What?"

Ellan scoffed with disapproval. "Don't you recall anything Mother told you these last few days? After breakfast you will be properly prepared to face Court for the rest of the day. You can't show up in breeches, looking a mess."

"I will only be gone a few hours at most."

"You're incorrigible. Your day is here and all you care about is making a fool of yourself by chasing stupid animals."

"How is hunting making a fool of myself? I've proven I'm capable."

Ellan's hands went to her hips. "You have other responsibilities and must face those starting today."

"You're not Mother or Father to tell me what to do. Just because you can't do anything but look pretty in gowns don't take your lack of skills out on me."

Ellan gasped in outrage, her fists balling in anger and she marched away.

Nigel arrived when Ellan stormed off. "What was that about?"

"She tried to tell what to do today, as if she has authority over me."

"She may not have the authority, but she knows what she's talking about in regards to today," he corrected her.

"I suppose," she begrudgingly said. "She's so bossy. She can never say anything nice. It's always 'Do this, Tristine. Don't do that. You can't act like this any more. You must act this way.' Well, I don't want to act like her! Boring and frivolous. Good for nothing but a dress mannequin."

Necie tried to stifle both a giggle and a yawn only ended up yawning.

Nigel chuckled at Necie's reaction yet spoke to Tristine. "You don't have to act like Ellan, but now that you are an adult, you will have to alter some of your behavior."

199

"I know, but I should be allowed to change in ways best for me, not to suit her."

He chuckled. "Can't argue with you there."

She took his arm. "Good, because I don't want to argue with you. I'm hungry. Let's go eat breakfast."

Ellan pushed past servants, soldiers, and anyone else making preparation for the banquet in an effort to leave the activity behind. Morrell weaved his way through the mass of mortals to follow her. Fortunately being seven and a half feet tall, he easily saw her head for the main gate. Once outside Waldron, he overtook her on the bridge across the dry moat.

"What upset you?"

"Tristine, who else? Ever since the boar she's been insufferable!"

"I thought she was always insufferable," he dryly commented.

She snorted in great annoyance. "Well, she's worse. You think she owned the world. I wish I could find a way to avoid the banquet."

He led her out of the way of traffic. "Are you so jealous?"

She shrugged, frustration filling her face. "I don't know. Everyone is so pleased by everything she does."

"That's not entirely true. She has tried your parent's patience on many occasions. Most recently in dealing with the prince and his relation to the Morvenian princess. After tonight, things will get back to normal and she'll have to behave like an adult."

She glanced up at him batting coquettish eyes and said, "Is there anyway you can help me avoid this evening?"

He sighed and scowled. "You know I help you within reason, but your responsibility to the king is not a area I want to interfere." Seeing she wasn't convinced, he continued. "It would be no different than Armus helping Tristine in the ways you find fault."

Annoyed, she stomped her foot and headed back inside the gate.

Morrell pursed his lips in irritation before turning to follow his charge. He just reached the gate when he became hit by intense pain and staggered into the wall, holding his head. A supportive arm encircled his waist. Wren.

"Morrell? What's wrong?"

He didn't answer, mercilessly rubbing his temples. He staggered a few steps before falling to his knees, Wren beside him. Concerned, she looked about for help and saw a pair of warriors sitting on a nearby wagon watching the mortals making preparation.

"Ewert! Bailey! Help me with Morrell."

The warriors responded to her summons. Each took Morrell by an arm and helped him to sit on a bench away from the activity.

"What happened?" asked Bailey.

"I don't know." Her focus was on Morrell, who looked pale.

He closed his eyes and swallowed back the pain. "It's passing now."

"What?" asked Ewert.

"I guess it's what mortals call a headache."

"We don't get headaches."

"Take him to the Guardian quarters. I'm going to fetch Eldric," said Wren.

"I don't need Eldric. I'm fine now." Morrell stood, but swayed and was caught by Bailey to keep from falling.

"Take him," she said Ewert and Bailey before heading off to find Eldric.

Although Guardians didn't require sleep, furnished quarters were included in the construction of Waldron. The rooms were mostly used for privacy during meditation or a retreat from dealing with mortals. Morrell sat on the edge of one of the four beds in the chamber. Ewert and Bailey remained with him. Wren arrived, bringing Eldric and Kell.

"You didn't need to bring Kell," chided Morrell.

"She didn't bring me. When a Guardian is hurt I want to know what's wrong."

"Let's take a look at you." Eldric lifted Morrell's head to look into his eyes.

"I'm fine. It's passed now. Ask them," he said of Ewert and Bailey. "I walked in the here on my own power."

Eldric ignored Morrell's tirade. "What did the pain feel like?"

201

"Er, sharp, stabbing all over my head, but especially behind my eyes."

"Have you ever felt that type of pain before?" Eldric examined Morrell's head for signs of injury.

"No ... er, maybe," he reluctantly answered.

"Maybe?" asked Kell.

Morrell shrugged. "I experienced all types of pain in Dagar's dungeon."

"Could this be a residual effect from the torture?" Kell asked Eldric.

The physician thoughtfully regarded Morrell a moment before replying. "No other Guardian has complained about lingering affects since being restored."

"Vidar wasn't tortured," chided Morrell in refute. "Gulliver only mildly beaten while I lost the use of my arm and some of my faculties back then."

"And Elgin? He was almost beaten to death," said Wren, defensive.

Morrell didn't reply. His sour scowl spoke enough of a disputing answer.

"Captain, I'd like to take him to Melwynn for further observation," said Eldric.

"No!" insisted Morrell, bolting to his feet. "I'm fine. See. I'm standing on my own two feet with no ill effects." He turned from Eldric to Kell. "Captain, I tell you I'm fine."

"Eldric's not so certain."

"This pain has never happened before."

"And blacking out and not remembering where you were at the fair?"

"That was traced back to the Morvenian stones."

For a moment, Kell studied Morrell. His pallor appeared fine and the familiar stubbornness shown in the amber eyes, so outwardly he appeared normal. "Very well. But if this happens again, you will go to Melwynn," he said in tone unwilling to accept any dispute.

"Ay, Captain."

Kell motioned for Eldric to leave with him, and in the hall, questioned the physician. "Did you sense anything wrong?"

"No, and I saw no sign of head injury. Still, his complaint is very unusual."

Kell nodded, still very thoughtful. "I'll tell the others to keep an eye on him."

Now at breakfast, Tristine didn't even get an opportunity to broach the subject of hunting when her mother began informing her of the day's schedule. Ellan arrived and Tristine saw the smug expression on her sister's face at hearing Shannan describe Tristine's duties. She glanced to Nigel, who heaved a careful shrug. She hated Ellan being right, more for the attitude it invoked than the sheer facts of the matter. Still, this was her day and she determined not to let Ellan's superior attitude ruin it for her. Ellan may not have the skills she did, but she was taught the same Court etiquette and requirements. If anyone had the advantage, she did. So, when breakfast concluded, she willingly accompanied Shannan.

All the same, Tristine never liked being fussed over, prodded and confined in the many layers of high Court fashion on those occasions requiring her presence. Now, it would become more frequent so she tried to pay attention to the instructions Shannan gave the servants waiting on her, first with a bath then selecting her gowns for the various activities. A few times, she grew impatient and Shannan intervened by speaking words of encouragement for her endurance, and praise for what the day meant. Finally her tolerance ended and she stormed away from the servants. Only partially dressed, she wore a corset, shift and underskirts with her hair in the middle of being pampered.

Shannan dismissed the servants, leaving she and Tristine alone in the chamber. Armus kept his vigil by the door. "You're doing very well. I thought you where going to lose your temper long before now."

"Am I to spend the whole day being stuffed into clothes with my hair burned and ripped from my head?"

Shannan laughed. "This is just the first step."

Tristine caught Armus' amused glance. "You don't need to enjoy this."

Shannan smiled. "He's recalling when I first became queen. I had difficulty adjusting to so many people helping me. Up until then I spent my life running free in the forest, not contained within a castle." She played with

Tristine's hair, a tender smile appearing. "Like me, you prefer the freedom of the outdoor life and he knows that. Right?

"Indeed. The stag and boar are only some of the ways you are like your mother."

Shannan continued her discourse, "But we were born for a purpose. I too reunited the Guardians and mortals and helped your father take back the throne. You were born to carry on the legacy."

"Nigel is to be king. I'm only third."

She took Tristine by the shoulder and looked her squarely in the eye. "The same royal blood flows through your veins. Your name bears witness to your heritage back to Tristan, Allon's most beloved king. In fact, your father named you after him. I named your siblings and chose another name for you; but when he held you for the first time, it was the name he uttered and insisted. Something he did not do with the others."

"Really?" asked Tristine, fascinated by what she heard.

"Ay, so just because Nigel is heir, doesn't lessen your position. Today you take your rightful place among the adults and begin fulfilling the duties and responsibilities to which you were born. To which your name entitles you. Do you understand?"

Tristine smiled and nodded. She took a deep preparatory breath. "I'm ready to continue."

Shannan grinned and motioned to Armus, who recalled the servants.

In the stables, Ellis, Darius, Nigel and Angus watched a groom attempt to brush and saddle Dunstan; only the horse acted contrary.

"You really believe he's suitable for Tristine?" asked Darius.

Nigel smiled in beaming confidence. "I'm certain he is."

Ellis smirked and shook his head at Darius. "You're the one who defended her for shooting the boar. Why doubt her in this?"

"Who said doubt? I'm just concerned for the horse."

Angus laughed, poking Nigel, who just rolled his eyes in amusement.

Necie came running into the stable. "Father! Mother wants to know when you're ready for her to bring Tristine down."

Ellis noticed the groom finished with Dunstan. "Tell her we're ready." Necie dashed from the stables.

"This should to be interesting," said Darius, merrily.

Ellis spoke a few words to the groom before Darius, Nigel, Angus and he moved to wait in the Grand Courtyard near the main entrance of the castle. Nigel grinned from ear to ear. "Keep smiling like that and she'll become suspicious."

"Sorry, Father. I can't wait for her to see him."

"Shh!" warned Darius.

Tristine emerged from the door with Shannan, Necie, Ellan and Arista close behind her. She wore a beautiful russet and gold gown, her golden hair fixed in a most becoming style. Gone was her tomboyish appearance, replaced by a beautiful young woman.

"Father. Mother said you wanted to see me," she said, a hint of excitement in her voice.

Ellis smiled, pride filling his gaze. "You look wonderful. I hardly recognized you."

"Indeed. You have passed from a child into a woman," said Darius. He kissed her cheek.

She blushed. "I'm not used to this yet."

"My precocious little sister all grown up," said Nigel, a bit affected in speech.

"She does clean up well," said Ellan, smiling.

Ellis took Tristine's hand, his smile turning a touch melancholy. "This is your day and I must admit I've looked forward to it with mixed feelings. Another daughter crossing the threshold. Seeing you, those feeling are well founded. There won't be a man able to keep his eyes off you this evening and I'm already worried."

Tristine flushed, an embarrassed grin plastered on her face.

Catching a prompting glance from Shannan, Ellis said, "Before the day gets away from us, we have presents for you. Now, close your eyes." When she did so, he began to lead her across the Courtyard. She balked at moving. "Have no fear and let me lead you."

"Where are we going?"

"Not far, but no peeking. You must keep your eyes closed until we tell you to open them."

"All right."

Once at the stables Ellis motioned to several servants. They came forward, each holding a large wrapped item. Shannan took the largest one while Necie the smaller gift.

"Hold out your hands," said Shannan. After Tristine did so, Shannan unwrapped the gift and set it across Tristine hands. She flinched at feeling the weight, but kept her eyes closed. "This is from me. Open your eyes."

Tristine gasped. In her hands, she held a beautifully crafted bow of rosewood with gold tip nocks, handle and arrow pass.

Shannan nudged Necie, who stepped forward, unwrapping her gift. "This is from me."

The gift was a leather quiver engraved with the royal crest and matching rosewood and gold accents.

"I think this is worth it, just seeing her speechless," said Ellan to Nigel.

Nigel widely smiled in anticipation, watching Tristine hug Shannan and Necie, repeatedly saying thank you. "Close your eyes again," he said when she finished.

"We'll take these for now." Shannan took the bow and quiver from Tristine and handed them back to the servants.

"I said, close your eyes," insisted Nigel.

Tristine did so, her smile beaming.

Nigel made a hand signal and nearby servants started making noise to cover the sound of hooves on the cobblestone as a groom brought Dunstan to Nigel.

Tristine flinched, startled by the loud noise. "What's that?"

Ellis quickly stepped in front of her to block her view in case she inadvertently opened her eyes. "Keep your eyes closed."

When the noise stopped, Nigel said, "This is my gift and I hope you enjoy it for many years to come." He took her hand and guided it until she touched Dunstan's muzzle.

Her eyes snapped open upon touching the muzzle and hearing the soft grunt of a horse. Her breath caught in her throat, thunderstruck surprise on her face. Dunstan was a fine looking sorrel gelding complete with a magnificent saddle and bridle. Tears swelled and her lower lip quivered. She flung her arms around Nigel's neck, unable to speak, a soft whimper against his shoulder.

Her reaction stupefied him. "I didn't mean to make you cry."

"I thought I'd be stuck with Caleigh and Malin the rest of my life!"

Ellis heartily laughed. "The horse maybe from Nigel, but the saddle is from me, and the bridle from Ellan."

Tristine embraced Ellis and even hugged Ellan. "This is the best birthday ever!"

"To think, all we got her was the gown she's going to wear tonight," quipped Darius to Arista.

"I thought it was from all of us?" said Angus.

"Of course that's what your father meant," said Arista.

Tristine looked with some confusion to Shannan. "I thought you said I was going wear my white and gold gown?"

"I had to tell you something to shut you up."

Dunstan snorted and tossed his head to get attention.

"I can't believe I now have a horse and not a pony. Can I get on him?"

"I don't think so. If you notice it isn't a sidesaddle. You can't ride that way for hunting," said Ellis.

"Just for a moment. Please, Father."

"Very well." He positioned himself to help her mount. When her weight touched the saddle Dunstan grunted in annoyance and pulled from Nigel's grasp. For a moment everyone became concerned when Dunstan appeared ready to bolt.

"Shut the gate!" Ellis ordered. He reached for Dunstan only the horse avoided his effort.

Nigel tried to get Dunstan from the other side.

"Stop it! You're making it worse. I've got him," snapped Tristine. She gathered the reins and shifted position when he backed up, fighting her control.

"Let her be. She knows what she's doing," said Shannan.

Tristine began to ride Dunstan around the Courtyard; persistent in what direction she wanted him to go when he became contrary. Once he bucked and another time tried to rear, but she stubbornly remained on his back. After about ten minutes he calmed down and submitted to her control.

"Well, I'll be," muttered Darius, impressed.

"I told you she rode Balin. If you don't believe me, ask Mother, she was there," said Nigel.

Ellis tossed an askew glance to Shannan.

"You didn't think Allard willingly let her ride his horse, did you?" began Shannan. "Once she showed she was capable, we had no trouble convincing him we wanted to select from among Balin's offspring. We knew you wouldn't agree if you knew his sire. You would keep her on Caleigh and Malin until they died of old age."

With a sarcastic snort, Ellis said to Darius, "We've been played for fools."

"Speak for yourself. She's your daughter."

Tristine returned to where they stood watching and two grooms immediately came to help her dismount. One groom placed a set of block steps so she could get off more lady-like. She scratched Dunstan's cheek.

"I think we're going to get along just fine," she said. Dunstan rubbed his head against her, snorting in acknowledgement.

"That's all well and good, but you'll have to change and fix your hair," quipped Ellis.

"I didn't intend to get filthy," she said apologetically.

He smiled. "I know. Now, go, there is only an hour before the presentation."

The presentation to the Council began the festivities marking the day. In the Council Chamber, the Lords of Allon assembled. Accompanied by the adult members of the royal family, Ellis officially presented Tristine to the Council of Twelve. In recognition, the lords offered gifts from their provinces to the princess. From the Highlands, Fagan presented a small box filled with unrefined gold to be fashioned to her specifications. From the Northern Forest, Ned brought a finely crafted wooden jewelry box. Vicar Uriah gave a copy of Verse specially hand printed for her. Bosley brought fine woolen material woven in Midessex and suitable for hunting attire. From the East and West Coast, Hollis offered delicate imported linen for Tristine's bed while Mathias brought rare spices to season her meat. Erasmus gave healing ointments made from the water of the Delta spas, good for those occasional cuts and scratches common to hunting. From Lowland artisans, Zebulon presented a beautiful tapestry depicting the downing of a stag. The Meadowlands was not only known for its horses, but also for glassmaking and smithing of all kinds. Thus Allard's present was a beautifully engraved goblet commemorating her banquet. The North and South Plains were jointly renowned for their bountiful harvest of grain and beer and wine production. They generously supplied the wine for the banquet, naming the year's vintage after Tristine.

She was overwhelmed by the gifts and the flowery speeches several of the lords made, specifically Allard, Erasmus and Ned. Zebulon's words were surprisingly kind and courteous.

The last to make a presentation was Darius. The stunning necklace of silver, diamonds and sapphires once belonged to his mother and foster mother of Ellis. This was the most personally touching gift. Tristine grew misty-eyed when he placed it around her neck. Her smile shook with emotion in watching him bow and resume his place among the lords.

By his affected expression, Ellis was unaware of Darius' gift. Shannan must have known for she sent a smile to Darius after hearing Ellis do a soft clearing of the throat to regain his composure.

"Thank you, my lords, for so honoring my daughter," said Ellis.

"Ay. Thank you, my lords," said Tristine.

Ellis rising signaled the end of presentation and Tristine left with her parents, Ellan and Nigel. She wore the necklace while the rest of the gifts would be catalogued and properly used since some dealt with the evening's banquet.

Barely any conversation occurred before the head chambermaid and lady of protocol whisked Tristine back to her chamber to change for the banquet. For this preparation, Shannan would not be present. Tristine hoped to take the time to digest the day so far, but once more she was stuffed, prodded, hair fixed and adorned from head to toe in a stunning royal blue and silver gown from Darius and Arista.

At several points, Armus' diplomatic intervention prevented Tristine's frustration from being vented and aided the ladies in better serving the princess. When it came time for her to be escorted to the antechamber off the Great Hall, she declined anyone's aid except Armus. She held tight onto his arm, not speaking as her irritation turned to nervousness as they made their way to the antechamber. From there she would enter the Great Hall on the king's arm for all of Court to see. Upon arrival, fear crossed her face at seeing her parents speaking to Kell. They had not noticed her arrival.

Armus leaned down to speak in her ear. "You have nothing to fear."

"I don't want to do anything foolish this evening."

"You impressed the Council."

"That's different. I just stood there. Tonight I must dance and keep to my manners."

"Misnich, mo beag na te."

She recognized *mo beag na te,* since he called her 'my little one' all her life. In his chestnut eyes were encouragement and affection.

"Are you ready?" Ellis' question brought her to face him.

She swallowed back her nervousness to take his arm. "Ay."

Ellis widely smiled and patted her hand. "They are here to celebrate with you, so there is nothing to be nervous or frightened about." His gaze grew doting. "I, on the other hand, will be watching like a father hawk at any bachelor coming within ten feet of you."

She bashfully giggled. "I'm not pretty. Ellan's the beauty."

Ellis lifted her chin, his expression serious. "You're wrong. Ellan does possess an outward grace and charm, but your beauty is enhanced by an internal strength of character that radiates in your face and smile." He stroked her cheek. "Just like your mother, those attributes will never fade. In fact, they grow more precious and desirable as the years pass." He kissed her forehead.

"No fair making us teary-eyed before we enter," Shannan playfully chided.

A trumpet summoned, calling those in the Hall to give attention. Ellis drew Tristine to the threshold. When the Hall became silent, Kell moved to the middle of the room and introduced the king and queen. Everyone stood. Ellis escorted Tristine with Shannan following, escorted by Armus.

All formality of acknowledgement was given the royals in passing. Many smiled and nodded at Tristine during the walk from the back of the Hall to high table. Nigel and Ellan were already there. This night, Nigel sat one seat down from the place of honor he normally occupied beside Ellis, vacating the place for Tristine.

Her nerves were at the height of excitement, a blushing smile plastered on her face. When they reached high table everyone turned to give attention.

Ellis spoke, "Lords and ladies of Allon. This night marks a special occasion, the coming of age of a member of the royal family. It is my pleasure as a proud father and your king to present my second daughter, Princess Tristine."

A loud round of applause and cheers rose, making Tristine turn beet-red, her smile hurting because it couldn't grow any wider.

Darius raised his goblet and said, "A toast to Princess Tristine." He waited for everyone to raise their goblets before continuing. "May Jor'el's blessings be upon you. May he grant you a long and fruitful life in his service. May Jor'el grant us, the Court of your father, King Ellis, the Son of Tristan, the ability to serve you as we serve him and the rest of the royal family."

They all drank. Ellis motioned for Tristine to sit. Once she did so, everyone else sat and the feast began.

She received attention like never before. Oh, being a royal princess, she was accustomed to being well-treated and respected, but this night, even her parents took second place to her, something unusual. In the back of her mind, she knew it was only for this night, but she reveled in it. The enjoyment became momentarily interrupted when Ellis signaled the dancing to begin. The first dance would belong to him and Tristine.

She tried not to let her anxiety show when he offered his hand to lead her to the floor. All eyes watched them, and her heart raced with nervousness. He signaled the musicians to begin playing. Even though she knew the preplanned dance, her feet froze to the floor and her legs became paralyzed.

"Just concentrate on me," he whispered.

She followed his lead in a traditional folk dance, simple, yet merry. Halfway through the dance others joined them, Nigel with Shannan, Darius with Arista, and Wess with Ellan. Soon the rest of Court took to the floor and the dancing continued for several hours. Tristine danced twice more with Ellis, then Nigel, Darius, Wess and at least a dozen noblemen of Court. She was grateful when the entertainment began so she could rest her feet and catch her breath. Jugglers, acrobats, actors, dancing dogs and a man who performed without speaking a word, greatly amused the Court.

At one o'clock in the morning, the banquet ended and Tristine made her way back to her chamber accompanied by Nigel and Ellan. To her surprise and pleasure, Ellan was civil the entire night, and they laughed, joked and enjoyed themselves.

"How wonderful! I wish it didn't have to end," said Tristine.

"Ay, it was fun. Maybe now you'll see, being an adult isn't all bad," said Ellan.

"How about we all go riding tomorrow?"

"Sounds good to me," said Nigel, turning at Ellan, who agreed.

Tristine hugged them both before entering her chamber. "Oh, Armus, I never dreamed it would be so grand!"

"This is just the beginning of a new phase in your life, little one."

She did dancing moves in front of the full-length mirror. After a moment she stopped to regard the dress, but more so the necklace. "I hadn't noticed before how well the necklace compliments the dress."

"Both the necklace and dress have more meaning than you were told."

"I know this belonged to uncle and father's mother." She touched the necklace to once more admire it in the mirror.

"Ay, and I'm surprised Shannan didn't tell you the history of the dress. The gown was Lady's Agatha's wedding gown and given to Shannan to wear the day Court was first held at Waldron."

Tristine regarded the dress in the mirror. "So this is a family tradition."

"No. Ellan didn't wear the gown for her banquet," said Armus, growing thoughtful. "Come to think of it, more sentimental value has been placed on your banquet than hers."

"I wonder why?"

Armus' expression was slow to change from pondering. "It could simply be mortals expressing themselves in ways Guardians don't fully understand. I can say you are more like your parents than Ellan. Oh, there is a family resemblance and common traits easily seen in her. But you exhibit more similarities to Shannan in nature and action, while I clearly see Ellis in your face and mannerisms."

She looked back at her reflection with a small smile of satisfaction.

"If you're going to ride in morning, you should get some sleep."

"Ay. Call the maid to come help me. I can't get out of all these layers by myself."

213

Chapter 13

FOR THE NEXT FEW WEEKS, Tristine rode everyday the weather permitted. The first two outings were short since Dunstan needed a firm hand to control his tendency toward contrariness. By the end of the first week, he settled under her handling and eagerly greeted her in the stables every morning. In short, she won him over.

Most of the time Nigel accompanied her while Ellan went four times. Three times Ellis, Shannan, Darius, Arista and Angus went, making it a family occasion. Necie wasn't much for riding since her pony wasn't good at keeping up with the others. Tristine understood Necie's frustration. In an effort to accommodate Necie, she rode Malin one day. Dunstan showed his annoyance at being left behind by pawing the stable floor and snorting.

The beginning of the third week, Ellis joined Tristine and Nigel in the stable to prepare for their morning ride when a courier from Lord Hollis arrived.

"A report from Ambassador Emery, Sire." The courier handed him the document.

"I'm afraid this means Nigel and I won't be able to accompany you today," said Ellis.

"I understand, sir." She spoke to the grooms, "Put the horses up."

"You don't have stay."

214

"No, this is official court business. I should remain."

Ellis suppressed a smile and headed for the study, Tristine and Nigel following. Once there, they waited while he read.

Seeing Nigel's nervousness, she spoke to him a lower voice so not to disturb Ellis. "It may not be bad news. If they don't accept the terms you don't have to marry."

Nigel said nothing in reply.

Ellis spoke, unaware of Tristine's comment. "Well, Emery is making headway with the emperor. However—"

"However, what?" asked Nigel, anxious at the slight hesitation in Ellis's speech.

"The emperor insists you visit Morven like Kaleana visited Allon before any final decision is made about an alliance."

Nigel grew rigid, his expression worried.

Tristine noticed the immediate change in posture. "Father, must he go?"

Ellis regarded his children. Tristine appeared concerned, but Nigel looked troubled and slightly pale. "I'm not sure yet. This is a matter for consideration and prayer."

"Whoever Nigel marries will be Queen of Allon someday. Shouldn't she at least believe in Jor'el and not some ugly stone statues?"

Nigel winced and grimaced at Tristine's statement, yet avoided direct eye contact when Ellis tried to look at him while answering.

"True. And that is one of the considerations, along with Prophecy and the security of Allon." Ellis steered Tristine toward the door. "Go. I want to speak to Nigel in private."

He just closed the door on her exit when Kell and Darius arrived.

"Sire. Ambassador Lanzo is here," said Kell.

"Wonderful," snorted Ellis in annoyance. "As if I couldn't guess what he wants."

"Perhaps Dante wishes to offer congratulations on our victory," said Darius, his words dripping with sarcasm.

Ellis didn't accept Darius' ill humor. "Dante never sends Lanzo unless he wants something specific." He indicated the papers. "Emery's report."

"You think his arrival has something to do with the Morvenians?"

"Ay. He may not be aware of all the finer points, but Dante would not approve of us making an alliance with his sworn enemy."

"He can't dictate our foreign policy."

"Of course not. The problem will be how to strike a balance in maintaining good relations with Tunlund while not insulting Morven and possibly causing further conflict."

A murmur of distress escaped Nigel's tightly pressed lips.

"Sire, the only way to learn the answer is to speak to him," said Kell.

"Ay. Fetch him."

When Kell left, Ellis watched Nigel move to the window overlooking the Courtyard. The situation grew more complex. Then again, that was politics. The duty of a monarch was to keep politics in check by weighing the advantages and disadvantages of situations by how it affected his kingdom. Besides the plea from Tunlund for help eighteen months ago, the Morvenian proposal was the most serious foreign crisis to arise since Nigel came of age. Unlike the war, this issue was more personal, and could require great sacrifice on Nigel's part. Something Ellis didn't know if he could ask of his son. Personally he hoped the marriages of his children would be as blissful and beneficial as his to Shannan. Alas, what the heart of a father desired conflicted with the realities of ruling as king. He would choose mates for his children from others of royal blood. However, Tristine's simple statement of belief in Jor'el struck a deep nerve, and why he struggled over the proposal. He could only guess Nigel shared his struggle, but a good guess since he was training to be a Jor'ellian Knight. Perhaps after speaking to Lanzo, he and Nigel could talk in private.

Ellis caught Darius' concerned regard. He gave his brother a small grin and pat on the shoulder when passing to his desk.

A few moments later, Kell returned, escorting a tall elegant man in his early thirties with dark hair, pale blue eyes, shrewd brow and impeccable taste in wardrobe. Lanzo flashed a gallant smile and bowed to Ellis.

"Sire. Your Grace."

"Ambassador Lanzo. This is an unexpected pleasure," said Ellis.

216

Nigel's approach caught Lanzo's attention. "Ah, Your Highness. You have grown into a fine figure of man since I saw you last."

"Thank you, Ambassador."

"Your mother, the queen, is she well?"

"Very well, thank you."

Lanzo's returned to Ellis, his smile never fading. "I hear Princess Tristine is now of age. Would you allow me to offer her the compliments of Tunlund with this simple gift?" He pulled out a small, velvet covered box from the pocket of his jacket and opened it to show an exquisite ruby and silver ring.

Ellis took the ring to examine it. "It is lovely. You may present it to her later." He returned the ring to Lanzo, who placed it back in the box and put it in his pocket. "To what do we owe the pleasure of your visit?"

"My Lord King Dante wishes to express his deep gratitude for Allon's recent victory against our most *hated enemy*," said Lanzo. "We feel the loss of those noble sailors and marines like they were our own. As such, my lord king has sent a token for the widows and orphans. We realize it cannot compensate for the loss, but will provide some means for the difficult days to come."

"That is generous, and will be appreciated."

"What of your own numerous casualties?" asked Darius.

"They too received small compensation, but their sacrifice was their duty to Tunlund. For a man to lay down his life for someone he doesn't know in a foreign land is considered the most noble of sacrifices. The Morvenians know no such nobility." Lanzo sneered the last sentence.

"We hold the same sentiments, my lord."

Lanzo smiled. "I did not believe otherwise, Your Grace."

"How long are you planning to remain in Allon?" asked Ellis.

"Long enough to carry out my king's wishes. Unless there is urgent business that calls me home, or Allon desires to further strengthen our relationship."

"You just said there is nothing stronger than the shedding of blood."

Lanzo slightly flushed at the correction. "Indeed, Sire. Forgive me if you thought I spoke wrongly."

Ellis grinned. "You spoke eloquently. His Grace will see you to your quarters and later we will determine how to distribute your token."

"Thank you, Sire. Highness," Lanzo acknowledged before leaving with Darius.

"He knows about the Morvenian proposal."

"How can you tell?" asked Nigel in surprise.

Ellis cocked a sly brow. "You didn't catch his references to the *hated enemy*? Or how the Morvenians lack nobility and wanting Allon to make some show to strengthen our relationship? In subtle ways he was making the Tunlundian position clear without making direct reference to the Morvenian proposal or hinting he knew anything about it."

Nigel shivered, wringing his hand as if to warm them.

"Are you all right?"

A look of deseparation overcame Nigel and he bolted out of the room.

"Nigel!" Ellis hurried after him and into the hallway. Nigel ran down the galley way to the stairs.

Kell and Avatar waited. Curious, Avatar turned from the vanishing Nigel to Ellis, the latter motioning for him to follow.

"I believe I know what troubles him. We'll fetch him back, Sire." Kell followed Avatar.

Ellis returned to the study. Nigel being troubled upset him because it mirrored his own discord over the situation. He had to make a point of discussing the matter and once and for all put an end to this unnecessary tension. He hoped Kell and Avatar could stop Nigel from running off again so that would be possible.

Upset, Nigel ran through the Courtyard and toward the Chapel. Reading prophecy about the Great King helped to ease his mind, while the nightmares ceasing for a few days renewed his spirit that he made a connection and could cope with the situation. However, since Tristine's banquet the fear and the nightmare returned, and with greater intensity.

Each day the battle to contain his emotions grew more difficult, to the point where he felt unable to control his reaction and words. He was about to lash out at hearing Emery's report when Tristine spoke. Her question delayed his outburst for the moment while during Lanzo's interview he kept his hands clenched, nails digging into his palms to stay quiet.

His hurried footsteps echoed in the quiet Chapel and he stopped at the base of the altar. "Why?" he shouted in anger. His abrupt arrival and shouting disrupting those gathered to pray or quietly converse, but he ignored them to further demand, "What do you want from me?"

Avatar drew alongside Nigel, and motioned patience to those disturbed by the prince's outburst including the priest of the Chapel. "Let me handle him, Master Hampton."

Nigel balked under Avatar's grip. Kell arrived and took hold of Nigel's other arm.

"Come, Highness."

Nigel shook them off and headed for the Chapel gardens. Lashing out only offered momentary release of tension, but did nothing to quell his anxiety or help him find an answer. He knew Kell and Avatar followed and moved to a far corner of the garden.

Avatar took hold of Nigel to stop him. "What's wrong?"

Nigel hesitated to answer, so Kell added his prompting. "Jor'el is testing your faith and mettle. Your outburst tells me you know that, and even the reason why."

Nigel sighed and turned to Avatar, his expression and tone sheepish. "I haven't been completely honest about my dreams. I know what I'm running from." He motioned toward Kell. "He said it. Jor'el. He won't let my mind and spirit rest but I don't know how I can turn my back on my family, on my heritage!"

"Who said you had to do that?" asked Avatar.

"How else can the Prophecy of the Great King come to pass if I am heir?" argued Nigel, his voice thick with emotion. "The more complicated the situation gets, the more terrifying my nightmares become. I don't how much longer I can stand it, or keep it from him!" He turned to Kell, desperate and pleading.

"Then perhaps it's time you told him," said the captain calmly.

"Ay. He asked me about the statue in relation to the magic stones," said Avatar.

Nigel became confused. "But the nightmare started before they arrived."

"It's hard to believe so many things are coincidental. Your nightmares, Tristine, Necie and Ellis attacked by magical beasts of unknown origin, Morrell's strange behavior."

"The question of whether you are to be king or not, will be answered in time. But by allowing fear to rule, you keep from fulfilling your responsibilities," said Kell.

"As heir, my marriage is a responsibility I bear!"

"Defending Allon and honoring your father are also your responsibilities. By focusing on the one, you neglect the rest, and perhaps in doing so prevent the ultimate answer from coming."

Stymied by the rebuke, Nigel stared at Kell, who continued speaking.

"You just admitted that in your nightmares you are running from Jor'el, from his desire for you. Or at least your willingness to even consider what divine revelation you have been granted. Not many mortals are so privileged. Your father is highly favored. The answer may come from the Son of Tristan and not Avatar or me. Guardians don't hold all the answers where mortals are concerned."

Thunderstruck, Nigel sat on a bench to consider what Kell said. Could his refusal to speak to his father be preventing him from finding the answer? "I hadn't thought of it that way."

Avatar sat beside him. "You bravely faced the consequences of your actions with the Morvenians and it turned out well. Do so with your father and the outcome may surprise you."

Nigel nodded, his face and body growing relaxed. "I should start by returning and apologizing for running out."

He wasn't as hasty in his return to the study as his departure, although his steps were purposeful and he entered without hesitation. Ellis stood before the hearth and whirled about when someone arrived. Nigel was quick to speak.

"Father, before you say anything, I owe you an apology, not only for running out, but my moodiness of late. I've been thinking a lot, perhaps too much. If you permit, I'd like to propose a hunting trip to discuss what's been happening. The meadow we like east of Garwood, near the river."

Ellis smiled in relief. "I thought the same. Hunting is good there this time of year. And it will be nice to get away for a few days. We'll leave after Lanzo departs."

That afternoon, Ellis, Darius, Kell and Wess were with Lanzo at the storehouses near the postern gate taking an accounting of the compensation brought from Tunlund. Rather than bringing foreign currency, the tribute consisted of unrefined gold, cloth, silverware, jewelry, finely crafted leather goods and other sundry items. All the goods were of fine quality and craftsmanship. Most of the sailor's families would not have been able to afford such items. This gave them the option to keep them or sell some to meet their needs.

"I must say, I am very impressed, Lanzo. Tunlund has shown great forethought in bestowing such goods," said Ellis.

"As I said, Sire, we appreciate the sacrifice."

"My thanks to Dante. This is an act I will remember."

Lanzo wore a smug, pleased expression.

"Sire," began Darius, he, Wess and Kell were conversing to one side. "If the gold is divided up there would be six measures per family. While the goods can be distributed as needed, which should be left to Hollis since he knows them."

"So you suggest transporting all this back to Leith?" asked Lanzo.

"That's where it's needed."

"I suppose I should have left the tribute aboard ship."

"No," said Ellis. "You did right by bringing the goods to Waldron. Before you leave to help Darius and Hollis with the distribution, I will compose a letter to Dante expressing my compliments."

"Of course, Sire," said Lanzo, looking deflated.

Ellis asked Darius, "How long until you're ready for departure?"

"Day after tomorrow. I'll dispatch word immediately to Hollis." He turned to Kell, who nodded an acknowledgement and departed to handle the dispatch.

Ellis smiled and clapped a hand on Lanzo's shoulder. "That wasn't too difficult. And you get to dine with us the next two evenings."

Lanzo forced a toothy grin when Ellis steered him toward the main building. "I always look forward to my visits with Your Majesty, they are so invigorating."

"Frustrating is more like it," quipped Wess to Darius.

<hr />

The next evening, after dinner, Ellis and the family gathered in the private salon. Lanzo took leave to retire and Ellis began laughing when the door closed.

"You found what Lanzo said amusing?" asked Shannan.

Ellis composed himself to answer. "Enjoying his thwarting and inability to deal with it. He thought to use this trip and the goods to remind me of our alliance and alter our dealings with the Morvenians."

"He said that to you?" asked Tristine in surprise.

"Not directly, he knows better. His actions and veiled speech were thin disguises for his true mission."

"Couldn't they simply send the goods in gratitude?" asked Ellan.

"Oh, I don't doubt they're grateful. But Dante and Lanzo never do anything without a hidden motive or attempt to turn things to their advantage. I merely turned the tables. Allon will not be obligated. What can he do? Take the goods back to Tunlund?"

"He wouldn't dare," said Darius, laughing.

"Of course not." Ellis saw Tristine fretfully gazing at the ring Lanzo gave her and she wore on her right little finger. "Tristine?"

"Does his gift to me fall under suspicion like the Morvenians gifts?"

"No. Kell sensed nothing during inspection of the goods." He took her hand to admire the ring. "It's very nice."

She smiled. "I like it, and I don't like a lot of jewelry."

"Father," said Nigel. He gave Ellis a nod toward Shannan.

Ellis grinned with understanding and spoke to Shannan. "Madam, after our guest has departed, Nigel and I are going hunting near Garwood."

Tristine gaped in disappointed surprise. "What? That's days away. I thought I was going with you next time?"

"You will. This trip is for a reason."

"What reason?"

"Nigel and I have important matters to discuss in private and it would be better done away from Waldron, among the peace and quiet of the outdoors."

Shannan grew skeptical, even a bit concerned. "You have made a decision?"

"No. This will give us the opportunity to discuss the subject at length without interruption while prayerfully considering all aspects."

Shannan studied Ellis. He appeared calm and confident. "Very well."

"Just save a good stag for me," complained Tristine, which made Nigel and Ellis laugh.

The following morning, Darius and Lanzo prepared to leave with the Tunlundian token. A company of royal soldiers joined those of Baron Hollis' command who escorted Lanzo to Waldron. Ellis and Nigel wore hunting attire and bid the group farewell. They planned to leave shortly after the departure. Shannan and Ellan joined them in saying goodbye, but not Tristine.

After the company left and the gate partially closed, Ellan complained to Nigel. "I knew she couldn't be depended upon to be consistent in her duties."

"You're being unfair," he refuted.

"What are you two arguing about?" asked Shannan.

Both appeared sheepish, not wanting to answer.

"Your mother asked a question," said Ellis.

"About Tristine's absence this morning, sir," replied Nigel.

"Ay, she should be here," said Ellis in annoyance.

"I told you," Ellan said to Nigel, although Ellis had not finished speaking

"I can't fault her entirely. I broke a bargain. However, that does not excuse her from her responsibility," he added at seeing Nigel about to say something to Ellan.

"No, sir. Just understanding her reason and disappointment."

"Come. Let's tend to our horses." Ellis steered Nigel from Ellan to the stables. "You can't continue to defend Tristine's behavior."

"I know, but as you take responsibility for breaking your word, I feel responsible for suggesting the trip."

Ellis cocked a grin. "I suppose there is enough blame to go around. Still, she must learn the actions of others should not prevent her from fulfilling her responsibilities."

Ellis was speaking when they entered the stables only Nigel spotted Tristine talking to the grooming before Ellis. She wore breeches and doublet.

"So this where you've been?" he said, alerting her to their presence.

She flashed a smile, which faded at seeing Ellis' anger.

"Why are you pressing the matter?"

"I'm not, sir. You know I go riding every morning I can."

"You expect me to believe such an excuse when you should have been with us in bidding Ambassador Lanzo and Darius farewell?"

She grew chastened and sheepish. "No, sir. I'm sorry. I suppose it wouldn't be right to say that I hoped you changed your mind and let me go?"

Ellis couldn't help a sarcastic chuckle. "No, it would not." Hurt, she averted her gaze so he lifted her chin to face him. "I know you're disappointed that I broke my word, but sometimes situations happen which cannot be helped. It is very important for Nigel and I to discuss the future of Allon undisturbed."

"I do understand. I'm sorry for acting childish," she said in all sincerity.

"Next time try fulfilling your responsibilities and wait for the outcome."

"Ay, sir."

When Ellis went to take charge of his horse, Nigel whispered in warning, "You're lucky you got off easy. He may have patience while you're adjusting, but don't push him. He doesn't like being forced."

"I know. I promise to do better," she said in whole-hearted agreement.

Nigel moved to join Ellis in tending to the horses. Tristine caught sight of Shannan in the stable threshold. Her expression firm when beckoning to her and she promptly complied.

"It is obvious what you were trying to do this morning, and completely unacceptable."

"I know, ma'am. Father and Nigel already said so, and I apologized for acting childish and said I'd do better."

"That's a start. Now go change. There'll be no riding today."

An hour later Ellis and Nigel left Waldron with only Kell and Avatar as escorts. Avatar led a packhorse loaded with all the gear required for an extended hunting and camping trip.

"Father, I hope you're not too angry with Tristine."

"She can't pull her innocent routine much longer."

"I made certain she's aware of that. Still, both Ellan and I went through an awkward adjustment period."

"Ay. But a firm hand guided you both. Do you expect me to do less with Tristine?"

"No, sir."

Ellis grinned. "I didn't punish her because I broke my word."

"We realize that, and she promised to do better."

"I'm sure she will. Now, let us focus on our quarry, both animal and circumstance."

"Which one first?" asked Nigel, uneasiness creeping into his voice.

Ellis noticed the anxious expression. "Animal first. I think we need to release some tension before we can focus our thoughts properly."

Nigel grinned in relief. "Agreed."

"At the gallop!" Ellis snapped the reins and the race began.

The rest of the day passed in traveling toward their favorite hunting ground in the Southern Forest. The topics they spoke about ranged from various lords and their antics, the Council, family members, past history or wild game. The subject of Morven and marriage never came up and Nigel was grateful. In fact, it turned into a surprisingly pleasant outing with no hint of impending doom or unclear future.

Perhaps Kell was right. Since deciding to speak to Ellis, Nigel felt better. Oh, there was an occasional twinge of discomfort when he thought of how to broach the subject, but the feeling passed when nothing happened. The pleasantness of the first day reinforced his decision. More surprising, and a boost of confidence, was he slept through the night. No nightmares, no worries, no trouble whatsoever. It was the most refreshing sleep he experienced in weeks.

Chapter 14

THE MORNING OF THE SECOND DAY of the three-day trip, and once more they were racing. Ellis' horse began to falter in step, forcing him to pull up.

Nigel drew Alden along side. "You didn't slow so I'd catch you, did you?"

Ellis dismounted. "Something's wrong with Cutler. Easy, boy." He patted his horse's rump and checked the left rear leg. "He threw a shoe."

Nigel dismounted. "Is he lame?"

"No, I believe I stopped in time. That wasn't fun, was it, boy?" He stroked Cutler's neck.

"Something wrong, Sire?" asked Kell. He and Avatar joined the mortals.

"Cutler threw a shoe. I suppose it's quite a distance to a smith?" Ellis glanced about but there were no sign of civilization.

"Maybe not." Avatar pointed toward some smoke rising over a distance grove of trees. "If not a smithy, maybe they'll know where one is."

"I'll have to walk him until he gets a new shoe."

A mile down the road, and around a bend, stood a modest cottage with an enclosed blacksmith's forge located off one side of the cottage. Two large doors opened to the forge. From what could be seen, the forge was easily capable of accommodating work on large projects, along with two stalls for horses located near the front entrance. The sound of striking metal echoed and the smell of smoke lingered on the breeze. An old man sat on a bench near one of the open doors working on some harness.

"Hello," called Ellis.

The man paused in his work. "Greetings to you, my lord." He was indeed old with thinning gray hair, tanned wrinkled face, friendly smile and a twinkle to his hazel eyes. "Looks like he's thrown a shoe."

"Are you the smith?"

"I am Fraser." He pointed to the sign above the shed. His gaze passed to Kell and Avatar. "Don't see many of their kind around here."

Ellis grinned. "They won't hurt you."

Fraser's regard lingered on Kell for a moment before he placed the harness aside. "Let's have a look." He grunted and slowly stood, then hobbled to the horse.

"He doesn't look like he can fix it," commented Nigel to Ellis.

Fraser smiled. "Appearances can be deceiving, young sir. If you listen, you'll hear my grandson does the hard work." He motioned inside the shed. By the light only coming from the forge fire, it was hard to see clearly into the shed. He appeared to be a tall, strapping young man and barely paused to acknowledge them with a nod.

Fraser patted the horse's rump. "Handsome fellow. Now, let me see your problem." He moved his hand down the right hind leg. *"Socair suas,"* he said and the horse complied.

Ellis, Nigel, Avatar and Kell were surprised to hear him speak the Ancient.

"Lost a shoe all right." Fraser moved to the other back leg where he repeated the Ancient command. He grunted to straighten after finishing his inspection. "As I thought. Whoever shod him last time did a poor job. He would have lost the rest of them within a day then you would be in real trouble, my lord. Take a seat." He indicated the bench then led the horse inside the shed. "Four medium standard," he said to the young man. He returned to Ellis and the others. "It shouldn't be too long. My grandson is fast and efficient. Still, let me fetch you some refreshment."

After Fraser entered the cottage by way of the front door, Ellis asked Kell, "Have you ever heard a smith speak the Ancient?"

"No. And there is something familiar about him."

"You mean the way he looked at you?" snickered Avatar.

"That and his name. Fraser is common enough, but I knew several mortals by that name before the final battle with Dagar."

"Time changes a man's appearance from youth to old age, whereas Guardians look the same even when they are over two thousand years old," said Ellis, with a wry smile and wink at Nigel.

"I tried to talk Avatar into shaving to look younger," bantered Nigel.

"After watching mortals suffer cuts and irritation, a blade will never touch this face." Avatar stroked his goatee. They laughed.

Fraser returned carrying a tray with tankards, a pitcher and some pastries. He placed the tray down on a second bench and poured the ale. "My lord. Young sir." He began to hand two tankards to the Guardians.

"Thank you, no. We don't require refreshment," said Kell.

Fraser appeared a bit disappointed. "As you say, Captain."

Kell's brows furrowed. "How did you know my rank?"

Fraser chuckled, and offered the pastries to Ellis and Nigel rather than answer.

"You haven't always been a blacksmith."

A hint of melancholy crossed Fraser's face when he turned to Kell. "No, Captain."

"You were the assistant priest to Master Boyd."

"Ay, Captain, a very long time ago."

"What changed that?" asked Nigel.

Fraser sat beside Ellis, his features soured in remembrance. "The king's mercenaries. I mean Marcellus," he hastened to add, and tossed an apologetic side-glance to Ellis.

At that moment, Ellis realized Fraser knew his identity, yet kept up the informal attitude. "During Tyree's rampage," he said and took a bite of pastry.

"Ay. What Fortresses he didn't destroy were abandoned. Such was the case at Ludlow."

Ellis stopped eating, turning to Kell. The captain's expression grew sober and thoughtful.

Frazer didn't notice the exchange since he kept speaking. "Alas, not before they slaughtered a half dozen of my brother priests. To spare the rest, Master Boyd ordered everyone to leave, but some of us crept back that night to give them a proper burial."

"Why didn't you return to the priesthood once Marcellus fell and the House of Tristan reestablished?" asked Nigel.

"I wanted to take my family as far from the carnage as possible. By the time everything was over, we were settled in our new life." He motioned at the cottage and shed. "I uprooted my them once, I didn't want to do it again."

"The horse is ready, Grandfather."

The young man led the animal to the forge opening. He would be considerably taller than Ellis' six feet two inch height, if he stood up straight rather than keeping hunched over and head lowered. Black hair reached his shoulder and his eyes light in hue, the color of which was hard to determine since he avoided looking directly at anyone. He handed the reins to Fraser and went back inside the forge. Nigel stared after him.

"That was quick," said Ellis. He finished the pastry and down the rest of the ale.

"I told you he was fast and efficient," said Fraser.

Ellis inspected Culter's new shoe. "Indeed, excellent work. How much, Master Fraser?"

"No charge, my lord."

Ellis cocked a grin to the contrary. "Oh, no. A fair wage for fair treatment."

Fraser met Ellis' glance and smiled. "Two talents."

Ellis took the coins from his purse and gave them to Fraser. "Good day, Master Fraser."

"My lord. Young sir." Fraser stepped back so Ellis could mount.

The young man came to the corner of the shed to join Fraser in watching the departure. This time he his stood to his full height.

"Remember this day, Tyrone. It's not everyday you shoe a king's horse."

"I'll remember."

A terrible coughing fit racked Fraser. He fell against the wall and Tyrone caught him. When the fit ended, Fraser could barely remain on his feet, his face almost ashen.

"Time for you go back to bed. You shouldn't have been out here to begin with." Tyrone easily lifted his grandfather in his arms to carry him back inside the cottage.

Fraser's voice and protest were feeble. "It was Jor'el's will I see Allon's future. Now I can die contented."

Nigel glanced back at the smithy before rounding the bend. "Strange finding a former priest turn blacksmith."

Ellis followed Nigel's glance. "Not really. Many were forced to flee during that time. I spent nearly two years on the run." An affected sigh of sympathy interrupted his speech and he turned to face Nigel. "He knew who we were. The way he looked at me when he spoke about the mercenaries and Marcellus was his way of apologizing."

"Why not use our proper titles?"

"The code of the priesthood is to treat everyone the same. Meeting him brought back so many memories. The Fortress at Ludlow was the second stop on my journey to gather my companions before confronting Marcellus, Latham and Dagar. We found it abandoned, except for Valmar."

"Valmar?"

"Former Guardian of the Highlands. He gave his life in battle."

"We lost many Guardians," said Kell in sobriety.

"But won a great victory." Nigel tried to sound encouraging.

"Victory doesn't always ease loss, Highness."

A new soberness settled into Nigel's spirit as they continued the journey. There was a sadness connected to the old priest that touched him and he didn't know why. He tried to discern his feelings. He had enough to worry

231

about with his own situation, so why should the hardship of an old priest turned blacksmith bother him? He thought about the grandson who kept his shoulders stooped and never made eye contact with anyone. He was enigmatic yet Nigel felt a baffling sense of affinity for him.

Nigel replied when Ellis spoke to him and even participated in another race his father initiated; but no matter what events or conversation transpired for the remainder of the day, couldn't shake the sense of gloomy empathy for the smith and his grandson. With divided attention and thoughts, he helped set traps and erect camp for the night.

Finally, they sat beside the fire eating snared and cooked grouse. Kell and Avatar joined them at the fire, but didn't eat. Nigel picked at the meat. Ellis' voice interrupted his thoughts.

"What are you thinking so hard about?"

"Uh? Oh, the smith. There was something usual about he and his grandson."

"I thought we already discussed them?"

"His story struck a nerve, especially with you and Kell."

"Some memories are more painful than others. Why should they trouble you?"

Nigel shoved a piece of fowl into his mouth rather than answer, as well as avoided eye contact.

"Are they the real issue?" asked Ellis, probing. "We came on the trip at your request. Granted I agreed because I too wished to speak to you. Perhaps now is a good time. What's wrong?"

The time arrived; a time Nigel anticipated and hoped would be the beginning of the answer. Only, he was suddenly at a loss for words.

Seeing Nigel's struggle, Ellis said, "Let me start because I believe we wrestle with the same issues. As your father, I don't want you to marry against your heart or faith, but as king this may be an opportunity to make an beneficial alliance."

"How can it be beneficial if they are so different?"

"Some consider trade a benefit, but there is also an opportunity to share our faith."

Nigel's features and movement showed his annoyance and his words were laced with vexed sarcasm. "How can you say that after what happened with Tristine and Necie? To you?"

"Let me finish. True, I could have lost two daughters—"

"And been killed yourself!"

"Possibly. At the least, injured. Because of the Guardians and Jor'el's mercy all of us survived. As a result we sent the counterproposal."

Nigel bolted up, his ire exploding. "They want to accept the proposal and that is what troubles me!"

"Obviously. The question is why?"

Nigel stared at his father, again visibly fighting to reply and greatly irritated at his inability to give a direct answer while warring with the knowledge he had to speak. He glanced to Avatar but the Guardian said nothing, although his return stare was prompting. Nigel had to answer his father on his own.

Ellis noticed the exchange. "Is it because they are of a different faith?"

"Partly," Nigel managed to say.

"Understandable. Such a marriage does go against our beliefs."

"You just said you saw an opportunity."

Ellis also began showing signs of frustration. "I did. So does Kell."

"He's not advocating marriage. Nor is he king, you are." Nigel scowled in frustration. This wasn't going well.

"So you believe I'm pressing you into this marriage?"

"Ay!"

Ellis stood and took Nigel by the shoulder, his expression firm. "As king I can order you to marry whomever I choose and you are duty bound to comply. That is not my desire," he quickly added before Nigel objected. "However, I wrestle with the fact it maybe necessary to secure the throne—"

"I don't want it!"

Thunderstruck, Ellis stared at Nigel. "What did you say?"

Nigel gaped at his father, his outburst also a surprise to himself.

Ellis studied Nigel in guarded disbelief. "Are you saying you don't want to be king?"

"I didn't mean to say it that way." Nigel fumbled over his words.

Ellis' ire rose. "You are my heir, the continuation of the House of Tristan."

"I know. But, Father—"

"No! I didn't fight to restore the house of my ancestor only to have my son turn his back on me, upon his duty!" He abruptly turned aside. In doing so, he saw Kell and Avatar, and both greatly concerned.

"Father—" he tried again, only Ellis interrupted him.

"I'm not the only me you disappoint, but the Guardians, your mother, sisters and others."

Nigel's regret turned bitter, as what he feared about hurting his father became reality. "Please, Father, let me explain."

Irate, Ellis snapped, "No, you said quite enough."

Nigel's desperate pleading gaze found Avatar, who stood to speak. "Sire, you misunderstand."

Piqued beyond measure, Ellis rebuffed Avatar. "What do you understand about being a father listening to his son's rejection?" He whirled about on his heels and left the campsite.

"No, Father!"

Kell kept Nigel from following Ellis. "He won't hear anymore."

Tears swelled, Nigel's voice cracking. "I didn't mean to hurt him! I swear! It came out wrong."

"I know. Perhaps in time, he will realize it and you can both speak calmly and plainly on the matter."

In great despair, Nigel sat beside the fire, his head falling into his hands. "I hoped this trip would provide the answer not make things worse."

Avatar sat, an arm around Nigel's shoulders for comfort. "Who said it wouldn't work out? There's an old mortal saying, 'It is always darkness before the dawn.' Did you expect him to simply accept what you had to say without hurt or anger?"

Nigel shrugged and wiped his eyes. "I hadn't thought about how he'd feel. I was too concerned for myself."

"Give him time."

Nigel turned to Kell to say something only he was gone. "Where's Kell?"

"Where do you think? He's not about to let Ellis wander too far alone."

Ellis didn't go far from camp, only enough to collect himself. He saw the campfire through the trees. In the darkness, he knew he could not be seen, that was until Kell approached. "Did you hear him?"

"I did, but I'm not sure you did."

"What do you mean?"

Kell's golden eyes were direct. "Do we speak as captain to king, or Guardian to mortal?"

"He's my son!"

"Ay, and like you, he doesn't like to be pushed into a corner. When you did so, he lashed out. Rather than listen, you responded in the same way."

Ellis swallowed back his emotion. "He might have misspoken, but in a way I never thought I'd hear from him. It hurt more than I can say to think he would reject the throne—"

Kell's grip stopped Ellis' speech. "He didn't mean it the way you took it and is truly sorry for hurting you."

Ellis let out a long, heartfelt sigh. "Maybe not, but now I must deal with those feelings."

"As you do so, search your heart. Nigel would never reject or betray you. Perhaps when you come to accept the truth, you can hear what he has to say and why."

Ellis sat on a log and hung his head. Kell was right. However, placing aside such intense feelings proved difficult. *I don't want it* echoed in his ears, but the words didn't sound right. "Please, Jor'el, show me it wasn't what he meant."

Images and conversation of the past few weeks flashed across his mind. Images and words of Nigel dealing with the Morvenians, of his conversation with Lord Bijan after running off, and of Nigel speaking to various Council Members. No, these were not actions of someone who rejected the throne. Suddenly, the worried expression on Nigel's face after the Council session came to mind. *He doesn't want the marriage contract,* he thought.

"But I know that," he spoke in frustration.

"Sire?"

"The marriage contract scrambled his words and he lashed out when I pressed him and it just happened when I said 'throne'. It's the only thing that makes sense. I already told him I don't like the idea, but he can't understand I may not have a choice?"

"Sire, there is always a choice. You could have chosen to listen and not become angry when he misspoke."

"Ay," grumbled Ellis. "I knew what troubled him, I just didn't realize how much."

"He ran off."

"It's his nature is to withdraw when angry or upset. I thought he dealt with the matter, but this runs deeper then I initially realized."

"Very deep and caused him many sleepless nights and nightmares."

Suspicious, Ellis turned to fully face Kell. "Do you know what it is?"

"In part because of Avatar's concern, but nothing precise."

"Blast your Guardian evasiveness! It can be so infuriating."

"I don't mean to be evasive, only at times I'm uncertain how much I should tell of what I know in respect to mortal relationships. It is a touchy area. In fact, Nigel hasn't been completely forthcoming with Avatar. Still, based upon what he told us, we convinced him to speak to you. Upon our advice, he suggested this hunt. Unfortunately, what he feared about offending you by speaking wrongly came to pass. He may withdraw again. All I can tell you is to speak calmly and listen with patience to everything he has to say."

Ellis tugged at his lip. "In the morning. I need to consider how to phrase my words so I don't provoke him, and ready myself to hear harsh words if he feels threatened." He sent Kell a stern glare and added, "Alone, without any Guardian influence. This is something Nigel and I must come to terms with."

"Understood, Sire," said Kell in pleased relief.

Nigel didn't sleep well and at dawn decided to get up to tend Alden. Ellis was already up and saddling Cutler. Nigel was torn between apologizing again and saying nothing. He opted for the neutral greeting; "Morning, Father."

"Morning. There's some breakfast near the fire, if you want."

"Thank you. I'm not hungry."

Ellis nodded and finished tightening the saddle's girth.

Avatar hastened into camp. "Sire! I saw some deer in the meadow near the far side close to river."

"Good. Nigel and I will take the forest route and swing up from the south to herd them this way and into the open. You and Kell remain in camp."

Once Nigel finished saddling his horse, they mounted and left camp, both armed with bows and quivers full of arrows.

"Is it wise to let them go alone?" asked Avatar.

"He say he wants to speak to Nigel without any Guardian interference."

Avatar suddenly winced in great pain, grabbing his head and staggered to stay on his feet. Kell caught him and helped him sit on the log by the fire. For several moments Avatar fought against the pain with Kell unable to do more than wait and watch. Finally Avatar began to relax, although the color was drained from his features and he perspired, something unusual for Guardians.

"How strange."

"What was it?"

"An intense stabbing pain through my head and I felt faint."

"Sounds like the same thing that happened to Morrell."

"There's nothing Morvenian out here."

Kell's eyes narrowed in consideration, staring in the direction Ellis and Nigel rode from camp. "Order or no, we can't leave them unprotected."

Upon standing, Avatar cried out in severe pain and fell unconscious, narrowly missing striking his head on the log. Kell knelt and tried to rouse him, but to no avail. Avatar hadn't vanished, so it wasn't fatal. Vexed and concerned, Kell gnawed on his lower lip. Whatever happened to Avatar may mean danger for Ellis and Nigel, but he couldn't leave Avatar vulnerable.

Meanwhile, Ellis and Nigel arrived at the large open meadow that ended at the cliffs of the Deigh River. The Deigh was a major river running from the icy mountains of the Highlands through the Northern and Southern Forests to the sea. The swift, deep water carved out the hazardous cliffs, allowing few places to cross. This served as ideal hunting ground with only three directions for the game to run, making it easier to follow and herd them for the killing.

They rode near an outcropping heading north. Nigel spotted three does and two bucks, one older, one younger judging by the antlers.

"Father." Nigel indicated the herd and readied his bow.

Ellis mimicked his son's actions. "Go east. I'll keep going north."

The deer didn't seem to notice them before or after they separated, which was good. Nigel rode more in the open than Ellis, who moved in the shadow of the tree line. Nigel continued to utilize the outcropping to screen his movement and draw closer to the herd. The wind came from the south so it kept the deer from catching his father's scent, on the east, but he would not be so fortunate if he became visible. Thus he needed to get as close to the cliffs as possible before changing course to herd them inland toward his father.

Nigel drew within twenty feet of the cliffs when he turned. If he continued to use the outcropping for a shield, he would lose sight of the deer. Of course, not seeing the deer meant he couldn't see his father and his father couldn't see him. Fortunately, both knew not to shoot until they had a clear line of sight.

Alden suddenly grew agitated. "Steady, boy. There's nothing here to be frightened of." It took a moment for Alden to calm down then Nigel caught sight of what startled the horse and chuckled. "Oh, is that all."

Alden tossed his head and violently reared and bucked, ripping the reins from Nigel's hand. He dropped the bow when he slipped forward onto Alden's neck to keep from falling. "Alden, stop!"

The horse kept backing up. Nigel attempted to grab the dangling reins to regain control of Alden, only the horse's agitated movement made it impossible. Alden's rear leg slipped and Nigel saw they were at the edge of the cliffs.

"Alden, no! Avatar!"

Kell vacillated on what do to when Avatar's eyes snapped opened and he called, "Nigel!" He used Kell's shoulder to push himself to his feet then moved off at an unsteady pace. Kell followed.

By the time they reached the meadow, Avatar regained his strength and balance. "Find the king!" he told Kell before heading toward the river cliffs.

Kell didn't need further prompting and went in search of Ellis.

Avatar stopped a few feet from the cliffs, anxiously turning his head from side to side to scan the area but no sign of Nigel. He glanced down for hoof marks or footprints. From the look of the skid marks and overlapping hoof prints something happened. The marks lead to ... A shiver of intense fear racked him and he stared at the cliffs. In two bounds he reached the edge. His breath caught in his throat. One hundred feet below Alden lay half submerged in the water.

"Nigel?" Ellis violently drew rein and Kell grabbed the bridle when Ellis leapt from the saddle before the horse stopped.

Avatar's stiff-arm stopped Ellis him from drawing too close to the edge, but enough to see the horse.

"Nigel? Where is he?"

Avatar gave Ellis to Kell before vanishing. He reappeared beside Alden. Even from the cliff he knew the horse was dead. Close up showed the violence of the fall resulting in a broken neck, broken legs and numerous wounds. He knelt to touch the horse, closed his eyes, and stretched out his senses. He grimaced at sensing Nigel was on Alden when the horse fell. Abruptly he stood, breathing hard with emotion. He swallowed back his discomposure. Nigel couldn't have simply vanished. The horse being half submerged meant only one thing, Nigel was caught in the swift whitewater current.

239

"Avatar!"

He heard Ellis call from above, but couldn't answer, not yet; not until he learned what became of Nigel. A mile downriver something bobbed in the water. At that distance he couldn't see enough to identity it.

"Avatar!" shouted Ellis, more insistent and frantic.

Again, he ignored the call and ran along the water's edge following the object. Soon it became caught on a fallen log over hanging the riverbank. He hastened into the shallow water and snatched it. Nigel's hat. The hat crushed in his fist. He closed his eyes and again stretched out his senses desperately searching for any sign of Nigel's life essence. The cold sense of tragedy gave way to nothingness. He hung his head, a lamenting groan escaping as he fought back the realization his charge was beyond his help.

At the cliff's edge, Ellis battled to maintain his composure watching Avatar examine the horse then run downriver and out of view. "He must find him!"

At a flash of light, Kell drew his sword. Something terrible already happened and he would protect the king. The light faded to reveal Avatar. Kell began to relax, but grew uneasy at seeing Avatar's stricken expression, and he carried something.

The desperate look on Ellis' face translated to his voice. "Nigel?"

Avatar couldn't speak and held the hat out to Ellis, who took it and fell to his knees weeping, clenching the hat.

Kell's painful, befuddled gaze shifted between a grieving Ellis and a distressed Avatar. "This can't be right. I didn't sense any finality."

"What does your sense matter? You were wrong and I failed!" Avatar hotly rebuffed.

"You didn't fail."

Avatar's unusually fierce snarl made Kell balk and fall silent, something that rarely occurred with the captain.

Ellis' voice was thick with emotions. "Kell's right. If there is any blame, it's mine. I told you both to remain at camp."

Kell helped Ellis to stand. "There is no blame. Avatar experienced pain and—" he stopped when Ellis waved him off.

"Nothing matters now, except returning home and telling my wife and daughters—" he couldn't finish. He snatched the reins, startling Cutler.

Kell prevented Ellis from mounting. "Let me fetch Darius from Leith before returning."

He nodded, words difficult. "Avatar and I will meet you in Dryfuss."

Chapter 15

A T WALDRON, Shannan, the girls, Arista and Angus enjoyed supper in the family dining room. Vidar, Wren and Armus were with them while Morrell and Mahon stood outside the door. Ellis, Darius, Kell and Avatar arrived. Their somber and sorrowful faces were in marked contrast to those assembled at dinner so Morrell and Mahon slipped in behind them, curious about the unusual mood of their comrades. Kell appeared foreboding, Avatar grim, bordering on mournful. The mortals had yet to notice anything until Necie squealed in excitement.

"Father!" She ran to greet Ellis with an enthusiastic hug.

Ellis held her, his expression bittersweet.

"That was a quick hunting trip," said Shannan. She became guarded and perplexed by his forlorn expression. Her gaze passed to a gloomy Darius. "Has Lanzo left?"

"No," replied Darius, unable to fully meet her eyes. His troubled gaze sought and found Arista.

"Darius, what's wrong?"

"Uncle?" asked Tristine.

At Tristine's inquiry and concerned expression, Darius nearly lost his composure.

242

Ellis left Necie to kneel beside Shannan's chair and took her hand. His face showed he searched for the words to speak. "There's been an accident."

"Wait! Where's Nigel?" asked Tristine in apprehension.

Shannan's breath caught in her throat, a look of dreaded anticipation on her face. "How bad is he hurt?"

Ellis shook his head, unable to look at her. "He's gone."

Her disbelief turned to tears of shocked grief.

Stunned, Vidar, Mahon, Wren and Armus turned to Kell and Avatar. Kell gave them a stiff nod of affirmation. Avatar stood rigid and pale, staring mercilessly at some unseen spot, avoiding eye contact. Morrell watched Ellan's somber reaction.

"Nigel's dead?" she asked.

Ellis' reply was choked. "Ay."

"No!" exclaimed Tristine in utter agony.

Necie wept. Angus sniffled and tried to comfort Necie. Mahon stood beside Necie though his focus was on Avatar, who still avoided looking at anyone, bitter pain evident on his face.

"We were pursuing deer near the river cliffs—" Ellis began to explain when Tristine ran at Avatar and began swinging wildly at him.

"You were supposed to protect him!"

Avatar stepped back in avoidance, but one of her blows struck him in the mid-section. Armus caught her about the waist and Ellis seized her hands to stop any more blows.

"It's not Avatar's fault! I told him and Kell to stay at camp while Nigel and I went hunting. It was an accident."

She sobbed uncontrollably.

"Take her to her chamber and try to calm her," he told Armus.

Tristine kept muttering when Armus escorted her from the room, "No, it can't be true. It can't!"

The scene greatly upset Necie, so Arista said to Mahon, "Take her to her room. Go with her," she added to Angus.

In sympathy, Ellis watched Mahon, Necie and Angus leave. When he turned back to Shannan he noticed Avatar's absence. "Where's Avatar?"

"He left while you were speaking to Princess Tristine, Sire," said Wren.

Avatar ran from the dining room upstairs to the family's quarters. Tristine had every right to lash out at him. He failed. Ellis could say what he wanted and Kell use whatever incapacitated him as an excuse, but he knew the truth. It lay with that ugly green statue. He should have ignored Nigel's protest and gotten rid of it the first night.

The door to Nigel's chamber burst open under Avatar's might, practically falling off the hinges. Drawing his sword, he approached the statue, raised the sword above his head and struck with all his strength.

Shannan loudly gasped in fear, turning pale. Ellis knelt beside her, but she ignored him, speaking to Kell. "Avatar!"

Kell raced from the room.

"What about him?" asked Ellis.

She shook her head, trying to put her senses into words. "I felt a horrible pain, then nothing." She began to cry. "Oh, not him too!"

Ellis spoke to Vidar, "Fetch Eldric, I'm taking her to our room."

Armus and Tristine were in the hall when they heard a loud explosion coming from Nigel's room. "Stay here," he told her before rushing to the chamber.

The door partially hung off its hinges. Stepping inside, he saw pieces of green stone scattered across the floor and a sword lying among the pieces. Some furniture was knocked over. Moving further into the room revealed Avatar lying huddled in the far corner. Armus knelt to examine the extent of Avatar's injuries. He found a large gash on the back of Avatar's head. He was ashen, unresponsive and felt cool. Not good.

"Avatar?" cried Tristine.

"I told you to stay in the hall."

She knelt beside Avatar, anxious. "He's not going to die too, is he?"

He didn't reply, rather looked with great consideration from Avatar to the shattered statue, then back to Avatar.

She seized Avatar's hand. "I'm sorry! I didn't mean to hit you."

Kell rushed in and knelt beside Tristine, opposite Armus. "What happened?"

"I'd say by the pieces, he struck the stone and it struck back."

"You didn't witness it?"

Armus shook his head; worry filling his voice. "We have to get him to Melwynn."

"Take care of Tristine." Kell lifted Avatar and waited for Armus to take her aside before vanishing.

Frantic, Tristine pleaded, "Avatar can't die! He can't!"

"He'll be in good hands with Eldric."

In the infirmary of Melwynn, Kell appeared carrying an unconscious Avatar.

"By the heavenlies, what happened?" Phoebe motioned for Kell to put Avatar on a bed.

"Morvenian magic."

Phoebe and another female physician examined Avatar. They discussed the possible reasons for him remaining unconscious so long, how to treat him, and the long-term effects if he didn't wake up soon.

"Enough!" snapped Kell. "Do you know what's wrong with him or not?"

"Honestly, Captain, we don't," began Phoebe. "We found no physical injuries, save a wound on the back of the head from impact. I'm going to the library to research Morvenian magic to understand its effects and how to combat it."

"How long will your research take?"

She shrugged. "I'm not sure. Brooke will remain with him and inform us of any changes." Phoebe stopped her departure when another flash of white light appeared.

Elgin arrived. "Armus told me to give you this." He handed Phoebe a piece of the green stone. "Part of the Morvenian statue."

"Good. Now I have a starting point." She held the fragment up for Kell to see before leaving the infirmary.

"How goes it at Waldron?" Kell asked Elgin.

"Eldric is trying to give Princess Tristine a calming tonic, but she refuses. The queen did accept the tonic, or rather, the king insisted. Princesses Ellan and Necie are holding up fairly well with Lady Arista and Master Angus' help. All the castle is in mourning."

"No doubt."

Concerned, Elgin turned to Avatar. "Will he survive?"

"We're not sure yet. Return and keep me informed."

Elgin stepped aside and vanished.

Kell told Brooke, "I'll be on the terrace. Fetch me when he wakes."

Melwynn was a massive structure built the same time as the Temple of Providence. Since dealing with mortals could be dangerous and frustrating, Melwynn served as a place of refreshment and recuperating. From the large terrace, unfolded a commanding view of the surrounding Highland countryside.

At the moment, Kell wasn't interested in the view. He did require a time of reflection and meditation. Something was amiss about the whole situation. He sensed what Nigel did concerning his future of not being king, but no hint of finality. Now Avatar lay unconscious. If the shattered pieces of the Morvenian statue confirmed Avatar's suspicions, then it possessed enough power to waylay one of the strongest of all Guardian warriors. Joined with the stones collected after each attack, a new, dangerous evil threatened Allon. This required serious and lengthy consideration.

What could the Morvenians gain by destroying the royal family? Revenge for defeat? A rather simplistic explanation if true. Then again, some mortal cultures considered revenge an honorable method to save face. Where the Morvenians failed with the others, they succeeded with Nigel.

"But we found no jewel. No crimson gem to link to the other attacks," he argued with himself. "Not does it account for Nigel's discouraging sense

246

of doubt or his nightmare." Kell winced at the thought of Nigel's death. His frustration and confusion mounted by the time he reached the eastern edge of the terrace "Why, Jor'el? Surely there is a reason. Am I that wrong?"

"No," said a voice that seemed to surround him. A misty figure with large opalescent eyes appeared.

Kell got down on one knee. "Jor'el. How did this happen? I sensed nothing."

"Do you rely more on your senses than my will, Captain?"

"Forgive me, I didn't mean to sound skeptical, rather I'm confused about Nigel's death and Avatar waylaid by some unknown force. If I sensed or knew the trouble I could have counseled Nigel and helped Avatar ..." Kell fought to keep vexation and irritation from his voice.

The eyes were kind in their regard. "Testing of a mortal's faith is done for a reason. In time, all shall become clear."

"What test? Nigel is dead. He can no longer be tested." Kell was slow to ask his next question, anxious about the answer concerning his friend and protégé. "What about Avatar? Will he recover?"

"Avatar is facing his own test. Only he can decide." Jor'el vanished.

Kell wanted to object and inquire further. For a moment he remained on the terrace, pondering what Jor'el meant. Guardians naturally grieved the loss of a mortal in their charge. Nigel was Avatar's first assignment as an Overseer. Still, he sensed something more; something connected to the Morvenians. Wandering the terrace proved of little help, thus he returned to infirmary. He wanted to be there when Avatar woke, if he woke.

"There has been no change in his condition, Captain," said Brooke.

Kell sat in a chair beside the bed. Brook had wrapped a bandage around Avatar's head, but he disagreed with her assessment. In his estimation, Avatar's condition seemed worse. Of course, he didn't take notice of Avatar's true state since the situation unfolded so fast and he rushed him to the infirmary. He mourned the demise of each Guardian since the beginning, but next to Armus, the loss of Avatar would be personally painful.

Aside from venting grief and anger, what was Avatar thinking when he struck the statue? Avatar came to him very upset upon learning about Nigel's deep seeded uncertainty. Unfortunately, he didn't have an answer and without an answer Avatar couldn't help to alleviate Nigel's anxiety. True, they eventually convinced Nigel to speak to Ellis, only after brooding and rising tension between father and son. Now he understood Avatar's fierceness at the cliffs. It was not simply a failure to protect, but an inability to counsel. If Avatar knew the answer earlier he would have told Nigel to speak to Ellis sooner and avoided the fateful hunting trip. Knowing his lack of information and advice added to Avatar's sense of failure deeply troubled him.

Kell leaned forward and laid hold of Avatar's shoulder. "Oh, my friend, I'm sorry I didn't have an answer for you when you needed one. Please, don't let my failure be the reason you give up. Fight! So together we can stop anything else from causing more harm."

"Captain." Phoebe returned and she looked disappointed. "It's a piece of rock."

"You got that from a book?"

"No. After reading about Morvenian magic I went to the laboratory and did a few experiments. Nothing happened. It contains no magical properties."

"Then what knocked him across the room and left him like this?"

"My guess is Avatar did this to himself," she replied, much to Kell's great chagrin.

In fact, the answer brought him to his feet, golden eyes narrow and harsh. "How's that?"

Despite how intimidating Kell appeared when angry or irritated, she calmly replied. "Avatar's name means *He of the Lightning Sword* because of the special power he commands."

"I know that! He's my aide."

"Let me finish, Captain. His power is a physical drain on his life force. The amount of drain depends upon the amount of power used. But," she added at seeing Kell's growing impatience, "once unleashed, his power must have a place to go. Don't you see? The statue possessed no evil for his power to combat, so it turned back on him. He nearly killed himself."

Momentarily stymied by the explanation, Kell stared at Phoebe, the words and implication sinking in and making sense. Avatar took out his anger, grief and personal sense of failure on a statue he believed contained evil. All his power focused in a single blow. It may not have been a conscience decision on Avatar's part, but that is what occurred.

"What can be done for him?" he asked.

"Perhaps some strengthening tonics will help. Beyond that I don't know. What I do know is it's a wonder he survived his own full power."

"Do what you can. I'm going to Waldron."

Armus finally convinced Tristine to take the tonic. The remedy proved so effective, she fell asleep within minutes. He sat beside the bed. He wanted to be nearby when she woke and not in his customary position by the door.

Thought of Nigel made his heart ache, both for Tristine and Avatar. He understood Avatar's grief and anger since he experienced the lost of a charge in the past. But if they were to lose Avatar also, his grief would multiply. Centuries of friendship and camaraderie forged a deep, personal relationship. He took consolation in the fact Kell was with Avatar; and he did not sense a spirit of demise.

He admitted surprise at Avatar's appointment as Overseer of the royal heir. After all, Armus had the privilege of guarding Tristan. Orders were orders and it would be disobedient to question the choice. However, when Morrell became appointed Overseer of the second born, he began to wonder if he would even play a role in the lives of the royal family. Then came the night of Tristine's birth. Nothing unusual happened to make the occasion stand out, except what Shannan told about Ellis naming her. What struck Armus was how he felt the moment he took charge and held her. The connection was immediate and the first time he called her 'my little one' because of her small size compared to his big hands.

There came a soft knock on the door followed by Kell's entrance. A mortal soldier accompanied him. Armus rose and met them by the door, away from the bed. "How's Avatar?"

"Alive when I left. I informed Ellis of his condition, along with what we must discuss. Lieutenant Brandon will stay with Tristine while we meet with the Trio Leaders. I sent Wren and Elgin to summon them."

Armus frowned in dispute and glanced back at the bed. "I don't want to leave. I've never seen her so upset."

"I wouldn't ask if were not important. Vidar, Mahon and Morrell are also coming." When Armus still resisted, Kell asked, "Did she take Eldric's tonic?"

"Ay."

"Then she will sleep peacefully until the morning, unaware of your absence."

Armus turned to Brandon. "Don't step a foot away from her bedside."

<hr />

At Arundine, Kell and Armus were the first to arrive and he sent Armus to the threshold to await the others. He wanted a moment alone to gather his thoughts and feelings before making such an announcement about Nigel and Avatar. He sat in high chair and bowed his head, closed his eyes, and took several deep breaths before slowly exhaling.

"Please, Jor'el, don't let Avatar die before we can figure this out."

He sensed the arrival of someone and barely lifted his head to see who it was. Priscilla. She started to speak, but stopped and quietly took her seat in the East Coast chair. Several times she regarded him in somber curiosity. Two others arrived, Gresham and Barnum. Then in short order, the rest of the Trio Leaders. A few others gave him similar looks to Priscilla, only no one spoke. Even Armus remained silent and assumed his place. Wren arrived last, and took her seat in the Southern Forest chair.

A long heavy moment passed before Kell spoke. "I called you here on short notice because of what happened earlier today. A tragedy that will deeply affect the future of Allon." He took deep breath, preparing to announce the news, catching Priscillas' sympathetic gaze.

"Kell?" she asked.

"Prince Nigel is dead."

Stunned muted, the Trio Leaders stared at Kell or exchanged glances until finally Zinna said, "What? How?"

"A hunting accident. He got too close to the cliffs of the Deigh River in the Southern Forest and … his horse must have slipped."

"What about Avatar? Where was he when this happened?" asked Zadok.

"The king ordered Avatar and I to stay behind while he and the prince rode off." Kell explained why Ellis and Nigel went hunting in the first place, the incident with Avatar at camp and their discovery at the river cliff.

"I thought you said it was an accident?" asked Chase.

"I sensed nothing unusual at the cliffs."

"What happened to Avatar was unusual," said Auriel.

"Sounds like what happened to me," said Morrell.

"There was nothing nearby to suggest the Morvenians. No stones, statues, nothing."

"There is only one power that seeks to destroy Allon," said Jedrek.

"Priscilla and I sensed activity around Ravendale," said Gresham.

Kell shook his head. "If this is the Dark Way then it acting in a manner I am unfamiliar with and that's not good."

"It may not be the Dark Way," began Morrell. "The Tunlundians claim to possess powers and certainly wouldn't want Allon to make an alliance with Morven."

"So Dante avoids suspicion by making a generous overture of gifts to disguise some form of evil power?" asked Armus.

"Why not? It's possible."

Mahon was unusually short-tempered. "We have no proof of either the Dark Way or the Tunlundians. All we know for certain is Morvenian stones were involved with the beasts and it was against a Morvenian statue Avatar focused his power."

Kell's glance to Mahon was sympathetic. Whereas he and Armus mentored Avatar for several hundred years before Avatar became his aide, Avatar mentored Mahon. "The statue contained no magical powers."

251

Armus vocalized Mahon's thunderstruck expression before the young warrior could. "How can that be? I saw the aftermath of the shattered pieces and Avatar knocked across the room, barely breathing."

Kell's empathetic glance shifted from Mahon to Armus. "He did it to himself."

"Come again, Captain?" demanded Mahon, not satisfied by the answer. In fact, his passion made him move too close to Kell for Armus, and was intercepted by the lieutenant.

Kell stepped down from the high chair to speak to Mahon. "Grieved by Nigel's death and believing the statue contained evil, Avatar focused all his strengthen in one decisive blow. You know that once our power is summoned, it must fight something. With no evil—"

"It turned back on him," said Armus in grim conclusion.

Although subdued, the conflict and confusion reflected in Mahon's face, so Kell reassured him. "Eldric left Waldron to help Phoebe. Together they will find a remedy for Avatar."

Mahon held Kell's gaze. "You don't sense the worst will happen to him, do you?"

"No. I would tell you if I did."

At Armus' nudge, Mahon moved aside and Armus resumed his seat. Kell remained standing.

"Captain. How has this affected the royal family?" asked Mona.

"Very hard."

"What about prophecy concerning the Great King? Nigel was heir," said Zinna.

Kell heaved a hapless shrug. "I don't know yet. But unless Shannan has another son, he won't come from the House of Tristan."

"That opens the door to any number of possibilities," said Barnum glumly.

"Ay. He's supposed to be *our* king along with the mortals," said Derwin.

"I don't know!" snapped Kell in exasperation. "At the moment there is uncertainty. Ellan is next in line. All we can do is watch and wait. Return to your provinces and keep a sharp eye. I'll send word when I know anything."

All began to follow Kell's instruction except Egan, who lingered, thoughtful for a brief moment, before approaching Kell. "Captain, about Avatar. I'd like to go to Melwynn and see if I can do something."

To this offer, Kell's expression softened into a smile. "I hoped you would, only I didn't want to assume. Losing a charge is never easy but tragic circumstances make it worse."

Together, they vanished.

At Melwynn, Kell and Egan saw Avatar move in short agitated bursts, although he appeared unconscious. Phoebe attempted to give him a tonic and Eldric did his best to restrain him. Unfortunately, the more they tried to get him to drink the more he resisted. In the process, the tonic spilt.

"How is he?" asked Kell

"Stubborn," chided Phoebe. "That's the fourth tonic he refused." She walked off, grumbling and wiping her clothes.

"Make him drink it."

"What do you think we've been trying to do?" rebuffed Eldric. "The few times we've gotten a little into him, he gags and begins choking. There is a very precise method of getting an unconscious individual to drink." His expression grew remorseful. "With what strength he has, he is fighting us rather than fighting to live. If we can't get him to drink soon—" He didn't finish his thought, he couldn't at seeing Kell's ire.

Kell gestured with a curt wave. "Leave us alone with him."

"If you're going try to get him to drink, let me show you how."

"Leave us!" Kell waited a moment for the door to close before approaching the bed. He balked at seeing the deterioration of Avatar's appearance: ashen, lips pale and near death. He sat in the chair. Egan moved opposite him.

With one hand Kell grabbed Avatar's right hand, the other hand he placed on the bandaged forehead. Avatar flinched and moaned to the touch. "*Avatar, eisd agus bi umhail,*" he spoke the Ancient. "Avatar, listen and obey," he repeated when Avatar tried to move from under his hands. At that moment, he understood the difficulty Phoebe and Eldric were having. Despite his greatly weakened state, Avatar's resistance was surprisingly strong. "Be still," he commanded in Ancient. He felt then saw Avatar relax, though his eyes remained closed. "Give heed to the voice of your creator."

"I have failed, Jor'el," whimpered Avatar, his eyes still closed.

Kell kept his hands in place and watched the hazy cloud of Jor'el appear at the end of the bed. Egan bowed his head in acknowledgement of the Almighty's arrival.

The eyes were sympathetic in their regard, the voice compassionate. "No, Avatar. You are not faulted for what happened to your charge."

"His sense of fear! I could not help him."

"Nor could Kell," said Jor'el, kindly.

Avatar moaned in lament, his eyes remaining closed.

"Do you trust me, Avatar?"

His voice choked in reply. "Ay."

"Then believe that I will reveal the reason in time."

"When?"

"You will know the answer only if you live."

Avatar weakly groaned, this time in pain and not resistance.

Egan added his entreaty. "Avatar, please listen! I know what it's like to lose a charge to an untimely death. I didn't understand why at the time! It wasn't until a few years later I saw the reason and Tristan became king. Don't let yourself die before learning the answer."

"Fight, Avatar! I don't want to lose you like this," urged Kell.

"It is his choice." Jor'el vanished.

Kell released Avatar and sat back in the chair. He and Egan exchanged sober glances of concern. Eldric appeared right beside Kell, startling him. Eldric held a cup. "I didn't hear your return."

"You maybe the Guardian captain, but I am the Guardian physician. Give him the tonic following my instructions." Eldric handed the cup to Kell. "Sit on the bed and cradle his head and neck in the crook of your arm so your hand is over his throat." Kell did so. "Place the cup to his lips and use your hand to stroke his throat in a downward motion to get him to swallow. Now, little by little give him the tonic. Easy. Let him swallow between amounts."

Kell followed the instructions. Some of the tonic dribbled down the sides of Avatar's mouth and he gagged once; but to Kell's relief, he accepted the tonic.

Eldric took the cup from Kell. "Well, done. Now lay him down. The rest is up to him."

"I'll stay with him, Captain. I'm sure you're needed at Waldron," said Egan.

"I want to know the moment he wakes." Kell stepped away and vanished.

Chapter 16

ELLIS HAD LITTLE TIME ALONE to reflect on the tragedy while tending to his wife, daughters and sovereign duties. He dispatched Guardian messengers to the Council, urging them to come to Waldron with all speed. Arrangements must be made concerning succession. This was not only for the good of Allon's national interest, but to secure it from foreign countries attempting to capitalize on the royal heir's death. He sent Gulliver, the most notable sea Guardian, to fetch Emery safely from Morven. This news would change everything and he hoped Kamu would understand the need to mourn before proceeding with any negotiations.

Finally, at the end of his physical and emotional endurance, he lost his composure and lashed out at Darius, Wess and Uriah. In a nearly uncontrollable rage, he shook off Darius' effort to contain him. Then someone seized him and in a commanding voice spoke, "Ellis!"

For a moment he didn't know who held him or spoke until his befuddled mind realized he stared up into a pair of golden eyes. "Kell?" The moment he spoke the name, his whole body sagged as every ounce of energy instantly drained away. He also noticed the sympathetic way Darius, Wess and Uriah regarded him. "I'm ... sorry"

"It's all right. We understand," said Wess.

"Kell, take him to his chamber," said Darius.

256

Ellis didn't resist Kell steering him from the room. However, once in the hall, he balked. "I need to go to the Chapel."

"Are you sure?"

"I must."

In the Chapel, Ellis made his way to the front pew. He ignored inquires and offers of condolences, nor did he notice Kell clear the Chapel to give him privacy. He wept. He had no words, only tears of pain, loss and exhaustion. He pushed Nigel too far and should have spoken to him sooner. Better yet, tell Nigel he was right and the marriage should never have been considered. What possessed him to believe that by compromising Jor'el's laws and Allon's heritage something good could come of it? Nigel tried to tell him. Even Tristine questioned him about marriage to an unbeliever who could one day rule Allon. His head snapped up, staring wide-eyed at the altar recalling Nigel's rejection of the throne.

In desperation he said, "What did I fail to do with my son that I could have done better? That would have avoided this?" His question was met by silence so he answered himself. "I didn't listen. Then again, many times I listened and accepted excuses I should not have. Perhaps in doing so I failed to stress the importance of his duty to you and Allon. Is that the answer? Was I too tolerant and indulgent?" He growled in vexation and futility. "That can't be it."

"What can't be?" Shannan sat beside him.

Her arrival surprised him along with her pale and weary features. "What are you doing here? Are you well enough?"

Her smile was plaintive. "I'm better. At least, I can function." Tenderly, she brushed his hair behind his ears. "You've been working so hard the last few days, you're exhausted and a mess. I apologize for not helping you."

He hugged her. "No need to apologize. We must all find our way through this tragedy, together and individually." He bit his lower lip to keep from speaking further.

She noticed his familiar action of avoidance. "But?"

"The void must be filled. Not in our hearts, Nigel can never be replaced."

"The next heir."

"Ay. Until all is secure and formalized I cannot rest."

"Ellis, you can't go on much longer."

"Once I have spoken to the girls, I will rest. Kell, summon Ellan, Necie, Tristine, Darius, Arista and Angus to the family salon."

"Ellis, I don't know if they are ready to accept this," she argued.

He fought to contain his temper. "There is no choice, don't you understand?"

"Of course I do. I'm simply concerned for the girls."

"As am I, but it can't be put off. I put things off with Nigel and looked what happened!"

The statement made her wince, wounded yet grew concern. "Did you and Nigel not speak?"

He grunted in annoyance. "Not to the point of resolving anything. He misspoke, I overreacted and he withdrew. I intended to listen better after—" Emotions briefly interrupted him. "I told Kell and Avatar to wait at camp. No Guardian interference. If I hadn't maybe—"

She hugged him to stop his speech. "Don't blame yourself. You don't know for certain."

He held her and kissed her forehead. "I can't change the past, but I can change how I act from now on. Beginning with telling the girls." He drew her to her feet and they left the Chapel hand-in-hand.

When Ellis and Shannan arrived in the salon, Darius and Arista were there. Shortly, Necie arrived with Angus and Mahon, followed by Ellan with Morrell. Tristine and Armus arrived with Kell. Normally the Guardians divided their duties, but this wasn't normal, so Ellis said nothing to all of them remaining.

In sympathy, he regarded the girls. Necie was unusually quiet and Ellan pensive. Despite the tonics, Tristine looked pale and worn out. Nigel's death hit her the hardest. She idolized him, mimicking him any way she could. Only a few weeks ago Nigel took her camping so she could earn the right to go hunting. A sudden thought struck Ellis. How much more horrible it would have been if Tristine had accompanied them and witnessed the

258

accident that killed her brother. He turned aside to suppress the new emotions caused by the disturbing thought before proceeding.

"Is there a reason you called us here?" asked Darius.

Ellis nodded and spoke to his daughters. "I realize how difficult this is but arrangements must be made and life continue. I dispatched word to the Council, informing them to come to Waldron at all speed. In fact, I sent Guardians to fetch them. In the morning we'll hold a memorial honoring the passing of royal family member."

"How can we memorialize him when he was taken by the river out to sea?" chided Ellan.

Necie whimpered and buried her face in Arista's side. Tristine stifled a sob by biting her lip. Darius held her shoulder for support.

Ellis grimaced at their reactions. "To honor Nigel's memory and give all of Allon the chance to pay homage. And ..." he paused to take a steady breath, "to introduce Ellan as heir to the throne."

"What?" said Ellan and Tristine together; Ellan in surprise and Tristine in anger.

"Life must continue. In our hearts no on will ever replace Nigel, but the royal family must move forward and Ellan is next in line." He approached Ellan, who still struggled to comprehend. He made her look up. "You are now my successor. All that Nigel once meant to Allon as heir apparent is passed to you, his mantle of duty to the people and responsibility to Jor'el."

Overwhelmed, Ellan couldn't speak, but Tristine could, and vehemently did so.

"No! Nigel is supposed to be king."

Shannan tried to keep her emotions in check. "Ellis—"

"This must be," he insisted then returned his attention to Ellan. "The memorial will be the best time to introduce you to the Council and Court."

Tristine bolted up. "No! She can't be queen. It's not right."

Ellis moved to calm her. "Please try to understand. Nigel is gone. Ellan is now my heir. The people—"

"No! It's wrong and I don't want them here!" She ran from the room.

Tristine ran down the back hallway and out the door and through the rear courtyard. She knew Armus would follow so she dashed behind a wagon to hide. She didn't want to avoid him, but she couldn't go back, she wouldn't.

She shrunk down at seeing Armus stop to survey the area. If he were distracted, she could leave through the open postern gate. While she considered what to do, she heard and then saw him speak to several soldiers and servants about seeing her, but none had. She couldn't elude him for long considering his superior tracking skills. Vidar might be the best Guardian hunter, but most of the elite warriors were masters at shadowing their foe or performing clandestine reconnaissance. For the moment, she watched and hoped for the best.

After a few moments, Armus hastened toward the stables. Perhaps thinking she would leave on Dunstan. Once he disappeared from sight, she ran out the postern gate. She continued running. The more distance the better, although she wished she could have gotten to Dunstan rather than trying to put distance between she and Armus on foot. Hiding from him would serve no purpose; getting far away from Waldron is what mattered. Far enough to think, to grieve, to be left alone! Nigel's death was bad enough, but hearing Ellis announced Ellan as his heir and future queen proved too much! It tore at the very core of her being.

She ran until her legs ached and she couldn't breathe. Even then she tried to push herself, but stumbled and fell to the ground gulping for air. Her heart pounded, ringing in her ears, or was it footsteps? She held her breath to listen, only that proved painful. She heard footsteps and the rustling of branches. Either Armus found her or a creature lurked nearby. If a creature, she was unarmed; so she had to move, and wobbled getting to her feet.

"You won't get very far dressed like that and on foot," said Armus.

She pouted at him and sat hard on the ground, speaking between breaths. "I'm not going back!"

"You absence will be difficult to explain."

She sniffled back her tears. "I don't care!" When he drew her to her feet, she swung at him, shouting, "Let me go!"

260

He easily caught her arms and subdued her, but gently, so not to hurt her. "Calm down. This isn't helping you or your family."

"It's wrong! It's wrong!" She cried bitter tears.

He knelt, took her face in his hands and searched her eyes. "Why do you say that?"

She sniffled and shrugged. "She doesn't have the temperament to be queen. She is so bossy, now she'll be impossible! And I'll have to listen to her! At least Nigel treated me kindly and didn't force his position on Necie and me. Ellan will."

"Are you jealous of her becoming queen?"

"No, no! It's just wrong."

"You keep saying that, but your reasons sounds more like jealousy."

She shook her head, whimpering in frustration. "No, it's more than that, but I can't explain it. I just know in my heart." She shivered, wrapping her arm about herself, her weeping growing almost to the point of uncontrollable.

"You're cold and upset. I need to get you back inside so Eldric can give you another tonic."

"I'm not cold. I'm scared! I can't face them. Please, don't take me back!" Her voice cracked and she fell against him weeping, her whole body violently trembling.

He held her. His expression pricked in deep sympathy upon hearing her pleas not to be taken back muffled against him. He tilted her head to look in her eyes. They were puffy and red but with the unmistakable look of sheer terror. "Very well. Only you can't go to Garwood. I'll take you to Melwynn. There you can rest and renew your strength and spirit."

She nodded, unable to speak, rather clung to him.

❦

A flash of white light appeared on the front terrace of Melwynn. Armus held Tristine, who swooned from dimension travel. It took a moment for her to regain her senses.

"Are you all right?"

261

She swallowed back a brief sickness. "I think so."

"Look out there and maybe you'll start to feel better." He indicated the spectacular view from the terrace. Snow-covered mountains flanked the castle and rose in the distance with beautiful Highland meadows and glens stretching in between the peaks for as far as the eye could see.

She stared in wonder and walked to the terrace railing. "I thought the view from Waldron's upper turret was magnificent."

Armus laughed, but stopped at seeing Kell approach. The captain's questioning glance passed from him to Tristine. Fearful, she ran to Armus and seized him.

"It's not Armus' fault! I ran off and he brought me here because I can't face them." She began to weep.

Armus comforted her. He tossed a compassionate glance to Kell and spoke under his breath, "The memorial and reception."

With a gentle touch, Kell lifted Tristine's chin to look her in eye. Her distress and heartache ran deep. "I'm not here to scold you. I came to find you at your mother's request."

"Then you won't make Armus take me back?"

"No."

"Thank you." She hugged Kell tight, fighting back tears.

For a moment Kell held her. He spied two vassals on the terrace. "Violet. Frey." They approached. He lifted Tristine chin to speak to her. "Go with them. Armus will be along after I speak to him."

Tristine did so and Kell waited for them to leave the terrace.

"I know Ellis will be angry, but—"

Kell's hand on his shoulder stopped Armus. "You don't have to explain. I saw in her eyes how deep the pain is and felt her trembling."

"What about Ellis?"

"I'll deal with him. Shannan will understand. What I'm more concerned about is what I have to tell him."

"What?"

Kell pursed his lips before answering. "Morrell is to be appointed Supervisor of the Overseers which places him in authority over you."

Armus was first stunned then frowned. "I've never subordinated to anyone but you."

"Only subordinate in respect to Tristine. You can still function as second-in-command without answering to Morrell."

"Who is replacing him as Ellan's Overseer?"

"That is the part I'm concerned about telling Ellis." Kell took a step back and said, "Don't let her take advantage and stay away too long."

"Wait! You're not going to tell me?"

"It's best you help Tristine deal with one major upheaval before confronting another change."

"Oh, please don't say you mean for me to take his place." Kell vanished while Armus spoke. "Kell!" he shouted in frustration.

For a moment Armus remained on the terrace, contemplating the dreaded possibility. Not that he disliked Ellan, rather the thought of what misery his reassignment would cause Tristine. He glanced skyward. "Please, don't let it be me, Jor'el."

He heard a vocal echoing of Kell's statement. *Help Tristine deal with one major upheaval.*

He left the terrace to find her.

※

After Tristine ran from the salon, Ellis allowed the others to retire. Ellan hastened to her room with Morrell on her heels. He watched her worried state as she paced the length of her chamber.

"Are you upset over being named heir and someday becoming queen?"

"I don't know what to think. Everything has changed so fast. Just a few weeks ago the Morvenians came offering a royal marriage between Kaleana and Nigel. Tristine's banquet, Nigel killed. Now this."

"You knew you were next in line."

"Ay, but not so soon! Or so sudden." Fretful, she sat in a chair.

Morrell's smiled with confidence and held her hand. "From the day you were born, I felt you were destined to ascend the throne."

His statement surprised her. "How? Did you foresee Nigel's death?"

"Not in those terms, although it is a Guardian's sense which guides him. Prior to the Great Battle, I was Overseer to another royal. I saw qualities in her that went beyond what her older sister possessed. She had courage, strength, determination, but most of all, confidence in knowing her own mind and what she wanted. You possess the same qualities as Queen Alycia."

Ellan was stunned at hearing the name.

"Ay. One of Allon's greatest queens was also my charge."

"Alycia," she repeated in awe. "She wasn't of the House of Tristan."

"So? She ruled for twenty years. When the opportunity came to ascend the throne, she seized it. Through her ingenuity, strength, and iron will, she guided Allon."

"You think I possess those qualities? That I can be as good as queen as her?"

"I do," he said in unwavering certainty. "The question is, do you believe it? Will you seize the opportunity like she did? Without regret or looking back?"

"How?"

"By embracing your new position and using it to your advantage in all the ways necessary."

"I don't know if I can."

He feinted disappointment. "Well, I suppose I could be wrong."

"What? Oh, no," she began in concern then spoke with a sudden thought. "Since Alycia was your charge you know what she did and probably helped her."

"Ay, in modest ways."

She gripped his hand, guarded anticipation and excitement on her face. "Will you help me? I'll listen to whatever you say."

He pursed his lips in feinting thought. "I admit I wondered why I was appointed your Overseer, now I know. Ay, I'll help you."

She hugged him. "Thank you. I'll try to do as well as Alycia."

"To begin with, you must get a proper night's sleep so you can look rested and ready to face your new life."

"Ay. Summon my maid."

By the time Kell returned to Waldron, Ellis retired; having taken a sleeping tonic Eldric prepared for him and left orders not to be disturbed. The news would wait until morning.

When most of the family took breakfast, Kell arrived, and he wasn't alone; Avatar accompanied him, fully healed. Ellis was not yet present, which was unusual considering he rose early and often partook of breakfast before everyone else. The others were relieved and happy to see Avatar. Ellis' loud, upset voice interrupted the reunion as he burst into the dining room. Darius followed, trying to calm him.

"Ellis, what's the matter?" asked Shannan.

Ellis saw Kell and Avatar so he didn't answer Shannan. "Avatar? When did you return?"

"This morning, Sire."

"I'm glad to see you are well," he spoke with distraction. His focus shifted to Kell and he demanded, "Have you seen Armus this morning?"

"Armus? What's wrong with him?" asked Shannan, anxiety in face and voice.

"Tristine's gone!"

"What?" she exclaimed, shocked and seized Avatar's arm.

"Not like that," refuted Ellis. "She left. Or least no one can find she or Armus anywhere in the castle."

Kell began to speak when Ellan complained, "She left because she's jealous I'm now your heir."

"No, she's very upset over Nigel," insisted Darius. He then spoke to Ellis. "It's only been a few weeks since they went camping and he gave her Dunstan."

"Because of that I have excused her behavior up until now, but not when her family needs her to be here!"

Necie wept, which brought Mahon to her side. Shannan also comforted Necie yet spoke, "Ellis, this is difficult for all of us. Necie expressed fear of the memorial and the reception."

Ellis' expression and tone softened. "Necie's a child."

"Tristine isn't much older. Just because she turned a certain age doesn't immediately make her an adult. I needed help in accepting Nigel's death, so why expect Tristine to be stronger than I?"

"I held a firm but fair hand with Nigel and Ellan, you want me treat Tristine different?"

"Danger and death didn't challenge them as they have Tristine. We could have lost more than Nigel!" Shannan's gaze shifted to Necie.

To this, Ellis' argument was subdued. He crossed to Necie and touched her cheek. "You may be excused from the reception. Although, I would appreciate you being at the memorial."

"I'll try, Father." Necie wiped the tears from her face.

"I'll help her, Uncle," said Angus.

Upset, Ellan asked, "Then I must bear this alone?"

"As I sometimes bear the duties of being king." Ellis took her hand and gave it an affirming squeeze. "But in this, you will not be alone. Your mother and I will be there beside you, as will Morrel, and—"

"Not exactly, Sire," Kell finally spoke over the conversation.

"Not exactly what?"

"Jor'el has issued new orders for Morrell and Avatar."

"What orders?" asked Morrell.

"You are to become Supervisor of the Guardian Overseers while Avatar takes your place in watching over Princess Ellan."

"What? No!" Ellan moved from Ellis to Morrell, seizing his hand.

"Are you certain of this, Captain?" asked Ellis.

"Completely, Sire."

Ellan's surprise turned to painful anger directed at Avatar. "He couldn't protect Nigel so why should I get stuck with him?"

Avatar's jowls tightened but Kell refuted her. "That wasn't Avatar's fault, Highness."

"Indeed not. They followed my order," added Ellis. He could see Ellan's distress but his focus was drawn to Necie, who spoke in a shaky voice.

"Mahon isn't going anywhere, is he?"

266

Kell's tone softened, and he smile. "No, princess. The only new assignments are Morrell and Avatar. Mahon, Armus and Vidar will remain as they are."

"No!" insisted Ellan. "Father, tell him no."

Ellis frowned in reluctance. "I can't. Kell is Captain of the Guardians and this order comes from Jor'el. I will not interfere."

Morrell bent down to speak to Ellan. "It's all right, Highness. If you think about it, I'm not going away. I'll still be here."

"It won't be the same."

"Nothing will be the same again," said Ellis soberly. Despite Ellan's objection to the change, he spoke to Avatar. "Very well, once more you guard the royal heir." Avatar nodded in submission and Ellis turned to Morrell. "I suppose your first assignment will be to find Tristine and Armus."

"That will not be necessary, Sire," said Kell.

"Oh?" asked Ellis in suspicious displeasure.

"Armus took her to Melwynn for rest and spiritual restoration."

"Why didn't tell me earlier?"

"I tried, but other voices were raised."

"At least she's safe," said Darius.

The clock on the mantle struck eight in the morning.

"Two hours to the memorial," groused Ellis. He began to leave.

"Aren't you going to eat something?" asked Shannan.

He didn't reply, the door loudly closed behind his departure.

"I lost my appetite." Ellan stormed from the room. Avatar followed but Morrell remained.

Shannan took Necie's hand. "Come. They need our help."

Arista and Angus followed Shannan and Necie in leaving.

Morrell confronted Kell. "Was being reassigned some form of punishment, Captain?"

Kell's tone and face were firm in reply to the effrontery. "No, it is a promotion. You have been given charge of four Guardians, including Armus and Avatar. Take heed of my second-in-command and aide."

Morrell's expression changed to thoughtful regret. "I'm sorry, Captain. It was a shock. I've grown accustomed to Ellan."

"You don't need to explain. I understand. This isn't easy for Avatar either. His charge is dead, and by Ellan's reaction, she isn't going to be kind to him."

Kell's statement of Ellan not being *kind* was too soft. She began mistreating Avatar from the moment he accompanied her back to her quarters. Finally after an hour of being barraged by insults and jeers, Avatar lost his temper.

"Enough!" His voice brought everything to a halt, the maids staring wide-eyed at him in fear. "Away!" He sent them scurrying out.

"How dare you?" began Ellan in protest, only to hiss in surprise pain when he seized her arm.

His silver eyes direct on her. "Listen well, Highness. I would gladly exchange my life for Nigel. So don't presume to think you're the only one not pleased by this assignment. Why the Almighty put us together is beyond me, but I intend to follow my orders to the best of my ability."

She winced, his grip on her arm painful. "Are you through?"

He loosened his grip, yet maintaining hold of her arm. "I think we have made our positions clear. Perhaps with that said, we can reach an understanding and make the situation tolerable for both of us. You can start by acting civil."

She jerked away and rubbed her aching arm. "You can't order me. I'm the royal heir. You're answerable to me the same way you were to Nigel."

Avatar snorted a sarcastic laugh. "After all these years, you still don't understand the relationship between mortals and Guardians, do you? I am a servant of Jor'el, subject to his orders. As such, I willingly place myself in position to aid mortals, not to be subservient to them." His eyes showed the truth and depth of his words.

She balked, shading her eyes from his stare. "Morrell didn't hold that fact over me."

"Did you treat him with disrespect?" When she didn't answer, he pressed her. "Did you?"

"No."

"Then he had no reason to say it. Nor did I to Nigel." Seeing her hurtful frown, he spoke in a softer tone. "Ellan. I realize this is awkward and you were accustomed to Morrell, perhaps even fond of him. However, Morrell is still here, only in a different role. The same can't be said for Nigel."

She sniffled back a wave of emotion.

"Can we at least try to make this work?"

She shrugged in uncertainty.

"Well, I suppose that's better than an emphatic no."

"Highness," came a timid voice from the threshold. It was the elder maid. "It's getting late. We must finish preparing you."

Ellan's mood changed to determined and she smugly glared at Avatar. "You cannot keep me from my duty." She recalled her maids.

The Chapel filled to the point of standing room only. On the front pew, Ellan sat to the left of Ellis, Shannan on his right. Necie sat beside Shannan with Angus next to Necie, then Arista; Darius sitting to the left of Ellan. Those of the Council and Court were arranged according to rank with prominent merchants and servants taking the rest of the seats. The remainder of the crowd was left to stand.

Before being seated, Morrell privately reminded Ellan of their conversation about Queen Alycia. But Ellan didn't need much prompting when it came to stirring Ellis' annoyance by speaking about Tristine's absence. After years of sibling rivalry she knew the ways in which to thwart her sister and get their father's attention. Perhaps she could finally corral Tristine, something Nigel failed to do in his position as heir and older brother. Oh, she didn't begrudge Nigel, nor was she bitter, she mourned his passing like the rest of the family. He was her brother and she would miss him. Still, she understood what Morrell meant about this being her opportunity. If used correctly she could counterbalance Nigel's over indulgence with firmness and honor him by turning their younger sisters into well-rounded adults worthy of their station.

When the service began with Uriah's prayer, she turned her attention to him. In graceful and eloquent words, he spoke about Nigel and his desire to become a Jor'ellian Knight. Uriah spoke with confidence concerning a divine purpose behind the tragedy. Next, Darius spoke. His voice grew thick with emotion, but he pressed on about a young man who may not have been his nephew by blood, but in heart and spirit would never cease to be thought of as kin.

Lastly Ellis stood to speak. He had difficult keeping too much emotion from his voice. "This day is both a day of sorrow and remembrance, and a day of beginning. We have lost a most cherished and beloved member of the royal family. He was our hope for the future, both as son and king. Although Jor'el gave him to us for a short period of time, he will live in our hearts and minds for the rest of our days. Memories of his laughter, his kindness and of his love for us, his family …" he voice nearly broke and he forced himself to continue, "will sustain us through this difficult time. Nigel would not want Allon to be without direction, without leadership, without a future. That is the beginning part, the mantle of heir passing to his sister, Ellan." Ellis briefly looked at her. "To honor him, I call upon the people of Allon to make a pledge to remember him in fondness and treat his sister with the same love and respect given him." He took a deep breath and this time fully looked at Ellan. "Lords and Ladies, the heir apparent, Her Royal Highness, Princess Ellan."

"Here, here!" said Darius, although his voice was cheerless.

Erasmus stood and spoke. "Jor'el's peace to the prince, Jor'el's blessings to the princess."

The rest of the Council Members followed his lead, stood and repeated his phrase.

"Thank you, gentlemen. You honor both my son and daughter." Ellis stepped down and Uriah delivered the closing prayer.

270

The royal family departed the Chapel and led the way to the Great Hall. At the door to the Hall, Necie stopped and tugged on Shannan's hand, her face apprehensive.

Shannan gently smiled. "You may go." She motioned for Angus and Mahon to accompany Necie.

"At least she has age as her excuse," said Ellan.

"Let's not make this more difficult than it already is." Ellis took Ellan's arm and escorted her into the Great Hall.

Once there, he made the formal introduction to Court according to Allon Law and Protocol. Each member of the Council pledged fealty while the higher rank nobility also made pledges. After an hour, Ellis made excuse for the family's exit but encouraged those gathered to continue. He steered Ellan and Shannan toward the rear hall and into the family salon. Nothing was said until they were alone in the room.

"You did well, and I'm very pleased."

Ellan flashed a humorless smile. "It wasn't easy. Especially when asked about Tristine and I had to lie. Necie was easy, she's a child and some were surprised to see her at the Chapel."

"I realize Tristine's absence made it awkward."

"Are you going to make excuses for her again?"

"I wasn't going to excuse her, I was going to praise you for your strength of endurance."

"I'm sorry, Father, but everyone makes excuses for her. Nigel always defended her and I believe by doing so, made it hard for her to stand up for herself."

Shannan became defensive. "You dishonor Nigel by speaking of ill of him?"

Ellis intervened at Shannan's hurt and anger. "Now is not the time, Ellan."

"I'm sorry," said Ellan, swallowing back her emotions.

"When Tristine returns, I'll deal with her, no excuses, I promise."

Ellan nodded, emotions choking any words.

"Now, I think it's best you retire for the day. Have Avatar send for food and drink."

She rolled her eyes at hearing Avatar's name.

"Come now. He's a fine Guardian warrior."

"He's not Morrell."

"I already told you, I can't change the assignments."

"I don't see why not, you are king," she chided, which made him annoyed.

"Jor'el is the Almighty who graciously allows me to bear the title, king, same as he will allow you to someday rule as queen. Don't forget that."

Shannan's hand on his arm stopped further words. In turn, Ellis nudged Ellan on her way.

"What will you do when Tristine returns?" asked Shannan.

He shook his head, his voice frustrated and hurt. "I don't know. I agree with what you said earlier about each of us being allowed to deal with our grief, but she should have been here."

"At least hear what she has to say before reacting."

His look turned sharp. "You mean like I didn't do with Nigel?"

She flinched in regret at his retort. "No, Ellis. It's not an accusation, rather an encouragement for the sake of her grief, for your grief. So you both can come to terms with the loss."

"Ay. Now, go rest. I still have some work to do before I join you."

She tenderly touched his face and kissed him. "Please, don't be too long."

Chapter 17

FOR FOUR DAYS, Tristine rambled all over Melwynn. The Guardians were willing and enjoyable hosts, who neither imposed upon her privacy or made too many demands. The refreshing freedom and relaxing peace of Melwynn made for a welcomed change from Waldron. The past few months her emotions ran the gamut from being uncomfortable around the Morvenians, nervous excitement about camping, utter joy on her birthday, painful grief and despair at Nigel's death, and finally to deep fear and concern at hearing Ellan named heir. Relaxation and peace weren't among those emotions.

At Armus' prompting, she joined the Guardians in daily meditation and the reading of Verse. As usual he proved of great help, first agreeing not to take her back, then allowing her the time she needed to come to terms with Nigel's death. He didn't say much, which was somewhat surprising since he normally offered advice. He listened on the occasions she voiced her thoughts and conflicting feelings. More often, he left her alone; though he lingered nearby, keeping her within sight, more for comfort than protection.

In times of solitude her mind drifted back to hearing the same Verses during the Guardian meditation she studied under Master Hampton. However, the words sounded different. Before they were words on a page, now they meant something, especially the Verses about sorrow, suffering and

273

enduring. Being a princess, she led a life of privilege and comfort. Naturally there were responsibilities. The last few months those responsibilities of duty, family, faith, trust and sorrow became reality. For the first time in her life, she felt overwhelmed and scared. Not like the fear she experienced when camping in the forest or when the beasts attacked, but a fear of not knowing what to do, where to turn, or who to turn to. She believed herself to be strong and independent, not cow-towing to Ellan's bullying, learning how to shoot a bow and hunt. With Armus, she felt protected, while with Nigel, she had an advocate. Reflecting on the past, she realized how she tried to avoid trouble or least the consequences; and often did so with Armus and Nigel's help. It was disturbing to realize how much she depended on them and only fooled herself with her view of self-sufficiency. In the eyes of her family and Court, she reached the age of adulthood and what did she do? She ran away rather than face reality.

Nigel ran away, her mind argued. *But he came back and faced it like a man.*

Thus her mind warred after overhearing a Guardian from the Lowlands speaking to his companions about what would happen to the Great King now that Nigel was dead? The day's topic of mediation concerned the future of Allon and how the Great King would unite mortals and Guardians. Once more, her mind and spirit were challenged.

She withdrew to what became her favorite spot on the far corner of the terrace facing southeast. Although no one knew she overheard, the conversation struck a nerve. She became so wrapped up in how Nigel's loss affected her that she did not take time to consider the larger meaning. The more she thought about it, the more she began to understand why the Morvenian marriage proposal disturbed Nigel so deeply. It wasn't simply the fact Kaleana didn't believe in Jor'el but how the marriage affected prophecy and the future of Allon. With Nigel gone, who would be the next king?

The man who marries Ellan.

She shivered at the fearful implications. She could envision Nigel as king, but Ellan as queen? No. It was wrong! Alas, that was the direction Allon now headed and her father would have to change everything to prepare Ellan.

"It's still not right," she murmured to herself. "Why do I feel this way? Why, Jor'el?"

"Tristine."

Startled at hearing her name, she whirled about, fearful of a personal and direct answer from the Almighty. Kell and Armus approached and she realized who spoke. "Kell."

"I didn't mean to frighten you."

"I was thinking," she fumbled over her words still recovering from the fright.

"What about?"

"Prophecy about the Great King."

"What brought that up?"

She was a bit sheepish. "I overheard some talk after meditation. I hadn't thought about it before, but what they said made me realize Nigel's death means more than just losing my brother."

"Ay. It alters the future of Allon."

"I'm beginning to see that."

A small kind smile crossed Kell's lips. "Good, because I've come to fetch you. It's been four days and the king's patience won't last much longer."

"Oh, he must be furious."

"He's not pleased. In this case, I don't blame him. Mind you, I understand your need for rest, but your absence hurt him deeply."

She looked stricken. "I wasn't thinking about his feelings. I just believe it's wrong for Ellan to be queen. Still, I know it wasn't right for me leave like I did."

"Sounds as if you've done a lot of growing up in a few days."

"I've had no choice."

"You always had a choice, little one. A choice of how you respond to events," said Armus.

She half-heartedly pouted at him. "I haven't made good choices."

"Starting now, you can change."

She took Armus' hand. "Time to go home." All three disappeared.

275

They reappeared in the captain's quarters at Waldron. Tristine leaned against Armus to keep from fainting. "I can't say I like dimension travel."

Armus chuckled. "It wasn't meant for mortals."

She stood on her own and took a few deep, steadying breaths. "Where is Father?" she asked Kell.

"In his study."

Setting her chin, she and the Guardians left the chamber and walked the short distance to the king's study. A royal soldier stood outside the door whenever the king was present. Her heart started to race, but she must face her father. She hesitated in knocking.

"Courage, little one," Armus whispered in her ear.

She knocked. A brief moment passed before she heard Ellis say, "Come."

Ellis stood near an open window reading some papers and not looking at who entered. To Tristine's surprise, Shannan sat at the desk writing. Tristine's mouth went dry so she licked her lips before speaking, "Father." Ellis looked at her and she saw what Kell meant. The stern features were tempered by a level brow and look of pain in his eyes.

"Tristine," said Shannan in relief. She left the desk to greet her. "Are you feeling better?"

"A bit."

"When did you return?" asked Ellis.

"Just now. Kell and Armus brought me back."

In agitated strides he crossed to his desk and tossed the papers on it.

"Father, I know you're angry."

"Angry doesn't begin to describe how I feel!"

"Ellis," warned Shannan and he pressed his lips in an effort to control his temper.

Tristine clenched her hands to steady her emotions. "I realize saying I'm sorry isn't enough, but I am sorry. I swear, I never meant to hurt you!" Her voice quivered and her eyes grew misty. This was more difficult than she thought, especially the way he regarded her, long and steady, although his voice was calmer when he spoke.

"Do you realize you abandoned us in a time of sorrow?"

Her knuckles turned white and her nails dug into her palms but she forced herself to reply "I acted selfishly because I couldn't see beyond my grief to how you or anyone else felt about Nigel—" She couldn't contain her emotions any longer and wept.

Ellis' anger faded and he comforted her. She clung to him, her sobs deep and poignant. "Shhh. I understand your grief." He took her face in his hands to wipe away her tears.

"I've come to understand your grief, not only as a father, but as king. Being at Melwynn helped me to see things in light of Prophecy and not solely personal."

He tossed a pleased glance to Shannan before speaking to Tristine. "Well, maybe some good can come of this. Not that it excuses you," he added at seeing Tristine smile.

"I understand, sir. What punishment will there be?"

Before he replied, there was a knock at the door. "Come."

Ellan entered. Her features were set and eyes hostile toward Tristine. "I saw Armus in the hall and I knew you were back."

Tristine's ire rose, yet she needed to keep her temper.

Ellis intervened. "Your sister explained her absence and I'm satisfied."

Ellan was taken back. "What? She disgraced us before the Council and Court."

"I am aware of what harm my selfish actions caused the king," Tristine spoke in her most formal manner. Her father's intervention gave her time to curb her initial reaction.

Ellan's rigidity instantly returned. "The king wasn't the only one disgraced and shamed."

Tristine turned to Shannan and continued with decorum. "Your Majesty, I humbly ask forgiveness for my absence. I behaved childish and I will seek to correct the behavior."

Shannan just nodded, the battle on her face evident.

"Tristine. Do not press my good graces," warned Ellis. "What you did was wrong and will not happen again. Like it or not, Ellan is now my heir and you owe her fealty along with an apology."

Tristine's jowls flexed. "Ay, Sire." She turned to Ellan and often a stiff curtsey. "I apologize for any disgrace and shame my action caused Your Royal Highness."

"That's a start. What punishment have you given, Sire?"

Ellis sent a private indulgent glance to Tristine and Shannan before replying to Ellan. "The punishment has already been done."

Tristine suppressed her impulse to smile at realizing he meant her acknowledgement of Ellan. "Sire, am I excused? I would like to freshen up."

"Ay."

Tristine's curtsey to him was gracious and willing. She departed, not glancing at Ellan on her way out.

Ellan began to protest when Ellis held up a hand to forestall her words. She made a quick curtsey and left.

"I'm glad you didn't' punish Tristine. She proved she is making an effort, but she won't change overnight," said Shannan.

Conflict played across his face. "Perhaps, but I can't take her excuses any longer. You may not like what Ellan said about Nigel, but she's right. His defense of Tristine and my tolerance of her behavior hampered her maturity."

She stared at him, stunned. "You can't mean that?"

"I do. As harsh and insensitive as it sounds, some good may come of this tragedy." She became upset so he took her hand to guide her to sit on the sofa. "From birth I groomed Nigel for his future. I don't have the same luxury of time with Ellan. In three years she comes of age to marry."

"She's been properly taught her entire life."

He shook his head in adamant refute. "She is now heir with new and different responsibilities than before. You should know that." She didn't look pleased so he persisted. "In order to accomplish what is necessary, I can no longer be the indulgent father."

"I don't agree."

"Shannan, this isn't easy for me. I don't want to become some bully, but the future of Allon is changed. In three years, Ellan will be of age to marry. Between now and then, she must be prepared for her future. Hopefully before the Great King of Prophecy is revealed. I can't do that if I continue to accept every excuse from Tristine in relation to Ellan or indulge her every whim that goes contrary to my effort. She must acknowledge Ellan and treat her with respect as my heir and the next queen. To accept less from her or to allow her disagreeable attitude to be publically demonstrated could cause dissension." Still seeing her difficulty he said, "Please, I need you to understand. The time is too short and my task too great."

"I do. I just don't agree with the way you want to handle it. It could go too far and cause harm to our family."

He kissed her hand. "With your help, and Jor'el's guidance, I hope to stay the course because I don't want that either. Still, I must do everything I can to ensure the future of Allon by grooming Ellan and molding Tristine into compliance."

"Very well. It'll be as you say. And may Jor'el help us

Armus approached Tristine when she emerged from the study. "How did it go?"

"Well, actually."

The conversation was interrupted when Ellan left the study. Ellan's angry, piercing look shot across to Tristine before turning on her heels to head down the galleyway toward the family quarters. Armus took Tristine's arm to move in the opposite direction toward the main hall.

"Did that change when Ellan arrived?" he asked.

"Ay! Yet I managed to keep my temper and Father told her my explanation sufficed, even though she wanted him to punish me, which he didn't." She widely smiled in triumph and added, "Well, unless you count apologizing to Ellan a punishment. That's all. But," she looked over her shoulder, "she's going to be more impossible."

He stopped her, his look direct and voice sober. "There is one task remaining to complete your return."

279

Anxiety filled her face. "Must I?"

"Ay."

She took his hand. "Will you come with me?"

"Of course."

Armus led Tristine to the Chapel. Inside they continued down the corridor beyond the altar to the back door. The door could be locked and barred from the inside since it was located on the eastern wall of Waldron. Beyond the door laid the royal crypt.

Tristine drew back. "I don't think I can. Beside, we don't have the key."

"The bar is off and the key is in the lock. Somebody must be here."

"Who? Father?"

"You left him and your mother in the study."

Fearful, she bit her lower lip and stared at the door.

He titled her head up. "For own good and piece of mind, you must face reality." He pushed open the door and guided her inside.

A single narrow window on the far wall allowed light and air into the crypt. A raised altar to Jor'el stood beneath the window with a marble cushioned bench in the center of the crypt facing the altar. Before a lone plaque signifying the name on a crypt belonging to Sir Niles of Pollux, Shannan's grandfather, who died helping Ellis become king. Now there was a new marker for Prince Nigel. Darius sat on the bench facing the altar.

"Uncle," she said in a near whisper.

Armus nudged her toward Darius.

Uncertainty etched on her face, she approached the bench. "Uncle."

"Tristine." Darius moved to embrace her and she wept. "You're back sooner than I hoped, and I'm glad." He held her face in his hands and kissed her forehead. "Have you seen your parents?"

She nodded and wiped her eyes. "I spoke to both of them."

"What did Ellis say? Was he angry?"

"At first, but mostly he felt hurt. I told him I was sorry, I never meant to hurt him, to hurt mother, or you . . . " she whimpered.

He held her again. "Shhh. I know this is difficult. Rest assured, you didn't hurt me, or Arista."

She wiped her face. "Nigel told me he acted like a child when he ran off, and came back to face the consequences like a man. Father was right. I abandoned our family in a time of crisis and no amount of apology will make up for my actions. All I can do now is what Nigel did, and face the consequences like an adult."

A touched, proud smile crossed his lips. "Indeed, you have grown up."

"What are you doing here, Uncle?"

"Call me foolish, but I believe it does one good to speak as if the departed can hear you. If nothing else, Jor'el hears, and often voicing one's feelings is a good release of the pain and to feel his comfort." He turned to the marker. "There may be no shared blood, but I loved Nigel." He returned to her, an affectionate smile on his lips and tenderly touched her face. "I love you and your sisters as if you were my flesh and blood."

She hugged him. "I love you too."

"Do you want to speak to him?" He indicated the marker.

She recoiled in uncertainty. "It's just a stone."

"Then why did you come here?"

She shrugged and didn't answer, so Armus said, "To face reality."

"I understand. This is very painful. Perhaps in time."

"I don't know, so much is changed," she complained.

"Much remains the same," said another familiar voice.

"Avatar!" She ran and embraced him, clinging tight and whimpering. "I'm sorry, I didn't mean to hurt you."

"You didn't. It was my foolishness." He lifted her face and brushed away the tears from her cheeks. He glanced to the marker and used a gentle hand to turn her toward it. "Nigel would be proud of you for returning and facing your father."

She grew tentative in her regard of the stone. "I'd like to think so."

He made her look at him and he spoke with certainty. "I know so."

"It's all going to be so different now."

"Ay, but as I said, much remains the same. Neither of us is alone. From that we can draw strength to move on."

"As if Ellan will let you do that," groused Darius.

"I think we've reached an understanding."

"What are you talking about?" asked Tristine.

"You are Morrell's replacement," said Armus and Avatar smirked. Relieved, he patted Avatar's shoulder. "I thought it was going to be me."

Tristine voiced her surprise. "You replace Morrell? But he's Ellan's Overseer."

"No, not Armus, me. Morrell is promoted to Supervisor of the Overseers, leaving me to deal with Ellan."

In sympathetic concern she gazed up at Avatar. "You? But—" she motioned and looked at Nigel's marker then turned back to Avatar. "Can you do that so soon after—I mean you both were so close."

"I can. Just like you can face reality," he took hold of her hand while speaking, "united in faith and support."

Darius took her other hand. "We will face reality together."

"Indeed," agreed Kell. He arrived unseen and smiled at Tristine. "Ellis is grateful to have you back. Go with Darius and prepare for supper. Armus will be along in a moment."

The door just shut on the mortals' departure when Armus confronted Kell. "Why didn't you tell me about Avatar rather than leave me wondering what impact my reassignment would have on Tristine?"

"I didn't know you thought that."

"I said so when you left Melwynn."

"Ah. All I heard was my name." He clapped Armus on the shoulder. "I'm sorry. I thought it best not to tell you and allow you to concentrate on helping Tristine deal with her grief."

"She has difficulty saying Nigel's name," said Avatar.

"Ay. Although she took your new assignment better than I expected." Kell moved to stand before Nigel's marker. Golden eyes narrowed and lips pressed in concentration. A long, heavy silence followed until Avatar and Armus stood beside him. "Either reality is mocking me or my senses are some how being influenced, for this is not right!"

"Kell—"

"No!" His head snapped around to Avatar. "Do not use the word *failure*, either in reference to you or me."

"I was going to thank you for *not* failing and giving up on me when I wanted to give up myself." Avatar's gaze shifted between the marker and Kell. "If this is not right, and I believe my captain, we will find out why. Until then, I will be as diligent in my duty to his sister as I was to Nigel."

"Ay, but hold back your attachment this time. I sense rising tension within the family."

"Between Tristine and Ellan is no surprise," said Armus.

Kell quizzically glanced at Armus and repeated, "Tristine." His focus returned to Nigel's marker.

Armus seized Kell's arm. "You don't think Tristine will end up here?"

Kell shook his head, his attention on the marker. "No. Yet some day she may provide the reason of what happened and why?" With that said, he led them from the crypt.

Explore the Kingdom of Allon

www.allonbooks.com

Featuring

- Original Character Art
- Interactive Map of Allon
- News and Events
- Photo and Video Gallery
- Links to:
  - o Facebook – Allon Group Page
  - o The Kingdom of Allon blog
  - o Contact Shawn Lamb

Allon
Book 4

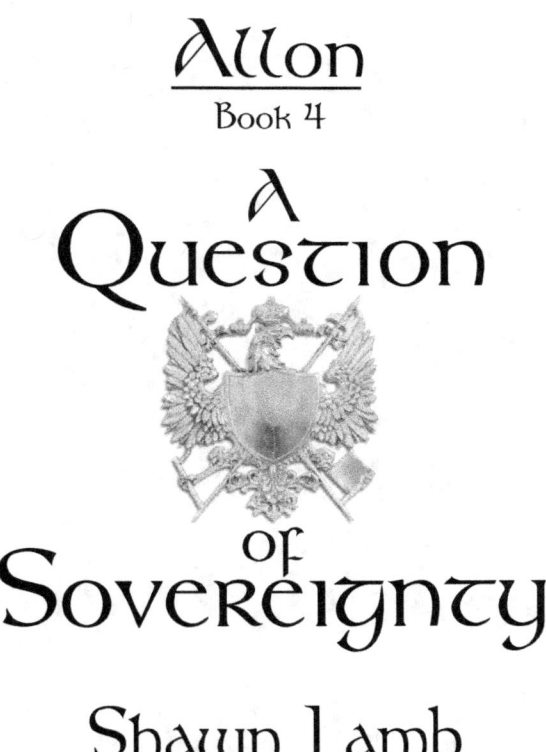

A Question of Sovereignty

Shawn Lamb

Using subtle craftiness, an age-old enemy returns, bringing dissension to Ellis' family, causing strife among the Guardians and conflict with the mortals. Those who resist or give warning are driven away or somehow rendered silent. Can Ellis and his family survive the unexpected coup? Or will they and Guardians finally fall victim to the Dark Way?

Summer 2011